PRAISE FOR VICTORIA PURMAN

'Heart-achingly raw yet filled with the beauty of the human spirit, this novel is a triumph that will linger in the heart and psyche.' — Karen Brooks, author of *The Good Wife of Bath* on *The Nurses' War*

'Heartfelt, heartbreaking, emotional and so very moving.' — *RBH Historical* blog on *The Nurses' War*

'Post-war Australia is captured brilliantly in all its relief and celebration, as well as the struggle and heartache … Victoria's characters are real women—complex and compelling. Once again, Victoria reeled me in to a richly imagined (and meticulously researched) world. I loved the characters and slowed down in the final pages, reluctant to finish the book and leave them behind.' — *Better Reading* on *The Women's Pages*

'Victoria Purman's books are always well researched; they never disappoint or leave you wanting more and are a pleasure to read … five stars.' — *Karen Reads Books* on *The Women's Pages*

'Seamlessly merging historical facts with fiction, Purman's focus is on exploring the postwar experiences of women in this enjoyable, moving, and interesting novel … Heartfelt and poignant, with appealing characters, *The Women's Pages* is an excellent read … an engaging story that also illuminates the real history of post-war Australian women.' — *Book'd Out*

'I consider Victoria Purman one of Australia's leading storytellers in the field of historical fiction … *The Women's Pages* is a rich historical fiction title that leaves a strong imprint on the reader.' — *Mrs B's Book Reviews*

'A richly crafted novel that graphically depicts life during those harrowing years. A touching tale and an enthralling read.' — *Reader's Digest* on *The Women's Pages*

'A powerful and moving book.' — *Canberra Weekly* on *The Women's Pages*

'An engaging tale about family life and relationships at this turning point in Australian culture. Dealing with the legacy of the old whilst carving out the new. It valiantly shone the spotlight on the women who fought to break free of a solely domestic role in search of greater independence.' — *Great Reads and Tea Leaves* on *The Women's Pages*

'This is an enjoyable novel to read ... The historical research is invisibly sewn into the world building. Most importantly, the characters are vivid and believable.' — *Other Dreams Other Lives* on *The Women's Pages*

'... an engaging tale from a foundation of extensive research that deserves its place in the canon of Australia's wartime-inspired fiction.' — *News Mail* on *The Land Girls*

'Moments of great sadness and grief, as well as moments of pure, radiant joy, unfold in this gentle, charming tale ... the genuine heartfelt emotion and the lovely reimagining of the way we once were ... makes *The Land Girls* such a rich and rewarding read.' — *Better Reading*

'A moving tale of love, loss and survival against the odds.' — *Better Homes & Gardens* on *The Land Girls*

'Purman's almost lyrical description of this particular point in Australia's history is a richly crafted treat veering cleverly through the brutal hardships faced at the time while also filtering in little moments of beautiful, historical nostalgia. It's a well-told story filled with multi-dimensional female characters.' — *Mamamia* on *The Land Girls*

'I would recommend *The Land Girls* for its historical significance, romance and power to make the reader feel proud to be Australian.' — *Chapter Ichi*

'A beautiful story with rich characters, vivid settings and the whole emotional range.' — *Beauty & Lace* on *The Land Girls*

'There is a wealth of detail woven into this novel ... Victoria Purman just seems to be going from strength to strength with her historical fiction.' — *Theresa Smith Writes* on *The Land Girls*

'What a lovely tribute this book is to all the women of the Australian Women's Land Army. ... I enjoy her style of writing, the characters and the in-depth description she gives to make you immerse yourself into her world.' — *Reading for the Love of Books* on *The Land Girls*

'A heart-warming novel ... The story of Bonegilla is a remarkable one, and this novel is a tantalising glimpse into its legacy.' — *The Weekly Times* on *The Last of the Bonegilla Girls*

'Victoria Purman has researched and written a delightful historical piece that will involve its readers from the first page to the last ... written with empathy and understanding.' — *Starts At 60* on *The Last of the Bonegilla Girls*

'Victoria Purman has written a story about people exactly like my family, migrants to Australia ... I came to this novel for the migrant story, but I stayed for the wonderful friendship Victoria Purman has painted between the four girls.' — *Sam Still Reading* on *The Last of the Bonegilla Girls*

'A story told directly from the heart ... *The Last of the Bonegilla Girls* is a wonderful ode to the bonds of female friendship and the composition of our country.' — *Mrs B's Book Reviews*

'... a moving and heartwarming story [and] a poignant and compelling read, *The Last of the Bonegilla Girls* is ... a beautiful story about female friendship and how it can transcend cultural and language barriers.' — *Better Reading*

Victoria Purman is an Australian top ten and *USA Today* bestselling fiction author. Her most recent book, *The Nurses' War*, was an Australian bestseller, as were her novels *The Women's Pages*, *The Land Girls* and *The Last of the Bonegilla Girls*. Her earlier novel *The Three Miss Allens* was a *USA Today* bestseller. She is a regular guest at writers' festivals, a mentor and workshop presenter and was a judge in the fiction category for the 2018 Adelaide Festival Awards for Literature.

To find out more, visit Victoria on her website, victoriapurman.com. You can also follow her on Facebook or Instagram (@victoriapurmanauthor) and Twitter (@VictoriaPurman).

Also by Victoria Purman

The Boys of Summer:
Nobody But Him
Someone Like You
Our Kind of Love
Hold Onto Me

Only We Know

The Three Miss Allens
The Last of the Bonegilla Girls
The Land Girls
The Women's Pages
The Nurses' War
A Woman's Work

The Nurses' War

Victoria Purman

FICTION
HQ

First Published 2022
Second Australian Paperback Edition 2023
ISBN 9781867255994

THE NURSES' WAR
© 2022 by Victoria Purman
Australian Copyright 2022
New Zealand Copyright 2022

Published by
HQ Fiction
An imprint of Harlequin Enterprises (Australia) Pty Limited (ABN 47 001 180 918),
a subsidiary of HarperCollins Publishers Australia Pty Limited (ABN 36 009 913 517)
Level 13, 201 Elizabeth St
SYDNEY NSW 2000
AUSTRALIA

A catalogue record for this book is available from the National Library of Australia
www.librariesaustralia.nla.gov.au

Printed and bound in Australia by McPherson's Printing Group

To Andrew Eckert

(20/10/62 – 2/4/20)

So dearly loved and so terribly missed

'Harefield is like a mansion of broken hearts ...'
—Letter from an Australian soldier, 7 September 1916

1915

Chapter One

12 May 1915

It was the trilling song of an English woodlark perched high in the gnarled and outstretched limbs of an ancient oak that reminded Staff Nurse Cora Barker that she was ten thousand miles from home.

For six long weeks on the RMS *Osterley,* she had watched birds she'd only ever read about in the encyclopedia soar and swoop and dive around the ship, an ornithological escort for the Australians on board. Enormous seagulls had hovered and screeched and called to her as the ship coursed its way across the Indian Ocean to England. Wandering albatrosses had floated overhead, so low that she had almost been able to see each individual feather in their silvery underwings. Trussed up in a stiff life jacket during a drill on deck, straining to hear the captain shouting above the wind and the roaring sea-splash on the hull, Cora had lifted two fingers to the sky to estimate the span of the impressive bird's wings. It must have been ten feet at least—bigger than any bird she'd ever seen in South Australia, bigger even than a pelican. The petrels, as broad as the albatrosses but with short stubby beaks instead of elongated ones, had speared into the water at sunset with such velocity that Cora imagined they might reach the sea floor with the power and propulsion of their dives. And the gliding shearwaters, brilliant white and shimmering silver, had skimmed across the waves whenever she tossed a bread crust or an apple core into the air for the pure pleasure of enticing the creatures closer.

The incessant roaring of the ocean and the pounding of the waves against the hull had created a soporific song that still sung in Cora's ears, even though her feet had already been firmly planted on English soil for two days.

How, she wondered, was it possible to already be pining for a kookaburra's belly laugh or the ear-splitting screech of a galah when she had only walked up the gangplank in Australia six weeks earlier? It wouldn't be long until those familiar sounds of home would once again be the soundtrack to her days and evenings, she was sure of it. The war was certain to be over by Christmas, according to the newspapers she was in the habit of devouring, and her adventure—and her duty—on the other side of the world would be complete. Her aim was to serve her country, and its soldiers, with pride and distinction.

And when her role was complete, she would sail back home across the vast oceans and return to the little cottage on the lane in Adelaide's inner west in which she'd been born and had lived all her life. She loved the place where the boobooks hooted at night and dark swarms of spindly bats emerged from the tall palms in the front yard of the old house across the street, swooping and stealing fruit while they navigated with their metallic squeaks.

Yes, she would be home for Christmas. Surely her sacrifice would earn her the good fortune of discovering the sixpence in her mother's Christmas pudding that year.

As the *Osterley* had sailed out of Port Adelaide at the end of March, Cora had waved an excited goodbye to her tearful parents, Arthur and Minnie, and her two envious younger sisters, Eve and Grace. She had promised them once again that she would stay safe and they had reiterated over and over how proud they were of her. When her dear family had shrunk into distant specks on the faded silvery wharf at the end of St Vincent Street, she had turned her eyes to the sky, breathing in the salty South Australian autumn air and memorising the broad sweep of the blue that her mother always told her was the same colour as her eyes. She had spread her arms wide and turned her palms up to the warmth of that March day. She was leaving behind the summer scent of jasmine, the antiseptic smell of freshly picked and crushed eucalypt leaves and the early fall of foliage from the plane trees.

'Do us proud, lass,' Arthur had whispered into her ear as he'd hugged her on the wharf, his cloth cap brushing against her cheek.

'With everything in my power, Dad,' she'd replied, brushing the drizzling tears from his face. Her parents hadn't ever ventured further than Victor Harbor—three hours south of Adelaide on the train—and the thought that their daughter would be travelling for six whole weeks to London was unfathomable to them.

How was it that she was already missing Adelaide's warmth? On the day after Valentine's Day (on which she had yet again failed to receive any token of affection from any young man—or old man for that matter), the daytime temperature had reached 107 degrees in the shade and it seemed that all of Adelaide had wilted, from backyard fruit trees laden with nectarines and peaches to the ostrich feathers on the black velvet hats of society matrons at the Adelaide Town Hall. How had they ever survived it?

After her shift at the Adelaide Hospital that hot and exhausting day, Cora had covered her uniform with the long black cape that fully disguised her nurses' dress and tied the white ribbons of the matching cap tightly under her chin. In the cloying heat, she felt as confined as an Egyptian mummy. She hadn't always understood the rationale behind the rules of nursing etiquette, but had learnt with a quick kick to the shin from one of her fellow students that it was not her place to question them, no matter how infuriating they were. Once properly and respectfully attired, she'd wandered into the fecund oasis of the Adelaide Botanic Garden just over the hospital's stone boundary wall, and found a quiet spot under a Moreton Bay fig. Its roots—huge, tangled tentacles resembling those of a creature from the depths of the ocean—created a shelter from the prying eyes of passers-by and she had tucked herself among them, leaning against the trunk, sucking in the chilled, oxygen-rich air in the tree's shade, and imagined she was floating in the ocean. When she was rested and cool, she'd retrieved from the pocket of her uniform little crumbs of shortbread biscuit that had been left on a drowsy patient's plate and scattered them into the hot wind. In an instant, the noisy miners flew in and fought a losing battle for the tidbits with the New Holland honeyeaters that were fine and delicate creatures but as bossy as old male patients. Later, she'd walked back through the gardens towards Palm House and watched the glint of the afternoon sun on the glass windows as the building shone back at her like a million stars had been captured inside.

How odd it was to look back and realise that the glasshouse that had been imported piece by delicate piece all the way from Bremen in Germany was most likely made by the very people the forces of the British Empire were now killing—and who were killing them.

'Sister Barker?'

Cora startled, her thoughts of home fleeing like a starling in flight. 'Yes, Matron Gray?'

'I wonder if you're paying attention to me or is your mind somewhere else altogether?'

Cora shivered. Was it from nerves at the thought that the matron already believed her to be scatterbrained? Or was it the biting cold that seeped up from the gravel of the driveway through the leather soles of her boots? It had settled right in the arches of her feet that frigid and dull Middlesex morning and yet it was supposed to be spring in the northern hemisphere.

'I apologise, Matron. I was only thinking how cold it is for May.'

Cora quickly glanced sideways at her three colleagues, Gertie North, Leonora Grady and Fiona Patterson. They stood like birds on a wire, their white veils waving in the wind, their attention completely focussed on the matron. The sudden need to redeem herself overtook every rational thought of staying silent.

'I was wondering if there will be sufficient heating in the wards for our patients,' she offered.

'A pertinent question,' Matron Gray replied. Appointed by the Australian Army Nursing Service to help establish a sixty-bed Australian convalescent hospital at Harefield Park, the matron came with a fine reputation. Tall and as lean as a greyhound, she had a beak nose and a hint of grey in the hair that peeked out from behind her white linen veil. She looked at each of the nurses in turn and shared a warm smile. 'I've been in the country six weeks and I don't think I'll ever get used to this topsy-turvy weather.' She shivered dramatically. 'When I made my first visit here in March for an inspection of the house and grounds, there was snow on the ground. I must admit I was almost speechless.'

Cora took Matron Gray's smile and manner as a welcome signal that the rules and norms of hospital hierarchy ingrained in the nurses during their training might be somewhat more relaxed here, half a world away, during a war.

'Truly?' Leonora laughed gaily. 'I've never seen snow. How exciting.'

Cora watched her as she spoke. Everything about Sister Grady was elegant. Had she been a ballet dancer in her youth? Her high cheekbones created shadows that would never need rouging with powder, and her long neck and fine features wouldn't have been out of place on the stage. She didn't walk so much as glide as elegantly as a swan on a lake.

'I wouldn't get your hopes up of seeing a white Christmas,' the matron replied, shaking her head. 'I fully expect that our work here will be done by December.'

'It *will* be a short war.' Cora cleared her throat and continued when all eyes turned to her. 'All the newspapers are saying so. The King's men will be victorious and there will be peace in a few months.'

'We do rule the waves, after all,' Gertie added with a grin.

Next to her, Fiona harrumphed. 'What a blessing that will be.' Her shoulders heaved and dropped with palpable relief. Was it wrong for Cora to think of Fiona as a crow? Her jet-black hair only looked darker under her snow-white veil and her deep-set brown eyes seemed to be perpetually narrowed in suspicion. Her unruly eyebrows resembled two caterpillars almost shaking hands with each other just above her nose.

When no one replied, she explained, 'It will be a blessing for the war to be over so quickly, I mean. I don't know if I'd survive a winter. I shall have to knit some warmer gloves to ward off the frostbite, not to mention the chilblains.'

'I'll take a pair if you're in the mood for knitting,' Gertie said. 'I never did master the art of it, or many other home-making skills, I'm afraid. Much to the disappointment of my mother.' She pushed her wire-rimmed glasses up her button nose and Cora tried not to laugh at her complete lack of embarrassment at such a revelation. Since they'd met on the *Osterley*, Gertie had become the voice of reason in Cora's head. Watchful. Wise. Steady. Cora couldn't help but think of her as an owl.

Matron Gray cleared her throat and the nurses took it as a sign that the chatter should come to an end. She looked over her shoulder to take in the imposing house behind them. 'We have a very important job to do here at Harefield Park, sisters. Our first and immediate task is to transform this manor house into a hospital.'

Matron Gray turned, clasped her hands behind her back and began to stride along the narrow gravel drive, which ran along the front of the building and was only wide enough for one vehicle before its edge met freshly cut grass. Her nurses obediently followed her.

'The Billyard-Leake family has graciously given up Harefield Park and all its buildings for our soldiers. Officially, it's to be known as the Number One Australian Auxiliary Hospital, AIF, but I believe Harefield hospital will be easier to remember, don't you? We're only twenty miles from the centre of London, and in between the Denham and Northwood railway stations—very convenient for patient transport but far enough away from London's temptations, which can only be a good thing.'

Cora had read all about those temptations and longed to see them for herself. The West End's theatres. St Paul's. Selfridge's. Buckingham Palace. Chinatown. The museums of South Kensington and the Underground railway. To think that those delights and many more undiscovered ones were a mere twenty miles away. Although she wasn't in London to be a tourist, if she were to have a day off she might take the omnibus and see the sites for herself.

London was close. But the war was close, too. Only thirty-one miles separated Dover from Calais. The war was on their doorstep.

Just over the Channel, fighting had been raging for almost six months. Belgium had fallen first—as easily as a house of cards—and refugees had flooded into England with nothing but the clothes they were wearing and a suitcase. There had been bloody battles in Ypres, and in France and Germany trenches were filled with troops shooting at each other over their parapets. When the nurses had arrived at Portsmouth, they'd caught up with the news of the sinking just a week before of the Cunard liner RMS *Lusitania*, which had been struck by German torpedoes in the waters off Ireland. More than one thousand people had been killed, including women and children. The horror of it was still evident in the eyes of every English person she'd met since arriving. *Women and children.*

Cora's father, Arthur, had rightly predicted Australian Prime Minister Joseph Cook's pledge to wholeheartedly support Britain in the war but had been in furious disagreement with it. When Cook had sent Australian troops to Egypt in preparation for defending the Suez Canal, Cora's father had taken himself off to the pub to drown his sorrows.

'Nothing good will ever come of it, Cora,' he'd said when he'd returned in his cups. 'Nothing.'

Now, there were boys from Adelaide and Sydney and Orange and Murray Bridge and Tibooburra and Perth and Brisbane and Dubbo and Bendigo and Longreach— and a thousand other places—fighting in Europe. All had volunteered to don a khaki uniform and take up arms for the King.

Cora was not naive. She believed herself to be practical and prepared and every bit up to the challenge of war nursing. She breathed deep, filling her lungs and exhaling in a whoosh to drown out the memory of Neville Pendlebury's hectoring about her enlistment. The further away from Adelaide she was, the more miles distant from his declarations about how she should live her life, the quieter his voice became, but it was still there, nagging at her.

'Why you? You're not young any more, Cora. Who knows what will happen to your prospects of marriage if you go off to the war? In all likelihood you'll come back coarse and unladylike after spending so much time with all those men.'

Cora pressed her fingers to the silver Rising Sun badge at her throat, which fastened the scarlet cotton cape draped around her shoulders. It was a reminder of why she had enlisted and the call to do her duty that had underpinned her decision. The war was closer now than it had ever been and she was ready for whatever challenges it might bring.

'The Billyard-Leake property is two hundred and fifty acres. This house and all its outbuildings are at the beck and call of the Ministry of Defence for the period of the war and six months after. The family specifically requested it become a place of recuperation and rehabilitation for Australian soldiers.'

'What a wonderful act of generosity and community spirit,' Gertie declared patriotically as her boots crunched on the gravel path.

Fiona glanced up at the stonework and eyed the windows of the ivy-covered three-storey manor. 'They must be very rich,' she said to no one in particular.

'Their good deed is inspired by their own family circumstances,' Matron Gray continued. 'The Billyard-Leakes have two sons *and* two nephews serving.'

'They have sons?' Leonora asked with a laugh as she cupped the back of her head through her veil. 'What a pity I'm already engaged. Do they have wives or are they still on the market? Cora? Gertie? Fiona? It sounds like there might be one of these rich men for each of you.'

'You'll be far too busy to entertain any such thoughts, Sister Grady.' Cora couldn't see the matron's expression but there was humour in her tone.

Fiona scoffed at Leonora's idea.

Gertie snorted, 'I don't think so,' and Cora rolled her eyes. It was the last thing on her mind. Then she remembered.

'Mrs Billyard-Leake is a South Australian by birth,' she said. 'Just as I am.'

Matron Gray stopped mid-stride and turned back to Cora. 'She is?'

'Her people are from the south-east, Glencoe, near Mount Gambier. I understand she's an heiress.'

'An Australian heiress?'

Cora found it hard to interpret the matron's expression. Was it derision at the idea that Cora might be a gossipmonger or disbelief that any young Australian woman might have inherited wealth in such a way?

Cora found it necessary to explain herself and stepped forward. 'I make a habit of keeping up to date with current events. I read the newspaper every day, actually.'

Was that a glimmer of acknowledgement in the matron's hint of a smile?

'Tell us then. How did she come to be so rich?' Fiona asked.

All eyes turned to Cora. 'The Leake family once had fifty thousand acres of prime grazing country with thirty thousand sheep on it. Cattle, too. When her father and uncle died, she inherited everything.'

'Everything?' Leonora asked, wide-eyed.

'Everything,' Cora nodded. 'Which meant, naturally, she had her pick of suitors. She married a solicitor from Sydney and they joined their two family names together and became the Billyard-Leakes.'

'Why wouldn't she simply take her husband's name?' Fiona grimaced. 'She isn't a suffragette, is she?'

'And what if she is?' Gertie huffed on behalf of every woman in Australia who'd fought for the right to vote. 'Perhaps she was proud of her own name, Fiona, and that of her family. And anyway, from what Cora says, she did bring much capital to the marriage.'

Before Fiona could reply, Matron Gray spoke. 'However she got it, and perhaps it's best if we're not seen to be gossiping, she's been exceedingly generous with it. The family have moved out of their residence for the duration into Black Jack's Mill in the village, but that doesn't mean they aren't keen to be involved here. We expect to accommodate sixty soldiers under winter conditions and one hundred and fifty during the spring and summer. We're to be a rest home for officers, warrant officers, non-commissioned officers and rank and file soldiers to recuperate after sickness or injury. And we're to act as a depot for collecting invalided soldiers who'll be heading home to Australia.

'Mrs Billyard-Leake has suggested numerous ways for our soldiers to be entertained while they're convalescing and Mr Billyard-Leake has taken a keen interest in the running of the hospital. He's very insistent that all ranks be treated equally here. There's to be no separation of officers and soldiers such as you'll find in the British hospitals. So, you'll be treating officers and soldiers side by side in our wards, sisters. When a patient's time here is at an end, they'll either be recovered and sent to rejoin their battalions or will be heading for Portsmouth to go home to Australia if they're deemed medically unfit to resume service.'

It was only logical to assume there would be injured men but the thought jarred Cora anyway. She had imagined deaths on the battlefield—of course she had. It was no surprise that war was brutal and there would always be a deadly cost. How disappointed those men would be, having come this far, to be forced by injury or debility to leave their friends, their units, to be prevented from further serving King and country. That realisation had her recommitting herself to her task. If it was in her power to see that a man could return to his unit, she would exercise that power. Her resolution gave her strength and she felt her spine lengthening, her chin turning towards the sky, her heart beating faster in her chest.

She had come to England to do a job and it was about to begin.

Chapter Two

Matron Gray lifted her gaze to the roof of the grand building before turning back to her nurses.

'I still can't quite wrap my head around how old this estate is. Just think. Harefield Park was built before Captain Cook landed at Sydney Cove. Families have been living in this place longer than the English have been living in Australia.'

'Hope it doesn't have damp,' Gertie whispered to Cora. 'It'll make my nurses' knees ache, you mark my words.'

Cora tried not to laugh.

The matron continued. 'I've scoured all of London for the supplies we need, sisters. Furniture, fittings, equipment and utensils are on their way to us. Soon, this place will be unrecognisable.'

The seventeenth-century manor house was more fantastical than anything Cora had ever seen. The stone building was covered in creeping ivy, which had been neatly trimmed around all the windows so no view out to the garden or the fields would be obscured. Upon closer inspection, Cora noted that each window was fitted with blinds and each of them was partially open so the windows took on the appearance of blinking eyelids set in their wooden frames. She stopped counting chimneys when she reached five.

On one side of the house an oak tree stood as high as the roof, and its budding spring branches grasped out over a vast lawn on which she imagined fancy people might have once played croquet and games of tennis in gleaming whites. A garden bed full of roses in neat rows, their leaves dark green and abundant, were dotted with tiny buds about to bloom. A fan-shaped sundial was set among the roses, and Cora thought how optimistic it was to expect to use it to tell the time when there seemed to be no sun at all to cast a shadow.

Cora's imagination took flight. What might be happening on this very spot if the Serbian who held a grudge against Archduke Franz Ferdinand, the heir to the throne of the Austro-Hungarian Empire, hadn't shot him on the twenty-eighth of June the year before; if the complicated web of alliances with Russia and Germany and Britain hadn't resulted in the declaration of war one month later?

Would the staff of Harefield Park be preparing for an elegant soiree that evening? Instead of Australian nurses in dark grey serge uniforms and scarlet capes, would the manor house and gardens be filled with elegant young ladies wearing dinner dresses of velvet or silk or chiffon, perhaps embroidered with beads or delicate flowers; a ruched silk headband decorated with small rosettes and perhaps a feather; a long strand of pearls or glass beads, with long white gloves to complete their outfits? And would there be handsome young men sporting black ties and tails, so many that the ladies' dance cards tied to their wrists with silk ribbons would be full before the orchestra had struck its first note?

'Follow me, sisters.' Matron Gray raised her hand in a wave and her nurses followed, lifting their skirts to prevent them dragging on the sodden ground. They passed the newly constructed mess hall and, at the rear of the house, the sounds of hammering and sawing accompanied by tradesmen's shouts filled the air. Then they turned another corner and Cora found herself unable to take another step.

In the near distance, two rectangular lakes reflected the dull spring sky. White swans floated gracefully, creating delicate ripples behind them on the water's surface. Birdsong rang out like pealing church bells and echoed off the stone house. Her eyes darted from tree to tree and she wished she could see the creatures that were singing their welcome greeting. Neat rows of elms grew alongside the lake, and in the distance cedars and horse chestnuts led to a pretty wood.

A grand house with lakes and swans. Had she landed in a fairy tale? 'How beautiful,' Cora whispered to herself, to the chill in the air, to the flat grey sky and the birds and the trees, to the creatures she imagined burrowing and scurrying in the earth, hares and puddle ducks and moles directly from the pages of Beatrix Potter's stories to this little idyll in Middlesex.

Leonora lifted a flat hand to her eyes, her graceful neck craning. 'I see a bench under one of the trees by the lake. What a delightful spot to sit and take in the fresh air.'

'Exactly what I was thinking, Sister Grady.' Matron Gray swept her arm out to take in the breadth of the vista. 'When the sun is shining and the men are in need of recuperation, this will be a very therapeutic place for them. It's a distance from the huts going up on the top field and the bustling comings and goings of the rest of the place. We know how important peace and quiet can be to injured bodies and minds.'

Leonora took up a position next to the matron so they could continue their conversation as they walked, and, falling back, Cora and Gertie exchanged smiles and fell into step with each other. Fiona hurried along behind them, her eyes darting. Cora wondered if she was keeping a furtive eye out for foxes.

When they returned to the main doors of the house, the women's leather boots click-clicked across the tiled foyer and through a doorway on the left into a spacious drawing room. The furniture, beautifully upholstered in tapestry fabric swirling with roses and deep green leaves, was arranged around the room so four different conversations could be held at once. Set by the largest fireplace Cora had ever seen, so large she might be able to walk into it if she were her mother's height, were two rocking chairs and a leather footstool. The rugs on the floor were elegantly faded florals and Cora's imagination took flight once again. On the way to England, the *Osterley* had stopped in Cairo to offload men and supplies, and Cora had dragged Gertie and Leonora on a tour of the city. Fiona had refused the offer of sightseeing, having heard too many stories of the white slave trade to set a foot on the ship's gangplank.

The narrow streets of Cairo had bustled with hawkers calling out in languages Cora didn't understand, their waving arms beckoning the women into narrow little shops filled from floor to ceiling with exotic wares, from copper tea sets to tarnished silver jewellery and sweets that smelled of honey and exotic spices. One establishment was filled with towers of woven rugs stacked so high that Cora half expected to see a princess on top complaining of a pea. The carpets had been stitched in geometric shapes of deep red and cobalt blue and sunshine yellow, and Cora wondered if any of the rugs decorating the floors at Harefield House had such exotic origins. Had they been hand-knotted in Persia from the finest silk and brought to England on a sailing ship a hundred years before?

Matron Gray's gaze swept from the fireplace to the dull and dusty windows. 'This will be our operating theatre. There is space over on the far wall for the instrument sterilisers and for cupboards in which to store dry dressings. I'm a little perplexed as to how we might dispose of waste water.' She searched each inch of the room and shrugged. 'We'll have to make do. We'll be carrying pails across the hallway, I'm afraid, and then emptying them into the nearest drain. There's a bathroom down that way on the left. That might be the solution.'

'What will happen to all the furniture, Matron?' Cora asked.

'Most everything you see will go into storage. The Billyard-Leakes have taken only bare essentials for their new home. They have, however, left the billiards room intact, which was very considerate of them. And the library. Wait until you see it.' The matron smiled and paused. 'The patients will no doubt make use of both, depending on their inclinations and their physical limitations.'

They moved out to the main foyer. Cora's attention flitted from portrait to portrait, from floor to ceiling, and then to the wide polished-wood staircase that separated into flights to both left and right. Light streamed down on them from a skylight high above in the roof. The nurses climbed the stairs and inspected the bedrooms—Cora lost count at six—each filled with antique furniture and beds made up in fancy linens. Sumptuous dusky pink velvet curtains hung over the windows, and artworks decorated the papered walls.

'The third floor will comprise staff accommodation but I'll be on the ground floor so I can more closely observe all the comings and goings. I'm not far from the nurses' quarters if you ever need me. Remember that.'

The nurses followed the matron back down the stairs and into the fresh outdoor chill where they reassembled in an obedient row. A cold breeze whipped their veils around their cheeks like freshly washed sheets resisting being pegged to a clothesline. Cora ached to get started on the task at hand, to transform this house full of rich upholstery and Persian rugs and billowing curtains into a sterile, functional hospital. Wasn't that why she had come to England?

Cora exchanged glances with Gertie and saw a similar expression of excitement in her eyes.

'I'll take you to your quarters now,' Matron Gray said. 'I'm sure you will want time to unpack. We'll then have supper in the mess and you may retire after that. You'll need your rest tonight, sisters. Tomorrow, our work begins.'

Chapter Three

The Australian nurses rose early courtesy of an alarm clock Gertie had brought from home, and by seven o'clock they were washed and breakfasted and had even managed to swallow down a hurried cup of tea before assembling in the main house to await further instructions.

The early morning sun created long shadows on the tiles in the foyer and Cora blew clouds as she breathed. She smoothed her palms down the sides of her uniform. Her starched bib apron was still white as a puff of summer cloud, her collar and cuffs neatly pressed. How long would that last and how much work would it take to keep them looking so pristine, she wondered? She reached a hand to the back of her head to ensure her square linen veil was still pinned firmly in place.

And then—she couldn't help it—she tried unsuccessfully to stifle a yawn.

'We keeping you up, then?' Gertie jabbed Cora with her elbow.

'I barely slept,' Cora explained and then lowered her voice to a whisper. 'Someone was snoring.'

Leonora laughed heartily. 'I'm so pleased I had some cotton wool to stick in my ears.'

Gertie looked from nurse to nurse, her eyes narrowed and lips pinched in confusion. 'I didn't hear any snoring.'

'Of course you didn't. You were the one who was snoring!' Fiona harrumphed.

Gertie gasped. 'Never!'

'You're hardly a reliable witness, Gertie,' Leonora teased. 'One can't hear oneself snore. It's a scientific impossibility. One can't be awake and hear oneself trumpet one's exhalations around the nurses' quarters.'

Gertie's hand flew to her mouth and she stared wide-eyed at Cora. 'Do you mean … all this time … for six weeks on the boat over from Australia,' Gertie slapped her cheeks with her palms, 'you've said nothing?'

Cora covered her mouth to hide her laugh. Leonora nodded sympathetically. Fiona didn't seem quite certain about taking part in the friendly banter and remained silent.

'We're teasing.' Cora giggled. 'It's really not that bad.'

'Well, I beg to differ actu—'

Cora cut off Fiona with a raised hand. 'I'm sure we can all borrow some of Leonora's cotton wool. We should find a ready supply here of all places.'

While it was true that Gertie's snoring did sound like a rutting bull roaring across a paddock, Cora wasn't certain that Gertie could be held solely responsible for the tumultuous night's sleep Cora had endured.

After the tour of the house and grounds the day before, the nurses had unpacked and made themselves at home in their quarters, a wooden hut situated on the northern side of the property, with a view out over the park. If Cora had been a little less tired, she might have gone for a walk in the fields to pick wildflowers, but after supper the nurses had turned in, not willing to fight sleep any longer.

At nightfall, as Gertie was setting her alarm clock, Cora had pulled the blankets up to her chin to ward off the night-time chill and tried to make her army-issued pillow the slightest bit comfortable by punching it into submission with a clenched fist. Sleep seemed to have come easily to the others: Leonora was the first to fall silent, then Gertie began to snore and, finally, Fiona began to mumble incoherently in her slumber.

But it seemed to have taken Cora hours to drift off. She'd tossed and turned, restless and full of anticipation, every thought swooping and curving and dipping like a murmuration of swallows in the distant sky. When would the first soldiers arrive? What condition would they be in when they did? Deep down, no matter how hard she'd tried to, Cora hadn't been able to brush aside the harsh judgement Neville Pendlebury had so unkindly shared with her, which had cause seeds of doubt to sprout. What if she wasn't up to the task? Why could she not stop thinking about what he'd said, when he was so wholly unimportant to her?

'Sisters.' Matron Gray's black leather boots struck the foyer's tiled floor like a metronome. 'Welcome to our first proper day here at Harefield Park. I'd like to introduce you to two ladies from the village who have generously volunteered to help us. They have come personally recommended by Mrs Billyard-Leake, who told me herself they are as hardworking and trustworthy as any women we'd find in the country. This is Mrs Chester and Miss Chester. We thank you sincerely for your help, ladies.'

Mrs Chester nodded towards Matron Gray. 'Thank you and please call me Win. This is my daughter, Jessie.'

'Thank you, Mrs Chester,' the matron responded and then turned to the younger woman and nodded. 'And you are very welcome too, Miss Chester.'

Miss Chester smiled politely and demurely. 'Jessie, if you please.'

'Jessie it is then. Thank you for coming.'

There was no mistaking the two women were related. They were the same height—a good head shorter than Cora, who had always been considered tall for a girl and then a woman—with the same shade of light brown hair, both wearing it swept up into a loose bun at the top of their heads. They had perfectly matched English-rose cheeks and bright blue deep-set eyes, although the daughter's were slightly brighter than her mother's. Between them on the gravel driveway sat a basket full of rags and two pails piled high with boxes of soap flakes and hog-bristle scrubbing brushes.

'Don't worry, Cora,' Gertie whispered from the side of her mouth. 'I have something for the blisters.'

The small but exceedingly energetic group of women spent the morning following their matron's instructions and their own quick-thinking initiative. They worked like Trojans, moving every piece of unusable furniture they could carry from the downstairs rooms into the large and light-filled billiard room, which had become a de facto storage area for pieces that would be moved upstairs into the offices and staff quarters the next day. They tugged at carpets with claw hammers, ripping them from the floorboards as easily as if they were peeling wallpaper from old walls. Once the clouds of dust had settled, the women discovered polished floorboards underneath and swept and then scrubbed them. When the floorboards had dried, they would be stained dark, almost black, in preparation for an application of beeswax. They would be easier to keep sterile that way and Cora knew that blood and fluids would be easier to clean from sealed and polished floorboards than bare ones.

On her knees, blowing a stray curl from her eyes, Cora dipped a scrubbing brush into a pail and swirled it around in the mix of water, vinegar and soap flakes, creating sudsy circles in the grime. The potion stung the broken skin on her palms and she chided herself for how soft her hands had become during the six weeks on the boat from Australia.

The intricacies of scrubbing dusty and muddy English manor-house floors might have been new to Cora, but she knew operating theatres and hospitals. Those places were her natural sphere. She had brought just one suitcase with her across the oceans, but she also carried something far more valuable: her well-regarded training at the Adelaide Hospital and ten years' experience on wards in all kinds of specialties.

From the first, Cora had taken her nursing education seriously. She had trained under the formidable Matron Margaret Graham, who was herself serving with the Australian Army Nursing Service. Matron Graham had sailed off in October 1914 and was now on a hospital ship in Egypt. The spirited, forthright, smart-as-a-whip woman—who always seemed to be fighting with the hospital board over the shabby treatment of 'her' nurses—had inspired Cora's enlistment. Cora had had the good fortune to have worked with women who had never been in any doubt that ideals worth holding are ideals worth fighting for, and their convictions had inspired hers. Unlike her father, Cora believed that England was worth defending, that the cause was righteous and that Australians should be fighting alongside their English cousins to help bring about victory.

To put it simply, if Australian boys were at war, Cora and the other nurses wanted to be there too. Who better to remind them who and what they were fighting for?

As she scrubbed sudsy circles, she thought back to the day she'd signed up, so many months ago in Adelaide.

She'd made the mistake of mentioning the exact date— 12 January—to Neville Pendlebury, who had promptly turned up on her doorstep that very morning at sparrow's to tell her she was making a mistake.

She had been stepping out with Neville Pendlebury for the previous two months. The bootmaker had been pleasant enough company even though she hadn't felt a glimmer of anything resembling attraction during their time together. But, Cora had reasoned, it was certainly nicer to have coffee at the Coffee Palace in Hindley Street or take in a matinee at West's Pictures with a man, rather than with her sisters. He was handsome, too, tall and always smartly dressed. How shallow she'd been to let those superficial attractions blind her to his true nature. She'd been flattered, and then humiliated by him.

A week before she'd enlisted to go to war, they'd attended a screening of *The Eagle's Mate* starring Mary Pickford. In the musty humidity of the picture palace, as smoke from pipes and cigarettes wafted languorously towards the ceiling and blurred the image of the blonde bombshell, Neville had used the cover of darkness to grasp her hand. Just as young innocent Anemone Breckenridge was being abducted by a lecherous band of mountain moonshiners, Neville took her fingers in his and whispered, 'Don't be scared, Cora.'

If only she had tugged her fingers from his right there and then, because the fact that she hadn't had become some kind of sign to him that he had the authority to tell her that her place was in Adelaide, not in the war.

'You can't possibly go,' he'd huffed. He'd stood on the front veranda. It was a hot Adelaide January morning and Cora squinted into the sun behind him, lifting her hand to shade her eyes from the burning sting.

'Yes, I can,' Cora replied. 'And I am.'

'But what about marrying me?'

Cora almost choked. 'We've never even talked of marriage.' For goodness sake, he'd never even kissed her— and in that moment she was very glad of it.

'Well, I …' Neville stammered, anger tightening his jaw. 'I was going to but now you're going to up and leave anyway, so why would I? No wife of mine will go to war, be around all those soldiers.'

'It's lucky you didn't get around to asking me then. It saved me from having to reject you.'

'You've just lost your last chance, Cora. No one else will want you now.'

There were footsteps in the hallway behind Cora and then a gentle hand rested calmly on her shoulder. She knew it was her father.

'Who's this then?' he asked, his gruff voice echoing in the hallway.

'This is Neville Pendlebury. He doesn't want me to go to war.'

Arthur looked Neville Pendlebury up and down, tipped forward on his toes and slipped his hands under his suspenders. 'Is that so?'

Neville Pendlebury whipped off his flat cap. 'How do you do, Mr Barker. Surely you, of all people, agree with me that the war is no place for a young lady and definitely not our Cora.'

Cora hissed in a breath. *Our Cora?*

Her father huffed. 'I don't believe war is a place for anybody—young lady or young man. But I don't have much of a say in world affairs from my front doorstep in Mile End now, do I?'

'But surely you'll stop her from going? I mean, what will the blokes say when they find out she's heading off? They'll say I can't keep a girl, that's what.'

Arthur's silence was deafening. Then, 'How long have you been stepping out with this bloke, Cora?'

'Three months,' Neville blurted.

'Eight weeks,' Cora clarified.

Arthur took a good long look at the man on his doorstep. 'Too long, if you ask me. You best be off, young man.'

Arthur took a step towards Neville Pendlebury. Neville Pendlebury took a step back. Then another, then another until he reached the front gate and stepped over it. He turned to walk away then stopped and looked back at Cora.

'What good do you think you'll be over there? You're not young any more, Cora. When you get back, no one will have you. You'll be nothing but a washed-up spinster.'

It was only when Cora felt her nails digging into her palms that she realised she'd been clenching her fists into tight balls. Her father tsk-tsked and then swore.

'Don't know what you saw in that bloke, Cora.'

'I let flattery get in the way of my good sense. How stupid of me.'

'You'd have to give up your job if you got married. That would never suit you, would it, love?'

And after that, Cora had done exactly as she'd planned, perhaps with even more fire in her belly. She'd walked into the city and pledged a solemn oath that she would well and truly serve her Sovereign Lord the King; that she would resist His Majesty's enemies and cause His Majesty's peace to be kept and maintained; and that she would in all matters appertaining to her service faithfully discharge her duty according to law.

Underneath the words SO HELP ME GOD in bold capital letters on her enlistment form, she had signed her name, proudly, dutifully, on the dotted line. She had signed her affirmation that she wasn't precluded from service due to being married, that she indeed fell into the category of single or widowed (single); and that she was well between the ages of twenty and forty-five years (thirty-one). In return for her service, she was to receive free passage to and from Australia, and any pay and allowances set forth by the AIF, as long as she was of service for the duration of the war or until sooner legally discharged or dismissed from military service.

At thirty-one years of age, five feet eight inches, nine stone one pound, with a chest measurement of thirty-two and a half inches, complexion fair, eyes brown and hair brown, Staff Nurse Cora Barker had been deemed fit to serve.

She hadn't been concerned then about what she might be faced with at a military hospital. She had seen her fair share of misfortune, disease and death. She'd treated patients with cancers of all kinds and tuberculosis and stroke and poisonings; broken bones on those who'd fallen off horses; injuries from attempts at suicide; the symptoms of syphilis and smallpox. She'd tended women with broken jaws and ribs and men with black eyes from late-night fights in Hindley Street. She had answered the call to serve with patriotism and pride.

She had so much more to offer than tending the ill back home when the boys at the front desperately needed medical care. She had left the knitting and the making of flannel garments to women who didn't possess the skills she had. They were doing their part and she would do hers.

Cora hadn't ever entertained second thoughts about her choice to go to war. If her parents had worried for her and her decision, they'd concealed it behind their proud smiles when they'd waved her goodbye. Those colleagues she'd left behind at the Adelaide Hospital had farewelled her with a gift of dried fruit from the Riverland and warm embraces on the ward.

The war was her chance to see the world and experience all its pleasures and challenges. She wasn't one of those daughters of the South Australian elite who were sent to England to learn manners and meet English men who they could marry once they were 'finished', spending just enough time in Blighty to cultivate an accent. Those young women had connections with the fashionable and the civilised, and always seemed to have an aunt or an older cousin who was available to act as chaperone. Who would Cora have chosen as a chaperone? And how would her parents ever have afforded it? Had those privileged young Australian women ever stayed at Harefield, she wondered.

'Cora.'

She looked up from her scrubbing brush, her thoughts returning to hog bristles and the cold sudsy water she was swirling around the floorboards. Gertie was motioning towards her. 'Come and see this.'

At the doorway to the new operating theatre, they pulled up to avoid running into two flat cap–wearing men struggling with a large sideboard.

'Watch out there, lassies.' One of the men winked generously and the other let out a low whistle. Cora smiled at their optimism. They were surely not a day under sixty and were moving as slowly as their age befitted. Despite the piece of furniture being heavier than the two of them put together, they still had time for humour.

'How is this so bleedin' heavy?' moaned the taller of the two.

'Might be beech?' the other breathed as he shuffled backwards.

'You're asking me? I'm a bootmaker, not a bloody arborist.'

'Can we help at all?' Gertie asked.

'Don't trouble yourself, sisters. You need those precious hands for nursing. Leave it to us.'

Cora and Gertie watched them struggle on, ribbing each other good-naturedly, and when they were out of earshot Cora said, 'I don't suppose there are any young men left in the village to do the heavy work.'

'I wouldn't expect so.'

'The papers are saying that a million young British men have already enlisted.' Cora felt a shiver ripple right through her, the hairs at the back of her neck pricking.

'A million?' Gertie whispered in disbelief, her eyes wide with shock.

Cora did a quick sum in her head. Australia's population was five million people: men, women and children. She couldn't imagine what a street or an office or a factory looked like when one in five people—and more if you took into account that half the population were women—had left to go to war. How many empty spaces were there in factories and at kitchen tables and in hearts and beds?

Your Country Needs You. Cora had seen the poster in the window of the White Horse Inn as they'd driven through Harefield on the day they'd arrived. It seemed Britons had heeded Kitchener's call, had answered his beckoning finger just as the children of Hamelin had followed the Pied Piper's melodic flute.

'What did you want to show me, Gertie?'

Gertie seemed to have forgotten and it took her a moment to find her train of thought. 'Oh, yes. The floor.' They stepped inside. The removal of the carpet had revealed the most intricate black-and-white tiled floor. Even covered with grit and dust, it was exquisite.

'It looks rather like an enormous chessboard, doesn't it?'

Gertie knelt down and ran her fingers across the cool tiles. 'It'll be easy to keep these clean. A scrub with some bleach should do the trick.' She stood, rubbed her hands together to sweep off the dust and then palmed them down her skirt.

'What's next?'

Chapter Four

Just before lunch, a convoy of grunting and groaning army trucks chugged up the Harefield Park driveway in a rumbling line.

The vehicles had ferried bed frames, mattresses, small bedside tables, desks, shelves and lamps up from London, and the nurses and the two Chesters dragged what they could up three flights of stairs to furnish the staff quarters, and arranged as many desks and chairs as they could find in the offices on the second floor.

'Just here, I think, Cora,' Gertie huffed. She and Cora steadied and lowered the piece of furniture to the carpet.

'This'll make someone a nice office.'

'I believe it's for one of the top brass. A colonel or a major or … I can't quite remember.' Gertie shrugged.

Cora flexed her fingers and moved to the windows. She couldn't resist taking a moment to admire the view. The nurses looked out over the grounds. The curtains had already been pulled down, folded and stored away, and the window frames—wide enough to be a perfect spot to sit with a pillow and a book—were covered with a fine layer of dust. Cora ran a finger down the pane, fighting the temptation to write her own name there.

'Whoever sits here will be able to keep an eye on everything. The comings and goings of trucks, of supplies …' Cora's voice trailed off and she swallowed the lump in her throat. 'And soldiers.'

Next to her, Gertie sighed and reached a hand to Cora's forearm, squeezing it softly. 'Yes.'

'The news in the papers isn't good. I expect we'll be full before long.'

The window afforded a superior view over the front lawns and the emerging little village of wooden ward huts that had been positioned there to accommodate their patients. Long and rectangular, all in a row, there was a covered area at the front of each, no doubt aimed at protecting the patients from the rain in the cooler months and the sun in the warmer ones. Cora wondered if the doors would be wide enough so the beds might be moved outside. Even the bedridden would need fresh air.

On the north side was an open parkland, sparsely decorated with birches and elms, and a cricket pitch with one lonely stump at each end. Cora knew there was nothing surer: the patients would want to play and, if she did say so herself, she'd learnt a few skills as a child by playing with the other children in her street. She smiled at the memory of boys in short pants kicking dirt up in their wake as they bolted between wickets. There was always a ball that flew up onto a neighbour's roof, never to be seen again. Those innocent days felt suddenly like a hundred years ago.

Were any of those boys in the army now, serving the King?

Would any of those boys become patients at Harefield hospital?

'Do you ever worry, Gertie ...'

'Worry about what?'

Cora turned her eyes from the view and searched Gertie's face for any signs of the doubts and worries that had been blooming inside her own mind since they'd arrived in England.

'I don't want you to think I'm not excited to be here. I truly am,' Cora blurted.

'And so am I, Cora. I can think of no better place to be a nurse than where our boys will need us the most. Can't say I'll miss the old men with gout and all the slow deaths from cancer. But.'

Gertie seemed so assured. Cora breathed deep. 'But. I've only ever treated one gunshot wound.'

'You've one up on me then. Who was it?'

'A farmer was climbing through a wire fence while holding a rifle. Shot himself in the foot.'

'Injuries?'

'Lost his big toe.'

Gertie chuckled.

'Which hardly prepares me for what we might have to treat here. I've been trying not to, but I find myself feeling a little ...'

'Nervous? Me, too. It would be entirely unexpected if we weren't.'

Gertie pulled Cora in for a sideways hug. 'We shall take each day as it comes. And that means waking every morning, washing and dressing, drinking tea and eating toast so we may steel ourselves for whatever is to face us. You're an experienced nurse, Cora. You'll excel, I'm certain of it. We all will.'

Cora tried to soak up some of Gertie's confidence to bolster her own wavering belief in herself. Everything suddenly felt real and close. What was to come? How would they be tested? All the courage she'd felt when she'd enlisted, when she'd stepped onto the ship, when she'd waved goodbye to her family in Adelaide, was wobbling. And they hadn't even seen a patient.

'Speaking of tea, I do believe it's time for a cuppa.' Gertie beckoned. 'You coming?'

By mid-afternoon, the nurses and the Chesters—a dusty but determined group—had left the main house for the newly constructed wards on the front lawns.

Cora stepped inside one and took a moment to study the unprepossessing space. Above, wooden beams and the silver of corrugated iron created only the flimsiest barrier to the cold or the heat. When it rained, she imagined it would sound like a herd of cattle passing overhead. The wooden walls looked more substantial and two stoves positioned in the middle of the hut would throw a decent sort of heat, she thought.

Outside, there was an orchestra of hammering and sawing, of raised voices and commands and the throaty rumble of truck engines. A warmish breeze moved through the hut and the women turned their faces to it, like sunflowers to the sun, breathing in the smell of sawdust and horse manure.

The beds they'd moved in that morning needed linen and blankets and plump pillows and a bedside cabinet for the men to store their possessions, however meagre they might be.

There was still so much to do to transform the estate into a functioning hospital but Cora was determined not to allow herself to be overwhelmed by it. Her left shin throbbed at the exact spot she'd come into clumsy contact with the curved leg of a mahogany piano stool, and she knew a bruise was blooming there. But she couldn't let herself be distracted by it. The work needed to be done and done swiftly.

'Cora,' Fiona called. 'Come and have something to eat.'

The Chesters had made a table of sorts on one of the bed frames, and a white plate filled with slices of fruitcake sat in the middle of it. Next to it, another bed provided somewhere for them all to sit. Mrs Chester poured cups of tea from a pot on the floor and passed them out. Cora held hers between her hands like a vicar might hold a cup of sacramental wine. She had always found something extremely comforting in a cup of tea.

Leonora cleared her throat, and her cup and saucer tinkled as she set them on the floor. 'While the silence has been a respite from all the noise outside, perhaps we should take a moment to learn a little about one other.' She made a point of nodding to the Chesters. 'We don't know you two from Adam.'

Mrs Chester and her daughter exchanged glances. Mother seemed to be urging her daughter on but Jessie remained silent.

Leonora sensed their nervousness and adherence to propriety and jumped to her feet anyway. She smoothed down her skirt and saluted before laughing gaily.

'Staff Nurse Leonora Grady reporting for duty.' She held her right hand in place at the side of her forehead, her palm out. Dirt had rubbed into the creases of her palm, like a fortune-teller's life lines. Having elicited the laughter she was after, Leonora dropped her arm and sat down so quickly on the bedsprings behind her that her skirt puffed up around her legs like a balloon.

'Well,' Leonora said, spreading her fingers wide on her knees, as if she were about to settle in by the bedside of a sleepy child and recite something beginning with 'once upon a time'. 'I'm from Sydney. I'm over here rather than being back there,' she cocked her head in a direction that may have been south but Cora really had no idea which way was anywhere, 'because my fiancé, Lieutenant Percival Jones—Percy to me and his family—is in France and by hook or by crook we're going to see each other soon. Even if I have to swim the Channel myself.'

Fiona gasped. 'But the sea mines, Leonora! It's far too dangerous.' She clutched a hand to her neck. Fiona seemed to foresee danger everywhere and in everything. As she spoke, her face grew paler and paler. Cora had never seen anyone who was more in need of a spot of sunshine.

'You'd make it if you swam as fast as Fanny Durack,' Gertie said, laughing.

'Who's Fanny Durack?' The words were spoken softly, almost in a whisper. The nurses turned as one, altogether surprised at the realisation that the young woman, Jessie Chester, had finally spoken. Her blue eyes were lit with a keen curiosity.

'Fanny Durack is an Australian Olympic champion,' Gertie explained. 'At the games in Stockholm back in 1912, she won a gold medal in the world's first women's Olympic swimming event.'

Leonora leant forward. 'It was in all the papers. She is extraordinarily famous back home in Sydney.' She jumped off the bed, her boots striking the wooden floor with a thud. She moved her right arm behind her, made an arc above her head and completed almost a full circle before lifting her left arm in similar fashion, as if her arms were windmills at her sides.

'That's the Australian crawl, ladies. Every young girl in Australia wants to be Fanny Durack and swim like she does.' Leonora sighed. 'My father would never let me go swimming at Bondi. He said it was indecent to appear in public wearing a swimming costume. He didn't want me parading around like that Annette Kellerman.'

'Oh, I love Annette Kellerman,' Cora sighed and turned to Jessie to explain. 'She's another Australian girl who upset people. They called her the Australian Mermaid. She wanted to swim just like the men, unencumbered by all sorts of clothing that only slowed her down. So, instead of wearing stockings, skirts and shoes into the water, she appeared in a one-piece outfit. Imagine the scandal! It revealed her legs and showed off every inch of her form. She tried a few times to swim the English Channel but never made it across.'

'She's an actress now,' Leonora added, looking quite envious of the fact. 'In Hollywood.'

Jessie straightened her back and glanced at her mother as if asking permission to speak, then proceeded anyway. 'I believe some of the suffragists exhibited their bathing suits in the Serpentine last year, in Hyde Park. In London. They were all arrested.'

'They were arrested for swimming?' Gertie was aghast.

'How dreadful,' Cora said. But she knew that wasn't the worst thing that had happened to Emmeline Pankhurst and her fellow suffragettes as a result of their battle to win the right to vote.

Mrs Chester laughed. 'Well, I know one thing, Sister. If you want to swim across the Channel to see your sweetheart, you'd better get practicing. It's thirty-one miles to France!'

'Oh, dear,' Leonora replied. 'I hadn't imagined it was actually that far. Perhaps I shall practice by swimming across the lakes here at Harefield Park.'

Win and Jessie laughed and Jessie clutched a hand to her stomach. 'I wouldn't attempt it. They're only knee deep.'

Leonora played at looking glum and Cora watched on, enjoying the reverie. She knew it couldn't last, this innocent joyousness, and that they would soon have more serious matters to speak of and much work to do, but it was cheering to see everyone determined to enjoy this moment while it lasted.

'Gertie?' Leonora glanced in her colleague's direction. 'Your turn.'

'Gertrude North from Wirrabara in South Australia. Everyone calls me Gertie except my grandmother and she's such a stern old thing I dare not ask her to do anything otherwise. My father and four brothers—I'm the only daughter—work at the timber mills and are still at home.' She dropped her confident gaze to her linked fingers. Gertie had long fingers. A piano player's hands, Cora's mother would have said. Gertie's long black hair was coarse as thatch and black as pitch and Cora wondered since the first day she'd met her how on earth Gertie tamed it under her veil. It always seemed to be springing out of its plait, which circled her head like a rope.

'My brothers are in protected occupations, you understand,' she added hurriedly.

'You have those back in Australia too, do you?' Mrs Chester asked.

Cora had often heard women explaining why their menfolk weren't in uniform, offering it up like a penance lest criticism or a white feather follow.

'Oh, yes,' Gertie answered. 'They're needed back home to keep the war going, too. I signed up to do my bit, just as they are. But in my own way.'

'Your father should be very proud of you, Gertie,' Mrs Chester said and, if Cora wasn't mistaken, Gertie's cheeks flushed the palest pink.

'Fiona. It's your turn,' Leonora urged.

Fiona shook her head in mortification. 'I've nothing interesting to say. I'm from Melbourne. Nowhere fancy. I'm a regular churchgoer and a nurse. That's all. Cora, it must be your turn.' Fiona turned to Cora, exceedingly keen to hand on the baton.

'My name is Cora Barker. I'm from Adelaide, a city named after a king's wife, I believe. William IV?'

Mrs Chester confirmed Cora's guess with a murmur of approval.

'Yes, he's the one. We have a street named after him, too. It runs right through the city, splitting the town mile halfway along, from north to south.' Cora reflected on her failure to know England's kings and queens off by heart. Surely Mrs Chester would think her some kind of heathen. The realisation made Cora wonder why she didn't feel more

British. This was the mother country, after all. And that diffidence wasn't about divided loyalties or any nascent doubt about the war. She wondered if there was something intrinsically different about being from a place so far away from the heart of the Empire. She had always felt more Australian than British, for as long as she could remember.

'I've been a nurse for fourteen years. I enlisted to be here for our boys who are sacrificing so much for us. It's the least I can do, to give up my comforts to ensure theirs. I don't have any brothers but I have two sisters, Eve and Grace. I'm a single woman so I was able to enlist.'

'There's no sweetheart waiting for you back at home? Or serving?' Win asked with a mother's mournful eyes.

'No.' Cora shrugged her shoulders and pushed thoughts of Neville Pendlebury from her mind. 'If I did have one, I wouldn't be here, so things work out the way they're determined to work out, don't you think?'

'I do believe you're right,' Win replied with a nod of agreement.

'So, am I the only girl here with a fiancé?' Leonora searched each face in the little party. 'Jessie? A nice village boy, perhaps?'

Jessie blushed. 'Oh, no. Not me.'

'Mrs Chester? Tell us about Mr Chester.'

Cora noted the shadow that flickered in the older woman's eyes. 'I'm widowed. Five years ago, my husband— Jessie's dear dad—died. Terence was a prince among men. He's buried right here in Harefield at St Mary's.' Her eyes welled and Jessie's gaze dropped into her lap.

Jessie looked up, hesitated, then explained. 'It was his lungs. Dad worked at the asbestos mill. It was the dust that made him sick.'

'We're sorry to hear it,' Cora said softly.

'I have a brother. Harry,' Jessie continued. 'He ... well, he's ...' She swallowed nervously and looked to her mother.

Win proceeded to explain. 'He was born lame, with an arm and a leg that don't work the way they do in other people. What he can't do with his body, he makes up for in being clever, though.' Win tapped her forehead. 'Smart as a whip, he is.'

The arrival of Matron Gray brought a swift end to the chatter.

'I hope you've enjoyed your afternoon tea. We have some supplies to unpack. Bales and bales of donated goods have just arrived from Australia. They've come up from Plymouth on a canal barge, would you believe. Imagine that! I understand there are blankets, pillows, linens and coats.'

At least our patients will be warm, Cora thought. And alive.

Chapter Five

20 May 1915

Jessie Chester struck a match.

She cupped her hand around it to protect the flame from the open window's draught and steadily held it to the wick of a long white tapered candle set on a chipped saucer, which sat in the middle of the kitchen table in a house on the high street of Harefield.

The Chesters didn't need the candle for light. The saucer sat right by the new oil lamp, a recent purchase that was an altogether more reliable form of lighting. The candle was decorative and solemn, lit every night after supper for the King, for all of England and for her soldiers. It was a tribute and a prayer for every young man from Harefield—and for that matter, nearby Uxbridge too—who was away fighting the Jerries.

When the flame flickered and took hold, Win murmured, 'God bless 'em,' and crossed herself before bowing her head in a silent prayer. Jessie and Harry paused a moment to do the same. Then Harry reached over with his good hand and swept up the box of matches. He pushed his chair back, got to his feet and limped over to the pine dresser against the wall by the back door. With his taut left arm tucked up tight under his armpit, he reached for the drawer's knob with his right hand, tugged it open and dropped the matchbox inside. He closed the drawer with a hip shove and a scrape of stubborn wood on wood.

Jessie sighed. 'I'll have to rub some Velvet soap on those runners. It'll make that drawer easier to open and close.'

Harry turned to her with a blush on his fair cheeks. A lock of strawberry blond hair fell over his eyes and he swept it back into position. He had never taken to applying brilliantine to his hair like other young men and he was all the more handsome for it. 'I can open it just fine, Jessie. Stop your fussing. I know it's the noise that bothers you.'

'No, it's—' Jessie bit her tongue. She hadn't meant to embarrass him and if she continued explaining that her only aim was to make the drawer easier for him to open and close, she would only make her sisterly concerns more obvious. Instead, she shook her head from side to side with a look of confected consternation. 'It squeaks like a mouse caught in a trap. It gives me the shivers.'

Harry chuckled and resumed his seat. As he returned to the newspaper, he brought an elbow to rest on the table and absentmindedly stroked his neat moustache as he read. He'd grown it when his father had died, as a tribute of sorts, and Jessie thought it suited him. From a certain angle, Harry rather resembled what she imagined a young Oxford student might look like. In another life, in another body, and if he had been born to a different family in a different time and place, he might have been able to fulfil that secret lifelong ambition. But he was from Harefield with a father who had laboured at the Asbestos Works and a mother who had sewn for the families who sent their sons to Oxford and had their daughters marry its graduates. He'd only ever shared his dream with his sister and, once he'd said it aloud, it had disappeared as quickly as a puff of smoke and he'd never mentioned it again.

The candle flame and the lamp flickered. Jessie glanced at the open kitchen window and pulled her knitted shawl tighter around her shoulders. She could not remember it ever having been closed.

'The miasma, Jessie,' Win had always insisted. 'The fresh air keeps the miasma out. It's the only way to stay healthy, my dear girl. To let the fresh air in. If it was good enough for Queen Victoria, it's good enough for us. You best remember that when you have young 'uns of your own.'

Sometimes Jessie's fingers became so stiff with cold that she could barely feel the sewing needle she was pinching between her fingers, but her mother simply refused to allow her daughter to close the windows. Jessie had always harboured doubts about Win's belief that the air outside was fresh and healthful, given that it comprised a combination of odours from rows of backyard privies and scrawny hens, fumes from the nearby mills and smoke from coal burning in every stove and fireplace along the street and in every street in the village. All the odours and clouds of vapour and dust swirled together to create a noxious winter fog. But her mother had been insistent and Jessie had never dared fully close any window in the house when her mother was home lest she jinx herself or Harry, who surely had been jinxed enough, or her poorly father when he was alive. Jessie hadn't ever wanted to ask, but if it was true about the fresh air driving away the miasma, why had her father endured a long, painful and rasping death?

The Chesters had lit a candle for the first time last November, on the night that news had come through that Harefield had lost its first son, Ronald Smith. Jessie and Ronald had been in the same class at the village school, and one of his four sisters, Rosemary, was Harry's age. Jessie remembered that Harry had been sweet on Rosemary for a time, but she'd married and left the village years ago and Harry hadn't turned his attentions to any other girl since.

Ronald had been a sweet and friendly boy at school and had taken up work with the village grocer until last August when, just weeks after war had been declared, he'd left Harefield for the recruiting station in Trafalgar Square, arm in arm with a bunch of other local young men. When the whole village had turned out to wave them goodbye—for word had spread quickly that the first boys had heeded Lord Kitchener's call and were going off to fight—they'd marched down the street waving to everyone they knew, looking as proud as a school soccer team that had just walloped the side from Uxbridge.

Wondering what the commotion was about, Jessie had stepped outside the house and right into a crowd of people on the street. She'd managed to make her way to the front to see the boys waving and shouting 'Cheerio'. She'd pulled a white handkerchief from the pocket of her skirt and unfurled it like a flag, and had begun to wave it furiously when Ronald had jogged over to her.

'Goodbye, Jessie,' he'd said, tugging off his flat cap, his cheeks flushed with the idea that he was on the cusp of a great adventure. His eyes were bright with excitement and the spirit infected her too. She laughed and said, 'Your country needs you, Ronald. Godspeed.'

And when he'd reached for her shoulders and planted a loud kiss on her left cheek, she'd let him and laughed as he'd done it, and as he'd walked away, the crowd's cheers becoming louder all around her, she had pressed her fingers to the spot where his lips had touched her skin and marvelled at the fact that her first kiss was from a brave young man who was going off to war.

Ronald Smith had never returned to Harefield, not even to be buried. He'd been killed somewhere in Belgium and his remains had been dug into the earth there, in a field so far away from his family that he may as well have been buried on the moon.

The Chesters had even lit a candle for Tommy McIntyre, although he'd been a right bully to Harry all through school. When she'd heard he'd been killed, Jessie had tried to feel guilty about the time she'd cornered Tommy after Sunday school at St Mary's and given him what for.

'I swear, Tommy McIntyre. If you don't leave my brother alone, I'll—'

'You'll what?' he'd spat back, brimming with the confidence only a fifteen-year-old bully possesses. 'You standing up for your stupid brother? That lousy cripple? Little Harry Chester goes whining to his sister. He's a right sissy.'

She'd breathed deep and panicked, feeling humiliated at her sudden cowardice. Her legs had become frozen to the spot, her breath had snagged in her throat. Which is why she hadn't realised that her best friend, Dottie Higgins, had stepped forward and shoved Tommy McIntyre so hard he'd stumbled backwards and fallen flat on his back in the long grass behind the church. Dottie had stood over him, her little fists clenched in indignation.

'You leave my friends alone, you hear me? I'll come after you, I swear. I'll shove you harder next time, you can bet on it.'

Dottie's show of rage—stunning to Jessie and downright humiliating to Harry—hadn't had the desired effect. Tommy McIntyre had only become more of a tyrant and he'd then bullied Dottie too, mercilessly. The torture had only stopped when he'd left school the summer after the incident, when he'd taken up a job at the mill and married Elsie Glover. She was never without a black eye or a limp, that poor woman, until the very week her good-for-nothing husband went to war.

Jessie had tried to feel bad that the Jerries had killed Tommy McIntyre, she honestly had.

Ronald had been the first of the Harefield boys to be killed and Tommy the second. And since then, there had been so many casualties that it had become too sad to pray for each of them individually, to think of the young boys who owned those names—the boys Jessie had played hopscotch with at the village school, those boys who'd run amok at the village fair and after church on Sundays, the boys who'd fished down at the canal with sticks for rods and freshly dug worms for bait.

So a solitary candle was lit every night for everyone the Chesters had known and all they hadn't, no matter which village or city in England they hailed from.

The Chesters were quiet, contemplative. Harry turned the page of the newspaper and peered closer at the fine print. Win sat quietly with her own thoughts and Jessie picked up a glove from the sewing basket at her feet and laid it out flat on the kitchen table. Its owner, Mrs Pickles from two doors down, had ripped the suede on two fingers of the left glove on a bramble hedge while walking to work at the asbestos factory, and there were three jagged tears. Jessie searched through her biscuit tin of cottons and found a perfect match.

Jessie sewed. As a very young girl at school, she'd been skilled up in the talents she would need to be a good woman and wife and mother. She'd also learnt it, more practically, at her mother's knee, a chore born of family necessity. In the years since, she had sewn all her own clothes. House dresses, a woollen suit each year for best, and her own nainsook petticoats and cotton chemises. And shirts and trousers for Harry, and aprons, of course, for herself and her mother. Those skills had become her livelihood. She was a woman now, but not a wife or a mother, and her adroitness had cemented her position alongside her own mother as one of the best seamstresses in the village. The sad truth of it was that the war had created business opportunities for many, and the Chesters found themselves benefitting from the fact that so many men were away and the women left behind had taken up working in numbers greater than ever before. Who had the time these days to spend keeping house and hearth clean or to do their own mending or sewing? And having taken to heart the exhortations to *make do and mend*, not a day went past when there wasn't a knock on the Chesters' door from one of the village women wanting a ripped seam fixed or a dress taken in—or out, in some cases. The little sign in the window that read *Chester Seamstresses* was a source of pride for both Jessie and Win. Their skills and acumen had kept them out of the almshouses in Church Street and the workhouse when Terence had died.

In every other house on their street, the front room, with a window framed with a pretty net curtain, was an inviting sitting room with an armchair or two, a few books on a side table and a wedding photo on the mantel above the fireplace.

At the Chesters', the front room was a sewing room. Light from the north-facing window illuminated bolts of satinised cottons and lawns and silks and serges and linens, haberdashery items from cottons to lace trims and ribbons to match every shade of colour imaginable, and in pride of place sat the Singer sewing machine that had served them dutifully since Win's mother had bought it back in 1891, direct from a travelling salesman who'd knocked on the door with a catalogue and offered her hire-purchase.

'Made in Scotland,' he'd assured her with a wink. 'Glasgow.'

That acquisition had changed her life and had provided independence and an income for the Chester family. They hadn't been forced into one of London's notorious East End sweatshops and every penny they earned was their own. It also meant Harry had been able to be cared for at home when he was a child rather than being sent away, an option Win and Terence would never have countenanced.

Jessie lifted her needle towards the light of the oil lamp, closed one eye to focus, and threaded a length of pale pink cotton through the tiny hole. As she created tiny stitches, drawing the jagged edges of the glove's ripped finger together, she created an interweaving pattern of threads, a warp and a weft.

How many stitches had she sewn in her life? As many as there were stars in the sky?

Harry sighed and turned a page. His movement made the candle flame flicker and shadows danced on the kitchen walls.

'What's the news of the war, Harry?'

He sighed again. 'There's still a lot about the Zeppelin raid on London last month. Some of the injured are still in hospital.'

'To think that the Germans made it as far as London, floating above the streets like butterflies.' Win shivered. 'I'll never forget that day.'

Jessie remembered it. The first Zeppelin raids had happened along the coast back in January and then London had been bombed, killing dozens of innocents. Weren't their guns or bullets or searchlights enough to keep people safe? After that incursion, people turned their eyes to the sky more regularly, not to feel the warmth of the sun on their cheeks or to check for rain or to watch a nightingale or a woodlark fly by. They were constantly on the lookout for the return of those deadly war machines.

Harry read on. 'The prime minister is calling for more volunteers.'

'I hear there's some land girls on a farm just outside Ickenham,' Win said. 'They're picking strawberries. For jam.'

'That reminds me,' Jessie said as she sewed, her eyes fixed on her tiny stitches 'We're almost out. I'll pop to Read's tomorrow and pick up another jar.'

'Any chance of a box of custard creams while you're there?' Harry asked hopefully.

'And some more Tickler's Marmalade?' Win asked.

Jessie huffed then smiled. 'What is this, then? You think we're made of money? Jam and marmalade and custard creams? And it's not even anyone's birthday or Christmas.' She winked at her brother. 'I'll see what I can find.'

His attention returned to the paper. 'Look at this. It's an article about the Australian hospital.'

'Really?' Jessie set the glove she'd been mending on the table.

Harry peered closer in the dim light. 'The first soldiers are on their way, it says. From Turkey.'

'They'll not find a more sanitary hospital in all of England.' Win nodded with pride. 'It's as clean as a whistle.'

Jessie smiled at the memory. 'We certainly scrubbed it from top to bottom.'

It had been a week since Jessie and Win had been at Harefield Park, or the Australian hospital as it was now being called in the village. It had been an honour to be asked to help prepare it. If Australian soldiers had come all this way to help defend the Empire, they should be given every care and comfort they deserved when they were injured.

'I know the grounds well enough from watching Mr Billyard-Leake's cricket matches but what's it like inside? Is it very fancy?'

Jessie lifted her eyes and fixed her gaze in the corner of the ceiling. She saw the house again in her mind's eye. 'It has very grand proportions, indeed, but all the fancy things were being moved out when we arrived. It didn't really look like anyone's home, did it, Mum?'

Win shook her head. 'The grounds are filling up with huts and other buildings. It's like a little village now. Soon your beloved cricket pitch will be built over, I expect.'

'Surely not,' Harry exclaimed, barely hiding his shock at the idea.

'Surely yes,' Jessie replied. 'There are ward huts for soldiers all over the grounds, enough for sixty men in the winter and one hundred and fifty in the spring and summer. And inside the house itself, the bedrooms and sitting rooms are offices now.'

Jessie had spent her time at Harefield in wide-eyed wonder. Not just at the elegant house but at the manner in which the Australian nurses behaved with one another and with their matron. They laughed and joked freely and used their Christian names when they addressed each other. It was such an easy familiarity and one Jessie wasn't used to. First names were reserved for family. Neighbours and shopkeepers and friends were always Mrs and Mr and Miss.

'All the fresh air will do them good.' Win nodded to the open kitchen window and Jessie and Harry tried not to look at each other lest they break into giggles. The men might not have been safe from the Kaiser's bullets but they would certainly be safe from the miasma. 'I can't think of a better place for them to rest and get better than right here in Harefield. We're a small village with peace and quiet in abundance. Who wants to be in the dirt and smoke of

London, I ask you? They'll be very comfortable there, you mark my words.'

'I'm sure they will be.' Jessie's mind raced with a million questions.

Who were these young men on the way to the Australian hospital and what might have happened to them in battlefields so far away?

Chapter Six

21 May 1915

'I'm in desperate need of summer day dresses for my daughters. You can't be that busy. Surely you can squeeze me in?'

Jessie propped open the front door with her boot and ushered Mrs Pritchard inside, out of the warm spring breeze. The stout woman had the great privilege of being married to a local merchant who had become wealthy through his ownership of a fleet of canal boats that shipped lime from the quarries around Harefield into London for the making of concrete.

'We will always make time for one of our best clients,' Jessie replied with a courteous smile. Mrs Pritchard had expensive tastes and a tight purse and she was fully aware that Jessie could make up a frock for a fraction of the price she might have to pay in any of the fashionable London department stores. Mrs Pritchard was more interested in the contents of her purse than the social cachet a designer label might attract. Jessie was glad of it, too.

'You're after summer day dresses, you say? Let me think,' Jessie said. 'I have some new lawn, if you'd like to see it. It's in the prettiest of white with fine yellow daises and I found satin ribbon to make waistbands and matching trim on your daughters' hats, if you'd like. Or perhaps this blue-grey light wool? Or grey-blue, depending on which way you look at it. In a summer suit, it would go very well with grey stockings.'

'I don't know,' Mrs Pritchard said, turning up her nose just a little.

'I think it's lovely to see colour on ladies' legs, isn't it, now that skirts are a little shorter. Especially in these warmer months.'

Mrs Pritchard manoeuvred her large girth around the sewing table, the Singer and the bolts of calico and other cloth. 'I can't say I approve of shorter skirts,' she declared, glancing down at her own ankle-skimming brown silk suit.

Jessie had sewn it herself four years before, when there were no thoughts of war and no such thing as austerity fashion. Women's hemlines still skimmed the ground then.

'This war is creating an excuse for some people,' Mrs Pritchard's emphasis was on the *some*, which clearly meant people like Jessie and not people like her own daughters, 'to go around exhibiting the kinds of behaviours I never thought I'd see. Why, Miss Chester, I hear young ladies are going to the cinema on their own these days, to sit in the dark with young men and get up to who knows what.' Her eyes bulged in an expression of pure horror and she clutched a fist to the voluminous lace bow at her throat. 'With no chaperone, Miss Chester. *No chaperone*. It's simply unheard of.'

'It matters not to me, Mrs Pritchard,' Jessie replied quietly. 'I don't get much opportunity to go the cinema.'

'We may be at war, but there's no need for our standards of decorum and propriety to slip. What are we fighting for if not to preserve our very way of life?' The older woman lifted her chin and looked down her nose. 'Nothing good will ever come of the moving pictures, I assure you. It's not something I would ever let my girls do, that's for certain.'

In the same way Mrs Pritchard didn't approve of rising hems or young people sitting in proximity to one another in a darkened cinema, she clearly didn't approve much of wartime-inspired austerity, either. She snatched the kid glove from her right hand and smoothed her fingers over a bolt of azure blue rayon that Jessie had positioned near the sewing table. Jessie pulled her lips together to stop her smile ruining the moment and the thought that Mrs Pritchard noticing the fabric had been mere coincidence.

'This is rather delightful, isn't it? Such a fetching colour.'

'It's very pretty indeed.'

'It's not silk, I expect?'

'Sadly, no,' Jessie replied. 'It's been difficult to source silk, with the war, but this rayon is produced in Coventry. All English, you see. I do believe it's our duty to support the country at a time like this, don't you, Mrs Pritchard?'

Mrs Pritchard's chest puffed out with patriotic fervour, which made her ample bosom appear even larger. Jessie took a step back to make room.

'Perhaps a dance dress for Arabella? Doesn't every young lady need to appear to her best advantage? It's more important than ever in these uncertain times.'

Jessie didn't need any explanation. Men were scarce and a young woman on the hunt for a suitable husband had to make use of every advantage to come her way. If Mrs Pritchard happened to believe that an azure blue rayon might help her daughters' chances at matrimony, who was Jessie to argue?

'If I recall,' Jessie moved to Mrs Pritchard's side and slid her thumb and forefinger down the smooth fabric, 'this is the exact colour of Miss Arabella's eyes. I ordered some ribbon for her, perhaps two years ago, and I remember you commented on it at the time. I might even have some left.'

Mrs Pritchard's eyes gleamed and Jessie was almost certain she could see a church and a wedding gown reflected in them.

Jessie continued. 'I can see this with multiple petticoats underneath, so it appears as if the young lady might be wearing hoops, but petticoats are far easier to negotiate, especially when dancing. Let me show you something.'

Jessie found a sketch on her desk. She had been inspired by a frock she'd seen in the women's pages of the *Illustrated London News*.

Mrs Pritchard snatched the sketch from Jessie.

'Oh, yes. That's exactly what I was imagining. Modern yet modest. It'll be perfect for dances during the summer. Who could possibly bear it if all our social occasions were put on hold too? I expect we'll go on having cocktail parties and dances and afternoon teas, as we always did.'

'I'm sure there will still be social outings,' Jessie replied.

'I fully expect there to be invitations to Harefield Park, in any case. The people I mix with in the village—and

Uxbridge—are most excited at the idea of being invited to see what the Australians have done to the park. Did you know the Billyard-Leakes have moved into the village? I had afternoon tea with Mrs Billyard-Leake last week and she informed me that a group of volunteers are organising activities for the soldiers. Of course, the girls will be donating some of their precious time to their recovery. Mrs Billyard-Leake was exceedingly pleased when I told her.'

'She is very generous indeed,' Jessie replied. While Mrs Pritchard's comment piqued Jessie's interest, she let it slip away like water off a duck's back. Jessie had learnt long ago that the likes of Mrs Pritchard believed that the young women of the village who laboured for a living were as unlike her daughters as a donkey was from a starling. She would, in her casual snobbery, not even consider that Jessie, or the women who worked at the asbestos factory, or in munitions, were young women for whom she had to give a single thought. Their lives were lived in a manner that was invisible to her and other women like her.

Jessie fetched her workbook and flipped it open to a new page. At the top, she wrote *Pritchard* and the date and then waited. 'When will you be wanting Arabella's new frock then, Mrs Pritchard?'

'Why, as soon as possible, of course. Invitations will be arriving at any time, I expect.'

Jessie scanned her list of orders. 'At the moment I can give you a two-week turnaround.'

'Surely you can do something with a little more haste.' Mrs Pritchard glanced around the sewing room. 'I don't notice you bursting at the seams with customers.'

Jessie bit her tongue. She already had a list of jobs a mile long, as well as mending from the drycleaners in Uxbridge, which had increased in a steady flow since the war had begun. And Win's time would be taken up with her voluntary work sewing undergarments for the army and the navy and knitting socks for soldiers.

'I'll do my best for ten days. I hope that suits. I'm assuming I'm to use the same measurements for Miss Arabella? Will she require a fitting? She hasn't grown taller since the last time you measured her for me?'

'Oh, no. She's as she ever was.' Arabella and her younger sister Lucinda never came in person. Jessie imagined it was because Mrs Pritchard had convinced them that the garments she purchased had been sewn in a fancy salon in Soho by a French émigré couturier, rather than a village girl with an old Singer. 'Fine,' Mrs Pritchard said firmly and then added, as if she were talking to herself, 'I must take a trip to Bon Marché in Uxbridge to choose a new hat for Arabella.' She tapped an index finger to her chin. 'Perhaps a sweet little toque with a net veil.' And then she snapped out of her millinery reverie as if she had just remembered where she was and glanced about the Chesters' front room with a little nod of condescending disapproval. It must be so different to her own house.

Jessie could only imagine the Pritchard home. Mrs Pritchard most likely drew fine silk curtains of an evening and sat on rich brocade upholstery. In a reception room kept specifically for the purpose, there would be a piano on which the young ladies of the household played amusing tunes to suitors, abundant light for embroidery and a particular comfortable chair reserved purely for the reading of books.

Jessie moved quickly to open the front door for Mrs Pritchard.

'We'll see you then.'

'You will, and ...' Mrs Pritchard paused, lowering her voice to a conspiratorial whisper. 'I have some words of advice for you, young lady, and I suggest you take heed. The village will soon be overrun by Australian soldiers. Your own mother might not think to say it to you, but beware, Jessie. I've heard all sorts of things from London about their true natures. You wouldn't want to know what I've heard. Let me just say, it's best that girls like you don't have anything to do with them.'

With that sage advice, and without even waiting for a reply from Jessie, Mrs Pritchard stepped out onto the street. Watching through the net curtain at the window, Jessie saw her glance quickly in each direction before scuttling away towards the top end of the high street.

'She's gone, Mum. It's safe to come out.'

Win emerged from the kitchen and Jessie rolled her eyes at her mother.

'Thank goodness for that,' Win huffed. She crossed the room and peered through the lace curtains at the window as if to make doubly sure. '"Girls like you." Why I ... to think you would need any advice from that woman. What a nerve ...' Jess had never heard her mother swear but it appeared she might be on the verge.

Jessie sighed as she sat at the sewing table, set her elbow on the table and dropped her chin to her hand. 'I didn't take it to heart, Mum.'

'I appreciate her business but the way she looks down her nose at us ... she's all fur coat and no knickers, she is.'

'Mum,' Jessie giggled and held a hand to her mouth.

'What?' Win asked, all faux innocence. 'You know it's true. Lucky for us she doesn't have any qualms about dressing so fancy when the boys are off fighting. It makes her look a bit suspicious, don't you think? People will look at her in the street and wonder where her money's coming from.'

'Her husband, of course,' Jessie replied. 'I expect his business has never been better.'

'Who's all fur coat and no knickers?' Harry came into the room from the kitchen, a newspaper tucked under one arm. His eyebrows shot up at the sight of his mother in such a tizzy.

'Mrs Pritchard,' Jessie managed before bursting into laughter. Both siblings watched on as their mother's face blushed a deep crimson.

'Oh, stop it, you two,' Win huffed good-naturedly. 'I wouldn't say it outside these four walls but I've never liked her and that's that. I took a set against her years ago and I won't change my mind.'

'Years ago? What happened?' Harry pressed a hand on the sewing table to steady himself.

'Oh, nothing in particular,' Win replied hurriedly, averting her eyes. 'Tell me, Jessie. What's she wanting this time?'

Jessie picked up a pencil and reached for the sketch that had caught Mrs Pritchard's eye. 'A fancy frock for Arabella. She's expecting to be invited to Harefield Park to meet all the important Australians.'

Win reached for her sewing apron, looped it over her head and tied it behind her back with a firm bow. 'Best we get to work then.'

Harry took the hint. 'I'll make tea, shall I?'

'That would be lovely,' Jessie called out as he went to the kitchen. 'And I've a mind to have a custard cream. Or two. If you've not eaten them all, Harry.'

Jessie opened her workbook. In it were the measurements of their customers and all the tasks they had completed for them. There were sketches of designs, notes on the lengths of material each needed, how much satin ribbon or lace had been incorporated, if there had been embroidery or rosettes attached.

As she wrote down the details for Arabella's new frock, her thoughts went to dances and azure blue dresses and the familiar realisation that she made beautiful frocks for others to wear to places she would never be welcome.

Chapter Seven

1 June 1915

For weeks, the Australian staff at Harefield Park had been on tenterhooks as they waited for the first injured Australian soldiers to arrive.

Cora had found sleep difficult. Once Gertie had turned off the lights and set her alarm, Cora's mind whirred with a million questions: about the soldiers, their medical conditions and her own abilities. She thought of home, of her parents and her sisters, Eve and Grace. What might they be doing this first day of June? As she lay in the dark, listening to Gertie snore and the other nurses breathe and toss and talk quietly to themselves in their sleep, she found herself trembling with a gnawing sense of expectation and unease.

Time felt strangely like turning one's gaze up to the sky while waiting for a storm to roll in, when the clouds were so visible on the horizon—heavy with rain, coloured with dark purples and greys, ominous and foreboding.

She knew they were in the eye of a hurricane, in the place where the quiet couldn't last.

Everything at Harefield hospital was ready. Matron Gray, the nurses and the Chesters had worked a miracle. There was now a functioning operating theatre on the ground floor and offices and staff quarters upstairs in the main house. In the four long ward huts on the expansive front lawns, there were twenty-two beds—eleven set out along each long wall— with a bedside cupboard alongside each. Cora had looked with pride at the exact hospital corners on each mattress. War or not, there was no excuse for standards to slip. Feather pillows had been plumped and positioned, open invitations for weary hearts and minds to lay their heads upon.

In the middle of the ward, a coal fire was ready to be stoked to ward off the overnight chill and, at the far end, a nurses' desk had been positioned in the best spot to keep an eye on recovering patients. Between the rows of beds there was a table or two at which soldiers might sit and read, or play cards or chess. Rows of windows set into the walls of the hut allowed for the movement of fresh air and precious light and provided a view to the world the soldiers hoped to soon re-enter. Each had a view across the lawns and the fields in front towards Rickmansworth Road, which led south to Harefield.

The floors were washed and clean, patient record systems had been established and the nurses had spent time refreshing the skills they'd learnt during their training. In a storeroom at the rear of each ward, cupboards were filled with options for pain relief, with bandages, slings and cotton wool. Scalpels and other items had been sterilised and the operating theatre was clean and waiting, ominously stark and sterile.

At lunchtimes and when their shifts were over, the nurses joined the doctors, officers and administrators in the mess and, while they ate their lunch of baked meatloaf and boiled vegetables, they scoured the newspapers for hints of what might come their way and, importantly, when. The officers always knew far more than they would ever tell the nurses, a fact evident in their shadowed eyes and tight-lipped grimaces. All Matron Gray would tell her nurses was, 'Be prepared, sisters.'

The papers were full of foreboding, too. The German attacks in Flanders had been repulsed by the Allies, and Australians were already on Turkish soil. Only a week before, it had been reported that sixteen thousand men had landed at Gallipoli at the furthest end of the Mediterranean to secure a supply line through to Russia. It had seemed to be a success, according to the official war correspondents' reports and other information from the War Office. The Allies were steadily advancing and, while the Turks were still claiming to have inflicted major losses on the Allies, and announced they had captured a number of Australians, no one believed that to be anything more than Turkish propaganda.

Cora had assumed the mantle of public pronouncer. She had taken to reading aloud any relevant particulars from the paper while the other nurses finished their lunches and sipped their tea.

'"The War Office in London states that despite continual opposition, the British troops have established themselves across the peninsula and are steadily advancing."'

'Hoorah!' Leonora exclaimed.

'Wait a moment.' Cora's finger traced a straight line down the column of newsprint. 'Here, further down. The Turks say the Allies have lost four hundred dead and two hundred captured.' She searched each face around the table. 'But that's what they would say, isn't it? Of course they want us all to believe they're victorious even though they can't possibly be.'

'What about the numbers of injured, Cora? Does it say how many?' Gertie knew, as they all did, that they wouldn't be treating the dead, God rest their souls. How many men were at this very moment on hospital ships in the Dardanelles, being tended to by nurses striving to keep their balance on the rolling seas? And when might those injured men make their way to Harefield?

At breakfast on the second day of June, the second day of summer, their waiting was over.

Matron Gray joined her nurses in the mess. 'Please, sit, sisters.' The matron always looked efficiently busy but never troubled. Something had changed. Her lips were pulled tight together and there was a clench in her jaw that made the tendons on her neck corded and obvious.

'You have some news, Matron?' Cora asked.

'I do.'

'Are we to finally have some patients?' Leonora asked. 'Are we at last able to do what we were sent here to do?'

The matron spoke gravely. 'We are to expect our first patients this afternoon. Men will be arriving by train and disembarking at Denham Railway Station. From there, they'll be transported here by ambulance and truck. And before you ask, I've no idea about the extent of their injuries. Each patient is to be issued with a suit, a flannel shirt, underpants, socks, slippers and pyjamas, two towels, a face washer, two plates, knife, fork, two spoons, a mug and a bowl. They'll be in desperate need of fresh clothes, I expect.'

Cora blinked away the thought of how much blood might be encrusted in their uniforms.

'I'm proud of you and the work you've done to turn this house into a hospital. You've earned the respect of the army and the doctors here. Please know that. You have been provided with the best possible training and you are all sensible and intelligent girls. I'm going to need you to be all that and more in the coming days and weeks.' Matron Gray paused, glanced at her entwined hands for a moment and then looked at each of them in turn. 'There is not much more I can say, but today's arrivals will only be the beginning. We've had word from the army that the beds we have prepared won't be near enough.'

Fiona squeezed her eyes closed and began to whisper, 'Our Father who art in Heaven.' She was as white as a freshly laundered sheet.

Cora took a moment to process the meaning of the announcement. 'The papers are saying that the Turks are claiming four hundred casualties on our side. Perhaps that's true after all.'

Matron Gray met Cora's gaze, directly, firmly. 'I'm afraid it's far worse. There were two thousand casualties by sundown on the first day of the attack in the Dardanelles.'

'Two thousand?' Fiona scrambled for a handkerchief from the pocket of her uniform and dabbed at her eyes.

'As many as five hundred men are on their way to us, injured in the assault on Gallipoli. They're being evacuated to barges right there on the beaches and then treated in hospital ships within striking distance of the battle. I can't imagine …' Matron Gray's voice trailed off. Her nurses watched her, hanging on every word. 'Every available bed in Egypt, every hospital, hotel and school in Greece is at capacity. We're next in line to take the injured. I've just spoken with Lieutenant Colonel Hayward. More ward huts are to be constructed urgently on the front lawns. A chapel is to be built by the courtyard to cater for those who need spiritual comfort but who aren't well enough to go into the village churches to worship. And, inevitably, we are to have a mortuary too, near the staff quarters, as far away from the wards as it can possibly be.'

But close to where I lay my head, Cora thought. She was no stranger to death. She had mopped the brows of people who had passed from cancer or tired hearts or exhausted lungs or sudden strokes. She had nursed those who had died of the diseases of poverty, like tuberculosis and septicaemia and syphilis. But she had never seen war wounded.

Fiona reached for Cora's hand and they gripped each other's fingers. 'Those poor boys. All their families. So far away from home. They'll need us.'

'Yes, indeed.' Matron Gray nodded. 'The nurses and doctors on board the hospital ships—the *Alexandria*, the *Sicilia*, the *Gascon* among so many others—have done the best they can in what one can only imagine are the most extraordinarily difficult circumstances. But they've only been able to provide the most basic care. Only the most urgent operations have been performed, as well as some stop-gap measures I must confess I've not heard of in modern medicine. Medical staff have been administering anti-tetanus injections because so many of the men had to lie where they fell, in the mud, at risk of disease. They could only be stretchered out under cover of darkness, you see, or risk being shot at. Carbolic lotion–soaked bandages are being used to wash the wounds in the field. Everything possible is being done to prevent sepsis, under very trying circumstances.' The matron paused, composed herself. 'The medical teams have been completely overwhelmed by the number of casualties and the imperative is to get the men to us before the next wave of injured arrive. We must prepare ourselves, sisters.'

Cora watched Matron Gray's resolve and steeled herself to feel it too.

Next to Cora, Fiona had begun to sob.

No. 1 Australian Auxiliary Hospital, AIF Middlesex,
England
June 1st, 1915

Dear Mum, Dad, Eve and Grace,
Hello from Blighty! I'm settled in, you will be pleased to
know, and we're up and running, ready to admit patients,
which we expect to arrive any day now. The hospital itself
is situated among a lovely parkland setting—if I squint my
eyes it might be my beloved Botanic Garden—and I'm told
there are places to take long walks and admire the scenery.
It's a little way out of Harefield itself, which is a quaint
old village just twenty miles from London, a pleasant little
place filled with even quainter old homes. The grounds are
full of English oaks and yew trees and birches and there are
two lakes behind the house which are home to swans and
the grounds are alive with birdsong. As you might imagine,
I'm in heaven.

The ladies of the village have rallied to support the
boys too and it's such a bright feeling to know that there
is so much assistance available to us. We feel we have
been welcomed into the village with kind hearts and open
arms.

The other sisters and I would very kindly appreciate
bandages, if you are able to rally people back home. We
will wash them until they fall to pieces. Washcloths too,
but assure everyone that we don't simply use them once and
discard them.

That's all to report tonight. My friend Gertie is about
to turn off the lights so I'll finish up now. I'm with a lovely
bunch of nurses and I feel honoured to be sharing the task

*ahead with them. We are primed and ready to exercise the
full array of our skills on our injured diggers.*

   *Please say hello to everyone at home and I promise to
write again soon.*

   Love,
   Cora

Chapter Eight

2 June 1915

The Australian nurses stood in a jittery line, their gazes fixed on the driveway leading from Rickmansworth Road, their ears tuned to the throaty rumble of the motorised ambulances growing louder as the vehicles made their way towards the hospital.

'Here we go,' Cora whispered to Gertie. Gertie clutched at Cora's hand and Cora held on tight. Cora tried to swallow away her nerves but they created a stubborn lump in her throat.

'We're ready,' Gertie replied.

As wheels crunched on the gravel of the circular driveway, Cora straightened her shoulders and tried to calm herself with a deep breath.

Harefield hospital's first patients had arrived and the nurses' real work was about to begin.

When the engines rumbled to a stop, the front doors of the first vehicle opened with a groan and two khaki-clad motor girls leapt out of the driver's cabin, scurrying to open the rear doors, which opened outwards like a cupboard.

Before the doors swung open and revealed their human cargo, one of the motor girls turned and spoke to Matron Gray in a quiet voice.

'These are only the first, Matron. There's more. Plenty more. We'll be making the drive back and forth from the station all day and night.'

The matron nodded her understanding and thanked the motor girl. The nurses standing behind Matron Gray craned their necks to see inside the open doors, looking for all the world like baby birds crowded in a nest waiting for their mother to descend from the sky with a morsel in her beak. There were men on those canvas stretchers, underneath the blankets and the uniforms, Cora reminded herself.

As the first ambulance drove off back to the station, the nurses prepared to admit the first contingent of eight patients. The day would bring more and more men, they all knew, so haste was imperative.

'First to the ward,' Matron Gray instructed the porters. 'Sisters. Follow them. The doctors arrived last evening. They're waiting to see these men.'

'You right there, Sister?'

Cora blinked against the blinding whiteness of the operating theatre and managed to speak beyond her shimmering nausea to reply, 'Yes, sir.'

Every single man who'd arrived that morning needed surgery and Rugg was the first that day, the first of the war. The early morning light bounced from wall to wall and obviated the need for lamplight, and the theatre had become a hothouse. Cora felt a trickle of sweat drizzle down her back between her shoulder blades and she dabbed her forearm to her top lip, where she felt beads of sweat now cold. How was it that only two weeks ago this theatre had been a sitting room, filled with well-worn upholstered furniture, Oriental rugs, leather footstools and silk curtains? Now, instead of the perfume of flowers or wood smoke from the fireplace, the air was filled with the tang of antiseptic and the metallic smell of blood.

'You looked a little wobbly there for a moment.'

'Please don't trouble yourself, sir.' Cora willed herself to keep her eyes focussed on the soldier on the operating table.

Was she green about the gills? Had the surgeon noticed? Wasn't it to be expected that one might feel both curious and sick at seeing a war wound for the first time?

The four other medical staff hovering over the patient wore surgical gowns and white linen caps over their hair. Cora was the only woman. The sleeves on the men's surgical gowns were rolled up, exposing their forearms, so as not to interfere with the patient and to aid in the viewing of the wound.

Standing at the top of the table, the anaesthetist dripped ether on a wad of folded gauze that covered the unconscious patient's nose and mouth. The patient lay on a narrow trolley with a stainless-steel top. His hands met across his chest as if he were naturally slumbering rather than knocked out, and his lower body was covered by a sheet, exposing only his right lower leg. Across from Cora, the two surgeons murmured to each other. Both worked deftly with fine fingers as they aimed their scalpels precisely to slice away slivers of rotten flesh from the patient's gangrenous leg wound.

Cora glanced at the tray on her left side that was covered with a clean white cloth. Instruments were laid out on it in neat rows, still gleaming from the sterilisation process. A silver dish on the tray was the receptacle for pus-filled swabs. Cora had been well-trained, had more than a decade's experience behind her and had believed she had seen almost everything, but nothing in Adelaide, nor the extra army training she'd undergone, could have prepared her for this sight.

Gangrene had engulfed the soldier's lower leg. To an untrained eye, it might appear that he was wearing a bloodied sock that had been pulled halfway up to his knee. At the top of it, a pink leg with a normal calf muscle, and dark hair in whorls that one would expect on a man's leg. But below this imaginary line the limb was bloated, the skin so taut it looked as if it might split open, and oozing at two oval-shaped spots. The doctors believed that shrapnel still lay jagged and trapped inside the soldier's flesh.

One of the most profound things Cora had learnt as a nurse was that inside a person's skin—when you stripped away the length and colour of their hair and eyes and skin and the shape of their nose and jaw, when they were naked of the clothes with which they chose to decorate themselves— every body was remarkably similar. Each person was made up of flesh and bone and sinew and muscle and organs. And, like the flesh of any animal, it could be cut and sliced just as easily.

In surgery, a patient was, by necessity, depersonalised. They were a lung or a uterus or a leg. A foot or an abdomen or a cervical bone. This knowledge helped Cora cope with the slick sound of the blades slicing through flesh and sinew and muscle, and with the overwhelmingly rancid smell of rotting flesh.

She wished she had a mask infused with lavender to cover her mouth, to disguise the odour, but no one else in the theatre wore one, so she soldiered on, the odour permeating her nostrils like the scent of jasmine had on a summer day back home in Adelaide. She wished it were jasmine.

Cora looked up at the sound of footsteps on the floorboards.

'Excuse the interruption, sir,' Matron Gray said.

The doctor who'd enquired after Cora, the taller of the two at the table, didn't raise his scalpel from the patient. 'Matron Gray, as I've mentioned to you before, please call me Captain. When you address me as sir I feel a hundred years old.'

'Of course, Captain. I'm wondering about your progress. Will you see to all the listed surgical cases today?'

He swore under his breath and Cora pretended not to hear.

'If the army wants us to perform more surgery, they'll have to send more doctors. Two of us arrived last night and we are both attending to this poor blighter. The two of us and … how many nurses do you have?'

'Four.'

'Four,' he replied with a frustrated exhalation. 'I'll send word up the line as soon as I finish in here that they'd damn well better send more people.'

'Yes, sir. I beg your pardon. Captain.' The matron closed the theatre door behind her.

Two doctors and four nurses? Cora was not afraid of hard work but the ratio of medical staff to patients seemed unworkable, especially since the latest reports indicated that five hundred men were on their way from the front. Cora was the only nurse with theatre experience and when the matron had asked the nurses who might be best suited to work in the theatre on that first shift, Cora had willingly put up her hand.

'Why is it important to note the odour in fungating flesh?'

The captain changed position to continue debriding the patient's wound. Cora flicked her eyes to his face. He glanced quickly at her.

'Odour can indicate the type of infection in a patient, sir,' she replied steadily.

He flicked a quick glance at her. 'Captain will do.'

'Yes, Captain.'

'Precisely,' he replied. 'We're smelling putrescine and cadaverine. The by-products of degrading tissue in an anaerobic infection. This boy, for he really is a boy, has no doubt been stretchered out from a trench in a place that might once have been home to cows or horses or even possibly goats. Do the Turks keep goats, Abbott?'

His colleague chuckled. 'Can't say I know much about goats, Kent.'

So that was his name. Captain Kent.

'More's the pity. So, Sister, the Anzacs come along, dig up those fields and shovel through all that shit. Then the heavens open and it rains cats and dogs and the whole damn lot becomes a swirling pool of filth. And if that isn't bad enough, the rats arrive, great swarms of them, nibbling through kitbags and eating anything they can. Once you toss in mortars and shrapnel and bullets, this is what we end up with. A mangled boy of, what must he be, twenty-two? A boy who'll never walk on this leg again.'

Was Captain Kent expecting a reply? His pronouncement was certainly a speech and not a question, so Cora remained silent. She knew her place and kept her eyes on the patient and her tray of instruments. While she had many opinions about boys of twenty-two being permanently invalided by a Turk's bullets, it was not her place to air them in front of these men.

'Clamp.' Captain Kent reached over the patient towards her, his hand palm up, and Cora swiftly placed the instrument in his palm.

It was quite common for surgeons to talk while they were operating, in Cora's experience. In her civilian life, she'd heard more than she ever cared to about this club or that, about investments that had paid off or had been a disaster, about pretty wives and not-so-pretty ones, sons who had lived up to expectations and daughters who had married well. She had been invisible to those men, a plain face peering out from a head fully wrapped in a white veil and a loose white dress that hit the floor. She could have been anyone or no one, nothing but a machine to them, there to do their bidding and mop up the blood afterwards.

'I don't believe we've been introduced, Sister. I'm Kent.'

Cora raised her eyes to the captain's, allowing herself to properly look at him for the first time. His cheeks were hollowed and held little colour, as if he'd been inside an operating theatre for months and not just since breakfast. His blue eyes were pale, the colour of an autumn morning back home.

'Sister Barker.'

'I'm very pleased to meet you, Sister Barker. And this is Captain Abbott.'

Abbott nodded. 'How do you do?'

'Captain,' Cora replied.

'Clear these swabs please, Sister.'

Cora blinked. Had Captain Kent just said *please*? She quickly tweezered sodden swabs from the patient's open skin and filled the kidney dish.

'I must say, Abbott, I was bloody well relieved when I heard Harefield was to be staffed with Australian nurses.' He glanced at Cora and their eyes met. 'Where are you from?'

'Adelaide.'

'Ah, the City of Churches,' he replied with a raised brow and a smile. 'Did you train at Adelaide Hospital?'

'Yes, Captain.'

'I hail from Melbourne. What about you, Abbott?'

'Sydney, me. Home of the SCG and Victor Trumper. Greatest batsman Australia has ever produced. Damn shame he boycotted the Ashes. He'll likely never play for Australia again, the way the war's going.'

'Look at us, will you? We're all three of us so far away from home with so much work to do and no cricket.'

The words came out before Cora remembered it wasn't her place to speak. 'Mr Billyard-Leake, the owner of Harefield Park, built a cricket pitch here a few years ago for the people of the village. There used to be matches in summertime.'

'Is that so? See, Abbott? You might get some cricket after all.'

The anaesthetist, who'd been so silent all this time that Cora had wondered if he'd inhaled some of his own ether and fallen asleep, piped up. 'The pitch is about to be built over. Too many buildings and nowhere to put them.'

'Damn shame.' Captain Abbott sighed. 'More evidence, as if we needed it, that the bloody war has ruined cricket.'

Captain Kent lifted an arm and wiped his brow with his sleeve. 'You wouldn't have time for it anyway, old boy. By my reckoning, we won't be leaving the theatre for twelve hours at least, I expect. And we'll be back tomorrow at first light.'

'Twelve hours without a shot of whisky and a cigar?' Captain Abbott scoffed. 'I might not survive it.' He winked at Cora and she allowed herself a smile, for it was better than weeping.

'Swab please, Sister.' Captain Kent's gaze flickered briefly in Cora's direction before he turned his full attention to the soldier on his operating table.

By midnight, the hospital was quiet. The ambulances had stopped arriving at nightfall and every bed was occupied. Freshly administered painkillers might also have helped the men drift off so easily and wordlessly.

Cora sat at the nurses' desk looking out over her sleeping patients.

Ward 22 was peaceful and quiet. At the windows, thin cream-coloured curtains hung still, almost but not quite meeting in the middle. Down the middle, a strip of plain linoleum had been placed like a red carpet at a theatre premiere, so highly polished Cora swore she might be able to see her reflection in it in the daylight. Chairs were scattered about the ward, nearest the heaters for comfort, and Cora thought it made the place look homely rather than hospital-like. Above her, an Australian flag hung from a beam, leaving no doubt as to how welcome the Australian patients were here in England.

On the table in the aisle between the rows of beds, a vase filled with fresh flowers threw a scent of lavender and roses. From one bed there was a soft snore. The coal fire had settled to a simmering glow. Even thought it was June and it had been a warm day, there was something reassuring, something homely about the flickering flames.

They'd had such a journey, these young soldiers. What horrors had they witnessed? What had they been forced to do in the name of King and country? Two were just eighteen years old. Another two were in their twenties, while others already bore hints of grey in their moustaches. Had they left behind wives and children? What agonies would families be enduring since the arrival of the army's telegram informing them their husband or father had been injured?

From behind the curtains, there was the faintest bleed of light that Cora guessed came from the half-moon and the northern hemisphere stars, constellations she hadn't yet come to know. Instead, she watched the silent broken bodies, eleven on each side of the ward, the dim light of the oil lamp at the nurses' desk casting flickering shadows.

After the men had been triaged by the doctors, they'd been relieved of their uniforms and given bed baths as quickly as the nurses could—who knew how long it had been since any of them had had a proper wash? The uniforms— jackets, trousers, vests, socks and undergarments—had been collected in a wheelbarrow and loaded into the incinerator for burning.

'It's the only way to get rid of the lice infestations,' Matron Gray had told Cora.

'I understand they live in the seams of their uniforms,' Gertie added.

Cora had shivered with disgust at the idea.

There was a snuffle and a loud snore and Cora looked out across the ward. Sleep, she willed them. Rest. Forget.

When she had enlisted back in Adelaide, Cora had had to declare on her Certificate of Medical Examination that she was clear of a number of medical conditions. She had signed her name to the medical report which confirmed that, no, she didn't have scrofula; phthisis; syphilis; an impaired constitution; defective intelligence; defects of vision, voice or hearing; hernia, haemorrhoids; varicose veins beyond a limited extent; inveterate cutaneous disease; chronic ulcers; or any other disease or physical defect calculated to unfit her for the duties of a nurse. As there were no specific forms for enlisting nurses, the doctor examining her had simply scrawled a line through the conditions that didn't pertain to her sex. Things to do with testicles, for example.

When these patients had proudly signed up to serve King and country, had they agreed to be willing to live in mud and lice or lose a limb or forsake their eyesight? Cora looked over the men's notes. One of the men, Luff, had lost his leg at the hip joint from infection after a gunshot wound split his shin bone at Gallipoli. Noble was mostly blind from chlorine gas, the discovery of which had disturbed the doctors at the hospital so dreadfully they'd used language in front of the nurses. They'd later apologised profusely. Two men had lost lower legs, and another three fingers on his right hand.

The shock was that these patients weren't the most seriously wounded. They had been deemed well enough to survive the journey to England to make room in one of the field hospitals for someone in more dire straits.

Cora checked the time, lifted her clipboard and stood. She would need to perform the men's observations, check their temperatures and wipe their brows if they were perspiring, monitor their blood pressure and their breathing.

As she pressed two fingers into the wrist of a patient, she recalled the discussion between two porters she'd overheard when the first ambulance-loads of patients had arrived. One had said, breathless, 'They were fearless, those blokes. I heard they landed under fire and got tangled up in the Turks' barbed-wire entanglements under the water right there on the beach. None of them waited for the command to charge—'

'They done us proud, hey?' answered the other man.

'Too bloody right. They charged up on to the beach singing "Tipperary" and counting out the Turks as they fell. Nothing stopped 'em. And then, when they were wounded, stretcher-bearers loaded them onto the barges and they were put on the hospital ships under fire. The stretcher-bearers were shot while they were rescuing men. Makes you proud, doesn't it?'

How proud she was of these boys, of their bravery and of what they had endured in the name of their country.

How many more were to come?

Chapter Nine

7 June 1915

Jessie Chester lifted her eyes from the fine seam she was sewing on Arabella Pritchard's new blue frock. She glanced to the mantel above the fireplace to check the time. The carriage clock that had sat in that exact position for the whole of Jessie's twenty-two years revealed it was half past ten. The clock had been a wedding present to her parents when they'd married in 1890 and her father had made a ritual of winding it every Sunday morning. 'Like clockwork,' he'd joked. That was Harry's responsibility now, as the new man of the house.

Jessie smiled, for she knew by both the knock at the door and the time exactly who it was.

'Hold on a moment,' she mumbled through clenched lips that held glass-headed pins in place, as she tightened the stitch she was sewing.

A moment later, she opened the door and Dottie Higgins threw her a cheery smile. 'Good morning to you, Jessie.'

'And a good morning to you, Dottie. How are you today?'

'I'm very well,' Dottie answered happily, her Cupid's bow lips wide and smiling, her eyes gleaming. She never looked prouder of herself than when she was wearing her new blue-grey serge post woman's uniform. It was smartly trimmed with red around the hatband and the collar, and there was a fine stripe at the seams on the long skirt. On a woman of average height, the hem would have fallen halfway between her knee and her ankle, revealing her black stockinged calves, but since Dottie barely scraped five feet it hit the tops of her black lace-up shoes instead. Jessie had more than once offered to alter it but Dottie wasn't fussed with such concessions to fashion. 'There's a war on, Jessie. This is a uniform, not a fashion garment.'

'Here's your morning post then.' Dottie handed Jessie a bundle tied with brown string. Jessie counted. Six letters.

'Why, thank you ever so much. You're like clockwork, you know that, Dottie?'

'Clockwork?' Dottie smiled and a blush flushed her cheeks. 'I aim to be.'

'Every morning at half ten. You knock on the door and I suddenly remember to stop and boil the kettle for a pot of tea. Are you sure I can't tempt you with one?' Every day Jessie asked and every day Dottie declined.

'Afraid not, Jessie.' Dottie patted the canvas post bag slung over her right shoulder. It was bulging and bumped against the folds of her coat as she walked the streets of the village. 'I have important letters to deliver.'

But not the telegrams, Jessie knew. The post women weren't entrusted with those.

'You know,' Jessie said, as she crossed her arms and leant against the door frame, 'I still can't believe you have the strength to carry that enormous bag around all day.'

'I've always been strong, even though I'm petite. All that farm work, don't you know? Not like you, sitting all day in front of that sewing machine,' Dottie teased.

Dottie and Jessie had waved farewell to schoolbooks and formal learning in the same month and year—October 1907—as soon as they'd turned fourteen years of age. Dottie had returned to the family's farm, formalising the work she'd always carried out before and after school and on weekends throughout her childhood. When war was declared, and seventy-five thousand post office workers had left to fight, women were called on to do their bit for England, and the rules were quickly changed so when women married they no longer had to give up their jobs. The post was far too important to let old rules apply. Women had answered the call to duty in droves. And these days Dottie walked the streets of Harefield with a purposeful stride, come rain or shine, delivering the mail. Efficient, loyal and trustworthy, Dottie carried out her duties with immense attention to detail and dedication. The only concession she made to being friends with Jessie was that while others in the village had to make do with having their mail slipped through the brass slots on their front doors, the Chesters always got a knock and a little chat.

Dottie's responsibilities had elevated her status to a place rarely reached by a farmer's daughter. She was the custodian of the King's Mail and a witness to everything that happened in the village. She made as important a contribution to morale as a patriotic film playing in the cinema. She delivered news of engagements and babies born, the latest from family who'd sailed abroad or who were serving in far-flung locations around Europe.

'Why, hello there, Dottie.' Win appeared at Jessie's side, wiping her hands on her apron. 'What a fine morning. Enjoying the sun, are you?'

'Good morning, Mrs Chester. It is indeed a fine morning to be out and about. Have you heard that Mrs Bosley on Newdigate Road had a bonny baby girl?'

'How lovely for the family,' Win replied. 'What name did they give her then?'

Dottie screwed up her face and lowered her voice. 'They've named the girl ... Bertha.' She waited for a reaction before continuing. 'I know it's not my place to say, but it's not a name I would have chosen. If I ever have children myself, I—' Dottie suddenly blushed beet red. 'Well, never mind that. I've just given Jessie the mail.' Her eyes darted to the pile of letters in Jessie's hands.

'I can see that,' Win said.

Dottie tapped the top letter in the bundle, tap tap tap, in the same rhythm as she'd rapped her knuckles on the front door. 'For goodness sake, Jessie. Look at that one! I couldn't help but notice it when I was packing my bag at the post office this morning. It's from the Australian hospital!'

'What?' Jessie undid the slipknot on the string and lifted the top letter. *AAH Harefield Park* was printed on the top left corner, and in the centre in an elegant hand was her name and her mother's and their address: *Mrs W. and Miss J. Chester, 12 High Street, Harefield*.

'What is it?' Dottie demanded, almost jumping up and down on the spot.

'I can't think,' Jessie replied, almost to herself. She hadn't had any further contact with anyone from the Australian hospital since she and her mother had helped the nurses set the place to rights for the arrival of the injured Australian soldiers. Since then, the Australian hospital had been the talk of the village. Someone had seen officers drinking at the Cricketers. Nurses had bought stamps at the post office and hand cream at the chemist. And, sadly, ambulances had rumbled through the village all day and all night the past few days on their solemn journey to the hospital. Jessie always made a point to stop what she was doing and look out the window as they drove by. There must be so many injured men. Harry said they'd been fighting in France and Belgium and Turkey.

'Why are they fighting there? I thought we were at war with the Germans?'

Harry looked up from the paper to explain patiently. 'The Ottomans are upping the ante in the Middle East. The Suez Canal is too important to let it get into their hands.'

All Jessie knew was that if the soldiers were coming from Turkey, it had been a very long journey to get to Harefield.

'Well,' Dottie demanded, checking her wristwatch. 'Are you going to open it? I don't have all day, you know, Jessie.' She smiled at her friend. 'Put a post-office girl out of her misery, will you?'

Jessie turned the envelope over. A red wax circle secured the flap and she pressed her index finger to it to trace the circles and patterns of the seal. She gently pried it loose and slipped out an invitation on a thick card.

'We've been invited to afternoon tea.'

Mother and daughter exchanged shocked glances.

'When?'

'July the fourth at three o'clock.'

Dottie clapped her hands together. 'Imagine that. Afternoon tea with the Australians!'

Win studied the handwriting, as if to confirm her daughter's summary. She returned it to Jessie. 'You should go, of course.'

'Me? But it's addressed to both of us.'

'I'm content to stay right here. You'll have a lovely time of it. It's been too long since you had an invitation.' Win sighed. 'To anything. It's been a while since we've all thought there was something to celebrate.'

Jessie slipped the card back into its envelope and then shoved the envelope into the front pocket of her sewing apron.

Dottie moved to grab the letter. 'What are you doing with that?'

'I'll look at it later,' Jessie replied, trying to brush off Dottie's curious desire to have an answer to everything right then and there, the second the thought popped into her head.

'I know you, Jessie Chester. You won't.'

'I will.'

'You won't.'

How could she go on her own to a place filled with strangers? And Australian strangers at that?

'Jessie?' Dottie asked incredulously, her fists on her hips. Her determined expression took Jessie back to their school days when Dottie had shoved that awful Tommy McIntyre, may he rest in peace.

'It's nice to be asked,' Jessie said finally, hoping to deflect her. 'But I'll leave it at that.'

'No, you will not, Jessie Chester, if I have anything to do with it.'

'Here you are, too busy to stop for a cup of tea but not busy enough that you can lecture me about going to a party I don't want to go to.'

Dottie grinned at her friend, waiting for an answer.

'What on earth would I say to all those people?' Jessie implored. 'You know how I am.'

'What are you talking about? You talk to *those* kind of people all the time.'

Jessie felt deflated. 'It's so much easier when I'm discussing muslin and ribbons and silks.'

'We could make something lovely for you to wear,' Win suggested.

Dottie winked at Win. 'You need something new. Every time I see you you're wearing that same old work dress and apron.'

'That's not true!' Jessie exclaimed, brushing a hand down her apron to smooth it out and catching her finger on the sharp edge of a pin. She clicked her tongue and sucked on her right index finger. 'I dress for church.'

Dottie leant in and her voice dropped to a whisper. 'I can't tell if she's telling a fib or not, Mrs Chester. I haven't been there much lately. Sunday's my only day off you see, and I don't mind a lie-in.'

Win whispered back. 'Neither have I. Don't tell God, if you happen to be speaking to him.'

'I won't if you won't.' Dottie laughed. 'Tell me you're going, Jessie. You deserve some fun and any girl these days would give her right arm to go anywhere at all.' Dottie's shoulders slumped, bearing the weight of disappointment that every single girl in the village carried. 'Go on, go. For every other young woman in the village. Talk to a soldier and then tell us all about it.'

'I'll see.'

Dottie patted her post bag. 'I'll be back this afternoon and tomorrow morning and every day after that to nag you until you do. You know I will. Say hello to Harry for me. Tell him I'll have his magazine tomorrow.' When Dottie's pale cheeks turned suddenly flushed, she turned away. 'It always comes of a Tuesday.'

Chapter Ten

18 June 1915

By mid-June, every one of the three hundred and sixty beds in the patchwork quilt of newly built ward huts on the lawns of Harefield Park was occupied.

Injured soldiers had been arriving in a never-ending stream, their young faces dirty, exhausted, wrapped in bandages or disfigured. Their skin had been flayed by bullets or flying shrapnel, their legs and arms and eyes destroyed by bombs or guns and their minds shaken by the things they'd seen and endured. The boys had been evacuated from the battlefields of Gallipoli and France and Serbia, via hospitals in Egypt and Greece.

As fast as ambulances arrived with new patients, they were filling them with patched-up soldiers for transport to the train station so they could begin their ambulance–train–ship journey home to Australia. Those injured men were destined for newly established rehabilitation hospitals, including Keswick in Adelaide, Randwick in Sydney and Heidelberg in Victoria.

There were extra staff too. A contingent of extra doctors and nurses and masseuses and porters and orderlies had arrived from Australia, dispatched when it had become obvious that Harefield—and every other military hospital in the AIF—was going to be overwhelmed. Cora now found herself among a general staff so big that there were more people whose names she didn't know than those she did.

Cora had been on Ward 22 in the morning from six forty-five and had then spent all afternoon and evening in theatre. The extra staff didn't mean double shifts could be avoided.

That evening, Cora sat wearily on her bed in the nurses' quarters. The springs squeaked beneath her as she bent double to untie her shoelaces. When she nudged off her boots, her stockinged toes pricked with pins and needles and she moaned. What she wouldn't give for a hot soak. With only a brief break for sandwiches and a cup of tea before going into the operating theatre, she'd been on her feet all day.

That morning, she and Gertie had admitted eight new patients to their ward with smiles and the warmest welcome they could summon. Eight new men were to fill the beds that had been emptied an hour earlier.

'Welcome to Harefield hospital,' Gertie had announced as the first of the stretchers and wheelchairs rolled in through the open front door. It had been a lovely warm June day and the windows had been thrown open to capture the fresh air.

'You've come ever such a long way and we're here to look after you. I'm Sister North and this is Sister Barker.'

A soldier had struggled to lift his head from his trolley as he whispered, 'It's bloody well true, then. You're Australian.'

Cora had gone to his side. The young man was attempting to smile but his mouth contorted in agony instead. Beads of sweat appeared on his top lip from the simple exertion of lifting his head. Her mind had gone immediately to fever and infection. She checked at his carotid for a pulse. It was racing. The jacket of his heavy khaki uniform was dirty, splashed with splotches of black as if paint had been flicked from a brush. But his trousers didn't look part of the set. They were clean and too big. Her answer was there in the pinned trouser leg, empty from the knee down.

He'd struggled to speak and she'd leant down, her ear almost against his mouth.

'Bloody hell but it's good to see sheilas from home.'

'We are indeed. Everyone here at Harefield is Australian. You'll feel right at home. Now, let's get you cleaned up.' She'd checked the paperwork attached to a clipboard on his chest.

'Norton?'

'Bill Norton.'

All these hours later, she hoped Private Bill Norton was fast asleep, as she longed to be. But all around her, her colleagues were still awake. Four beds, four nurses. The hut had already become the nurses' home away from home. There was a small square table near the front door, with a chessboard on it, the pieces set mid-game. Gertie and Fiona had started a match but three weeks later hadn't had the time or energy to finish it. There was a washroom at one end of the hut, and a fire. Each of the nurses slept on straw-filled mattresses atop white wrought-iron beds, with room underneath for the trunks they had brought from Australia.

In the bed next to Cora's, Gertie looked up from the pages of a novel. The low light from the lamp on her side table cast dark shadows under her eyes. Her long black hair lay twisted into a plait that hung loosely over her left shoulder like a ship's rope. 'Hello, Cora.'

'Hello, Gertie,' Cora replied and yawned. She didn't have to hide her exhaustion from her friend and, even if she'd wanted to, she simply couldn't summon up the energy.

'How was theatre?'

Cora sighed. 'Long. Too many patients.'

'I'd love to hear about it.'

'I'll give you chapter and verse if you like, but tomorrow. When did you get in?'

'Twenty minutes ago. One of the boys in the ward had … an episode. I couldn't leave him.' Gertie set her book down on her lap.

'An episode?'

'I'll give you chapter and verse if you like, but tomorrow.' Gertie managed a smile and then cocked her head towards Cora's bedside table. 'You have letters.'

'They're probably from my sisters. Or the nurses back at the Adelaide.' There was a bundle of envelopes, two inches thick, tied together with twine, next to a glass jar filled with tiny rosebuds she'd purloined from the garden when no one was looking.

'Eve or Grace?' Gertie asked.

What would Eve and Grace be doing right now, Cora wondered? At home, it was late on a winter's morning.

The trees would be bare of their leaves. If it had been a cold night, gardens would be whitened with frost and the motley collection of backyard chooks who scratched in the vegetable patch in the backyard would be huddled inside their coop in quivering togetherness. Was it Grace's turn to stoke the fire? Would Eve scrub the kitchen floor the next day and beat the rugs? Would they squabble good-naturedly about whose turn it was to make the tea for their mother that evening?

'I hope both. They each give me their own side of whatever spat they're in the middle of and I try to find the truth of it somewhere in the middle.'

Cora desperately wanted to hear news from home, to read of what her sisters and her parents had been up to. She wanted to know the news of the street and Adelaide and what was happening at the hospital and what films were being screened at the cinema.

But all that would have to wait. She needed to sleep.

On a bed across the hut, Leonora sat cross-legged, flicking through a magazine, her face rendered a ghostly mask by the thick layer of cold cream she'd slathered on her skin. She lifted her hand and waved.

'Hello, Leonora.' Cora sighed. 'Why aren't you asleep?'

'I just got in too.' Each nurse had tried in their own way to make their little spaces in the hut their own. Leonora had raided the pages of magazines for pictures of glamorous outfits and had tucked them into one of the uprights of the hut's wooden framework. Gertie had a pile of books stacked on her bedside table, tall and teetering. After hunting down a nail from one of the hospital's porters, Fiona had hammered it into the wall with the heel of her boot and hung a painting of Jesus Christ there, one she'd brought with her from home. Every morning and night, she dropped to her knees and prayed to Him.

'And,' Leonora said, 'Fiona is a night owl, as we all know by now.'

Fiona sat on the end of her bed, a pair of knitting needles clacking against each other, a half-formed sock bobbing up and down as she purled. The needles sounded like the clicking of her tongue in approbation. 'It'll be at least midnight before I feel even the least bit tired,' she explained. 'Reading makes my restlessness worse, so I knit.'

'I'm sure the soldiers will appreciate new socks,' Gertie said. 'They'll be very thankful for your insomnia, Fiona.'

'You look like you've had a horror of a day, Cora,' Leonora mumbled through lips she was trying not to open too wide.

'I'm certain I'm no orphan in that regard.'

'Let me show you this,' Leonora said through pursed lips as she walked to Cora's bed and spread a magazine open on the blanket. 'This will cheer you up.'

Cora wondered with the slightest bit of envy where Leonora found her energy.

'Look, Cora! There are photographs of women wearing trousers. And this.' Leonora poked the page and it fluttered. 'An advertisement for a brassiere. Aren't you desperate to try one?'

Cora flopped backwards on her bed and stared up at the corrugated-iron roof, lines of shadows at this time of night. Nurses would never be permitted to go without their corsets or their dresses so there seemed little point in even thinking about the possibility. 'Can't say I am.'

'What about you, Fiona? What do you think? Would you try it?'

'I don't think so,' Fiona replied curtly. 'I quite like being confined, thank you very much. A corset holds everything in and aids with one's posture and general digestion.'

Cora turned on her side and propped her chin in her hand, her elbow on the bed.

'What does it look like, this brassiere?' Gertie asked.

'Comfortable. That's what,' Leonora announced. 'See here. "It is highly recommended by Doctors and Nurses—"'

Fiona snorted.

Leonora ignored her. '"—is most comfortable to wear and can be worn with or without corsets. There is not that unpleasant feeling when taking exercise and it can be worn during the night next to the skin."'

'I don't wear a corset at night over my camisole,' Fiona said. 'So why on earth would I wear a brassiere?'

'Oh, look. They're for sale at a shop called Joujou in Portman Square. Shall we go into London on our next day off, do you think?' Leonora asked her colleagues. 'Perhaps we might even find some trousers. Imagine that. No stockings!'

Cora moaned. 'When will this mythical day off be, exactly?'

'What next?' Fiona's tongue clicked above her knitting needles. 'Trousers on nurses like those munitions ladies or the land army girls?'

'And why not?' Leonora challenged. 'Wearing trousers would certainly make riding a bicycle more comfortable. Why on earth do we still wear such long skirts?' She studied the advertisement more closely. 'They don't appear to be too complicated, actually. There's no boning. I believe I could make one myself with two handkerchiefs sewn into triangles and some elastic for the straps.'

'Hah. That's fine for you to say.' Gertie laughed. 'Some of us are more, shall we say … ample in the bosom than others. I don't think a couple of handkerchiefs would do me at all. I need more support than that or I'll be distracting all the patients.'

Cora and Leonora laughed too.

Fiona put down her knitting. 'If you ask me, it's all a bit too …' She searched for an expression, pinching her lips together as she concentrated, '… *suffragette* for my liking.'

Gertie scoffed. 'Oh, Fiona. Next you'll be saying that women shouldn't have the vote.'

'They don't here, you know,' Cora said, pushing herself to sitting. 'That's why the English suffragettes have been marching and picketing the Parliament and going on hunger strikes. Don't you think we take it for granted as Australian women? If we have the vote, why can't British women?'

'I'm not for one moment saying that's a good thing,' Fiona replied. 'But the hunger strikes? Those women took things a step too far. What did they achieve? All it did was give doctors at Holloway prison an excuse to shove rubber tubes down their noses and throats to force feed them. It was dreadful.'

Cora had read about the treatment meted out to the suffragette prisoners. They'd had their teeth broken and had choked as liquid food had been poured down their trachea into their lungs instead of down their oesophagus. It had appalled her to think that it had been in any way acceptable for doctors—doctors!—to inflict such appalling medical treatment on any human. But things had settled in the past twelve months. When war had been declared, the suffragettes' leader, Emmeline Pankhurst, had announced that militant actions—the very actions that had led them to being arrested in the first place—were to be suspended for the duration and the government had responded to that olive branch by freeing all suffrage prisoners from jail.

'We do take it for granted, don't we? The right to have a say in who governs us?' All eyes turned to Cora. Being the oldest of the group gave her a certain authority, which she took seriously. Her role was not only to be friend and colleague, but mentor and teacher. She'd had such a person when she'd trained in nursing, in Matron Margaret Graham. She hoped she might be half as inspiring to the younger nurses. 'Most of you were mere babes during Federation—'

Gertie scoffed and looked up from her book. 'Not me but I thank you for the compliment.'

'Let me think.' Leonora looked towards the ceiling. 'In 1901 I was eight years old.'

'When all the States came together to create the Commonwealth,' Cora explained, 'our prime minister Andrew Fisher said that we can only have a true democracy when women as well as men have the vote.'

'I think the English need a good dose of Australian democracy,' Gertie said.

'Think of all the young women working now,' Cora said. 'The munitions girls right here in Harefield. They're doing as much as any other worker in England for the war and they don't even have a say in who the prime minister is.'

'What difference would it really make?' Fiona put down her knitting. 'I've had the vote, have exercised it myself since the federal election in 1903 as a matter of fact, but ... who asked *me* if we should go to war?'

Fiona's voice cracked on her last few words and the other women fell suddenly silent.

She was right. Cora knew it. Powerful men in high places had made the decision to go to war while ordinary men—and she'd seen so many of them already and the war wasn't even a year old—were paying the price for it.

What had been a happy conversation had become a sombre reminder of why they were in England and a few moments later books and magazines and knitting were put away and the lights turned off for the night. Cora changed into her nightdress and fell into exhausted sleep staring at the glow of the wood fire and dreaming of an Australian sunrise.

Chapter Eleven

19 June 1915

'Sister North. Do you have a moment?'

Cora kept her voice calm and low and, from the next bed along in the ward hut, Gertie looked up, her eyebrows raised in a question. Her fingers were pressed to the wrist of a new patient who'd arrived earlier that morning. He'd been the talk of the ward because he was so tall his foot hung over the end of the bed.

Gertie placed the soldier's wrist at his side and tucked the sheet over him. 'Lay back there, Private Naylor,' Gertie said. 'Enjoy that fluffy pillow. I'll be right back.'

'No worries, Sister,' Naylor murmured. 'Your blood's worth bottling.'

'Just doing my job. We want to see you well enough to go home to that fiancée of yours as soon as you can, don't we?'

Naylor turned away from her and spoke no more.

Gertie joined Cora and the two nurses examined the fine red line on a thermometer Cora had just pulled from between her own patient's lips.

'Tell me that says 104.' Cora blinked and squinted and held it closer to her tired eyes. 'I've checked it so many times I think I'm seeing double.'

Gertie took the thermometer from Cora and held it up towards the window and the fading afternoon light.

'Yes, that's what I'm seeing.'

'Half an hour ago it was 99.'

They exchanged glances and Gertie nodded, seeming to know immediately what Cora had called her over to do. 'I'll fetch a doctor.'

As Gertie walked briskly away, Cora pressed the soft skin of her wrist to her patient's forehead. Private Roderick Koop had suffered a compound fracture of his left femur from a gunshot wound and had been treated in an Australian field hospital, where doctors had hurriedly amputated his left leg. He was burning up and sweating but was almost unresponsive. Aside from a slight moan, he hadn't made a sound for an hour. Cora had tried not to worry too much—at first new patients often slept well and long. There was something about the comfort of a real bed in a real hospital that induced a deep sleep in men who'd been without it for months on end, but this was different. Koop didn't rouse at her touch. She quickly filled a bowl of cool water and set it on his bedside table with a flannel. She dipped the flannel, squeezed it out and lay it across Private Koop's forehead. She pulled back the sheet and blankets to his foot and undid the buttons on his pyjama shirt, revealing a chest so young there was not even a shadow of chest hair.

'You'll be right, Roderick,' she reassured him and herself. Even if she wasn't sure they were listening or could hear her, Cora needed reminding that each man lying in her ward was someone's brother or son or husband or cousin or sweetheart or husband. They were so much more than their injuries or their afflictions.

She heard bedsprings squeak and grate. Cora looked up. Private Naylor was looking over to Private Koop.

'He'll be all right, won't he, Sister?' he asked in a gravelly voice.

She smiled and lied. 'Of course he will. The doctor is just coming to check him over. Nothing out of the ordinary. Do you know him, Private?'

Naylor coughed, wet and painful. 'Not from a bar of soap, Sister. It's just that he ... well, he seems like he's in a pretty bad way.'

Before she had the chance to answer Naylor's well-meant enquiry, Cora looked up at the sound of footsteps coming towards her so fast it seemed as if the ward itself was jumping on its stumps. Captain Kent strode towards her, grim-faced. Gertie was hurrying after him, her white linen veil lifting behind her as if caught in a breeze.

When he reached the bed, he gave Cora a quick nod of acknowledgement and asked, 'Pyrexia?'

She explained what her observations had revealed.

Captain Kent listened intently. 'His temp is?'

'104 a moment ago.'

'Please refresh my memory. What injuries did he sustain?'

Cora reached for the patient's notes and scanned them, flicking page after page, including some notes scrawled in pencil all the way across Europe in Turkey. 'GSW. Compound fracture of left femur. Lower limb amputation.' She cleared her throat. 'Obviously.'

There was a sudden pounding in her chest. 'I checked his wound when he was admitted, Captain. It appeared to be soundly healed. There was no inflammation or discharge. The stitches were neat and clean and I applied fresh bandages.' She tried not to let panic rise in her. Had she missed something? Was Private Koop slipping away in front of her because of a mistake? There had been so many men and so many decisions. Had she made the wrong one?

'My concern here is a flare of latent sepsis. We'll have to open up the wound to take a look to be absolutely certain. We're seeing cases of osteomyelitis setting in after compound fractures like this one.'

Cora's mind was whirring so hard that she took a moment to remember what osteomyelitis was. Gertie whispered in her ear, 'Bone infection.'

'Indeed, Sister. It's often a bullet fragment or sometimes just the tiniest sliver of bone. Try as we might, we don't always remove all the shrapnel, especially when those first surgeries happen in a hurry in a field hospital. We'll likely have to go in and drill the bone.' Captain Kent stood and propped his hands at his hips, his expression distracted as if there was too much thinking going on in his head all at once.

'Sister Barker. Organise an orderly to take this man to theatre. I'll head over there right now and scrub in. We need to do this now.' He exchanged quick glances with both nurses and then fixed his gaze on Cora. 'You're not rostered to theatre at the moment, I see.'

'No,' she replied.

'Good work,' he said, and strode away.

'I'll alert the orderly,' Gertie said and left the ward without another word. Cora sat on the edge of Koop's bed, stroked his cheek and whispered quiet words of comfort until the orderlies came and whisked him away.

At midnight, Cora and Gertie lay turned towards each other in their separate beds, talking. Leonora and Fiona had been asleep when Cora and Gertie had come in from the evening shift and they'd tiptoed around the ward so as not to wake them. Sleep was too precious to be interrupted.

Outside, the wind shook the tin roof and the windows rattled in their frames. Cora didn't know how on earth she would sleep. All she could see when she closed her eyes was Private Koop's pallid face. The young soldier would likely remain in intensive care until he was no longer critical. His fast-deteriorating condition had rattled her confidence in herself and her abilities, made her realise there was still so much she didn't know. Harefield hospital hadn't lost a patient yet and some part of Cora feared he might be the first. And under her watch. 'How do you think he is, Gertie?'

There was a long pause and when Gertie replied, her quivering voice gave her away. 'He'll come good, Cora.'

The next morning on the dot of six, Cora, Gertie and Fiona sat together in the mess, sipping strong black tea and devouring warm and creamy porridge for breakfast. They were all on the early shift that day and they'd quickly learnt that if they arrived early enough to eat, the golden half hour before the patients roused and their shifts began in earnest was a brief respite. After her relentlessly restless sleep, Cora was learning that these might be the only thirty minutes in the whole day in which she was able to be still. She had learnt to appreciate every second.

Fiona had her Bible open in front of her, murmuring to herself. Gertie was staring off into the distance and Cora was still thinking about Koop when Leonora arrived at the table, her cheeks flushed, her eyes wide with excitement.

'I have news,' she blurted.

Cora, Gertie and Fiona looked up in unison.

'There's to be an afternoon tea and we're all invited.' Leonora floated to her seat and set her cup of tea and bowl of porridge on the table.

Cora was confused. 'There's afternoon tea here in the mess every ... well, every afternoon.'

Leonora rolled her eyes. 'Not that kind of afternoon tea, silly. The kind with invited guests and entertainment and a bowl of punch and little sandwiches with the crusts removed. It's to cheer us all up, apparently. Especially the men. There's some kind of local volunteer entertainment committee and they've organised it all. People from the village will be invited, too, I hear.'

'That sounds very diverting,' Gertie said, lifting her cup to her lips. 'Just what we need. More tea.'

Cora immediately warmed to the idea. Their patients were growing bored with relegation to their beds and their wards. Those who could manage on crutches were able to venture out a little further but those still in bed had been staring at the tin ceilings for far too long. They could surely do with some semblance of normality, of civility. A reminder of the entertainments they used to enjoy before the war.

'When is it planned?' Cora asked.

'July the fourth. At three o'clock. The weather should be positively balmy by then. Lucky I brought a summer frock with me.' Leonora leant into Cora and poked her with her elbow. 'Perhaps you might share a dance with your handsome doctor, Cora.'

Cora stilled. 'I beg your pardon?'

Leonora winked at her. 'I'm talking of Captain Kent, of course.'

'You've been reading too many magazines, Leonora.'

Leonora sighed dramatically and raised a wrist to her forehead, cocking her head to one side. 'If I can't dance with my Lieutenant Percival Jones, someone should be dancing with a man, don't you think?'

Cora and Gertie exchanged smiles. Who needed the stage for entertainment when they had Leonora?

'Speaking of Captain Kent, I had noticed …' Gertie began. 'Oh, never mind.'

Cora straightened her back. 'Noticed what?'

'He does seem to pay you particular attention.'

'That's not true. He's attentive to all the nurses.'

Gertie smiled and shrugged and Fiona snapped her Bible shut. 'For goodness sake. We are here to tend to our patients, not flirt with doctors.'

Cora's hackles rose at Fiona's implication. 'I have not ever once flirted with Captain Kent, Fiona. I've barely had time to brush my teeth and I don't appreciate being accused of being on the hunt for a husband.'

'That's not what I said,' Fiona replied tartly.

'But it's what you meant.'

Tension hovered over the empty porridge bowls and teacups until Leonora pierced it.

'Wait until my father discovers I'm engaged.' Leonora's smile wavered.

'Your family doesn't know?' Fiona was flabbergasted.

Leonora shook her head. 'I've decided what I do with my life is none of his concern. Of course he'd be horrified. He was horrified when I became a nurse. And when I enlisted? He was apoplectic. "Daughters are for marrying and producing grandchildren" he told me. He assumed I would leave school and join my mother's garden club or the church fete committee until I received a proposal. He told me … he told me nursing would make me barren. He said no daughter of his would be a bluestocking.'

Cora's heart smarted a little at the idea that she had judged Leonora to be a flighty society daughter. She was clearly so much more than that.

'Do you know what my mother said?' There was an uncharacteristic wobble in Leonora's voice, a crack in her confidence. '"Why on earth does she want to *work*? And in such an undignified profession?" As if my only worth were as an ornament.'

'You would make a very pretty ornament, Leonora,' Gertie said from across the table. 'You'd look quite ravishing on a mantel above a roaring fire in a fine sitting room somewhere.' She paused, then added with a wry smile, 'Gathering dust next to a carriage clock and a set of *Encyclopaedia Britannica*.'

Leonora smiled warmly at Gertie. 'That's the problem, you see, Gertie. Ornaments don't move or speak or dance or laugh. They don't have opinions and they crack in half if manhandled. I was always determined to be so much more than that. I was determined to marry who I wanted to, not someone my parents chose for me.'

'Percival,' Gertie said.

'Yes.' And for the first time in the conversation, Leonora's eyes lit up with something other than anger.

'I was going to be a nun.'

Cora, Gertie and Leonora were suddenly silent at Fiona's declaration.

'You were?' Cora said.

'Clearly you didn't become *that* kind of sister. What happened?' Leonora asked.

Fiona's bottom lip wobbled and tears welled in her eyes. 'I fell in love and became engaged. That put an end to thoughts of the convent, much to my grandmother's approbation. She raised me.'

No one had to ask the question. Fiona volunteered it in a whisper. 'He was trampled by a horse a month before our wedding. My grandmother told me it was God's will.'

The nurses were silent.

'That's abominable,' Gertie whispered.

Fiona stood, pushing her chair back with a scrape on the wooden floor. She clutched her Bible to her chest as if it were a shield. 'I thought so too. I never spoke to her again.'

As the nurses bustled through the grounds to their wards, they passed ambulances loading patients, horse-drawn carts driven by land girls delivering milk and delivery trucks dropping off the meat and vegetables and fruit and bread required to feed more than four hundred people each day in the small village within a village the hospital had become.

Cora looked up, breathing in the fresh morning air and the smell of an English summer. The sky was already blue and cloudless and she thought she might get some of the men outside that morning. She'd need a porter's help but that could be arranged. Fresh air would do them wonders.

Unbidden, her thoughts returned to Captain Kent.

Your handsome doctor.

'Gertie,' Cora asked, hesitating. The two women were striding arm in arm.

'Mmm?'

'Do you really think he's handsome?'

'I presume you're talking about Captain Kent?'

Cora let herself blush. She nodded.

'He's tall and fair-haired with the loveliest blue eyes. He's courteous to nurses and compassionate with patients. In my mind, that makes him extremely dashing.'

'When you said you'd noticed that he's paid me particular attention, what did you mean?'

'Exactly that. He seems to notice you in a way that he doesn't notice any of us.' Gertie laughed. 'Even the glamorous and eye-catching Leonora.'

Cora mulled over the thought. Captain Kent's manners were definitely appealing. She had to agree with Gertie that he was handsome. He stood taller than she was, which made her feel less awkward about her own stature, and when she'd allowed herself to look directly into his pale blue eyes she felt something she hadn't ever experienced in her life. It was a giddiness, an excitement that fluttered inside her chest and sent something unfamiliar coursing through her. She had rationalised it as a biological reaction to the intense gaze of a member of the opposite sex. She had never before in her life felt so seen.

'It's nice to be noticed, I suppose,' she said, almost to herself.

'Yes, it is.'

'But I'm not here to find a husband, you know.'

'I know that. But who's to get in the way of a little flirtatious admiration? For goodness sake, we need something to distract us, don't you think?'

'Indeed.'

Since her first day on a ward, Cora had been fully aware that any romantic attachment that might lead to marriage would end her career. For those who loved the profession so much—and the independence it gave them—the idea of being forced to leave it upon getting married was a wrench they couldn't bear. And anyway, there had been a bright side to her spinsterhood: the mere fact of her marriage would have prevented her enlistment.

It was diverting to imagine such things but as they approached their ward, stepping onto the duckboards that formed a floating path above the mud, Cora pushed such thoughts to the back of her mind. There were other men who needed her attention that day.

As Cora and Gertie stepped through the front door of their ward at precisely six forty-five, Matron Gray looked up from the nurse's desk. She smiled wearily.

'Does she ever rest?' Gertie asked under her breath.

'I can't imagine when,' Cora whispered in reply.

The women exchanged greetings.

'A quiet night?' Gertie enquired.

The matron nodded as she looked across the room and over her patients. 'As quiet as can be expected. I'll be in my office if you need me.'

And with that, Matron Gray tucked her hands under her scarlet cape and departed.

Chapter Twelve

24 June 1915

The warming days and nights of an English summer had not only caused the cornflowers and forget-me-nots and violets and foxgloves to bloom in the fields around the hospital, but the hospital itself was growing as if it were one of those wildflowers.

Every time Cora lifted her eyes from ministering to a patient, another building was under construction, appearing as quickly as field mushrooms. Towards the end of June, more ward huts were erected, a pay office and a post office had opened for soldiers and staff, and a Red Cross store had been created to handle the myriad donations sent from back home. The catering demands of the hospital had become so great that a field kitchen had been erected and a second mess near the staff quarters had opened. The nurses now found themselves waking in the morning to the tantalising scent of freshly baked bread.

When the mortuary had been built—as necessary to any hospital as a bedpan—Cora could hardly bear to walk by it without her heart thumping wildly in her chest. They hadn't yet lost a patient and everyone at the hospital had taken pride in that knowledge, but how long would it be before a soldier succumbed to his wounds? Would it soothe a family's sorrow to know that their son or father or brother was buried among friends, rather than in an unmarked grave in a foreign country? Wasn't death still death no matter the lines on a map determining which country owned the soil?

She finished her shift in the ward that evening to calls of 'Night, cobber' and 'Goodnight, Australia' from her patients, which never failed to lift her spirits. How the men found it in them to lift hers when theirs had been so battered was humbling.

When she arrived in the nurses' quarters, Leonora rushed to her and handed her a letter.

'Thank goodness you're here. We've all been absolutely bursting with curiosity about this package.' Leonora pointed to a large tea chest that sat at the side of Cora's bed. The words *Assam MT Co* had been stencilled on the side with an upside-down triangle and Cora leant forward, running her fingers over the rough-hewn plywood, breathing in the malty scent of loose tea leaves. If she wasn't so tired she might have craved a cup.

Cora turned her attention to the envelope in her hand.

Sister Cora Barker, 1st AAH, Harefield, Middlesex.

Cora swiped a forearm over her forehead to move the stray strands of hair that had come loose from her veil. Her heart leapt in her chest. 'It's from my sister. I know the handwriting.'

Gertie yawned. 'Eve or Grace?'

'Eve.'

'The middle one.'

'Yes. She's four yours younger than me and Grace is ten years younger. And before you ask, Leonora, yes. She was a change of life baby, as they say.'

Cora tugged open the envelope and read the letter silently for a moment. Then, she couldn't help but burst out laughing. 'Oh, bless her. Eve has joined the Red Cross. It's now having large meetings of all its members at the Keswick Barracks in Adelaide and they've packaged up some supplies for the boys.' Cora ran a finger down the list in Eve's letter. '"36 flannel shirts. 36 sets of pyjamas. 36 pairs of socks. Seven dozen handkerchiefs. Two dressing gowns."'

'Only two?' Gertie asked, puzzled. 'All those pyjamas and not enough dressing gowns. Continue.'

'"Two pairs of bed socks". They must be for me, but I'll give a pair to you.' She winked at Gertie.

'Excellent,' Gertie replied.

'"Four pairs of slippers. Eight face washers. One eye bandage."'

The nurses exchanged glances. If the people at home only knew that one wasn't enough.

'"One bar of glycerine soap. Old linen."'

'Good for bandages,' Leonora noted.

'"And sixty packs of cigarettes."'

The women laughed.

'Sometimes I wish I smoked,' Gertie said, flopping back onto the bed. 'It looks so relaxing, don't you think, Cora?' Gertie drew two imaginary fingers to her lips, breathed in and then exhaled slowly. 'Imagine. At the end of a shift. Sitting down with a cup of tea and a cigarette. I wonder if it might help me sleep.'

Cora turned to Gertie, who was staring at the corrugated-iron ceiling. She knew her friend hadn't been sleeping. If Cora wasn't in the same boat, she wouldn't have heard her tossing and turning at night in her narrow cot, muttering under her breath in the wee small hours of the morning. Cora wondered if the same thoughts and anxieties kept Gertie awake.

'A cup of warm milk will have to do me,' Cora sighed. 'I can't imagine ever taking up smoking.'

She cleared her throat and began to read.

Dearest Cora,
I hope you will be able to make use of the supplies I've sent to you on behalf of the Adelaide Red Cross Society. The ladies were most impressed to hear the news that my clever sister was in England tending to our boys. They took it upon themselves to gather up a collection from their own homes to send off to you immediately. I shall thank Mrs Dripps, Mrs Gifford, Mrs Hankinson, Mrs Muntz, the Misses Maude, Renie and Muriel Muntz, Mrs McClelland, and Miss Jean Robertson especially for the bar of soap. Mrs McClelland insisted that the old linens might be useful for bandages or some such and she insisted I make it clear that they had already been boiled within an inch of their lives in her very own copper before they were folded and sent off to you.

Cora heard her sister's voice as clearly as if she were standing next to her.

There was some other news of home, little things about their neighbours, and how well their parents were faring, about how their father devoured the newspapers each and every day for news of the war. And then her best wishes and three crosses under her signature.

Cora folded the letter and slipped it into its envelope. 'It appears, sisters, that we have some unpacking to do.'

Harefield Hospital
Middlesex
England
July 4th, 1915

Dear Dad, Mum, Eve and Grace,
A quick note of hello from Harefield, where the weather is glorious at present. The days are lovely and warm—some might even say hot—and the nights are wonderful as it's twilight until nine o'clock. When I have a moment to spare, I try to take a walk around the beautiful grounds. This morning, on my day off, I was out and about for hours. I believe I heard my first cuckoo and I was transfixed. I keep listening out intently for a nightingale but no luck as yet.

The meadows are a carpet of colour, like an Oriental rug. There are primroses and bluebells and buttercups and anemones. Grace, I'm certain that if you were here you would have collected up every single one and put them in vases all around the house.

Thank you, Eve, and to the Adelaide Red Cross Society, for the very welcome supplies. They are sincerely appreciated by all the nurses here at Harefield.

We are busier than ever but the boys' spirits are high. I must go. Kindest regards to all who remember me.

Love,
Cora

Chapter Thirteen

Jessie and Dottie walked arm in arm to the crossroads in the middle of Harefield on a humid June Sunday afternoon and chose a spot on the village green for their picnic. Jessie had packed cheese-and-pickle sandwiches and two bottles of lemonade, and Dottie had brought a picnic rug, which they stretched out taut between them and lowered to the grass with a flutter.

The green was both the physical locus of the village and the centre of its social life when the weather was pleasant—and even when it was not. Houses were perched along Northwood Road, which bounded it, and there was a pretty wood on the opposite side where Jessie, Dottie and Harry had played hide and seek when they were children. Behind the smithy sat the Kings Arms and a smattering of village shops on either side. A little further along Rickmansworth Road—as it turned into the Harefield high street—the Cricketers welcomed lunchtime drinkers who might be in the mood for a Wellers pale ale, and parishioners made their way from the morning service at St Mary's Parish Church, sauntering in the sunshine, young children skipping around their parents.

One could see everyone and everything in the village if one sat on the grass long enough.

It had been so long since Jessie had seen Dottie out of her uniform that she'd looked twice when Dottie had knocked on the front door and beckoned her out. How young she seemed once again. They were both twenty-two years old, young spinsters according to those in the village who took it upon themselves to judge the circumstances and life choices of young women. The war had taken so many young men that women's opportunities for socialising were constrained to events with each other. There was church on Sundays for those who observed, afternoon tea in villages all over England filled with polite hellos to all the other young, single women, or jam-making, bottling and pickling in village halls up and down the length of the country. Men were to fight and defend. Women, it seemed, were to do everything in their power to ensure the populace didn't go hungry.

'Do you think we'll see any Australians today?' Dottie popped the lid on a bottle of lemonade and poured its contents into two glasses balanced precariously on the rug. The sun caught the lemonade's effervescence and the bubbles sparkled.

'Perhaps,' Jessie replied.

'I've heard this has become quite the spot for them. That is, those who are well enough to get out and about. It must be nice to leave the hospital and for them to see real English people. I mean, the Australian hospital is full of Australians. Imagine coming all this way and not meeting any villagers?' Dottie scanned the green. 'Can you see any, Jessie?'

Jessie squinted into the sun then quickly turned her head back to Dottie, placing an index finger perpendicular to her lips. Dottie understood her meaning and remained silent.

'It's Arabella Pritchard,' Jessie whispered. 'I don't want to talk to her.'

Dottie casually glanced over her shoulder and, with a small nod in Jessie's direction, seemed to confirm her friend's observation.

'She's with a gentleman,' Dottie mouthed.

A moment later, Arabella's cut-glass accent wafted towards them. Jessie surreptitiously cocked her ear to listen. She wasn't usually a busybody but Arabella was wearing one of the dresses Jessie and Win had made for her and Jessie wondered where she might be going in it.

'Is that yours, the big black one?' Arabella asked flirtatiously.

The man's voice was too deep and low to be heard distinctly but he must have said something hilarious because Arabella burst into singsong laughter. 'You went to school at Harrow?'

And then, there was a lull in the cheering from a boys' game of football, and Jessie heard him say, 'Yes, darling, I did. Played rugby and I have the scars to prove it.'

'You simply must show me the rugby grounds when we get there. After lunch, perhaps?'

Jessie waited before she looked up. Arabella and her gentleman friend walked arm in arm across the green. He opened the passenger door of a black motor car and waited for Arabella to climb in, before they drove off with a roar.

'Same as she ever was.' Dottie shook her head. 'You should see all the invitations she gets in the post. Not that I'm allowed to mention them, of course.'

Jessie rolled her eyes. 'Of course. I find myself making the new frocks she needs for all her engagements.'

'Never mind them. Can you see any Australians?' Dottie insisted.

'Look for their khaki uniforms and their hats. They wear them at a jaunty angle. Like this.' Jessie tipped her cloche hat to one side and Dottie laughed then gasped.

'I think I see some! Look over there!'

Jessie saw them too, khaki-clad troops in khaki hats, gathered in twos and threes. The puffs of smoke from their cigarettes rose and drifted in the breeze.

'Are you very excited about the afternoon tea party at Harefield?' Dottie sat up on her knees, her legs tucked beneath her. A breeze picked up and she slapped her hand on her straw hat to stop it blowing away. 'It's not long now, is it?'

'It's on July the fourth. I'm not excited at all. I'm nervous more than anything.'

'Oh, Jessie!' Dottie exclaimed. 'Why on earth are you nervous? Do you think you might have forgotten how to drink tea?' Her laughter pealed across the green.

Jessie poked her tongue out at her friend. 'It's all going to be such … such a fuss. I wish Mum wasn't making me go.'

Dottie's eyes widened. 'Jessie Chester! You're being such a ninny. What I wouldn't give to be invited.'

'Then you should go in my place. You could pretend to be me.'

'If I could get away with it, I would.' Dottie sighed. 'Just think, Jessie. There might be dancing. In the afternoon! I hear there's going to be a concert by a soprano who's coming up all the way from London. Foot? Frost? Something like that, anyway.'

Jessie flopped back on the rug, her back pressing into the grass, and stared up into the sky. Sometimes she wished she were a bird. That way she could flap her wings and raise her feet and fly away from any situation in which she felt nervous and skittish. From any conversation in which she had nothing to add. From people who made her feel less than. How she would love to fly away from Mrs Pritchard. Imagine that? Turning into a swallow the moment the woman knocked on the front door of their cottage, Jessie would swoop through the house and out the open window in the kitchen and into the trees.

'You'll have a wonderful time. And you simply have to go so you can tell me all about it.'

Jessie sighed. 'Who will I talk to? What will I say?' What on earth could she possibly say to an injured Australian? What if she was repulsed by their wounds and embarrassed them—and herself—with her reaction? They were in no more need of a simple village girl trying to make conversation than they were of an English rainy day.

'It's simple. You just walk up to them, put out a hand to shake theirs and introduce yourself. "Hello. I'm Jessie Chester. How do you do?"'

'That's easy for you to say, Dottie. You talk to people all day. It comes naturally to you.'

'Not with everyone.' Dottie fell silent. 'Especially not with the one person who matters the most.'

Jessie propped herself up on her elbows. Dottie's smile had inverted into the kind of frown Jessie rarely saw on her friend's face.

'Are you trying to tell me something, Dottie?'

'The thing is …' she began and then stopped. 'I've found that someone.'

Jessie shot up to sitting. 'You have? Is it someone from the post office? Wait a moment. Are there any men left in the post office? Haven't they all enlisted?'

Dottie blushed. 'No, he's not from the post office.'

'Then where? And who is this lucky man?' Jessie was relieved the conversation had steered away from her own shyness. She had hopes and dreams of her own, to be sure, but she'd never voiced them to anyone. In her mind's eye, she had a vision of herself in the future, in which she welcomed a husband into the kitchen at night with a warm kiss. She was never able to make out the face of this imaginary young man, except that he was tall with brown hair and a lovely smile. He always stopped to pat the children's shoulders—a boy and two girls—and as they ate their dinner he would turn to his wife and smile a smile that held a world of secrets within it, secrets only they shared. At night, she and her husband would walk up the stairs holding hands and they would cuddle up in bed together and kiss and do the things married people did. She tried not to think about that part too much, as the thought of that intimacy made her embarrassed, but she wanted to feel strong comforting arms about her, and she wanted to pass on that feeling of warmth and security to her own children. That was how she'd been raised and she wanted to give her own children that comfort too: of knowing in their bones how much they were loved.

But as the years between leaving school and the war had passed, invitations from young men had become fewer and fewer as those in the village had married or moved away and now, with so many gone to fight, the chances of receiving any offer at all seemed as elusive as ever.

Dottie sucked in a lungful of air and burst into quick and heaving tears.

'Oh, Dottie. It can't be that bad, surely.' Jessie reached across the sandwiches and lemonade bottle and took her friend's hand. 'You really are heartsick, aren't you?'

Dottie nodded and sniffed.

'Tell me everything. Has your heart been broken?'

'No. Well, it might be. I'm not sure.'

'You're sounding like a puzzle and I don't have all the pieces.'

Dottie covered her eyes with her hands for a moment, took a deep breath and then looked tearfully at her friend. 'It's ... it's a man I don't believe has ever looked at me twice.' And then she blurted out her revelation. 'It's your brother.'

Jessie felt winded. She was silent for a long moment. 'You're sweet on *Harry*?' How had she not put all the clues together? The knock on the front door every morning when Dottie was delivering the mail. It was to see Harry. The way her cheeks flushed each time she spoke to him or mentioned his name.

Of course it was Harry.

'And I have been for ever such a long time.'

Jessie had tried to conjure a life for herself outside of her family and the cottage and her sewing but had never imagined one for Harry. Because of how he was. How cruel had she been, how unseeing?

'Oh, Dottie,' Jessie said. 'I don't know what to say.'

'I've been right miserable about it, to tell the honest truth. I haven't been able to tell if ... well ... if he's sweet on me. Sometimes I get a little smile and a laugh and that keeps me going all day. But then other times ... well, other times he never seems to want to talk to me when I come round in the mornings. If I see him in the village, he says a quick hello and shuffles away.'

Jessie swallowed the pang of envy she felt. What was it like to feel that rush of heartsickness, of longing, of hope for a life better and more fulfilled? She wished she had, just once, experienced the blush of first love that had rendered Dottie so tongue-tied. Was her heart palpitating too at the mere mention of her sweetheart's name? Were her hands clammy with sweat?

'The thing is, Jessie, I have to put myself out of this misery. I have to know.'

'You want me to ask Harry?'

'No. Well, yes. Harry probably thinks no girl would look twice at him on account of him being how he is, but that doesn't matter to me. Honestly. It never has and you know that to be true. His eyes are ever so lovely and he always makes me laugh. I get a warm feeling right here every morning because I know I'll see him, even if only for a couple of minutes when I knock at your door.' Dottie lay a hand on her heart and then wiped her eyes. 'Will you tell him, Jessie? Will you tell him that I could love him just as he is?'

This was a lot to take in and Jessie thought it over for a long moment. A football went whirling past, chased by two boys so light on their feet they looked as if they were flying.

'Are you certain about how you feel? It's not just because so many boys are away and so many have been lost? Do you have in mind that there might not be many to choose from when all this is over?'

Jessie had seen the new newspaper, *The Link*, in the village newsagent. It carried classified advertisements from people looking for companionship and Jessie had studied them, envious of those brave enough to put their feelings into words in such a way. Was it fascinating or horrifying that women had resorted to such measures to find themselves a husband?

Lonely Sybie (London SE) 30, sincere, lover of animals, all nature, would be glad to hear from sincere gentlemen 35–40. All letters answered.

Or:

Peg (London) 28, dark, short, working class, would like to correspond or meet man of same class, short, 27–33. Someone please write.

Someone please write. Was she herself so desperate? There were others offering to marry the blind or the incapacitated or a disabled man who might need cheerful companions or pals. So many lonely people were searching for affection. It broke her heart.

Dottie uncovered her eyes, looking stricken, and quickly crossed herself. 'I swear on my grandmother's grave, Jessie, and you know how much I loved my nan. It's not just the war. Harry's the only boy I've ever met who gets me to thinking about marriage and having a family of my own one day. It's all I can think about. Well, that and delivering the post on time.' She laughed through her tears and Jessie was relieved to hear it. 'I've even thought that if we marry, you could make my wedding dress. I've only ever wanted those things with him. Truly.'

Dottie clutched at Jessie's hand and squeezed hard. 'Will you tell him? Will you tell him I love him?'

In that moment, Jessie heard the truth. Her friend had never lied, not in all the years they'd known each other. There wasn't much in the way of true love going on in the village these days, nor in the whole of England, for that matter. Wasn't it incumbent upon Jessie to do all in her power to see her best friend's dream come true?

'Will you be patient?' she asked. 'I'll find out but I'll have to do it my own way. He's stubborn sometimes and I'll have to let him think it's his idea.'

'Would you? I'd be ever so grateful, Jessie. If Harry could love me, I'd be the happiest girl in England.' Her eyes sparkled. 'And just think. You might be my sister-in-law one day!'

Chapter Fourteen

3 July 1915

As the weeks passed, a steady stream of injured men continued to arrive at Harefield from Turkey and Egypt. Some days, this constant movement of men in and out, of arrivals and departures, of admissions and discharges, reminded Cora of a circus. The hospital was a giant canvas tent; she and the other nurses, doctors and staff were the performers, and the men were the constant cavalcade of audience members in and out, in and out, for performance after performance, day after day.

Cora had found herself performing the part of a loyal Australian nurse. Each day, she lifted her lips in a smile that she kept in place until she fell asleep. No matter what she was faced with. It was her job, her calling, to welcome the soldiers, to tend and treat them, to watch over them and then send them on their way with words of comforting reassurance.

Men continued to arrive from Gallipoli, murmuring conspiratorially to each other in the dark about what a disaster the landing back in April—and every day since—had been. Many of those soldiers had undergone rudimentary surgery on the hospital ships before arriving in England and would never go back to their battalions, their wounds career-ending. Others, recuperating from minor wounds and infections that were more safely treated away from the battlefields, found themselves in a strange interregnum, lying between clean sheets in a place in which it was safe, indeed encouraged, to look out to the horizon.

Cora had just completed a week's rotation of long days in theatre and hadn't had much time for anything else. Letters from home sat on her bedside table unanswered and she tried not to let guilt gnaw away at her. Her parents and sisters would be desperate to hear from her and she resolved that it would be her first priority the next spare minute she had.

That morning, she'd risen at six, dressed and had breakfast before hurriedly making her way back along the Long Ramp to Ward 22 just as the six forty-five Reveille sounded. She had always loved the tune. The hospital's bugler played his heart out every morning and it sent a frisson of energy through her, which was always appreciated at that time of the morning. Most days, she needed more than tea to keep her awake.

Cora stepped into the ward hut, planted her hands on her hips and called out, 'What time do you call this? And you boys all still in bed?'

From the other end of the ward, Gertie looked up at Cora and shrugged her shoulders with a smile, as if to say *I tried*.

Moans and groans filled the ward.

'Just half an hour more, Sister,' one patient implored in a ragged voice.

'You'll get no such thing,' Cora announced. 'It's nearly seven. The sun's been up for hours. Can't you hear the skylarks and the blackbirds calling?'

While the soldiers in their beds may have also been proud to have been serving in His Majesty's Army, they also knew very well that Reveille meant they had ten more grace minutes until Rouse was played, after which those who were able to were expected to be out of bed, complete half an hour of physical jerks on the lawn (weather and health permitting), and then get dressed for breakfast. Those who weren't able were Cora's priority.

Gertie motioned for Cora to meet her at the nurses' desk and together they looked over the night's observations, having a surreptitious conversation without looking at any one particular patient. There wasn't much privacy for the men but they could be afforded this much, to have their own particular problems respected, without announcements to every other man in the ward.

'An eventful evening, it seems?' Cora noted

Gertie nodded and kept her voice low. 'Brown—Colin, that is, not Walter—had a rough night. He's been trying to scratch that elbow of his that isn't there. And Prentice snored heartily, as per usual, which certainly kept me awake if not everyone else.' Gertie handed her clipboard to Cora. 'And no comment from you on that score, thank you very much.'

Cora tried to supress her smile.

'Duffy and Jones are being discharged today.'

'Oh, truly? They'll miss the afternoon tea tomorrow.'

Gertie signed deep and heavy and when she muttered, 'Poor blighters,' Cora knew Gertie wasn't talking about the concert.

The two men had been blinded by shrapnel. What kind of work could a man with no sight do? She'd heard stories when she was a child of blind people having no other choice but to beg on the street. There had been change in the past few years, fortunately, but was it enough? Would Duffy and Jones be satisfied or even capable of making brooms and brushes at special workshops for the blind? How would they go about learning Braille at their age, especially Duffy who'd lost half a hand as well.

'Oh, and keep an eye out for young Wagner. The blondie from Echuca with the arm gone?'

Cora remembered him. How could she not? He told the most ribald jokes to the nurses and turned it into a bet with the other men. They'd placed cigarette bets on which of the nurses would blush the reddest.

'About two am,' Gertie continued, checking her notes, 'he roused and shot out of bed like a cannon. I tried to get him back into to bed but … you know what happens to some of the men if they're woken while they're sleepwalking. Those who don't scream and throw fists are as frightened as little children. You can never tell. Anyway, the moment I touched his arm, Wagner fell to the floorboards like a sack of potatoes. Then he curled up in a ball and lay there, whimpering, on the floor right next to his bed.'

Cora didn't look up from the notes. 'Might be best to leave him in bed for a little longer this morning then.'

Gertie nodded. 'I'll call a doctor to come to take a look at him today.'

'And night shift is supposed to be quiet.' Cora studied Gertie's sallow face. Dark shadows had developed under her eyes, as if she might have a broken nose. 'You all right, Gert?'

Gertie shrugged off Cora's concern. 'Nothing a good night's sleep won't cure.'

'Go and have a cup of tea and then go to bed. You'll need your eye mask. It's going to be a beautifully sunny day.'

'I plan not to see a ray of that sunshine.' Gertie took her scarlet cape from the back of the chair at the nurses' desk, flared it over her shoulders and fastened the Rising Sun badge at her throat. 'All the things we took for granted before the war, hey?'

Cora sighed. 'I can think of a million things I miss about home.'

Gertie's face softened into a dreamy expression. 'I miss a hot bath. A really steamy hot bath. When the war is over, I'm going to check into a fancy hotel in London, lie in the bath and drink French champagne until I can drink no more.'

'I hear the afternoon tea at the Ritz is quite something.'

'The Ritz. Claridge's. The Savoy. I don't care which one. I'm willing to blow all my savings on a hot bath.'

Cora sighed at the idea of such luxury. 'If you do, I'll be right there with you. Although I'm not sharing your bath water.'

'You shall have fresh water of your own. We shall treat ourselves like princesses.' Gertie yawned and didn't bother to hide it.

'Go to bed, Princess Gert. You'll need your rest for the concert tomorrow.'

'Oh, the concert!'

Cora nodded. 'Would you bring your box Brownie? The men might like to have a photograph taken to send home to their families.'

'Will do.' Gertie saluted Cora sleepily, clicked her heels together and left. As Cora watched Gertie go, a wave of gratitude swept over her. The war had brought her many challenges but it had also brought her the joy of Gertie's friendship.

Cora turned her attention to her patients. None of them had made any attempt to get out of bed. She clapped her hands together three times, which elicited another round of half-awake groans.

'Good morning, everyone.' She rounded the desk and walked the aisle between the beds, taking detours to each window to lift the blinds, which alternated between rolling up energetically with a snap or dawdling up with a squeak.

'Fair dinkum, Sister,' McCoy pleaded, pulling the sheets and blankets over his head. 'Ten more minutes can't hurt, can it?'

'Rise and shine, soldiers. I don't know what you're all thinking but this isn't a holiday camp. It's not Sorrento or Victor Harbor or Manly Beach, you know. You've all got work to do.'

Cora was a firm believer in waking her patients with a smile and a laugh. God knows they had enough to endure during their waking hours—the awful slap of reality every time they looked at their bodies—and if some humour first thing in the morning helped their mood for just a little while, what was the harm? She wanted to encourage them, not berate them, and the boys responded in kind, with jokes and teasing of their own.

'White with two sugars, love,' one called. She guessed it was Prentice. He must have come to know her voice for his war injuries meant he would never see anything again.

'Toast with raspberry jam and loads of butter.' That was Walker, who at night cried and called out in his sleep, but was a teasing devil during the day.

Bright morning light seeped into the ward. Twenty-two beds. Twenty-two men. But there weren't forty-four legs or forty-four arms.

'Gentlemen. You might have forgotten what today is.'

'Struth, is it Christmas?'

'It's my birthday, Sister. How about a kiss on the cheek and a cuddle?'

Cora crossed her arms under her red cape and looked over her patients. 'Good try, Private. Rise and shine, boys. The hospital is full of excitement and activity for the afternoon tea and concert tomorrow. And today, you shall have your choice of needlework, painting, photography or, as always, you may avail yourselves of the services of the library. I'm told there are more than nine hundred books there and no, I've not counted them personally.'

'Any Banjo Paterson? "There was movement at the station, for the word had passed around, That the colt from old Regret had got away …"'

'What about "There once was a man from Nantucket …"'

'And …' Cora continued, trying not to laugh, 'there will be French lessons in the mess.' There were more groans but when Cora responded with, 'I understand a Miss Tarleton from the village is conducting that class,' the ward erupted in wolf whistles.

'Ooh lah lah.'

Chapter Fifteen

4 July 1915

At a quarter to two the next day, Cora pushed Corporal Prentice's cane wheelchair along the gravel drive to the lawns out the front of the main house. The chair's thin metal-rimmed wheels weren't designed for navigating such terrain and when she muttered 'Good grief' under her breath and gave the chair a shove, Prentice turned back in the direction of her voice and said painfully, 'I'm very sorry, Sister.'

Cora felt shame burning her cheeks.

'Oh, Corporal. It's not you.' She had learnt to think quickly on her feet around the injured men. If they saw tears in her eyes, she said the antiseptic made her sniffle. If her hands shook, she told them she was in desperate need of a cup of tea. 'I have a wretched piece of this gravel in my shoe and it's positioned itself right under the ball of my foot.'

'You sure, Sister?'

'Absolutely. Ah, look at that. There's a position right here with your name on it.' She leant down to whisper in his ear as she manoeuvred his chair into a space off to the side. 'The empty stage is in front of you and slightly to your left. Well, stage may be a slight exaggeration.' She narrowed her eyes to make sure she was correct and then laughed. 'It's a wooden table! There's an upright piano right next to it with, let me see, perhaps one of the local ladies waiting there, and on the other side, a chair. I expect that's to help the singer climb up on the ... stage.' She giggled. 'There are boys sitting on the grass all around in a semi-circle with their crutches and their wheelchairs and their slings. They're wearing their uniforms and looking smart. As do you.'

Cora patted his shoulder and under her fingertips she felt him shaking. 'I'll be ten paces right behind you at the front doors to the main house. You sing out if you need anything.'

Prentice reached up with his right hand and covered hers with it. Her heart ached when he gave her fingers a gentle squeeze. 'You're bonza, Sister.'

She swallowed hard. 'Enjoy the performance, Corporal.'

As the crowd grew, the excited chatter grew louder and the clouds of cigarette smoke thicker. Some men sat cross-legged on the lawn, others had their backs to the ward huts, their legs splayed out in front, their crutches flat on the grass. The house, with the ward huts on one side and a towering tree on the other side, created a kind of little amphitheatre and when Cora closed her eyes for a moment, she imagined herself to be back at His Majesty's Theatre in Adelaide. She felt a familiar excitement: the murmur of a crowd, the cigarette smoke, the anticipation of knowing the curtain would soon rise on a performance.

That day's tea party and concert had been all the patients and staff at Harefield had been talking about for weeks. The soldiers had placed bets on whether the visiting songstress would be a blonde or a brunette; on her height; on which songs she might perform, with 'Keep the Home Fires Burning' already a two-to-one favourite over 'When Tommy Comes Marching Home'.

Cora had some inside knowledge that she hadn't shared with the men so as not to ruin their surprise. Leonora had heard from one of the cooks that the performer, a Miss Fiske, was actually an Australian living in London.

Leonora had taken great delight in sharing her gossip with the other nurses.

'I can't say I've ever heard of her.' Fiona tended towards the suspicious in all things and this was no exception. 'Is she actually a proper singer?'

'Well, she's obviously no Nellie Melba, Fiona,' Leonora had replied. 'But Mrs Graves says she performs regularly in London establishments. She must have *some* talents.'

'And,' Leonora had added, 'apparently this Miss Fiske is quite the philanthropist. As well as performing for soldiers all over England, she holds regular morning teas for Australian soldiers at Stoke Newington. And she feeds the poor older women of Hackney. All out of her own purse.'

'Is she an heiress like Mrs Billyard-Leake?' Gertie asked.

Leonora had shrugged. 'I haven't a clue. I shall ask Mrs Graves in the kitchen next time I go past. She is quite the fount of information.'

A rousing round of applause and loud whoops and cheers arose from the crowd when Lieutenant Colonel Hayward, the officer in charge of the hospital, escorted Miss Fiske across the lawn to the makeshift stage. He held out a hand and she took it before daintily stepping up onto the chair and then, with another light step, climbed up to the tabletop. Miss Fiske acknowledged the applause with a gracious curtsey.

From her position at the rear of the crowd, standing in the doorway of the house, Cora studied this philanthropist songstress. Miss Fiske was definitely no ingenue—she was perhaps forty years or so, and Cora wondered if the boys might be disappointed, but they were showing no sign of it in their rousing applause. She was glamorously dressed for an afternoon-tea concert, in a straw boater with a dark pink ribbon around it, and a white frock gathered high at the waist in the fashionable style. She wore white shoes, which Cora immediately coveted, and her dark upswept hair could just be seen under her hat. She was ruddy cheeked and smiling and, in her right hand, she held an unfurled lace fan. Cora wished she had one to cool herself with in this humid English July heat.

Miss Fiske bowed and waited for the clapping and cheering to die down before speaking.

'Good afternoon, men.' Another burst of applause forced her to wait before she raised her hand and continued when quiet descended. 'Please, it is I who should be applauding you. As a colonial, I am naturally extremely proud of all of you, and my modest efforts today, in providing a diversion and an afternoon tea to all of you and those who care for you, will never repay what your country and Britain owe you.' She raised her hands and clapped the men before her. 'If you're ever within cooee of Stoke Newington, on furlough, or on your way home, there is an Australian morning tea every Wednesday and you will always be most welcome. There are a good deal of young Australian lady volunteers who help me. I wish you all good luck and a safe return home.'

Miss Fiske and her pianist didn't wait for the men's exuberant cheers to die down before she launched into her first song, something Cora recognised from a Gilbert and Sullivan operetta.

She relaxed a little, leaning back against the cool stone walls, letting the music and Miss Fiske's thin but enthusiastic voice wash over her.

Cora closed her eyes, reached her hands behind her back and pressed them against the ivy, relishing the fresh coolness of the leaves against her fingers. Her hands had become calloused and dry from so much scrubbing with soap and the coarse bristled brushes supplied by the hospital, and no matter how much Vaseline petroleum jelly she massaged into them each night—a routine that had been highly recommended by Leonora—they remained red and rough.

The men cheered and her thoughts turned to Corporal Prentice. What would he hear? Singing? The piano? The chatter all around him? The strike of a match? Footsteps? Coughs?

'Can't say I know this number. Do you, by any chance?'

Cora's eyes flickered open. Captain Kent was at her side, in full uniform and bearing a dashing smile. He spoke surreptitiously out of one side of his mouth and she immediately noticed something was different about him. He'd shaved off his moustache. Somehow his eyes seemed brighter, his cheeks ruddier. She felt a little quiver of excitement and turned her gaze away from him lest he notice it and think she might be flirting with him.

'It's "Three Little Maids from School" from *The Mikado*, Captain Kent. You don't know Gilbert and Sullivan?'

He cocked an ear. 'I do. But I'm not so familiar with this version. Bloody hell,' he winced. 'What she lacks in talent she makes up for in … gusto.'

'It's very kind of her to come and stage the concert. I believe we should be very grateful to her.' She threw him a chiding glance.

'You're absolutely right, Sister. Beggars can't be choosers and the men are enjoying it. That's what matters, after all.'

'It certainly is.'

'I hear that Miss Fiske is quite the patriot. She's paid for the entire afternoon tea. All the ingredients have been shipped over from Australia, from the wheat for the flour for the scones to the jam and even the tea.'

'How extraordinary,' Cora replied. 'I wonder if they will taste like home.'

They listened respectfully to the last verse and chorus and when the pianist ended his accompaniment with a dramatic flourish, Miss Fiske placed one foot behind the other and bowed deep. The men responded as if she were Nellie Melba.

Next to her, Captain Kent slipped two fingers into the corner of his mouth and let fly with a piercing whistle, which set the men off even louder.

Cora laughed heartily at the gesture and he smiled warmly at her. The concert was supposed to be a diversion for the patients but it was clearly having the same effect on staff as well.

'It's heartening to see the men enjoying themselves, don't you think?'

'There is no prescription better than this: sunshine, music and fresh air.'

'Undoubtedly.'

Cora paused. 'I can't stop thinking about Prentice.'

Captain Kent met her eyes. His own were jocular no longer but intense and dark. 'How is he?' He moved closer, lowered his voice.

'He puts on a jolly front, as they all do. From a medical perspective, I wonder ... do you believe all the other senses are heightened when one is lost?'

He stared at her for a long moment. 'I think all the senses are heightened in war, Cora. Every emotion seems bigger, grander, funnier, sadder. And lovelier.'

He came closer, whispering against her hair, 'Close your eyes for me. I'll show you.'

She felt his breath on her cheek. She held hers.

'You don't have a field mouse in your pocket, do you?'

'No tricks, I promise. Close your eyes.' His voice had dropped deep and low. 'Now. What do you hear?'

Cora stilled her breath and took a moment to concentrate. 'Singing. The piano, which, I've just realised, is out of tune. Or perhaps that's the player. Oh, and you're laughing. With me, not at me, I hope. There's chatter among the men. Someone's mentioning cake. Cups of tea.'

'Now,' he asked. 'Tell me what you smell.'

Cora took in a deep breath. 'Cigarette smoke. Smoke from a wood fire, possibly from the kitchen. Antiseptic.' She always smelt antiseptic, even in her sleep. 'Talcum powder. Brilliantine. Your uniform. There's something particular about the way uniforms smell. Perhaps it's the wool.'

At her side, she felt the pressure of his thigh against her hip, and then the gentlest stroke of his thumb on the inside of her wrist. His caress was like a trickle of warm water.

'Now, touch,' he whispered into her ear and she held her breath. 'What do you feel?'

He pressed his fingertips into the soft skin there. He was searching for her pulse. Was he looking for a physical sign of his effect on her? Could she feel it racing at his touch?

She wanted to tell him that she felt his fingers, his caress, his breath, but couldn't. Instead, she gently moved her hand from his. She had been fooled by handsome before. And anyway, she was too old for flirtatious games and too professional to want to be seen acting in this manner in front of her patients.

She met his eyes briefly and then turned away. 'Excuse me, Captain Kent. I believe Corporal Prentice is calling.'

Chapter Sixteen

Jessie had never felt so out of place in her twenty-two years on this earth. How could she have let her mother and Dottie talk her into this?

She was a village girl who worked all day and night in her front room to make pretty frocks for other women. That was her place and she had been comfortable with her lot, satisfied with glimpses into the lives of others, through their satins and silks and bonnets and peacock feathers. She was the person behind the curtain on a stage who urged the stars out under the proscenium arch to shine.

So what on earth was she doing at Harefield Park in a pretty floral frock and straw hat adorned with matching ribbons of pale blue and white?

The house looked so little like the place she had seen back in May that for a moment she wondered if she might have become discombobulated and taken the wrong turn off Rickmansworth Road. Back then, there had been a pretty manor house, rolling lawns and fields nearby filled with grazing cows. Now there was a village where a fine residence once had taken centre stage. Wooden huts had sprung up like field mushrooms, joined by wooden walkways like bridges that linked them together, as if each hut were a charm on a bracelet, and there were people and trucks and motor vehicles coming and going in every direction.

Jessie swallowed and gripped the handle of her purse. One cup of tea and she would leave. That way she would have shown her face, honoured her mother's request and the hospitality of her Australian hosts, and she could slip away. She knew every road and lane and path in Harefield and could leave without anyone knowing or noticing.

This place would always seem like another world and it was not and would never be hers.

She closed her eyes for a moment to steel herself and heard Dottie's voice in her head. *Talk to a soldier and then tell me all about it.*

Near the ivy-framed entrance to the house, Jessie spotted Mrs Billyard-Leake and her daughter chatting to Matron Gray and some of the nurses. Jessie had never met Mrs Billyard-Leake herself—she didn't move in those circles—but recognised her, of course. The Australian was a tall woman, with light brown, upswept hair and an elegant bearing. She and her husband had been the talk of the village when they'd purchased Harefield Park back in 1898.

Glasses tinkled against each other and teacups clattered against saucers in gloved hands. The scent of the rose garden wafted over her and she inhaled it, deep into her lungs, hoping it might calm her nerves.

'Excuse me, miss. Can you give a digger a hand?'

Jessie stopped in her tracks.

A gravedigger wanted her assistance? She turned in the direction of the man's voice to see a soldier with an eye patch pushing another in a wheelchair. It seemed to be bogged at the other side of the rose garden.

Talk to a soldier and then tell me all about it.

'Miss?' the pirate asked.

'I'll fetch a nurse for you.'

The patient seated in the wheelchair laughed. 'We don't need a nurse. Just a push. Think you can manage it?'

'Yes, of course,' Jessie replied, exhaling her nerves. She had at first feared some kind of medical emergency. 'Here. Let me help you.' She made her way around the rose garden and quickly assessed their predicament. Instead of pushing him forwards, as the one-eyed soldier had tried to do, she cocked her head over her shoulder and instructed, 'Let's pull him backwards, get him out of this soft dirt.'

And with a two-handed tug, the wheelchair was back on solid ground and the man in it was whooping. 'Watch out, Shorty. I reckon this little lass is stronger than you!'

Shorty let fly with a curse before pulling himself up and apologising profusely. 'Sorry, Sister. I didn't mean to offend.'

Jessie waved it away. 'I'm not a nurse. And no offence taken.'

'We're sorry to keep you,' the soldier in the wheelchair said. 'You going to the concert?'

'Yes. I am.' She smiled down at him. He smiled up at her. He had the brightest of blue eyes, a wide and cheeky grin, and a slightly crooked nose.

'What's your name, miss?'

'My name?'

'Everyone's got one.' He grinned. 'Shorty here's real name is Lionel but we call him Shorty on account of him being so tall.'

'And I hate Lionel,' Shorty groaned. 'Shorty will do just fine, Blue.'

'Blue?' Jessie quizzed.

'The hair.' The man in the wheelchair pointed at his closely cropped head and Jessie saw the light, sparkling orange of it, the same in the growth on his chin and on the fine hair on the back of his hands.

'Do you have any Scottish blood by any chance? Is that where the colour comes from?'

'Oh, my kin are from somewhere in the mother country. Don't know exactly where. I'd better write and ask my mother. I'll tell her a pretty girl from Harefield wants to know.' He held out a hand. His palm was huge and his fingers long and she hesitated before stepping forward to shake it. She could have put both hers in that paw of his.

'I'm Miss Chester.'

'Miss Chester.' He doffed an imaginary cap. She had a flash of how he might look in a slouch hat tipped romantically to the side, the strap so tight on his chin it would look as if it were aimed at keeping him quiet.

'I'm Private Bert Mott, 10th Battalion.'

'How do you do, Private Mott. Please accept my best wishes for a speedy recovery.'

'Very kind of you to say, Miss Chester. I'm a lucky bugger. A bullet hit my leg but the docs say I'll be back fighting the Turks in no time.'

Shorty let fly with another curse and ended it with, 'Stop making eyes at her, you big mug,' which only elicited a bigger grin from Bert. Or Blue. She wasn't sure which name she might use if she were to ever run into him again.

'You have a lovely day, miss.' Bert nodded and as Jessie turned to make her way to the big house she couldn't resist the urge to look back over her shoulder.

Shorty was lighting a cigarette into a cupped hand. Bert sat in his wheelchair, looking back at her.

He waved.

Jessie waved back.

Near the huge tree by the main house, Jessie spotted the tall Sister Barker. The idea of a friendly face helped settle her just a little and she made her way across the lawn. The sister was speaking to a man in a wheelchair and, as Jessie approached, Cora turned and waved.

'Miss Chester! How lovely to see you. We were so hoping you would come today. And is your mother with you?'

Jessie felt herself flushing at the attention. 'No. But she asked me to pass on her thanks for the very kind invitation. She isn't one for parties like this.'

Cora nodded her understanding. 'Please tell her we think of her with great fondness. So what do you think? Do you recognise it at all?' Cora swept an arm wide.

'Barely at all. There are so many soldiers. You must all be very busy.'

'We are indeed. There are more nurses now, thank goodness. And doctors and porters and clerks. But we're still run ragged. Which has the effect of making us ravenously hungry. Shall we taste Miss Fiske's scones?'

Part of Jessie wanted to retreat inside her shell like a snail yet ... a tiny part, a blossoming part, felt a flickering. 'That would be lovely.'

'Jessie!'

She turned to see another nurse approaching her. The beautiful one. Jessie chided herself for not remembering her name.

'It's me! Leonora. Sister Grady.'

'How do you do?' Jessie stammered. In her nervousness she'd seemed to have forgotten everyone she'd ever met. Perhaps she shouldn't have come after all if all she was going to do was embarrass herself.

'Don't worry.' Leonora patted Jessie on the shoulder. 'I expect we all look very much the same in our uniforms. Like penguins. Speaking of clothes, that's a very pretty dress you're wearing.'

'Thank you.' Jessie glanced down at it, swallowing the nervous lump in her throat. All the attention was overwhelming and she felt a little faint.

'It's lovely,' Cora added, and the nurses reached for the hem on the sleeve, running thumbs and forefingers along the fabric. 'So light and what a beautiful floral pattern. The blues and white suits your complexion.'

'Is there a dress shop in Harefield you could recommend? I only brought one summer frock with me. How silly was that?' Leonora laughed. 'Why did I think that all it would do in Blighty was rain and blow cold draughts direct from the North Sea? I hadn't expected this heat and the humidity. It curls my hair.'

Jessie's feet felt more firmly anchored now that she was talking clothes. She exhaled. 'There's a department store in Uxbridge you might like to visit but I made this dress myself.'

'You did?' Cora and Leonora exchanged surprised glances.

'I'm a seamstress. My mother, too. We would be more than happy to make you something if you like.

Leonora clapped her hands in delight. 'That's very kind of you. Where are you in the village?'

'On the high street. Number 12.'

Cora linked an arm through Jessie's. 'We were on our way to find some scones, Leonora. Won't you join us?'

Cora, Jessie and Leonora settled at a table laid out with a sumptuous display of freshly baked scones, clotted cream and strawberry jam on plates. Their cups were steaming with fresh tea and it wasn't long before the scent beckoned Gertie and Fiona to join them.

'Miss Chester,' Gertie called out as she approached the table. 'How lovely to see you again.'

Oh dear. What was this one's name? 'And you, Sister.'

'You remember Gertie and Fiona?' Cora said.

'Of course.'

Fiona reached for the largest scone on the table and lathered it with jam and cream, so much that half of the cream threatened to slide off into her lap. She noticed it just in time and cupped her free hand underneath the morsel to save her uniform. After she'd devoured a large bite, she set the remainder on a china plate in front of her. 'While the scones are delicious, I'm still not certain it's appropriate to be having a party.' Fiona's brow furrowed as she took a furtive glance about. 'I mean, look at us. There's a war on and we're sitting about at a grand country house eating scones and listening to opera singers. What would people at home in Australia be thinking if they saw us now?'

'Oh, come now, Fiona. Aren't we allowed one hour to forget the war?' Leonora pleaded.

'Do you think a concert and some warbling will help the men forget?'

Jessie looked at the soldiers sitting at other tables and on the lawns. She shifted her gaze from face to face, from missing limb to bandaged head, from men laying prostrate in metal beds with wheels to those in wheelchairs to those trying to negotiate their crutches while balancing on one good leg.

'It's good for their morale,' Cora said. 'All the medical evidence says so. Just like all the other therapies we encourage them to participate in.'

Fiona sighed. 'I hardly think that needlework will do them any good when they get back home.'

Cora began to speak but Gertie quickly silenced her with a hand on her forearm. It seemed to be signal, like a code.

'It's good for our morale as well, Fiona. Perhaps you should have spent a little more time listening. I think you would have found it rather diverting.'

Leonora elegantly licked a finger on which a dab of clotted cream had smeared. 'Tell us about Harefield Park before the war, Jessie. What was it like? Did princes and princesses, dukes and duchesses and marquises and … goodness me, what's the wife of a marquis called?'

'A marchioness,' Jessie replied. She'd made a frock for one, once.

'Were there fancy balls here every weekend?'

Jessie had to laugh at the idea that she might have been a regular guest at the Billyard-Leake's parties, or any parties in the big houses of Harefield for that matter. 'I don't know. I would never have been invited if there were.'

'No?'

'People like me don't mix with the types who live in houses like this. The Billyard-Leakes are a little different, I grant you. We all put that down to the fact that they're Australian and not used to English ways. My brother, Harry, loved coming here to sit in the shade of the oak trees and watch the cricket matches.'

Harry loved the game above anything else in his life but had never been able to hold a bat with any strength nor run without tripping over his lame leg. The teasing and taunts that had followed his first and only game at school had made him shy of ever trying again. Watching him hobble off the field, his bat left lying at the crease, the shouts and laughs ringing in her ears as loud as church bells, had broken Jessie's heart in a way she had never recovered from, either. He'd been ten years old—half his life ago—and she knew she would never be the only one imagining the possibilities for his life if he'd not been born the way he was.

He'd made up for it in other ways, acting as scorer every summer since for the local Harefield team, happy to sit in the shade and mark each run, each boundary and each wicket with precise enthusiasm. But he'd been bereft that summer of 1915. The 1914 season, twelve months before, had been cut short and there hadn't been a match played in a year. Hundreds of first-class cricketers, county players and promising boys just out of school had enlisted so there were no players left for the competition. And anyway, who could go on playing cricket at such a time? When WG Grace had patriotically called on the young men of England to do their part for the war—he himself being already too old to serve—Harry had wept uncontrollably at the fact that he wasn't able to answer the call from the grandfather of English cricket.

'He has a physical condition, doesn't he?' Jessie heard kindness in Gertie's question rather than judgement.

'He had a troublesome birth. He's lame on one side because of it.'

'Is it a birth palsy?' Cora asked.

'I believe so. He's smart and funny ... it's just that parts of him don't work as well as they do on other people.' Harry had never received a white feather from any of those women who pounded the streets of England wearing straw hats and self-righteousness, searching for young men to humiliate. They'd been known to pass out their poisonous symbols to injured men, soldiers on furlough in street clothes and men who were exempt from service. Jessie had no time for women who shamed men into fighting. Harry had come across a group of the white feather brigade once, in London. They'd stared at him with disdain instead of compassion, as if he might have chosen to be born lame to avoid a war twenty years later. It had taken him a long time to tell Jessie the story and she'd wept for him when he had.

'You should have brought him along too,' Gertie exclaimed. 'He could have met some of our boys. Many of them are in the same boat, even if the reasons are different. Although, it might break his heart to see the cricket pitch built over with all these wards.'

'He's glad the games have been cancelled. He says, who can think about cricket in times like these?'

'Quite right,' Fiona added. 'Australia and England may fight over the Ashes every four years, but right now, we're all on the same side.'

Cora lifted her cup. 'To King and country.'

Gertie clinked her cup to Cora's and waited while the others did the same. 'Cheers to our boys,' she said. 'And all our girls who are tending to our boys, wherever they lay.'

Leonora scoffed. 'I've drunk enough tea tonight to last me a lifetime. I wish we had a sherry.'

When the scones had been devoured and the concert was over, Jessie bade farewell to the nurses and agreed when they insisted she visit again soon. As she left, she looked out for Private Mott, searching every wheelchair for his sparkling blue eyes, but he wasn't to be found.

As she walked down the hospital's long drive towards Rickmansworth Road, Jessie felt a frisson of excitement shiver up her breastbone and tingle on her tongue.

How do you do.

She'd managed it. She'd talked to an Australian soldier.

Wait until she told Dottie.

Chapter Seventeen

9 August 1915

Jessie sucked the pad of her left index finger and cursed silently. She'd pricked herself with a needle for the umpteenth time that afternoon and was both annoyed with herself for being distracted and frustrated that the ribbon she was hand stitching to a straw hat seemed to have a mind of its own. She turned away from the window and tossed the hat onto her worktable, where it upset a roll of thread that went tumbling to the floor.

Sometimes she would be happy if she never sewed another stitch in her life.

Perhaps she should knit more. Wouldn't England's soldiers need woollen garments to keep them warm on the battlefields of France and Belgium as autumn and winter approached? She was a better seamstress than she was a knitter but she was certain she could manage balaclava helmets, mufflers, gloves, knee bands and socks. What man wouldn't be grateful for a new pair of socks?

Jessie heard voices and, letting them distract her, she went to the window and tugged aside the lace curtain.

A group of young women from the Asbestos Works was walking down the high street and, after a glance at the clock above the mantel, she guessed they had just finished a shift. They walked arm in arm with their friends, not just to hold each other up at the end of an exhausting day, but out of a sense of comradeship she could hear in their chatter and see in their laughing faces. And they were wearing trousers like men. It still shocked Jessie to see women wearing men's clothes—she herself had never donned a pair—and she wondered what such freedom from wearing a corset would feel like.

She envied the factory girls their trousers. It seemed to create in them a purposeful stride, a determination and confidence. What must it be like to walk off to work each day on a production line alongside friends with whom you might share a silly joke or an intimacy, perhaps about the young man you fancied? And then at lunchtime, sitting together in the factory cafeteria engaging in conversations about who was stepping out with who and what magazines you read and what films you might have seen. When she was a child, she'd had friendships with other girls and they'd played hopscotch and skipping rope at lunchtime and in the high street after school, with victory being handed to the first to make one hundred skips without tripping on the rope.

And while Dottie remained her best friend, her life since finishing school—eight years now—had existed in her cottage. There were trips to Uxbridge for notions and occasionally into London to buy fabric, but she was rarely allowed to linger. She had been far too busy to take time looking in the shop windows of Harrods or to visit

Selfridges, so famous and popular since it had opened seven years before. Home had been her workplace, her safe place, a haven for Harry and a comforting idyll for each of the Chesters.

Jessie moved away from the window, opened the front door and stepped out into the street. Everything about it was so familiar. The village had barely changed for a hundred years and she knew it like the back of her hand. But there was something stirring in her, something unfamiliar and urgent. In this little pocket of England, time had always travelled slowly. Until the war changed everything. Now, girls worked in factories and shops and Dottie delivered the mail. Just the week before, Jessie had noticed the bus from Uxbridge was being driven by a lady and Harry had mentioned that the last time he'd caught the train into London the conductor was a woman.

'A conductress,' he'd announced authoritatively. 'I gave her my shilling and she handed me my ticket just as well as any man.'

Her little life seemed smaller than it had ever been.

'Jessie!' Harry called from the kitchen and she turned. The sun was warm on her face and she didn't want to close the door and shut the outside away. Not today.

'What it is, Harry?'

'I'm looking at the account for Mrs Pritchard. Has she paid? It's a week overdue.'

Jessie was a competent and talented seamstress but the part of the job she had always liked the least was collecting payment. Especially from women like Mrs Pritchard, who seemed to believe their time to be far more valuable than hers and the small detail of a payment of an account for summer dresses for her daughters something that could be easily delayed and then forgotten.

'She hasn't paid.'

Harry shuffled to her and looked over Jessie's shoulder at the street and the activity. 'Nice day.'

'It is.'

'Why don't you go for a walk? It'll do you good.'

She turned to Harry. 'I'm fine.'

'No, you're not. You sit at that blasted machine too much. Why don't you go and see Dottie and have another picnic? Anything. But you should leave this house while the sun is shining.'

Jessie knew this was the moment she'd been waiting for.

'Harry. There's something I've been meaning to talk to you about.'

He looked perplexed. 'Me?'

'It's about Dottie.'

'What about her?' He moved to turn away but Jessie was fast. She reached a hand out and grabbed his good arm.

'Don't go. Dottie likes you very much, Harry.'

When Harry blushed and looked away, Jessie chided herself for having been so blind. He did harbour an affection for Dottie after all. She had always prided herself on knowing her younger brother's needs, on helping him lead as independent a life as possible. But had she really been listening to him at all? Had she only seen what she'd wanted to see? He tried to shake off Jessie's grip but she held on.

'Don't talk such rubbish, Jess.'

'It's not rubbish. Of course she's always been my best friend and a friend to you and our family. But it's you she looks at the most now, Harry. When she sees you, she gets a little blush in her cheeks. She favours you above all others.'

'She does not,' he replied angrily. 'Stop talking so.'

'I've seen it, Harry. And just now, judging by your reaction to what I've just said, I think you might be fond of her too.'

Harry tugged his arm hard and Jessie let go. He walked into the kitchen and she closed the front door, and the rest of the world out, before following him. Harry pressed his good hand into the kitchen table to steady himself and she waited a long while before he spoke.

'You know what they say, Jessie?' When he turned back to her, his eyes were filled with unshed tears. 'He who serves wins the girl. I can't serve and I don't deserve the girl. Plain and simple. She won't want a man like me. What good am I to someone like her?'

Jessie willed her feet to stay in place. What she wanted to do was go to him, put an arm around his shoulders and comfort him as she had when he was a little boy and she still had the authority of being his older sister. But he was a man now, and she knew if she touched him in that way, he would want to squirm out of his skin and shrug to make her go away. She swallowed the words she so desperately wanted to say: that he was a truly wonderful man, a kind man, a compassionate man, a man with a heart as well as a head.

'Oh, Harry, she doesn't think that, I know it.'

He slapped his hand on the table, stumbled, then steadied himself. The account books he'd been working on and the pile of thin paper invoices fluttered. 'A man should be strong, to provide for a wife and protect his family. If the Jerries come marching into Harefield, what good would I be to any woman?'

Harry reached for an apple from the bowl on the table, slipped it into his trouser pocket and limped to the back door. 'I'm going to feed the hens.' The door swung closed behind him. Jessie watched him through the open window. The chickens flapped their wings in delight and gathered around him greedily. He took small bites of the apple and spat them into his hand before tossing them to the ground, the hens squawking and squabbling around his feet.

The knocking on the Chesters' front door was determined and angry.

Jessie and Win looked up from their lunch plates and exchanged startled glances.

'Is there an emergency?' Jess asked as she stood, careful not to knock over her cup of tea. She and her mother had taken a half-hour break from working to have a bite to eat and a cuppa and even that was to be interrupted.

Win huffed. 'It better not be another peddler. I sent two away yesterday.' She bustled to the front and peered as surreptitiously as possible through the lace curtains out onto the street.

'Mrs Chester? Mrs Chester? Open your door this instant.'

Win grimaced. 'It's Mrs Pritchard.' She wrapped her woollen shawl tight around her as if it were a shield and sighed. 'Let her in then.'

Jessie opened the door to a red-faced Mrs Pritchard, who all but knocked Jessie aside as she rushed inside, lugging an enormous carpet bag.

'Good morn—'

'Yes, yes. I've no time for that. You and your daughter will have to drop everything you're doing and see to these dresses this instant.'

She opened the wooden handles on her carpet bag, reached in and tossed a pile of fabric onto the sewing table. It fell in a tangled heap. Jessie recognised the pale blue wool skirt she'd sewn earlier in the year, as well as a brown woollen dress with a lace collar and a cream-coloured fine cotton shirt with pintucking at the breast.

'These garments are too small. I don't know what you did but until you make what I ordered I won't be paying for them. It's far too hot for such tight garments.' She hesitated, pulled her lips in tight. 'Arabella has taken to not wearing a corset. I blame that Mrs Pankhurst,' she spat. 'All that voting nonsense. Things were fine the way they've always been. We need morals, not votes. We need discipline, not this new world in which young women gambol about the streets, thinking they have freedom to go out on their own. And don't even get me started about riding bicycles. I've seen those Australian nurses from the hospital, up and down Hill End Road all the day and night, their skirts flapping up and revealing their legs like harlots in Soho or some such. And those Australian soldiers? They don't look injured to me. They're in every shop in the village, and don't talk to me about what they get up to with those factory girls at the Cricketers.'

'I've found them to be polite young men,' Jessie said, feeling the heat rise in her cheeks. She knew some of the factory girls from the village too, and understood they wouldn't appreciate Mrs Pritchard's insinuation.

'Polite?' she exclaimed. 'They're nothing but utterly low-class and foul-mouthed louts. I certainly have nothing in common with them and find it exceedingly difficult to put up with their wantonly pointless, witless and filthy conversations.'

The woman suddenly burst into tears.

Jessie searched her mother's face for an answer to Mrs Pritchard's unusual behaviour. Jessie stepped forward, thinking it only polite to console the woman. 'I do apologise, Mrs Pritchard. I didn't mean to upset you.'

Mrs Pritchard snatched up the frocks she'd thrown on the sewing table and clung to them, pressing them to her chest. 'They've done nothing but prey on …'

Win stepped forward and placed a comforting hand on Mrs Pritchard's. Her voice was gentle, calm.

'Jessie, why don't you put the kettle on?'

She took the hint and left the two women to talk.

Half an hour later, Win came into the kitchen. Jessie folded the newspaper she'd been looking at, grateful for an excuse to stop reading about the war.

'That was unexpected.' Win brushed down her apron as if she'd walked through an alleyway full of cobwebs instead of having just survived an encounter with Mrs Pritchard.

'A cuppa?'

'Yes please, love.' Win sat down, her face a picture of weary resignation.

Jessie knew her mother. Win would sit on her thoughts for a while and in her own good time would open up about whatever was troubling her. It had taken two whole days before she had told Jessie and Harry that their father was sick, that he would finally succumb to what ailed him. Win never jumped the gun when it came to serious matters. She deliberated before opening her mouth to speak, just as she'd taught Jessie to measure twice before cutting fabric and ribbon and thread.

Win studied the tabletop while she considered her conversation with Mrs Pritchard. Jessie spooned loose tea into the pot and took it to the stove for the boiling water. She slipped the knitted tea cosy over it and took it to the table.

Win heaved a huge sigh. 'I know what she's like. How she's always been. I wish we didn't have to do business with her, but in a village as small as ours, beggars can't be choosers. But … what she said to me when Harry was born? Well. I will never forgive her for it.'

Jessie waited a moment before asking. 'What did she say to you?'

Win narrowed her eyes in anger. 'That I must have offended God to have carried a child with such an affliction. That your father should send him away so the rest of the village wouldn't have to look at him.'

Jessie struggled to hold her anger inside. Mrs Pritchard had been snobbish and priggish for more years than Jessie had been alive. She'd looked down on the Chesters for their occupation, their situation in life, their address, the fact that they weren't regular churchgoers. To add insult to injury, she was always late paying her accounts and Harry had angrily suggested once that they refuse her business. It wasn't that easy in a small village, Win had explained. People like Mrs Pritchard would talk and she was the kind of person others listened to. While Jessie knew her mother was right, it didn't grate any less. Jessie had always believed that Mrs Pritchard would criticise the brand of soap flakes they used for the washing if she'd had a chance.

'Not Velvet soap, Mrs Chester. You should be using Sunlight. They're soap makers to His Majesty.'

Jessie couldn't think of a time when the woman had displayed one skerrick of kindness to them or compassion to anyone else in the village.

And now, this revelation about her brother had Jessie feeling a hatred of the woman that she never thought possible.

'She's had a terrible shock, that's for certain,' Win said through gritted teeth.

Jessie waited. 'It sounds like she has.'

'It's …' Win leant across the table and lowered her voice. 'It's Arabella. She's in the family way.' Just saying the words sent all the blood draining from Win's face. Was there no greater humiliation for a family like the Pritchards than a daughter pregnant out of wedlock?

'Oh, my.'

'The Pritchards are sending her up to Scotland immediately. There's a great aunt or a grandmother or godmother. I must admit I was so shocked to hear the news that I can't exactly remember which relative will help them hide the disgrace for the duration of her confinement.'

Jessie had never cared much for Arabella either—she took too much after her mother for Jessie's liking—but she found some sympathy for the poor girl, knowing how close she was with her sister. They were two peas in a pod, Arabella and Lucinda, who had taken to wearing matching summer frocks at parties and tea dances as it brought them twice the attention. They were barely an inch apart in height and wore their blonde hair, as thick and long as horses' swishing tails, piled generous and high on their heads, adding to their rosy-cheeked lushness that attracted the affections of young men from all over Middlesex. That and their father's business, of course.

No matter how unfriendly she'd found them over the years—and how much she now hated their mother—Jessie couldn't wish Arabella's fate on any young woman.

'Poor Lucinda,' Jessie said.

'She'll be a lonely young woman this winter, that's for certain.'

Jessie picked up a biscuit and took a gulp of tea. 'Poor Arabella.'

'Don't you go breathing a word, Jessie.'

Jessie was horrified her mother thought she might betray such a secret. 'Mum! Of course not.'

Win pulled her lips tight. 'As much as I love Dottie— and you know I do as if she were my own—not a word. She loves a story, that girl.'

'Of course.'

'There'll be enough shame heaped on Arabella without half the village knowing.' Win dropped her head into her hands and moaned. 'They're lucky they've got money, that's all I can say. They have the means to send Arabella away but while everyone in the village will nod their heads when they're told she's going to be a companion to a dowager aunt or some such, everyone will know the truth.'

'They'll believe Mr and Mrs Pritchard, won't they? They do when it comes to everything else.'

'Oh, make no mistake. They'll smile when they see Mrs Pritchard at the tearooms and they'll sidle up to her and ask politely, "How's Miss Pritchard faring up in Scotland?" And she'll tell them a story about all the sights young Arabella's been seeing and all the things she's learning and they'll say, "How marvellous. What a lucky girl". And then they'll walk out in the street and laugh behind their hands. People are cruel, as we well know.'

Win pushed back her chair and took her teacup to the sink. She cranked the tap and rinsed it out, leaving it to drain, all the while muttering under her breath. When she turned, her cheeks were beet red.

'You promise me one thing, Jessie, my girl.' Win wagged a finger at her daughter.

Jessie felt exactly as she had when she was ten years old and had been scolded by her mother for washing one of the chickens in the kitchen sink. 'What does Arabella's situation have to do—'

'You're to stay away from those soldiers.'

'The Australians? From the hospital?'

'That's exactly who I mean. They're all a long way from home and they're running wild in Harefield. Everywhere you look, there's another boy with a peculiar accent stepping out with a local girl. Walking around the green hoping to meet a local lass. What's going to happen at the end of the war, when they all go back to Australia?' Win's voice rose higher and breathier. 'They're going to leave every young girl in the village broken-hearted. Or worse: in the workhouse with a babby and no father to look after it.'

'Mum …'

'Where is this soldier who got Arabella in the family way, hmm? I don't see him knocking on the Pritchards' door asking for her hand to keep her safe from disgrace.'

Jessie waited. Win pulled a handkerchief from the pocket of her apron and dabbed at her eyes. 'It's fine for the Pritchards. Their money will see them right. If it happened to you? If one of those Australians took advantage of you? What would we do?'

'Mum.' Jessie went to her mother and stood next to her, their backs pressed against the kitchen sink. She squeezed her mother's hand.

'I don't think it was an Australian soldier.'

Win stared at her daughter. 'Of course it was.'

'It's just that … I've seen Arabella with a man in Harefield.' Jessie was torn but it wasn't fair for the Australians to be maligned in such a way.

'Yes, that's what Mrs Pritchard said. It was an Australian man. A soldier.'

Jessie shook her head. 'Dottie and I were picnicking at the green and Arabella walked past, arm in arm with some toff. They were talking about driving to Harrow. That's what I heard, anyway, and I remember it because I thought that he must have a motor car. And then they did hop into a motor car, black, I believe, and they drove away.'

'How can you be sure he wasn't an Australian, Jessie?'

'I heard his voice. As plummy as the King.'

Win didn't have much faith in God but she crossed herself just in case.

Chapter Eighteen

23 August 1915

On Cora's only day off in the week—a sunny and warm Tuesday—she decided to remedy her racing mind and her restlessness by practising what she preached to her patients.

She couldn't face lying in bed all day with her letters or stack of Leonora's cast-off magazines, as tempting as it might have been given how exhausted she felt, and had decided to take in the fresh air. She wore a straw hat, her hair tucked up into a low bun, and carried with her on her expedition a paring knife and a wicker basket. She hoped to use the first to fill the second with flowers for the ward.

It had been almost three months since she'd believed herself to have landed in the middle of a fairytale landscape in England, filled with storybook manor houses and swans a-swimming and wildflower-filled meadows. Most of the grounds between the main house and Rickmansworth Road had been swallowed up by new buildings, but when she rounded the manor house and strolled north, she was able to take herself back to the wonder of that first day.

The lakes at the rear of Harefield House sparkled in the bright sunshine, reflecting the Wedgwood blue sky. Cora thought ahead to winter and wondered if the shallow man-made lakes might freeze over. Did people skate there? She had never strapped on a pair of skates—with either blades or wheels—but had seen a performance at the Tivoli back home in which Nellie Donegan and Earle Reynolds had skated to music like two ballroom dancers. The crowd had gasped and cheered as they'd glided gracefully across the stage like swans and then twirled with dizzy cleverness as spinning tops might. Cora thought it must be the closest a person might come to flying, to feeling weightless and free like the birds she loved.

Drawn by its perfumed scent to a lavender hedge in what might once have been a carefully tended garden, Cora set her basket on the grass. She chose carefully, looking for blooms that were about to open, and snipped two dozen or so before laying them in the basket. When she tried to stand upright, she tried to ignore the sudden pulsing spasm at her side and paused, holding herself at an odd angle before slowly moving upright. She winced and pressed her fingers into the small of her back, lifting her chin and arching herself forward to determine if that awkward posture might help with the pain that had set in a month before and hadn't budged.

Nurses' back, that's what it was known as. All the lifting and leaning and grabbing and pulling and tucking took a toll on nurses even in civilian life, in which the hours were shorter and the wounds not as severe. Army nursing was another kettle of fish. Longer hours, longer weeks and the severity of the injured meant more lifting, not less. The flow of injured men had continued its devastating pace and the hours—and the men's faces—had blended into a mishmash of blue eyes and brown, of days and into weeks.

A visit by the King and Queen the week before had lifted everyone's spirits for the day, but once the fruitcake had been devoured and the fresh blooms had wilted, reality had settled in once again upon their weary shoulders.

Most nights, after a day which had begun at 6:45 am and ended at eight, Cora had dragged herself to bed in the nurses' quarters and fallen into fitful sleep.

Her heart was breaking just a little bit more each day.

Fresh air and a good walk. That's what she needed, as well as some time to herself. To quiet her racing mind. Some time to think.

Rather, some time to forget.

There was so much she would like to forget, to erase from her mind and her heart.

She had slept in a little that morning, pulling the blankets over her head when the others were rousing to go over to the mess. She had taken a late breakfast alone, untroubled by the groups of other staff laughing and chatting. While her second cup of tea cooled, Cora had leafed through a pile of Australian newspapers. Her colleagues and the patients devoured them story by story for news of anyone they knew. They were surreal souvenirs of home, a reminder that among all the chaos and carnage across the Channel, there was still some sense of normality in the world, even if they were so far away from it. She'd sorted through them—the *Port Macquarie News* and *Hastings River Advocate*, the *Stawell News* and *Pleasant*

Creek Chronicle, the *Gippsland Mercury*, *The Capricornian*, the *Burrowa News*—until she found a copy of *The Register* from Adelaide. Its date was late June but it was the most recent news she was going to get.

Vaudeville shows were being performed at the Tivoli and Mary Pickford and Charlie Chaplin movies seemed as popular as ever, judging by the large advertisement and all the weekly sessions listed. More than £170,600 had been raised for the SA Soldiers' Fund and, to her great disappointment, Cora noted that she had missed the June Stocktaking Sale at Fitch's. At page nine, she'd stilled. The column Call of Duty included the numbers of men who had enlisted on just one Tuesday of the previous week.

Volunteers	191
Men accepted	153
Week's applicants	443
Fit for service	333
Enlistments to date	10,973

Tears stung her eyes at the realisation that more than ten thousand South Australian men had already enlisted. These were men she might have sat next to in school, or brushed past on a busy Rundle Street on her way to Birks the Chemists, or seen picnicking in the shade of the Moreton Bay figs in the Botanic Garden. She might have walked in their footprints in the sand at Henley Beach or marched past them on a climb up Waterfall Gully, juggling her umbrella to avoid poking them in the eye.

Would she nurse any of these South Australian recruits at Harefield? Would the Fates bring two people who might have walked past each other ten thousand miles away into close proximity on the other side of the world?

Cora closed her eyes, breathed deep and long, and took in the earthy scents of pasture and earth. It had rained only once during the past week and there was no threat of it that day, the sky above streaked with fine gossamer clouds. Above her, robins darted and tits flitted by, teasing her with their freedom.

Cora cast her eyes down to the array of colourful flowers in the basket on her elbow. She knew lavender and roses and cornflowers but not the others, a kaleidoscope of bright pinks and whites and yellows. The gardens of Harefield Park had presented her with a rainbow of colours and shapes and scents for the little vases she would set on each soldier's bedside table. Sometimes comforting words and flowers were all she could provide her patients. The worse the injuries, the more helpless she and her colleagues felt. So many of their patients would have to endure months and possibly years of medical care, massage and general rehabilitation if they were to get back to any semblance of normal life. Captain Kent was predicting that some might need six months at Harefield to become robust enough to survive the journey home and, even then, they would likely spend many more months in hospital in Australia.

Since their conversation at the concert, she'd thought over and over about his flirtatious behaviour. She'd been embarrassed at first, that she might have been seen being too familiar with a doctor. She knew doctors—those who assumed themselves to be irresistible to anyone with a female form, and their assumption that anyone with a female form would find them the same. She had brushed off wandering hands on her bottom, suited arms brushing across her breasts and outright requests for 'relief'. But Captain Kent had never been inappropriate with her in that way. They'd continued to work alongside each other in theatre when she was rostered there. They'd consulted as colleagues about patients and said convivial hellos to each other when they'd passed each other in the mess. For two weeks earlier in the month he'd been away from Harefield and Leonora had passed on the gossip that he'd been in London doing something official with the army.

She had tried not to see what Gertie had observed, that Captain Kent noticed Cora in a way he didn't seem to notice Leonora or Gertie or Fiona or any of the other nurses. She'd finally had to admit to herself that it was true. But, simply, there was nothing to be done about it. She hadn't come to England to seek a romance. She had come for duty and honour and all her attention was to be properly directed towards her patients. She had purloined a gramophone from the main house and, in the afternoons, in that sleepy hour between activities and dinner, she played records as loud as the men could bear. One afternoon last week, a couple of soldiers had hopped up and down the aisle together, their arms about each other's shoulders, and called out, 'Sister. Look at us! Tom's got a left leg and I've got a right. Together we make a whole bloke!'

And she'd laughed and laughed along with them, and later that night cried herself to sleep.

Flowers. That's what she could do today. She couldn't bring back limbs or minds but she could aid a man's recovery with kind words and music and flowers.

Cora picked up her basket and strode out. Rounding a copse of trees, she spotted a person in the middle distance stretched out on the grass. With his knees bent upwards, the trousered legs made a triangle, and they moved gently in the breeze like a boat sail on an almost still lake. He held a book over his head, as if to shield his eyes from the sun, and a curl of smoke rose from a cigarette between his lips. As she kept on her path, with the full intention of walking right by and leaving him to his reverie, the man stood, propped one hand on his hip and waved at her.

'Sister Barker!'

Had she conjured Captain Kent out of thin air with her thoughts of him?

He beckoned her over with a wave and, as it would have been impolite to walk by, she made her way across the grass to him, an arm looped through the handle of her basket. 'Captain. I do apologise. I couldn't make you out at first,' she lied.

He held his arms wide. 'It's me. How nice to see you out here. I must admit it took a moment to recognise you, as well. We are different people out of our uniforms, are we not?'

Cora's free hand flew to the back of her head, where her veil would normally drape. Instead she felt her nape, warm and flushed. 'We are. I'm sorry to have interrupted your solitude. I know how hard it can be to find any these days.'

The captain chuckled and swept back his hair. 'I'm glad you did. I swear I've been reading the same chapter over and over without any of it sinking in. I don't know if it's me or the book. I suspect it's the former.' He stepped forward.

'Won't you come and sit with me? I have cigarettes, if you'd like one.'

'Thank you but I don't smoke.'

'Bugger. I wish I had tea and biscuits then. Something to entice you to stay.' He gazed at her for a moment and then, without asking, he stepped forward and lifted the wicker basket from her arm. With a wave, he motioned she should follow him to the tree where he had created a little idyll for himself. A green and blue tartan blanket covered a square of grass. On it, his book lay open and a pack of cigarettes was half-crumpled next to a pair of shoes. She glanced at his feet and saw khaki socks. He wiggled his toes inside them which made Cora want to laugh. 'To be honest, I can't wait to get my blasted shoes off.'

Cora wondered how he might cope with a corset.

'I've seen so many cases of trench foot that I seem to have become slightly obsessed with getting fresh air to my feet.'

'Entirely understandable.' She'd seen them, too. Boys who had been forced to stand in water for days without having the chance to dry their feet or change their socks developed swollen, red, fungal skin which sometimes split and became infected. The situation was made worse by their leather boots, which shrank when wet, constricting the blood flow to their feet even further. In the worst cases, gangrene had already set in, rendering the digits on the foot black. They would have to be removed—something she had observed Captain Kent do many times in surgery—so she fully comprehended his attention to his toes. For patients with less severe cases, the nurses encouraged them to walk to return circulation and prescribed a daily foot rub with turpentine and olive oil. Cora had grown to detest the smell of the concoction.

'Please, Sister Barker. Won't you sit?'

Cora glanced around. He'd chosen a beautiful spot. The leaves on the trees around and above them flickered and swayed in the warm breeze. The sound of them swishing, and the view to the pastures and meadows in the distance, enabled Cora for just a moment to banish all thoughts of muddy trenches and gangrene. Perhaps if she sat and listened, she might hear the birdsong of a nightingale or a cuckoo.

'Are you certain I'm not intruding?'

'The absolute exact opposite, in fact. I thought I was in need of my own company but I'm already rather sick of myself. And besides,' he nodded dismissively at his novel, 'I think I've already figured out who did it.' The sunshine had made his cheeks ruddy and his eyes bright and for the first time since she'd met him, Cora thought his expression resembled something close to serenity.

'How clever of you.' Cora lowered herself onto the corner of the rug, her legs coyly bent on her right side.

'Are you a reader, Sister?'

'I used to be. Voracious, in fact. But even though there are more books in the library here at Harefield than I could ever read in a lifetime, I've lost my enthusiasm for it. I sometimes ... well, I sometimes find it hard to concentrate. Newspapers are about all I can manage at the moment.'

'Yes,' he murmured. When she turned to him she saw sincere understanding in his expression.

'What's the book?'

'Conan Doyle. *The Hound of the Baskervilles.*'

'I haven't read him.'

'He served in the Boer War, you know.'

'Perhaps that's why our patients like him so much. I'm more of a Jane Austen devotee, myself.'

'She's very famous, I understand.'

'Very.' Cora smiled to herself.

'For a woman author.'

'Oh, most definitely,' Cora chuckled. 'Just as Sir Arthur Conan Doyle is, for a *male* author.'

Captain Kent laughed warmly. 'Touché.'

They sat a sensible distance apart and admired the view for a moment. The captain scooped up his novel, turned down the corner of a page to mark his spot, and then reached for his cigarettes.

'You don't mind if I …?'

'Not at all,' Cora replied. 'I'm quite used to it. The men smoke like trains. If cigarettes and tobacco aren't being delivered in packages from the Red Cross, they're arriving in parcels from home.'

'I don't know what we'd do without the damn things.' Captain Kent slipped a cigarette between his lips and struck a match. His hands trembled as he lit his cigarette, she noticed. He drew in and blew the smoke out, lifting his chin and turning his head away from her.

'Do you find it relaxing, Captain?'

He nodded. 'The funny thing is, I never smoked back home. I didn't like the idea that patients might smell tobacco on my clothes or see nicotine stains on my fingers. But now? I smoke like a chimney and drink like a fish. The war, hey?'

In the sombre silence that followed, Cora took a moment to study him, his long legs outstretched, his socked feet moving from side to side to some music only he could hear. His hair was unkempt and his jaw looked like it hadn't had a razor scrape against it that morning. The top button of his shirt was undone and, underneath his knitted vest, his shirtsleeves had been roughly rolled up to mid-forearm.

And she herself wasn't dressed in grey and white, but a soft brown dress and lace-up boots. If she let herself, it would be so easy to forget for that moment who they were, where they were, and what they were in England to do. What if they were two people who happened upon each other at a concert, a walk, an afternoon tea party? Might he have noticed her then? Might she have let herself be noticed by him in a way that she wasn't sure of all these thousands of miles away in the middle of a war?

She let herself imagine, for a moment, the possibilities of such a meeting and then tucked the thought away.

'Just before you walked over, I heard a cuckoo. Can you believe it?'

'Really? Did it remind you of one of those German clocks with the little doors?'

'Yes! It actually did. Although in that case, I suppose I shouldn't have enjoyed it.'

'I suppose not, Captain. It might seem, I don't know, traitorous.'

They smiled at each other.

'Sister Barker,' he sighed. 'Since we are both off duty this afternoon, perhaps you might call me by my first name. Standing on ceremony here, in the middle of all this ...' He waved his arm around and Cora knew instinctively that he didn't mean the gardens or the manor house or Middlesex. 'There's no need.'

She only used first names for her friends. Were they becoming friends?

'I would, Captain. If I knew it.'

He lay back, resting on an elbow, and looked at her. His eyes sparkled. 'You don't?'

'All I know is the initial. W.'

'Why don't you take a guess?'

Was he flirting? Was she enjoying it? 'I'm thinking it might be … Wilberforce?'

He chuckled and took a drag on his cigarette. 'No, thank god. I should never have forgiven my parents if that were the case.'

'Walter?'

'Not even close.'

'Wolfgang?' Cora ventured.

'Not likely. And if it was, I'd admit it to no one.'

'Perhaps it's … Winston?'

'No.'

'I've got it.' She snapped a finger. 'You're a Wilfred.'

'Wrong again.'

'I find myself rather out of options.'

He leant across the rug, extending a hand to her. 'It's William.'

'William,' Cora replied slowly. She slipped her fingers into his. His palm was warm and broad and his fingers strong. She'd seen them stitching a wound with fine thread and knew they were dextrous and nimble, but hadn't anticipated them being soft.

He grinned widely. 'Thank you. I need someone to call me by my name. It reminds me that I'm young.' He chuckled. 'Relatively young, anyway. Every time I hear someone calling me sir I think of my father.'

'Your father is a doctor too?'

'Yes. And my grandfather.'

'Goodness. Such a long line. And …' She hesitated. 'Have you have any sons to continue that fine tradition?'

He met her eyes. 'No sons. Or daughters. For that matter.'

It didn't escape her notice that he hadn't mentioned if he was married.

'And your name, Sister?'

'Cora.'

'Cora.' How had he made two syllables sound like four? He'd almost enunciated each letter of her name as he'd said it, as if he had taken it apart and examined it to see what was between them. As if he were committing it to memory.

Cora reached for a stem of lavender from her basket and began knotting its bare stalk.

'May I ask you something?' Cora said.

'Of course.'

'Where were you serving before you came to England?'

William took a long drag and looked off into the distance. He stubbed out his cigarette on the grass and lit another with trembling fingers before he told her.

'The Dardanelles. And lately, at Number Two Australian Hospital in Egypt.'

He'd been at Gallipoli. The realisation forced her questions out in a tumble. 'You must know so much more than what has been printed in the newspapers.' She paused. 'How bad is it really?'

William returned her gaze with a curious expression and he stared at her for a long while.

'You don't believe it's a nurse's place to ask such questions?' Was she not allowed to be curious about her patients' injuries? In her weeks in theatre, she had seen the results of hastily performed field amputations: filthy bandages that covered weeping wounds on limbs that appeared as if they'd been hacked off with a farm implement, increasing cases of sepsis and the liberal use of carbolic lotion–soaked gauze wrapped around wounds. In the operating theatre, William himself had spoken of a wound having been 'bipped', and when Cora had investigated what the treatment involved, she'd made a wonderful discovery. BIPP—bismuth iodoform paraffin paste—had first been created by the English pathologist Dr Helen Chambers, who was treating wounded soldiers at the Endell Street Military Hospital in London. When she'd rushed to tell Gertie about her discovery, Gertie had huffed with impatience.

'Is it any surprise that those women doctors—working at the only British hospital entirely staffed by females—should come up with such a practical solution to infection on the battlefield?'

'Isn't it fascinating?' Cora had exclaimed. 'The paste is smeared into a wound after it's been debrided to create a kind of seal to prevent further infection. I've seen it myself on some of our patients.'

In Cora's experience, there was a secret language that the doctors were reluctant to share with their nurse colleagues, which Cora had always found perplexing and unfair.

William reached for his pack of cigarettes and slipped one from the wrapping. 'It's not that at all, Cora. I admire your curiosity. I know some more senior colleagues of mine might think that way, but I don't. Then they are of a different era and of a different generation. A nurse in my operating theatre is as vital to a patient as my scalpel is. On a ward, as important as any padre. Having seen firsthand the work of your colleagues on the ships off Gallipoli, so close we could hear the gunfire … well, they didn't flinch. I have nothing but the highest regard for members of your profession.'

She averted her gaze from his, discomfited that she'd leapt to a conclusion he'd so swiftly rebutted. 'I apologise. I didn't mean to be defensive. It's just that, in my experience, not many doctors appreciate such questions from a nurse. Nor men in a woman.'

'Perhaps all those Wilberforces and Walters and Wilfreds don't, but I admire it tremendously.'

She held the lavender blossom to her nose and breathed deep. 'Things are getting worse, aren't they? You officers are told much more than we nurses ever are.'

He puffed on his cigarette. 'You're right. Things are getting worse. Not that we're supposed to notice or talk about it. No one expected this many wounded. And the extent of the injuries … they're unfathomable.'

Cora twisted her fingers together in her lap. 'I'm an experienced nurse, William, but I couldn't have imagined what shrapnel and bullets do to bodies. The perforation of bones. The way in which the soft organs are ploughed up. How the men survive long enough to get to us, I'll never know.'

'It's worse if the bullet hits broadside.' William pointed his finger at his side and traced a line across his stomach.

She watched his movement, frozen at the idea of it.

'The track in the soft tissue is much larger. We're seeing the walls of the wound pulped with large exit wounds and any bones in the way are almost ... pulverised. Shrapnel worms its way into everything. I find myself removing bits of the blasted stuff months after a wound was inflicted. Its power to destroy ... that's why we're seeing more amputations in the field. And when the organs are pulverised in that way, the stomach and bowel contents spill and the risk of infection is so high there's almost nothing to be done for those men.'

So many thousands of men. So much unbearable suffering.

'It's bad here, Cora, no doubt. But in the field hospitals?' He shook his head as if the very action might slough off the memories. 'I never imagined what heavy artillery could do to a man's body until I saw it with my own eyes. Until I held the remnants of legs and arms and torsos in my bloodied hands.'

'Good lord,' Cora whispered.

'Those poor bastards die right there where they were standing. They're shredded into a thousand pieces in an instant. Ever heard a patient say that he looked away and heard an explosion and then looked back and his mate was gone?'

'I have,' she blurted. 'One of the men was describing it to me and he said "He was gone, Sister". He said there was an explosion and that when the smoke cleared, his pal was ... gone.'

'Do you know the patient Lingley? Gunner Lingley? Tall bloke, bright red hair?'

Cora had seen so many men come through the hospital that she couldn't be certain. Perhaps he'd been on another ward. Perhaps all the men were blending into one? 'I can't say I do.'

William lit another cigarette. 'He copped a bullet across his temple. France, I think. It barely penetrated ...' His voice was shaky. 'So, you might think it would knock a chap flat for a few days, give him a crashing headache for a week or so. But what we're seeing in these men is something different. They're dull ... they look at you but you just know they're not taking in a single word you're saying to them. They can't concentrate. They don't remember their rank or the town they were born. It's as if they revert to childhood.'

'That poor lad. His poor family.'

'He's nineteen years old, Cora.' William lowered his back to the rug and turned his eyes to the sky. 'What kind of men am I sending back to Australia? All those families who stood at railway stations and docks and waved goodbye to their strong, brave boys. Their sons and lovers. Each one a courageous, willing young man. And I'm sending them back half a man.'

'Aren't we all doing the best we can in the circumstances?'

'How can any man not think they'll be next when death comes so randomly? What kind of a weight is that to carry? You ask your mate for a smoke one minute, and the next he's blown to bits. And you don't want to know what happens to those boys who stick their head above a parapet. Some of them have their entire faces shot off.'

What possible treatment or words of comfort could anyone offer a person so disfigured?

'Yet the men arrive in a seemingly unending stream, don't they, bearing every conceivable kind of injury. On an average day I'm doing twenty procedures. Twenty.' He cursed and reached a hand up, flexing his fingers. 'I don't think I'll ever get the blood out from under my nails. And after a day in surgery, I can barely move my bloody fingers.' He cleared his throat. 'I apologise. I shouldn't air my frustrations to you.'

'If it helps you, I'm all ears.'

William turned to her, his eyes soft, his hair unruly, his body languid and loose. His intimate gaze, his pose, was too much and she felt confused by it. She shouldn't be looking at him that way, imagining he might be something other than a colleague. A friend with whom she might share secrets and intimacies. She turned away, afraid her cheeks were aflame, afraid he might notice.

'Really?'

'Of course.'

'You won't think me selfish or churlish if I moan at you?'

'We all have our frustrations. With the hospital, with our colleagues and yes, sometimes even with doctors.'

He chuckled. 'What have my learned colleagues and I done this time?'

'Nothing that doctors haven't been doing since Florence Nightingale flexed her muscle in the medical sphere.'

'In that case, I apologise on behalf of my entire sex.'

'We need more doctors, that's clear.'

'If only we could find them.'

'I know where they are. Did you know there are women doctors in Australia whose offers of service have been refused by the army? Wouldn't their help be useful somewhere? You said yourself you're performing too many surgeries a day.'

William propped himself up on an elbow. 'You think women doctors should be allowed to enlist?'

'Why ever not? Nurses are.'

'Some of my army colleagues say women are too hysterical and illogical to serve as doctors or surgeons. And that they'll only distract the men.'

Cora paused and tried to calm her frustration at sentiments she had heard many times in her career. 'And men are never hysterical and illogical?'

He thought on it. 'Touché again.'

'The British War Office will have them. Endell Street Military Hospital, for instance. Not to mention the Scottish Women's Hospitals, which are run exclusively by women. They've served in Macedonia and Serbia. Why on earth should Australian women not be able to serve under the Australian flag? I'm perplexed.'

'But what if they're killed or taken prisoner? I'd hate to think what the Jerries might do to a woman, Cora. It would be unspeakable.'

'You've seen what they've done to men. Isn't that unspeakable, too?'

'I wouldn't want my ...' William paused, words frozen on his lips.

'Your what?'

'Nothing.' He shook the thought away.

'The more doctors and nurses we have, the more lives we can save. To me, it's as simple as that.'

'I wish there was no need for us to be here in the first place, if we're being honest.'

'On that we can agree.'

They were a long way from the fighting but not from the consequences of it and the realisation weighed heavy on them both.

'So you don't smoke. Do you drink?'

'Not much.'

'What's your poison, then?' William took a drag and the trembling in his fingers returned.

'My poison?'

'What do you do to help you forget?'

Cora gave the answer that was expected of her, the answer expected of any woman. 'I pick flowers for the men.' She wouldn't tell him that she cried herself to sleep some nights at what she had seen or heard or been told.

She pointed to her wicker basket. 'I take long walks and I drink copious amounts of tea.'

'If only that were enough for me,' he said bitterly. 'I'm a miserable bloody sod, aren't I?'

'Perhaps simply more honest than most.'

'And here you were, innocently picking flowers and I've gone and brought you back down to earth with a crashing thud.' William sat up, met her eyes, imploringly studying her face. Her eyes, her mouth. 'Forgive me, won't you?'

She felt her own voice trembling as she answered. 'To be honest, it's nice not to have to pretend that this is all going to be over by Christmas.'

'It won't be, Cora,' William replied. 'There's nothing surer.'

Chapter Nineteen

10 September 1915

The new Harefield hospital canteen was a low-ceilinged hut that had been built near the wards and close to the recreation hall to provide a place of comfort to the recuperating men. It was filled with tables of all shapes and sizes—Cora guessed they had been rescued from the main house or donated by the people of the village—and around each sat regulation army wooden folding chairs with canvas backs.

At the far end of the room, the serving counter always had a queue and volunteers could be seen rushing back and forth through the curtained doorway to the kitchen beyond. Patients could come in at all hours for refreshments or to buy stamps or even postcards, and no one was ever heard to complain about having to pay a few shillings for their purchases as all the staff were volunteers and all the profits went to a canteen fund to improve amenities for the men.

Cora and Gertie had taken to heading there after a morning shift for a cup of hot chocolate and a cheese-and-pickle sandwich. Cora enjoyed the convivial atmosphere of the canteen. There was always a boisterous game of cards or draughts at one table or another and she enjoyed hearing groans of disappointment at having lost a game rather than groans of agony in the wards. Patients with a musical bent pounded away at the piano and gratefully received any applause that might come their way. Others sat quietly writing letters or reading.

Steam rose from Cora's cup and powdered cocoa had clumped at the top in swirls. She reached for an Australian newspaper that lay folded and discarded on the table.

Opposite her, Gertie held up a copy of *Woman's Life*. The bright red and blue on the cover caught Cora's eye for a moment. Its cover featured an illustration with the headline 'Betty's uniform for the war-worker': a young woman wearing a red shirt, a navy scarf shortened and tied at her neck in the manner of a man's tie, and a navy skirt. With one hand propped cockily at her hip, Betty looked determined and proud. Good for her, Cora thought, before turning the first few pages of *The Age*, skimming over the classified advertisements until she reached the international news pages.

It was a relief, in a strange and confusing way, to see so many headlines about the war. She often wondered if indeed distance didn't make the heart grow fonder at all; if the miles between Australia and England, the weeks and weeks it took for news to reach home, might mean that the events happening in the muddy battlefields of the war would somehow seem as unreal as a fairytale to people at home.

But no. According to the headlines, 'The Turks are losing their morale and it is now much easier to capture their trenches'. At Gallipoli, the stalemate between the British, French, Australian, New Zealand and Indian troops who made up the Commonwealth forces and the Turks continued. So many months of fighting, with neither side being able to claim a victory, and the loss of tens of thousands of men. What a price to pay. Earlier in August, the British transport ship *Prince Edward* had been sunk by a German submarine and 861 British soldiers had perished. That was more men than there were patients in Harefield hospital. Cora read that more troops were on their way from Australia, New South Wales specifically, and all Cora could think was that they would become lambs to the slaughter the minute they set foot on the Continent.

And it seemed there were already discussions at the highest levels about the question of providing jobs for returned and disabled soldiers, with a plan to give preference to patriots. There were items about fundraising drives and details of battles in places Cora struggled to remember and news of new munitions factories and bigger naval guns and starving civilians in Germany.

She felt a tremor behind her breastbone and closed the newspaper with shaking hands. She couldn't read any more. She stared at her cocoa and wished it were something stronger. Self-restraint was a virtue in normal times. In war, it was a hindrance and she felt herself straining against its conventions.

'I'll read yours when you're done,' she told Gertie.

Gertie peeped over the top of the *Woman's Life*. 'I shall be a while. I'm reading a fascinating article about the correct way to lay the dinner table.' She dropped the periodical on the table. 'I think I'd rather read about the war.'

No matter where they turned, there was no respite.

The flow of injured from Turkey had continued its devastating pace and by September Harefield had more than five hundred patients—ten times more than the army had anticipated. So many troops were being injured that they were bypassing field hospitals and arriving in England directly from the front, disembarking at Plymouth and then travelling by train and ambulance to Harefield. Their swift evacuations meant no time for any remedial treatment of their injuries near the battlefields so the conditions of the soldiers grew more severe and horrifying as the weeks went on. Fractures, lung infections, gangrene, shrapnel and gunshot wounds, diarrhoea and trench foot: every man who arrived had at least one, and more likely a combination. Their treatment was painful, ongoing and sometimes futile, which meant amputations and a steady flow of departing ambulances filled with broken boys bound for the six-week journey home.

The original group of nurses had been joined by fifty-one others who hailed from all over Australia, but each time Cora became used to a name and a face they seemed to disappear to field hospitals closer to the front or to other hospitals in England where their skills were needed too.

'Sister Barker. Sister North.'

Cora straightened her back in reflex at being addressed so formally and looked up.

'Captain Kent,' she said. His uniform was crisp, his hair neat and trim as if he'd just had a haircut. He held himself upright, his chin forward, as if he were standing at attention at a parade.

'Good afternoon, Captain.' Gertie nodded.

'That looks comforting.' He looked at their cups. 'Nothing better at the end of a long shift, I expect.'

Gertie snorted. 'A gin might do better, but beggars can't be choosers.'

William smiled briefly and his attention turned to Cora.

He notices you in a way he doesn't notice anyone else. Gertie's words had been in her head constantly for months.

'Sister Barker.' He paused. 'I was wondering how Gower is faring?'

The private had come in the week before. He'd been shot in the feet at Suvla Bay and had lost three toes on one foot and half the other. He'd been evacuated as quickly as possible, but by the time he'd arrived in England, he'd developed severe sepsis. He'd arrived at Harefield delirious with fever and in agony, his feet swollen as if he was wearing red balloons for shoes.

'No change, I'm afraid.' Cora looked at Gertie for reassurance. There were so many men now, she would be mortified if she inadvertently passed on incorrect information about a patient.

Gertie nodded her agreement. 'I'm sorry to say. While I would always defer to a medical opinion, it seems by my reckoning that he might lose both feet. If we could save just one, at least he might be able to walk, to negotiate crutches and a prosthetic leg.'

William lowered his chin, his expression transforming from serious to sombre. 'I have no reason to doubt your assumption, Sister North. He's lucky, in one sense, to have been sent here to Harefield. The artificial limb workshop is getting up to speed and doing such marvellous work. We'll just have to save that foot. Well, that's enough shop talk.' William lowered his eyes and with the slightest of nods, said, 'I hope you both have a pleasant evening.'

When he was out of earshot, Gertie raised her eyebrows at Cora.

'Don't,' Cora got in quickly.

'Are you not tempted?'

'Tempted to do what?'

Gertie smiled at her friend. 'You can speak the truth to me, you know. I don't know about you, but I've learnt a thing or two from the boys. Pain seems to liberate them from all the expectations around what they're supposed to do and what they're supposed to say and how they are supposed to behave. A man is never more honest than when he's in agony and crying for his mother.'

Those cries had come to haunt Cora's dreams.

'The rules that once applied to us are being shattered each and every day, don't you think?'

'Sisters.'

Harefield's benefactress Mrs Billyard-Leake suddenly appeared and Cora and Gertie shot to their feet. Cora had to stop herself from curtseying. Mrs Billyard-Leake was a handsome woman, elegant in her bearing and tall. Her hazel eyes were direct and open and her upswept light brown hair gleamed with good health. She wore a long navy frock with a long white apron over it, distinguished looking even in plain clothes.

'Pleased to see you again, Mrs Billyard-Leake,' Cora said with a nod.

'And you. Please resume your seats, sisters. How are you enjoying the new canteen?'

'Your volunteers make the best cocoa in the hospital,' Cora replied. 'Not that I would ever admit that to the Australian staff in the mess.'

Mrs Billyard-Leake laughed. 'I well understand your patriotism.'

Gertie waved her hand from left to right, taking in the sweep of the canteen. 'What you and your volunteers have done here, for the men? It's truly wonderful, Mrs Billyard-Leake. It's all they can talk about.'

'We had always hoped it would become a place for the men to relax and recover and, perhaps, if they close their eyes and imagine, they might see Mount Gambier or Warrnambool or Bathurst outside the windows and not the English countryside. The canteen committee is only too aware that not all of the men are able to travel into the village or even London for their diversions. We hope this gives them a taste of normal life and activities. To help them forget, for just a little while at least.'

'A very admirable aim, Mrs Billyard-Leake,' Cora said. 'And I know how much the men appreciate it.'

'May I introduce you to my volunteers?' Mrs Billyard-Leake stepped back and held out a hand as if presenting young ladies at a debutante ball. 'This is my daughter, Lulla. Mrs Steddall and her daughters, Miss Steddall and Miss Alice Steddall. Mrs Breakspears from the village, the Miss Tarletons and Miss Harland.'

The women exchanged greetings before the group of volunteers departed for the kitchen.

'What a remarkable woman,' Cora said.

'You're remarkable too, Cora Barker, and don't you ever forget it.'

Chapter Twenty

12 October 1915

Cora was relieved she wasn't the only one sobbing but, honestly, she wouldn't have cared if she was.

Outside, the October night-time winds whipped around the nurses' hut causing it to shriek and shift on its foundations. Inside, she and Gertie and Flora and Leonora each sat on their own beds, sobbing into their handkerchiefs, their shirt sleeves. Whatever was at hand.

Beside Cora that day's edition of *The Globe* lay crumpled and half-folded in the tangle of her blankets. Someone had left it on a table in the mess and she'd scooped it up after dinner, hoping she might be able to remain awake long enough to skim the pages. She had tried to read Conan Doyle's *The Hound of the Baskervilles*, which William had given her, but her mind was scattered. At the end of each day, her thoughts flew and crashed in a thousand directions. She found herself far too distracted to read the novel she'd been attempting to finish for the past month. She hadn't been able to stop thinking about patients and their wounds and their state of mind, of admissions and discharges, of nonsensical instructions from doctors and churlish spats between nurses and porters, who were being pushed beyond the limits of their endurance by the workload. A newspaper suited her; she was able to take in the meaning of a few paragraphs before attempting to sleep.

But tonight, only the stars would rest.

When Cora had turned over the front page, skimming over the listings for opera at the Shaftesbury Theatre and plays at the Aldwych and the Queen's Theatre and the Savoy that she was certain she would never have time to attend, her gaze drifted to page three and the headline: CRIME WHICH HAS STOPPED THE NATION. MISS EDITH CAVELL EXECUTED IN COLD BLOOD.

Cora's own blood ran cold.

She had gasped and clapped a hand over her mouth. And when she had cried out, 'Oh, dear God. No, no,' her friends had startled and roused.

'What is it?' Gertie had asked sleepily.

And when Cora had begun to read the article aloud, the other nurses in the hut began to weep quietly too. They had been following Cavell's case—as had the whole of England—and the news of her murder, for that's what it was, felt like a turning point, a juncture from which Cora knew she would never recover. She had, of course, seen the injuries the German weapons and tactics had inflicted on her patients. She was not naive about the damage war wrought. But men across a battlefield, all wearing khaki, were anonymous, uniformed foreigners.

A nurse, one who administered care, was someone altogether different.

The Germans had captured Cavell, kept her in solitary confinement and court-martialled her.

'It's brutish,' Fiona sobbed from across the room. 'Inhumane.'

'Wasn't there to be some kind of diplomatic intervention?' Leonora tugged a blanket around her shoulders. 'The Americans or some such? She was helping British soldiers, caring for them. She was doing her job as a nurse.' Leonora's voice faded away.

Cora blinked away the double vision caused by her tears. In the dim light, she lifted the newspaper.

The Earl of Desart in the House of Lords said, 'Miss Cavell was tried in cold blood. She was convicted in cold blood. She was executed in cold blood.'

The men of the German firing squad had aimed their rifles at her, looked her right in the eye and murdered her. A British nurse. A woman.

Gertie's voice was brittle. 'She was helping British soldiers escape to Holland. That's why she was arrested. She must have known the risks but went ahead anyway. How many men were saved by her sacrifice?'

Cora continued reading.

She may by her conduct have rendered herself liable to punishment—perhaps severe punishment—for acts committed in violation of the kind of law which prevails during war. But she might at any rate have expected that measure of mercy which in no civilised country would have

*been refused to one who was not only a woman, but a brave
and devoted woman, and one who had given all her efforts
and energies to the mitigation of the suffering of others.*

Nausea roiled in Cora's stomach and she pressed her hand
there to settle it. The newspaper drifted to the floor.
Tomorrow, she would twist it into wands for the fire. If only
it would be so easy to destroy the truth on its inky pages.

Her war and her world had suddenly spun on its axis.
Such a callous and brutal act. On someone just like her.
Had Edith seen death so often, and so brutally, that she was
no longer afraid of it? Is that what would become of Cora,
too?

Chapter Twenty-One

25 October 1915

Death lurked everywhere.

On the day that news of the loss of two more boys from Harefield swept through the village like clouds of dust from the brickworks, word also came through that cricketer Dr WG Grace had died two days before.

Harry had been at school with the soldiers, Colin Quinn and Harold Arkwright, and had played with them in the schoolyard. But he wasn't crying for them. He was crying over the passing of his favourite English cricketer. At the kitchen table, Harry sat with his head in his hands, inconsolable.

Jessie and Win exchanged concerned glances.

'There, there, love,' Win tutted.

'He was the best of the best,' Harry managed. 'He held the record for the highest score in an innings for nineteen years. Three hundred and forty-four. In 1876 for the MCC against Kent.'

Jessie daren't say a word. Her knowledge of cricket was limited at best and she feared upsetting her brother further in his present state with an insensitive question. She knew how it grieved him that he wasn't physically able to play the game he loved so much. Jessie looked over Harry's shoulder at the headline. 'A cerebral haemorrhage. I'm not sure I know what that is.'

If Harry knew, he didn't answer.

'Who knows if we'll ever see cricket played again. Not until the war's over, at least, and who knows when that will be?'

Jessie's heart broke for him. Harry didn't have much in his life. He lived with his widowed mother and his spinster sister. He had no sweetheart and had rebuffed Jessie's entreaties about Dottie so vehemently that she hadn't mentioned them again.

All he had was his cricket. Autumn and winter were always long without the game he loved, but he spent those short days and long, dark nights poring over his Wisden's Almanacks, memorising statistics and team lists and bowling figures. He was never so happy than when the first game of the season for the Harefield Cricket Club was approaching.

'I'll make a cuppa,' Win announced and took the kettle from the stove to the sink to fill it.

Jessie didn't feel like tea. She understood without him having to say it that Harry was embarrassed by his tears and that the last thing he wanted was his sister and mother fussing over him.

She suddenly found the excuse she needed to give him his privacy. There was so little of it in their house.

'Mum. Why don't I walk up to the hospital and deliver those socks we've knitted?' On the dresser sat a brown paper package tied with string. Inside it were the twenty pairs of socks Win and Jessie had knitted in the evenings while Harry had read interesting snippets about the war from that day's paper.

At the sink, Win looked over her shoulder and smiled. 'You might not even need an umbrella with that weather today.'

Jessie swept up the package in her arms and paused a moment. 'I'm ever so sorry about Doctor Grace, Harry. He sounds like a sportsman beyond compare.'

Harry lifted his head and met her gaze. There was such loss in his expression that it gripped Jessie's heart.

'He truly was.'

'I expect there'll be more to read about in the newspapers in the coming days. For his funeral and such.'

'And the next edition of Wisden, too, when that's published. We've lost Grace and Victor Trumper this year already. There'll be a big tribute in the next edition. There'll have to be.'

'Who's Victor Trumper?' Jessie asked. He looked up, eyes wide and wet and stared at her a moment as if she was a simpleton.

'The Australian batsman, of course.'

'Of course.'

'Trumper. Now Grace. Cricket will never be the same,' Harry said quietly, his voice hoarse from tears. His world had changed forever. The game he so loved had been halted for the war in September the year before and no one could really say when it would resume. WG Grace himself had said that in wartime it wasn't fitting that able-bodied men should be playing cricket and that pleasure-seekers should be looking on. Cricketers had enlisted just as shepherds and clerks had, and were losing their lives on the same battlefields.

Harry scooped up the newspaper, tucked it under his weak arm and stood. He turned and left the kitchen and a moment later the front door closed behind him.

'Shall I put the kettle on before I go, Mum? Make you a cuppa?'

Win pulled out a chair and slumped at the table. 'Can't say I feel like much of one, either. Not after seeing him so upset.'

'He loves his cricket,' Jessie said.

'Like nothing else,' Win replied with a heavy sigh. 'That's the trouble, I expect.'

'Well, I'll be off then.' Jessie clutched the parcel to her chest.

'The fresh air will do you good. And pass on my regards to Matron Gray for me, will you?'

At the entrance to Harefield House, Jessie looked through the main doors into the black-and-white chequerboard-tiled foyer and hoped no one saw her jaw hit the floor.

The place was busier than the Harefield high street.

Doctors in white coats strode violently through the entrance hall, brushing past nurses in their flowing linen veils holding clipboards and juggling arms full of supplies. Young women drivers in khaki lingered by the tall doors and an orderly pushed a trolley piled high with fresh sheets through the lot of them as if it were a bowling ball and they were pins.

'Can I help you?'

Jessie searched the teeming crowd to find out who had made the offer of assistance. A short man with horn-rimmed spectacles clutching a clipboard looked across at her.

'I have some items for the patients. Socks. If you could direct me as to where I should deliver them, I'd be most grateful.'

He nodded curtly and lifted an arm, pointing to his right. 'The library.'

Before Jessie had a chance to thank him, he turned and scurried off. She found the wide wooden doorway leading into what was now, according to the handwritten sign tacked to the door, the 'Newspaper Room and Library'.

As she stepped over the threshold, she lifted her eyes to the ornate ceiling then followed the curves and shadows of the plasterwork to the elegant light fittings and the plush curtains. The room was almost certainly bigger than the Chesters' entire house. It had remained untouched when the park had been transformed back in May and Jessie was glad of it. It seemed a calm and quiet oasis.

'Jessie?' a light feminine voice trilled and Jessie turned and laughed in surprise.

'Enid? Why am I not surprised to see you in a library?'

Enid Howard smiled warmly at Jessie as she pushed her wire-rimmed spectacles back up her nose. At school in the village, Enid's glasses had always seemed slightly too large for her petite features and were constantly on the verge of slipping off and landing in the pages of whichever book she was reading that day.

'I heard the hospital was in need of some assistance and I was happy to oblige. I take great satisfaction from seeing men with their noses buried in books. There can be nothing better for a recuperating soul than to escape for a few hours within the pages.' Enid's gaze drifted off dreamily to the shelves, each packed with leather-bound volumes. 'Don't you think?'

'There are so many.' Jessie craned her neck to the ceiling. 'I don't know how anyone would possibly have the time to read them all.' The two women's joyful voices echoed in the vast room, bouncing between atlases, dictionaries, Shakespeare, Austen, Dickens and Defoe.

'I don't know if they did. They probably came with the house, just like the paintings, the furniture and the curtains. Imagine moving them all! Over there are the Australian newspapers. Sometimes the Casualty Lists are the only way the patients find out if someone they know has been killed.'

'How dreadful.' Jessie couldn't remember the last time she'd read a book. Harry was the reader in the family, whether it was reading aloud any items of interest from the newspaper or from his cricket almanac or sporting magazines. Every spare minute in her daylight hours had always been consumed with work and, when the sun set, the light from the oil lamp on the kitchen table was hardly conducive to reading. And anyway, by that time of day her eyes stung from concentrating on stitches and threading needles and all she wanted to do was shut them and press a camomile compress to her closed lids. She had never been a bookworm.

'The men love their books.' Enid pondered her statement for a moment. 'Well, most of them. This one's exceedingly popular.' From the top of the pile in her arm, she lifted a volume and passed it to Jessie, who turned it sideways to read the spine. 'They always request this one. I'd never heard of CJ Dennis and his *The Sentimental Bloke* before I started volunteering here. There's a waiting list on account of us only having one copy. It was donated by one of the Australian officers whose wife sent it over in the post all the way from Australia.' She paused. 'Forgive me for prattling on. Don't get me started on books. I'll never stop.'

'Don't apologise, Enid. I'm sure the men are grateful for your efforts.'

Enid lowered her voice. 'I'm glad I can help them. What do you have there?' She balanced the pile of novels in her arms and nodded to Jessie's brown paper–wrapped package.

'My mother and I have been knitting. With winter coming, we thought they might be useful. Being Australian, they might not be used to how cold it gets here. I imagine many of them have never seen snow.'

'They have deserts in Australia, just like the Sahara,' Enid replied, and Jessie believed her.

'Miss Chester?'

Jessie recognised Matron Gray's voice and fought the urge to curtsey when the matron approached, her boots clip-clopping efficiently as she crossed the room.

'Matron. I hope you're well. My mother sends her best regards.'

'And please send mine to her. How are you?'

'Very well indeed.'

Matron Gray's eyebrows lifted as her gaze moved to the package in Jessie's arms.

Before she could ask, Jessie explained, 'Socks.'

The matron clapped her hands together. 'Wonderful. Thank you and thank you to Mrs Chester, too. We're getting supplies from all over Australia. It's heartening to know that people back home are thinking of the men. A huge delivery has arrived today from an Australian Red Cross Society. Goodness knows who will have the time to sort through it. I believe we have pyjamas, flannel shirts, dressing gowns and cigarettes. I can't imagine what the men will pounce on first.'

'The dressing gowns?' Jessie offered. 'The mornings are growing quite cool.' Her voice sounded soft and doubting to her ears, which embarrassed her. She felt suddenly small and useless surrounded by these capable women: all the sisters she'd met—and even Enid her librarian friend was playing an integral part in the running of a hospital. Before the war, it was something she would never have imagined, much less seen with her own eyes.

Matron Gray laughed. 'If only! It's the cigarettes. Tobacco isn't a luxury here, Miss Chester. It's a necessity. It's almost the first thing the men reach for of a morning and the last thing they want at night. It helps with their nerves, you see.'

Nerves? Why would the men be nervy?

'Miss Chester, I have an idea.'

Jessie held her breath. She had the sudden realisation that the matron's idea might involve her.

'Why don't you accompany Enid to the wards as she distributes her books? You could then deliver your socks in person. I expect such a gift, knitted right here in Harefield by local ladies, will be treasured. And I'm certain your presence will cheer them up as well.'

Jessie's throat felt thick and she swallowed.

'Do,' Enid said excitedly. 'These Australian boys will make you laugh. You just wait. Cheeky as monkeys, most of them.'

Jessie nodded. The matron thanked her and whirled off. Enid scurried towards the library door, turned and said, 'Come on then.'

Holding her package, now slightly damp from her sweating hands, Jessie dutifully scurried after her friend. Enid navigated the hospital grounds so adroitly she didn't have to once stop and ask for directions or read a sign pointing this way to the ward huts or that way to the stores or the laundry.

Jessie had never been in a working hospital before. The doctor came to them at home if anyone needed seeing to, and even then it cost money her mother didn't always have. She'd been born at home, as had Harry, seen to by a midwife from Uxbridge. She had imagined a hospital to be a quiet place but this was the exact opposite.

When they reached the conglomeration of wards, they stepped up onto a long wooden ramp with smaller walkways attached to it like ribs, each leading to its own wooden hut. Patients wearing pale blue pyjamas and a range of different coloured dressing gowns loitered together, smoking and chatting with good humour. Some sported bandages around their heads or covering one eye or the other. Others carried their arms in slings or limped on crutches. Other soldiers looked smart and neatly pressed in their uniforms and Jessie wondered if they were ready to be discharged.

'Apologies.' A man bustled past Jessie, almost knocking her off the ramp onto the grass below. He wore a khaki uniform with red lapel flashes, a flapping stethoscope around his neck and a grimace on his face. Before she had time to offer her apology for being in his way, he was out of earshot. When she turned back, a patient approached her, balancing awkwardly on wooden crutches that were jammed up into his armpits. When her eyes flickered down his body to try to figure out why he was using the devices, she saw that he only had one pyjama leg. She hastily swallowed her gasp.

When she blinked and lifted her eyes, she found him flicking a painful grimace in her direction.

'Good … good morning,' Jessie stammered and then averted her gaze, lest he think she was staring at him and curious about his misfortune. No one here needed her pity, she was sure of that.

'There are so many injured men,' Jessie said quietly to Enid, her voice trailing off until it disappeared in the sounds of men and conversation and footsteps on the wooden boards and trucks and ambulances coming and going. Jessie looked around her and felt very small indeed. Harefield had become a huge conveyor belt, on which troops and supplies moved in and out, around and about, and every day she had watched it through her front window. Trucks rumbled up and down the high street on the way to the hospital at all hours of the day and night. All the activity around her had become urgent and vital—and she had been watching it all happen through a window.

Enid moved in close. 'You'll get used to it.'

Jessie wondered how anyone could.

'And here we are.' Enid pushed open the door to the ward hut and Jessie followed her inside. Rows of beds on either side were pushed up against the wall, covered with gleaming white sheets stiff with starch. Some men were asleep, others stared at her with glazed eyes. Another, propped up in bed with pillows, lifted his eyes from the book he was reading and sat forward slightly.

'Why, hello there, Miss Howard. Aren't you a sight for sore eyes, you and your books.'

'You're one of my best customers, Private Cornwall.'

'And who's that with you?'

Jessie clutched her package to her chest. Its brown paper crinkled noisily.

'This is Miss Jessie Chester. She's a friend from the village.'

Private Cornwall set his book on his lap and opened his mouth to speak but he was interrupted by a booming voice from across the room.

'Bloody hell. Is that really you, Miss Chester?'

Jessie spun around. Something clenched inside her chest, squeezing her breath from her lungs. It was Private Bert Mott. She would know his laughing blue eyes anywhere. He was no longer using a wheelchair, she noticed, as he rose from a wicker chair by the side of his bed and limped over to her.

Before Jessie had thought through the protocol for responding to such an exclamation while in the presence of recuperating men—and slightly thrown by his choice of words—Bert's smile almost split his face.

'Well, this has made my day.'

She hadn't forgotten Bert and their conversation at the party back in July. Why was he still in the hospital? She tried not to feel guilty at the pleasurable thought that he hadn't gone back to the front.

'You're still here, Private Mott? How are you?' Heat prickled her face.

'I'll be right as rain before too long. Back fighting the Jerries, that'll be me.'

'That's good news,' Jessie said. 'Good news indeed.'

'You two know each other?' Enid asked.

Jessie swallowed nervously. 'We've met. Here, actually. At the afternoon tea and concert a few months ago.'

'Miss Chester has some handknitted socks in her package there. You might be her first taker.'

Jessie felt a gentle shove and she stepped forward. 'Would you like a new pair of socks, Private Mott?'

'Did you knit them?'

'Not just me. My mother and me. At night.'

'Then I'd be honoured.'

Bert beckoned Jessie to a small wooden table that sat between the rows of beds in the middle of the ward. She placed the package on it and quickly untied the brown string that held it together. The paper fell open and the two dozen pairs of socks, each one turned neatly into its partner so they resembled cocoons, tumbled out. They were dark grey and light grey and brown and even khaki.

'Which ones did you knit?' Side by side, they looked over the array of choices.

'Oh, you won't want any of mine. My mother is a much more proficient knitter than I am.'

'I want a pair of yours. You choose. And please, no khaki. I'm sick of the bloody sight of it, if you want the honest truth.' Bert laughed and the sound of it was joyous. How could he be so happy about socks?

She reached for a pair the colour of heavy winter clouds. 'These are mine. Promise me you won't look too closely.' She held them out and Bert reached for them. For a moment, they held each other's gaze, their fingers close but not touching. Neither seemed to want to be the one to let go first.

'I'll save them for best,' Bert said with a glint in his eye. 'Maybe there'll be another concert. Or some other occasion when I might see you here at Harefield.'

'I couldn't say.' Was she standing too close to the fire? Her cheeks flamed. Jessie scooped up as many pairs as she could handle and turned to continue distributing her handiwork, keenly aware of Bert's gaze on her back.

When her gifts had been deposited into the hands of their very grateful new owners, Jessie left the ward hut and made her way across the hospital grounds to the main building. Her quick steps suddenly felt too slow and she began to sprint. Her boots clomped on the wooden ramp and then thudded dully against the grass and dirt and gravel as she made her way to the main house. Her skirt flew around her calves and she jammed her hat firmly on her head as she ran.

With each step, images flickered. Men without legs. Men without arms. The blind. Those too ill and injured to move from their beds. The man who had burst into tears when she'd given him the simple gift of a pair of socks.

She had seen the posters imploring young women to join the war effort. Nurses, cooks, kitchen-maids, clerks, housemaids, ward-maids, laundresses, motor drivers and so on were urgently needed but she hadn't heeded the call until now.

The war had made other women courageous. She thought of the factory girls who strode confidently through Harefield and took proud delight in spending their own money, the pounds and shillings they'd earnt themselves, on things they wanted to buy. She thought of Dottie, doing her part to keep the post flowing back and forth to citizens and soldiers. And she thought of her own mother, who had kept her family fed and warm and clothed with her own labours. Jessie had been wondering lately whether life had something more in store for her and, in that moment, she knew the answer.

She was about to do something braver than anything she'd ever done. With a quick and breathless stop at the main doors to ask a passing porter for directions, Jessie ran to Matron Gray's office.

She knocked three times.

'Enter.'

Jessie swung open the heavy wooden door and the matron, pen in hand, looked up. 'Miss Chester. Is everything all right? You look flushed. Do you have a fever?' Matron Gray stood and rounded her desk and held out a wrist with the aim, Jessie surmised, of pressing it to her forehead.

'I'm perfectly well, Matron. I've run. I'm ... I'm a little out of breath. I should ... I should like to volunteer. Here at the hospital.'

Matron Gray stepped back, adjusted her sleeve at her wrist. 'You would?'

'I'm young and energetic. I have no attachments. You need help. I can see it. Please let me help the men. I can sew and knit. I'll do whatever needs to be done. So many are making sacrifices so we can win the war. I can, too.'

'You would be most welcome, Miss Chester. You impressed me that first day we met as a hard worker and as a polite and trustworthy young woman.'

'Thank you, Matron.'

'Take a seat, won't you, and we'll discuss how we might be able to make use of your talents.'

Jessie pulled up a chair and remained silent to catch her breath.

'You must be a popular young woman in the village.'

'Oh no, not really.'

'Surely you must know everyone? It's a quaint little place but it's a small place.'

'Not quite,' Jessie replied. 'And anyway, Harefield is full of strangers now.'

'They won't be strangers for long. And you'll never be a stranger here. I can't tell you how welcome you will be. We are nearly one thousand beds now. We have more than seventy nurses. We're so frantic they are struggling to pick up some of the more menial tasks. It'll be hard work.' Matron Gray raised her eyebrows, as if she was asking if Jessie was shy of it.

Jessie quickly moved to reassure her. 'I'm not afraid of that, Matron. Since my father died, it's been only me and my mother and my younger brother and he needs things done for him sometimes. That's been my job since he was little.'

'So, you are not totally ignorant of the male body, I take it?'

Jessie felt her cheeks heat and she didn't know how to respond.

Matron Gray laughed. 'I apologise if I've offended. It's just that I've had some other lasses offer themselves up but when I've mentioned that part of the job will be to give the men a blanket bath ... well, you would have thought

I'd suggested they walk down the Long Ramp in their petticoats. I don't need anyone who's squeamish. It's about the men's dignity, Miss Chester. A man who's scarred from shrapnel or who's lost a limb or an eye or … other parts of his most intimate self … does not need a nurse who baulks or, much worse, faints when she sees him. They do not need ridicule. They need understanding.'

Jessie lifted her chin. 'I understand completely what you mean. More than you can ever know.'

'You won't mind changing linen, cleaning floors, swilling out bedpans?'

'Not at all. It's not like I grew up with people doing things for me.' Not like some of the other young ladies of Harefield, she thought. Miss Arabella Pritchard had grown up with servants and a cook and people to wash her clothes and do her ironing and mending and a governess. It hadn't made her happy. Nor was her mother. But Jessie knew what it was like to be looked down upon for doing a hard day's work with your hands and she had tried not to be ashamed of it.

'We would be very pleased to have you whenever you can make yourself available, but I'm sympathetic to the fact that you have responsibilities at home, with your work and to your mother and brother.'

'I'll do whatever I can, Matron.'

'I'm very pleased to hear that.'

'All the Australians have come from so far away to defend England. I wanted to say thank you to them, and all the others to come.' Jessie shrugged. 'This is the only way I know how. I'm not a nurse or a cook or anything like that. And I'm certain the men don't need summer frocks or evening gowns.'

Matron Gray laughed. 'They won't but you never know, I might one day.'

She studied Jessie for a moment then pushed back her chair and stood. She reached a hand across the desk and Jessie leapt to her feet. They shook firmly and the matron said, 'Welcome to Harefield Park, Miss Chester. Or should I say, the Number One Australian Auxiliary Hospital, AIF.'

Harefield Hospital
Middlesex
England
October 18, 1915

Dear Mum, Dad, Eve and Grace,
All is well in Harefield. Thank you a million times for the recent supplies, for both me and the men. I thought I'd send a postcard so you can see for yourself what a haven this place really is. The four photographs—the house, the lake, and games of cricket and bowls—are true depictions, although the black and white images can't capture the stunning beauty of the gardens. It remained green right throughout the summer and now autumn has arrived in all its glory there is a show of colours so vivid I could stare at them all day. Alas, it is not me on the reverse playing cricket and bowls with the men. You're more likely to see me taking a turn around the beautiful lakes, home to swans and ducks and waterfowl. A swan had a clutch of cygnets over the summer and they follow their mother around delightfully. I'm running out of space. I assure you all is well.

   My sincerest love to all.
   Your Cora

Chapter Twenty-Two

21 November 1915

'Good afternoon, Jessie.'

'Hello, Dottie.' Dottie's silhouette was dark against the gloom and mizzle outside, but Jessie noticed immediately that she was wearing a brown coat and hat, not her usual blue workday coat.

'Where's your uniform?' A gust of cold air swept inside and Jessie shivered, pulling the sides of her woollen dressing gown tighter around her waist. Underneath, her thin cotton nightdress wasn't much protection from the cold.

Dottie narrowed her eyes and looked puzzled. 'It's Sunday, Jess. I don't work Sundays, you silly thing.' Dottie paused and propped her hands at her hips. 'You've been doing too much, Jessie Chester. Working all hours here with your mum and then every other spare bit of time out at the hospital. You're burning the candle, you are.'

'Oh no. It's Sunday.' Jessie slapped a hand to her cheek. 'I'm going to the hospital today. Did we make plans? I'm dreadfully sorry. I must have forgotten.'

Jessie's mind spun. How had she lost track of the days of the week as well as the hours? How had she forgotten she'd made arrangements with Dottie? What had they arranged? A walk along the canal? Surely not. It had rained all week and the entire village was a quagmire. Jessie decided right there and then that she did indeed need more sleep. She'd had barely a free minute since she'd begun volunteering at the hospital. And while she was tired more often than not now, how could she complain when so many were doing so much? At home, she had been keeping up with all her work and her chores. Win was knitting and making bandages in her spare hours. The nurses were run off their feet caring for the flow of men in and out of the hospital. Porters were constantly ferrying men to and from wards and ambulances and trucks. Doctors rushed from patient to patient. Laundresses constantly ferried sheets and towels to and from the laundry in huge wicker baskets on casters. And men were fighting and dying.

At the hospital, she had done everything that was asked of her. She had stoked fires. Washed dishes in the wards. Darned socks and jumpers and fixed buttons to shirts. Mopped floors of vomit and blood and lit the cigarettes of blind men and pretended to scratch limbs that no longer existed, limbs that had been blown off somewhere in Turkey.

The war had not only come to Harefield but Jessie herself was right in the thick of it. She had never felt sadder or more alive. That contradiction was a secret she had kept to herself.

'You haven't forgotten anything,' Dottie said, her gaze drifting to her brown lace-up shoes for a moment. When she looked up, her cheeks were blazing.

'What about a cup of tea? I think we have some cake …'

'Thank you, but no. I'm ... well, I'm here to fetch Harry, actually.'

'Harry?'

Dottie beamed and whispered, 'We're going to the tearoom for some scones.'

'You are?'

Dottie nodded so hard Jessie thought she might cause herself an injury. What had happened in the months since she'd had the conversation with Harry about Dottie's affections? Jessie remembered it clearly. Harry had angrily brushed her off, his feelings bruised, and not a word had been spoken between them about Dottie since. What had been going on between her brother and her best friend that she'd been too busy or obtuse to notice?

'When did all this happen, then?'

'On Tuesday last. You were at the butcher's, I believe, and when Harry opened the door to take the mail, I thought, blow it. A girl shouldn't have to wait forever to be asked to tea, should she? So I took matters into my own hands. Things have changed, haven't they? With the war and everything? Why should a girl have to wait around pining when she can jolly well pose the question herself?'

Jessie felt happiness bloom inside her. 'Harry. Dottie's here.' She reached for her friend's hands, clasped them in hers, and leant down to kiss her warmly on the cheek.

'I'm so happy,' she whispered.

'You and me both.'

'Afternoon, Dottie.' Harry's boots clomped unevenly, echoing his gait, and when Jessie searched Dottie's face, she knew Dottie could not have cared less. Harry looked as handsome as ever and Jessie's eyes filled with tears when she realised, with a pang, that he was wearing a tweed jacket and trousers that had belonged to their father.

'Hello, Harry.'

Jessie stepped back, allowing her best friend and her dear brother to greet each other with shy smiles.

'The weather's rotten out but I don't mind,' Dottie said cheerily, her fingers gripping the straps of her handbag. Harry donned his flat cap and his Adam's apple danced at his throat.

'Have a wonderful time, you two,' Jessie said as she stepped back. 'I have to get ready to go to the hospital.' She went into the kitchen but positioned herself by the doorway so she could hear their conversation. Could this really be happening?

'You look lovely in that suit, Harry.'

Harry cleared his throat. 'And that's a very nice coat you're wearing.'

'That's very kind of you to say. Shall we go?'

'I'll just get my walking stick. It's by the back door.'

'No need,' Dottie replied gently. 'I figure if I slip my arm in yours, you can steady yourself on me. If that's all right with you.'

After the front door closed, she waited a moment and then ran to the window, peering out to see them make their way down the street. They looked like any other courting couple and when tears welled in Jessie's eyes, she wiped them away with the sleeve of her dressing gown.

Since their father had died, Jessie had pessimistically thought ahead to their mother's passing, to the days when the only people living in this house would be her and Harry. From the time she had first realised as a child that Harry had limitations, she was aware that he would be her responsibility, that it would fall on her to care for her brother when both their parents had died. And she'd never minded that. He was family. It was her duty as a sister. She didn't need her mother to express her concerns about Harry's eventual fate either—Jessie had always made it clear to her that should she marry, Harry would be part and parcel of her hand in marriage.

She had told her mother more than once, when worry and fear had overcome her, 'Don't worry, Mum. He'll always have me.'

And Win's response had always been variations of the same. 'What if the young man you marry doesn't want him? What if they see him as a burden, what with him not being able to work like other men?'

What if he didn't need her in the way everyone had anticipated? What would become of her then? The idea of any young man wanting to marry her had become more philosophical than practical these days. She'd never had a sweetheart, even before the war when there were men aplenty. That was the consequence of a small life, she always reckoned, that she'd simply never had the opportunity to meet any young men other than those she'd gone to school with, or those who worked around the village. They were nice enough—decent, hardworking men—but none had turned her head and, evidently, she hadn't turned theirs.

The world she lived in was filled with women, children, old men and ghosts. And injured young men from a long way away.

She held on tight to what Lord Kitchener had said, that the war would be over by Christmas. And then, everything would go back to the way it was before, all the rest of England's young men would come home and she would surely find someone to love.

'Mudgeeraba.'

Jessie's nib was poised over the page like a hawk waiting for its prey. 'I beg your pardon?'

'Mudgeeraba. I was born and bred there. Twenty-three Foster Street. Make sure you write that at the top of the page there so the letter reaches my mum and dad. And my nan. She lives with them, you see. In the room out the back, ever since my pop passed. She'll be just as keen to know what I'm up to in old Blighty as they are. She was at the station waving me off when I left. I swear she burst out singing "God Save the King" right there on the platform.'

Jessie sat at the bedside of Private Walter King, a young man with the whitest hair she'd ever seen who hailed from a village in Australia with a name that was unpronounceable.

'Mudgey Robber?' Jessie shot the digger an innocent smile. She liked to make them laugh. Along with making them comfortable, it was the highlight of her time at the hospital. She loved writing letters for the patients. Not only was it an insight into a place half a world away, but she found she could make them smile at a memory or even laugh and think of home and those who were waiting for them to return. With her innocent prodding, they recalled streets where kangaroos surely hopped and trees in backyards that were full of koalas, as abundant as blackbirds were in the skies above Harefield.

'You bloody Poms.' The boy soldier with bandages wrapped around his eyes, in a wad as thick as a piece of bread from a freshly baked loaf, smiled, finally.

'A Pom?' Jessie asked.

'You're a Pom on account of you being, you know, English.'

'Well, there you go,' she replied. 'I'm learning something new every day.'

'Oh, I don't mean nothing by it, honest. Back home, it's what we call the new Jimmy Grants. The immigrants. You know, you spend a couple of hours in the sun and go red as a pomegranate. The fruit?'

'Oh, the fruit.' Jessie shook her head, trying to follow the convoluted logic of Private King's explanation.

'I travelled a bit before the war, up and down the east coast. The last job I had before I signed up was a wharfie on the docks in Melbourne. Funny thing is, that's where I left for the war. From those same docks in Port Melbourne. Anyhow, the blokes I worked with? The coal lumpers and the wharfies? They had a million nicknames for people. I suppose I picked it up from there. I don't mean nothing by it.'

'It sounds like you've travelled a lot. You've definitely been to more countries than me.' How could she be envious of a young man blinded by the war? Jessie blinked away the thought. 'Now, let's write this letter. I have Twenty-three Foster Street at the top left corner of the page but you'll have to help me, Private. I'm a little stuck as to how to spell Mudgey Robber.'

'It … it starts with an …' Walter's smile faded as his chin dropped. 'I'm not sure. Never was that good at the reading and writing.' He was suddenly shy. Jessie wished she could see his eyes, if only to reassure herself that there wasn't shame in them. Any man who had signed up to serve his country should never feel shame. He should feel the pride of a nation, not approbation because he'd never learnt to spell.

'Oh, that's no trouble at all, Walter.'

'And the docs reckon I'm a bit of a head case, as well, to top it all off.'

Jessie didn't know what he meant. This man seemed to be speaking another language. 'Don't worry. I happen to have something here that might help.'

Her makeshift desk was a leather-bound atlas that balanced on her knees, a volume Enid had sourced for her from the Harefield library. Jessie had loved geography as a child. She'd studied the source of the Nile and the pyramids of Egypt. She'd pored over stories of Cleopatra and Julius Caesar and all the kings and queens of England, which she could recite in historical order from the Saxon Egbert to King George V, although she sometimes muddled up the Plantagenets. But she didn't know much about Australia. Except for kangaroos.

Jessie had always started with London, in yellow and part of the United Kingdom of Great Britain and Ireland and she found it again, sitting by Private King's side. She traced her finger from town to town, along the lines of rivers and tributaries, and then to the coastline along the English Channel and up towards the North Sea. Across the Channel, the French Republic was fuchsia pink, Belgium lavender purple and the Netherlands apple green.

There was fighting in almost every single name on the map. Next to it, the German Empire was coloured red, which Jessie thought appropriate for all the blood that had been shed. Right in the middle, Switzerland, and below the Kingdom of Italy. She chided herself for not knowing the name of the king of Italy, or Spain or Portugal. Or, for that matter, Serbia. She hadn't realised Austria-Hungary was quite so big and wondered how many people lived there. She hadn't heard of Croatia or Bosnia-Herzegovina or Romania or Bulgaria until the war and now the Empire was fighting those countries and their people. Over what?

And then, she traced right—or east—to the Ottoman Empire. She knew that's where Gallipoli was. That was another name she hadn't heard until the war.

Jessie turned the pages on the war until she'd found Australia and her mood lightened.

'Here's Australia. My, it's a big place.'

'Up the top, on the eastern coast, that's Queensland. And that's where Mudgeeraba is,' Walter said.

'I know how to spell it, Sister.' The patient in the next bed along called out the letters and Jessie wrote them down with great concentration.

'Why, thank you.' She looked over her shoulder. 'How do you know how to spell it?'

'I'm from Brisbane.'

'Are you just?' Walter asked. 'What's your name, digger?'

'Ern Smith, 12th Battalion.'

'Walter King, 45th. Everyone calls me Wally.'

'Pleased to meet you, Wally,' Ern croaked.

'You too, Ern.'

Jessie closed her eyes and took a deep breath to steady herself. She couldn't look at Private King for too long without wanting to run into the store cupboard and sob. He had remained prostrate in his bed without so much as even a pillow since he'd arrived. A blanket was tucked up under his arms, and in the space on either side of his torso, where elbows and hands and fingers should be, there were two odd stumps of different lengths. He'd lost one arm below the elbow—likely hacked off at a field clearing station to staunch the blood pouring from his wound, a nurse had told her—and the other arm was gone just past his shoulder. Yesterday, she'd shaved him with a strop razor and a kidney pan of lukewarm water, more for the comfort of a woman's touch and the splash of warm water on his skin. He was so young he barely had a beard.

'So, we've successfully spelt …'

'Mudgeeraba,' Ern and Wally said in unison.

'Now, Private. Tell me what you'd like to write home.'

Wally swallowed and Jessie observed the angular Adam's apple at his throat bob up and down, up and down.

'Home,' his voice cracked. 'Oh, boy. Here we go. Dear Mum, Dad and Nan. Thank you for your letters. They really do buck up a bloke when he's lying in a hospital bed. It's beaut to read all the news about Dad and the chooks. They sound like they're laying up a storm.'

Jessie wrote in a fluid hand, her nib scratching against the thin paper, a sound like chicken's feet scratching in the dirt in her own yard.

'I wish I had some of those eggs all the way over here for breakfast. I miss those bright yellow yolks and Nan's sponges.' At the long silence, Jessie lifted her eyes from the page.

'That's no insult to the food here, you understand, Miss Chester.'

'No offence taken.' Jessie dipped her nib in the inkwell resting on the atlas.

'Things here at Harefield hospital are good. It feels like a holiday, to be honest, to be out of the mud of the trenches and here in old Blighty where the care is A1 and everyone is doing their best to look after us boys. I've got a warm bed and a soft pillow and that's better than a lot of blokes have. There's plenty to do. There's a shooting gallery and a billiard room as well as a regular cinematograph show for our entertainment. Some of the fellows are learning woodwork and even sewing from the lovely ladies of the village. We've been promised motor rides to London, too. Can you believe that?'

Wally gasped and his mouth contorted in a sob that came from somewhere so deep within him Jessie barely recognised it as a man's voice. She quickly set the atlas on the floor.

'Oh, Wally' Jessie reached for his shoulder. With her other, she slipped a handkerchief from her pocket and pressed it to his mouth to wipe away the saliva drizzling from his lips. The poor, poor boy. He would never shoot and play billiards or see a picture or be able to hold a hammer or a needle. How was she to provide comfort to someone so forever broken?

'You'll be right, Wally,' Ern said from the next cot. 'You'll be right.'

He sobbed his final sentence and Jessie scrambled for her atlas and the letter and her nib.

'I hope you're all well,' he cried. 'There's not much else to say except that I'm tickety-boo and hope to see you all soon. I'll write again as soon as I can.'

And as Jessie finished scratching his last words onto the page, a small offering from a son to a mother and father and grandmother so far away, Wally suddenly screamed as if the bomb that had shattered his eyesight had detonated right there under his bed.

Jessie dropped the inkwell. Ink splattered over her uniform like black droplets of blood. The atlas landed with a thud on her boot and the letter skittered off under the cot. Then there were quick footsteps, boots on the wooden floor and running steps that shook the whole hut.

'What's happened?'

A nurse was at her side, quickly pressing a wrist to Wally's forehead.

'I don't know. I was writing a letter for him and—' Jessie made room for the tending, and then stepped back again until the backs of her knees hit the cot next door. She jerked her head around to apologise but the bed was empty.

She hoped and prayed that the boy soldier who had been in it hadn't died.

As soon as she could without making a scene, Jessie walked out the front door of the ward. She moved quickly sideways so she couldn't be seen and pressed herself against the wall between the door and front window.

Every part of her was shaking and she looked down at her hands, willing them to stop. Her vision blurred with tears. That poor boy. That poor, wretched boy. Would it be better that he were dead? How was such a boy ever to recover enough to go back to his life?

'Miss Chester?' A hand was on her forearm. 'Is everything all right?'

It was Bert. She couldn't cry. She couldn't. Not in the presence of a man who'd been shot and survived, who had made the long journey to England and who was no doubt returning soon to face gunfire once again.

'You look like you've seen a ghost. Come with me.' Bert took Jessie's arm and led her down the steps towards the rose garden.

As they walked, Jessie's head pounded with every step. Or was that every heartbeat? She'd gone home more than once the past few weeks with a headache and had gone straight to bed with a wet flannel on her forehead.

'You're doing too much,' Win had fussed. 'I can't spare you here, Jess. I wish I could, for those boys deserve it. But you need to rest.'

Perhaps her mother was right. Perhaps she wasn't strong enough to cope.

'You've seen some things,' Bert said quietly. 'Some pretty terrible things.'

Jessie nodded. She scrambled for a handkerchief in the pocket of her dress and blew her nose.

'It's a lot to take in. You shouldn't feel embarrassed about having a little cry, Miss Chester. Honest.'

'What I've seen is nothing compared with what you boys have to put up with. I should be stronger. I wish I could be like the nurses. I don't know how they do it, I honestly don't.'

Bert looked ahead to the bare branches of the towering tree and the main house beyond.

'It doesn't get any easier. Not even for us blokes. Not that they'll ever tell you that, the ones lying in bed in the wards. We have to put on a brave face for the nurses and the ones like you, who don't get paid to come in and do for us but still come in anyway. You're all angels, you know that?'

Jessie breathed deep. Her tears had stopped. She managed a weak smile at Bert.

'How's that leg?'

'Getting there.'

'Are you scared of going back, Bert?'

He met her eyes. A dark shadow crossed his face. 'It's what I signed up for, Miss Chester.'

'You're all so very brave. Do you know that?'

Bert chuckled. 'If there were blooms on those empty rose bushes over there, I'd pick you one. To say thanks.'

'It's nothing, really. Sometimes I don't know if what I'm doing makes any difference at all.'

He reached for her hand, lifted it to his lips and kissed the back of it. 'More than you can ever know.'

The next day, Jessie stepped quietly along the duckboards to Bert's ward and gently pushed the door open.

The flames from the stove flickered soft light across the ward and she searched the beds for Bert's familiar form. She wanted to say goodnight before going home.

As she approached his bedside, he smiled at her. 'Hello, Miss Chester.'

'Good evening, digger. You're already in bed?'

Bert shook his head ruefully. 'There's a new rule. We have to be indoors by six and in bed by eight-thirty. They're treating us like schoolboys, if you ask me. Someone's even come up with a rhyme about it. *The head of the staff is the colonel, whose ideas are strictly nocturnal. He suddenly said, Eight-thirty to bed. One would think that his cares were paternal.*'

Jessie narrowed her eyes. 'He's trying to keep you away from the Cricketers, isn't he?'

'Me? At the pub? Never.' Bert winked. 'You on your way home, then?'

Jessie nodded. 'I wanted to say goodnight before I left.'

'That's very nice of you. I'm glad you stopped by.'

'Your leg. Does it still ache? I don't want you to overdo it.'

Bert chuckled. 'Look at you. Fussing, fussing, fussing.'

Jessie felt her cheeks heat. 'It's my job to fuss, Bert Mott.'

'My mother used to fuss over me like you're doing. She would be doing exactly the same if I was home, I bet. And my dad would be telling her to leave it.' He laughed at the thought.

'I bet they're missing you this Christmas.'

His face fell. 'And I'm missing them, that's for sure.'

'What would you be doing for Christmas if you were home?'

A shadow passed over Bert's face for just a moment. He smiled too quickly and Jessie knew he hadn't wanted her to see that he was homesick.

'Mum would have made her Christmas pudding weeks ago and my brothers and me would have got in trouble more times than you can count for holding up the bowl and sniffing it through the muslin. Bloody hell, there's no pud like my mum's. We would have taken bets on which chook dad would put on the chopping block for Christmas lunch. I'd have put in a full day at work on Christmas Eve, with everyone coming into town to get their fruit and veg. I might have gone down to the river for a swim, if the weather was good. There's a long rope that hangs over the water. Someone, I don't know who, hoiked it up over one of the branches of a huge river red gum years ago, and we swing out on it and toss ourselves into the water with a giant splat.'

Bert chuckled at the memory, his focus across the room, as if he was conjuring the water in his mind's eye.

'Tommy—he's my youngest brother—I swear, he swings out so far sometimes we reckon he's going to land on the other side of the river.'

'What's Tommy's up to?'

Bert beamed. 'He's an apprentice bootmaker at Rossiter's up in Adelaide. The big smoke. You know what's funny? Rossiter's makes boots for the army. He might have made the very boots I was wearing when I was hit.' Bert's attention drifted. 'One of Tommy's boots, made in Adelaide, worn by his brother, was left in a trench in France and was buried there in the mud. A little bit of South Australia there in the trenches.' He met her gaze and her heart stopped at how vulnerable he looked in that moment. He wasn't a digger or a soldier in uniform. He was a son and a brother, a boy who swam in the river, a boy who missed his mother's Christmas pudding. A man in blue pyjamas tucked up in bed, waiting to recover enough to go back to the mud.

'And the cherries. Christmas doesn't feel like Christmas without them. You've never tasted a cherry like ones from Norton Summit, Jess. As big as apples. Every lady in Murray Bridge wants a bowl of cherries for her Christmas table and that meant a grocer like me was run off his feet in the lead-up.'

Christmas in a place called Murray Bridge. Cherries as big as apples. Swimming in the river on a hot day. Australia sounded like a magical place.

'My Nanna and Pa—Mum's mum and dad— would be on their way from their farm to spend Christmas with us. We usually have a right old slap-up.'

They sat in silence for a while but Jessie didn't feel the need to fill it. 'It sounds lovely,' she said finally.

'Bloody oath it is,' he murmured. 'Since I can't be there, me and a couple of the other lads have hatched a plan. So many blokes are a little lonely this time of year. Especially the cot cases. We're going be like Father Christmas, going from ward to ward handing out cigarettes, have a smoke with the blokes and a natter. It's a bit rough when you can't even get up to go to the mess for your tucker.'

'What a lovely idea. How kind of you.'

Bert studied her face. 'You look dead on your feet. Go home. How can I drift off into the land of nod if you're here distracting me?'

Jessie struggled to her feet, her bones weary and creaking inside her. 'Goodnight, Private.'

He lay back on his pillow, his hands behind his head. 'Night, night.'

On her way home, as her feet crunched on the frost underfoot on the streets of Harefield, Jessie tried to distract herself with thoughts of cherries as big as apples and swimming in a river in the warm sunshine and Bert's smile.

But in her mind's eye, all she could see was a solitary army boot half buried in the mud on a Flanders field so far away.

Chapter Twenty-Three

5 December 1915

In the weeks leading up to the second Christmas of the war, the nurses of Harefield hospital had come up with as many activities as they could invent for their patients so their wards felt a little more like home and a little less like a corrugated-iron hut in a field in Middlesex.

The war that everyone said was going to be over by Christmas had only become more intractable. A week before, Matron Gray had told her nurses that the flow of injured from Gallipoli would cease. The Allies had begun an orderly evacuation of the Gallipoli Peninsula.

'The Turks have held on,' she'd announced. 'It's defeat. Eight months. A quarter of a million dead and who can even guess about the number of injured. We've certainly seen our share of them here in Harefield. And all for nothing, not one mile of territory.'

'That can't be true.' Leonora had looked to the matron for confirmation. 'I can't imagine that many men gone … it's unfathomable.'

Matron Gray was grim. 'You've seen the casualties through here. Imagine all those we haven't seen.'

When word about the Gallipoli retreat spread among the patients, many of whom had fought on that wretched stretch of beach and up those towering cliffs, there were difficult silences and then long walks in the bitter cold around the grounds of Harefield Park. For days afterwards, groups of men had huddled together in whispered conversations that came to an immediate halt if a nurse walked by within earshot. Did the men believe the nurses were too delicate in constitution to hear the truth? Was it a generous attempt on the men's behalf to spare their feelings, to protect them from the truth of what they'd seen and what they'd done?

It had been a long and dark year for so many, Cora knew. In January, before she'd even arrived in Harefield, German Zeppelins had bombed England. The Turks' attempts to invade Russia had been thwarted so they had moved into Armenia instead. In February, the battles on the Western Front had killed 240,000 French soldiers, and in April, at the second battle of Ypres, poison gas had been used for the first time and 58,000 Allied troops had lost their lives. Then Gallipoli, then the battles on the Eastern Front and Mesopotamia and Serbia. So many dead. So many grieving mothers and fathers and sisters and brothers and grandparents and friends. How did they bear it? Where once she had imagined the countryside of France to be full of rolling hills and grapevines, all Cora imagined now was mud and rubble and graves. The pace of the bad news was unrelenting, the death toll already so large as to be overwhelming.

There was so much to forget and regret but surely Christmas was a time to come together and celebrate the lives that remained. The nurses' task had been to convince the men, through encouragement, cajoling and downright browbeating, to take part in creating decorations for the ward. Anything to have them look forward with hope rather than backwards with regret. There was also something fundamentally important about making Christmas—this holiest of days to some of the boys, who prayed each night and begged God to make them well—a special day. She knew that there were all kinds in the ward—Church of England, Methodist, Roman Catholic—and all seemed to have put aside any ecclesiastical differences to pitch in together to decorate the ward.

One of the boys, Sapper Charlie Parks, a stocky young thing who'd been a clerk in an office in Perth, had told Cora while they sat together making paper chains out of old newspapers that he didn't mind helping out but he'd been an agnostic way before he'd landed at Gallipoli.

'And I've got to tell you, Sister, that after what I saw, I consider myself a full-blown atheist.'

'You can't mean that.' Fiona's scissors stopped mid-cut and the two ends of her broadsheet drooped over the blades.

'Sorry, Sister, but if there really was a God, where was he when we needed him?'

Cora had never met an atheist before, and she'd never met a Jew, either. Young Alexander Stern from Melbourne was a slight man of twenty-four who'd been shot through the foot during the landing at the Dardanelles. She hadn't known he was Jewish until he'd told her himself one afternoon during craft activities on the ward. The nurses had set out a long trestle table in the aisle between the rows of beds and the men sat facing each other. Fiona had rolled out a long sheet of butcher's paper and alongside it had set brushes, red paint, a pot of glue she'd mixed from cornflour and water, and a bowl filled with bolls of cotton.

'Now, gentlemen,' Fiona announced. 'I know you can all handle a gun, but can you demonstrate the same precise aim with a brush?'

The boys jostled for brushes, grumbling good-naturedly as they chose.

'See the words I've marked out at the top of the paper here ... "Merrie Christmas"? Your job is to fill it with cotton wool so it looks like the words are spelt out in clouds.'

Cora was hovering beside Fiona, ready to help if she was needed, when Alexander had beckoned her over with a sideways jerk of his head.

'What is it, Stern?' She leant down and he turned to speak quietly in her ear.

'This might be the right time to tell you that I'm Jewish, Nurse Barker.'

'You're Jewish?' Cora asked, louder than she had meant, and all around her the other boys fell silent. Her cheeks burnt and she straightened, not quite knowing what to do. Had all this talk of Christmas, for weeks and weeks, offended him? She exchanged a quick glance with Fiona, looking for guidance from her friend who was more acquainted with God than she was, but Fiona looked more shocked than Cora.

All eyes were on Stern. He lifted his chin. 'Yes, I am.'

'Come on, Stern,' called Pappas from the end of the table, taking a deep drag on his cigarette. 'We'll teach you about Jesus, won't we, boys?'

A chorus of laughter erupted.

'Don't look at me,' Adams joked. 'You think I ever paid attention in church? My nanna used to drag me by the ear every Sunday, praying that Father O'Reilly would find a way to put the fear of God in me but it never took.'

'Nor me,' called out Smith as he dipped his brush into a pot of red paint and began creating long strokes on the paper. He admired his work for a moment and looked up. 'I only ever went for the morning tea in the church hall after. And to kiss Mary Reynolds on the way home.' He winked at Cora and she smiled despite herself.

Near the end of the table, Bassett cleared his throat. 'If you're interested, Stern ...'

The boys, Cora and Fiona waited.

'Mazel tov, Bassett, but I'm not in the market for a new faith. Perfectly bloody happy with my own. Just like General Monash is, fellas.'

'Fair enough.' Pappas nodded and picked up a boll of cotton. 'If we're still here at Easter, I'll explain Orthodox Easter to you.' He let out a booming laugh and someone lit up a cigarette.

'Will you still come to Christmas lunch?' Cora asked. 'I understand it will be a proper feast.'

Stern laughed. 'I'll never say no to a feast.'

Cora stepped back, letting the men talk among themselves. She'd noticed that two of the men at the opposite end of the table, Allen and Moulds, continued whispering to each other, and the sudden sneer on Allen's ruddy face unsettled her. She tried to shake it off and looked to Stern to see if he'd noticed. He was looking down at the butcher's paper, stabbing his brush into a pot of glue.

She couldn't know what Allen and Moulds had gone through, really, and tried to find some generosity in her heart to excuse their rudeness. Had war turned them into different people than they might have been had they not been on the receiving end of an enemy's hatred?

Or did war simply amplify who people really were at heart?

On Christmas Day, Cora's feet hit the frigid floorboards and her toes shrank up inside her socks, the pair her sister Eve had sent in the package from home. They'd proved a godsend. She checked her brooch watch on the bedside table. It was six o'clock and as cold as charity. Behind the curtains, the sky was still dark and Cora wondered if her dream of a white Christmas had come true. She would have to check at first light.

Next to her, Gertie flung back her blankets and leapt out of bed with an enthusiasm that was infectious. She slipped her arms into the sleeves of her tartan woollen dressing gown and then opened her arms wide to Cora.

'Merry Christmas, Cora.'

'And to you, too, Gertie.' The two friends hugged, shivering in the embrace, reluctant to let go.

'Here's to a wonderful day.'

Gertie's eyes welled with tears. 'And here's to being home for the next one.'

Cora began to cry and tried to laugh instead. 'From your lips to God's ears.'

Around them, Leonora and Fiona were still asleep.

'I have a parcel from home I've been keeping until this morning,' Cora whispered. 'Would you like to open it with me?'

'Of course!' Gertie replied. 'I don't know how you had the patience to wait so long. I opened mine a week ago and I've already devoured all the biscuits.' She sat on Cora's bed and lifted her feet so her legs were horizontal in front of her. She turned circles with her socked feet. 'New bed socks. My aunt made them. They're not the most elegant things I've ever seen but, my goodness, are they warm.'

'They look absolutely toasty. Although … the colour is interesting.' Gertie's socks had been knitted from the finest baby pink wool, the colour used for newborn's layettes. Perhaps the colour had been chosen for someone's baby that had turned out to be a boy instead. Or perhaps the aunt had been keeping it for Gertie's daughters and had finally given up hope and used it for something more practical.

'I have something for you.'

'For me?'

'Yes,' Cora smiled. 'Don't get your hopes up that it's anything very grand. Like those socks.' She knelt at the side of the cot and pulled her suitcase from under it. She retrieved a small present wrapped in brown paper and tied with a length of string.

'You needn't have,' Gertie exclaimed, her voice catching.

'I warned you. It's not much but go on and open it.'

Gertie tugged at the string and peeled back the paper. 'Oh, Cora. A bookmark. That's so thoughtful of you.'

'I know how you love your reading and I was mightily sick of seeing your handkerchief left between the pages to mark your spot. I sat with some of the boys in one of the craft classes and I made one for each of us. I even pressed the flower myself. See? The one glued to the front? It's a forget-me-not. We dried some in the summer.'

Gertie looked to Cora, her eyes welling with tears. She sniffed loudly and unselfconsciously. 'I shall treasure it.'

There were footsteps and exclamations and then Leonora and Fiona leapt onto Cora's bed.

'Merry Christmas!' they cried and the cot's metal frame swayed and squeaked dangerously, which elicited a burst of laughter from them all.

After breakfast, the nurses walked down the Long Ramp to Ward 22, quietly opened the door and tiptoed in. They waved a silent hello to the night nurse, crept quietly in single file to the fire and stood in a practised formation.

'Ready?' Cora whispered, and after nods from the others, they began a hearty rendition of 'We Wish You a Merry Christmas'.

It was as perfect a Christmas as could be expected and Cora knew her heart wasn't the only one that was full. From bed to bed, the men slowly woke with yawns and tired blinks, either propping themselves on their elbows, or hopping out of bed to watch the spectacle. When the nurses sang the final words and bowed deep, their scarlet capes billowing like Christmas costumes, the men cheered and whooped.

'Merry Christmas, cobbers,' Pappas shouted.

Bassett slipped out of bed, dropping to his knees on the frigid floorboards, and prayed, his elbows on his blankets, his palms pressed together, his eyes squeezed tightly shut.

'You, too, you lovely girls,' Adams called out. 'How about a Christmas kiss, then?'

'Father Christmas told me you're the cheeky one,' Cora called out. 'Let's see if he's left you a lump of coal.'

The other men cheered and whooped. As they each slowly rose, smoked their first cigarette of the day and washed and dressed, the nurses offered help where help was needed.

'The ward's looking just perfect, isn't it?' Leonora sidled up to Cora and gave her a nudge. 'We've created a little slice of home.'

Every spare space on the walls of the ward had been decorated. On each panel between the windows, the men's paintings had been pinned to the wall, decorated with strips of red crinkled paper the colour of Father Christmas's suit. Each picture bore the name of a victorious battle spelt out in hand-drawn outlines and filled in with white cotton wool. The names of the brigades and their colours decorated each one. Gaba Tepe, Cape Helles and Lone Pine. They were three victories, three battles in which the Australians had proudly fought and vanquished the King's enemies.

So much holly was suspended from the ceiling that from certain angles the ward appeared to be in the middle of a wood. Union Jacks and state flags hung suspended too, quivering a little in the updraught from the fire. Behind the nurses' desk at one end of the ward, there was a large map of Australia, blue ribbon creating its ragged coastline, a kangaroo and an emu drawn remarkably accurately in the centre, with two flags, the Union Jack and the Australian flag, crossed over them. Above, a rising sun had been drawn and the words *Home Sweet Home* had been painted in blue.

Next to it, a southern cross looked over the men, fashioned from yellow painted stars.

At the other end of the ward, there was a tribute to fallen comrades. The boys had especially wanted to honour friends lost, so the cotton-wool cross with a laurel wreath underneath it read *In memory of our fallen pals*, written large in a neat curlicue.

It was the best home away from home anyone could have imagined.

Cora felt hot tears drizzle her cheeks and a glance at her fellow sisters confirmed she wasn't alone. A laugh rose in her throat, which became a sob and then another laugh, and she quickly wiped her tears.

Cora stepped forward and lifted her hands to calm everyone.

'Good morning, boys, and a very merry Christmas to you all. We might not be at home with our families and loved ones today, but let's spare a thought for all those still on the battlefront.'

The room fell quiet. Chins lowered and eyes closed in silent contemplation.

Cora breathed long and deep. How could she capture in words the emotions roiling within her, much less the experiences of all her colleagues and these men, who had seen the worst of what humankind had to offer?

'Today, we remember the men fighting in France, in Belgium, in Serbia. We remember the doctors and, in particular, the nurses at the battlefront, who tend to those men. We honour those who have been lost. We think of all the families and loved ones back in Australia who mourn, or who are missing you so dreadfully.'

Cora hadn't realised Bassett had got to his feet until she heard his deep baritone. 'Our Father who art in Heaven ...' His prayer echoed in the ward just as if he'd been reciting it in a house of worship, and those who believed—and even those who didn't—recited the words of the Lord's Prayer with him, because it seemed like the fitting thing to do and it gave them something to say when there were no adequate words at all to remember those who were lost.

Cora waited for Bassett to finish, and then told them all, 'We have a very busy day ahead, so let's get going, shall we?'

The Harefield hospital Christmas dinner in the mess was grander than the patients, nurses or doctors could have imagined. There was turkey with all the trimmings, jellies and custards and fresh fruit and plum puddings, and each man received a bag of gifts containing a pipe and tobacco and sweets.

A huge fir tree, recently cut from a field on the estate, was laden with toys for the village children and gifts for the men, its tinsel sparkling and its baubles bobbing like sailboats on a lake. Each table had been decorated with menus created in Australia and each featured real gum leaves adhered to the front. Some of the men couldn't resist and quickly tore the leaves away, snapping them in half and holding them to their noses, breathing deep to take in the much-longed-for scent of home.

Cora and Gertie and Leonora and Fiona sat with their boys, who needed a family as much as they did, and what else was Christmas about if it wasn't being with family?

Chapter Twenty-Four

25 December 1915

The spray of holly in a glass jar on the kitchen dresser at the Chesters sparkled in the light of the oil lamp set in the middle of the table. Tied to its branches were crackers Jessie and her mother had fashioned from scraps of butcher's paper and tied with pieces of ribbon from the scraps basket. The cards they'd received had been poked through with a knife and threaded with ribbon so they could decorate the tree: greetings from people in the village and a distant cousin of Jessie's in Leeds.

Next to it, there was a gathering of little presents, wrapped modestly in paper but tied with the ribbon flourishes only two seamstresses could manage in a time of such austerity.

Win hovered over the stove, stirring the gravy. The Chesters had managed to secure a goose for roasting, turnips and potatoes, with green beans and peas. They were making a special effort because for the first time since Jessie and Harry's father had died, there would be four people at the dining table to celebrate Christmas.

'Harry,' Win called. 'What time did you tell her?'

Harry emerged from the bathroom, patting down his hair with his functioning hand. 'There's a bit that's sticking up at the back, Jessie. Can you comb it for me?'

'Of course.' She took the comb from him, reached up and smoothed it through his crown. She laughed. 'It's your cowlick, Harry. I wouldn't worry. Dottie is hardly likely to be able to see the top of your head. She only reaches to your armpits anyway.'

There was a knock at the door and all three Chesters laughed. They were as familiar with Dottie's particular knock—a knock knock knock-knock-knock—as they were with the sound of the church bells from St Mary's.

'She's here!' Win exclaimed and moved to whip off her apron before remembering it was only Dottie and she knew Dottie wouldn't mind if she wanted to protect her good dress from splashes of fat from the spitting goose.

Jessie studied Harry and straightened his tie. 'You look exceptionally handsome, dear brother.'

Harry blushed and waved her away. 'Oh, stop it.'

'I'll get the door,' Jessie said quickly and rushed through the sewing room, flinging open the heavy door.

'Merry Christmas, Dottie!' Had Jessie ever seen a bigger smile on her friend's face? 'Come inside out of that wind. It's icy tonight.'

Dottie stepped in, the wind whirling around her, and Jessie quickly shut out the world. 'Oh, it's warm in here. I can't feel my nose,' Dottie giggled, poking it with a gloved finger. 'You think I'd be used to it by now, walking out and about in every kind of weather to deliver the post. What if I get frostbite? Imagine having to walk around without a nose!'

Jessie laughed at Dottie's whimsy. 'You've been busy then?'

Dottie widened her eyes as she tugged off her gloves and shrugged out of her coat. 'There's so much mail and that's not counting the packages. All the boys away and everyone in the country sending them letters and cards for Christmas, as you can imagine. Can you guess how many letters the Royal Mail delivered in the past week just to our boys? Go on, have a guess?'

Jessie took Dottie's coat. 'I can't even imagine.' Dottie's pride and joy was infectious. She had never complained about the blisters on her heels from her sturdy boots, about stomping up and down the streets of Harefield in all kinds of weather, of having to navigate the manure trails that followed the horse-drawn carts that rattled and clopped all day. Not once had she grumbled about starting her workday at six o'clock, or even five if a busy day was to be expected, walking the streets to the post office with the milkmen and the road sweepers and the occasional policeman.

'Well!' she exclaimed, her cheeks flushed pink. 'Twelve million letters. That's how many. We couldn't rest knowing that there was a soldier out there who might miss out on a letter from home. Can you believe that, Jess? Twelve million!'

So many were so far from home, in the cold and the mud and the rain. How could that be right? How could it be right that there were so many families with an empty chair at Christmas dinner?

'I think you're all just marvellous. A credit to His Royal Mail. I'll hang your coat. Mum and Harry are in the kitchen. Why don't you go through?'

Dottie all but bounced up and down on the spot. 'I've been looking forward to tonight for weeks.'

'We're so happy you're here to celebrate with us,' Jessie replied. She remembered the day Harry had told his family he was planning to invite Dottie for Christmas dinner. Outside, the rain had been steady and the street was slick with mud. He'd been sitting at the worktable in the front room, poring over columns of pounds, shillings and pence, calculating which customers still owed them and how much they themselves owed the draper, when he'd put down his pencil and cleared his throat.

'Mum?'

'Yes, love?' Win had been sitting on her work chair near the window, her favourite place to sew when the days grew short. She'd found a position to take advantage of every available ray of the thin winter light that leached in through the windows. Her attention had been determinedly fixed on her needle as it slipped effortlessly through the piece of silk fabric she was smocking for a christening outfit for the first child of the grocer and his wife.

'I wonder if … well, if you and Jessie wouldn't mind …'

When Harry seemed to lose his train of thought, Jessie looked across at her brother. She'd been pinning a pattern. 'Mind what?' she'd mumbled, keeping her lips pulled together so the pins between her lips wouldn't fall.

'I'd like Dottie to join us for Christmas dinner.'

Jessie would have gasped if she were able to open her mouth. Or smile. Of course she knew that Harry and Dottie had been spending time together. There had been meetings at the tearooms. At least one Sunday lunch at the Cricketers.

Picnics at the village green before the weather had grown too cold. Harry wasn't up for long walks, which Dottie had insisted she didn't mind a bit—'I walk all week. I'm perfectly happy to sit'—so they never ventured far from home. Jessie had been washing the lunch dishes one afternoon and she'd heard them chatting while they fed the chickens, laughing as the hens flapped their wings and attempted to take flight in pursuit of an apple core. Jessie hadn't been able to make out what exactly they had been saying to each other, but she realised in that moment that they'd developed an intimacy. She saw it in the way they spoke to each other. It was there in the deep undulations in Harry's voice and the giggling exclamations in Dottie's.

When Win had recovered from the shock, she'd leapt to her feet and rounded the worktable to plant a smacking kiss on Harry's forehead, which embarrassed and pleased him in equal measure. 'Of course she can, my dear boy.'

Jessie hung Dottie's coat on a hook by the front door, alongside her mother's and her brother's and her own and wondered if, one day, Dottie might just become her sister-in-law. She turned, not caring if her expression revealed what she'd just been imagining.

'Harry,' she called. 'Dottie's here.' And then to Dottie, 'Come through.'

Harry was waiting by the table, gripping the back of one of the kitchen chairs either for balance or to keep himself from crossing the room to throw his arms around Dottie, Jessie couldn't be certain. The two lovers beamed at each other and Cora and Win stepped back, allowing the stars of the show to have their place in the limelight.

'Good evening, Dottie,' Harry said, his tone so sincere it was as if every word he'd ever utter again would only be for her.

'Hello, Harry,' Dottie whispered. She gripped the handle of her purse with both hands and swung it from side to side.

'You look lovely tonight.'

'Oh, this?' Dottie looked down at her light grey woollen dress, its belt buttoned at the front with three ivory ovals. It was fixed with a wide lace collar in gleaming white and she wore a pearl brooch at her neck. Jessie wondered if it was new. She, at least, had never seen it before.

When there was the smallest moment of silence in the kitchen, Win filled it. 'Hello there, love. You're so very welcome in our home, as ever.'

Dottie went to Win and kissed her cheek. 'It really is lovely to be here. I hope you don't mind but I have something for all of you.' Dottie pulled a gift from her handbag, a small package about four inches by four inches.

'Oh, dear girl,' Win spluttered. 'How very kind of you, but you shouldn't have.'

'Oh, yes, I should,' Dottie replied adamantly. 'I can see you and Jessie have been working your fingers to the bone preparing dinner. It's the least I could do. Anyone looking around would think nothing less.'

Jessie was proud of all the work she and her mother had put in that day to make this a Christmas to remember. The plain kitchen table wore a white tablecloth and was set for four. Gleaming sherry glasses, which Jessie had polished until they had almost worn through, sat at the head of each plate. Four tall white candles decorated the centre, their wicks still limp and fresh. Small branches of holly had been twisted in on themselves and the prickly dark green leaves formed a circle at the base of the candles. The shiny bright berries looked as juicy as redcurrants. Tinsel hung from the window to the back door and across the top of the dresser to the doorway to the front room. It was lovely and homely and they were warm from the heat emanating from the stove and they had a goose and all the roast vegetables they could want and a Christmas pud that had been sitting for six weeks.

Jessie felt overcome by a wave of gratitude. How blessed they were. England was filled with families for whom Christmas would be a day of unimaginable grief, who had woken that harsh and bitter morning to the full knowledge that there would be no more Christmases for a son or a father or an uncle or cousin or neighbour. For those families, there would be a place missing at their Christmas table forever, a loved one they might have expected would one day bring home a sweetheart, then a wife, then children and even grandchildren to share their Christmas bounty. And in the Australian hospital down the road, there were doctors and nurses so far from home and soldiers who couldn't turn to the arms of their loved ones for comfort at such a time.

'Sit down, won't you?' Win pulled out a chair and set the little present on the table. 'I'll open it after dinner. Who'd like a sherry, then?'

Jessie scraped her dessert spoon around her bowl in a weary attempt to collect every drop of cream she'd drizzled over her share of pudding. She was already full to the brim, her stomach pressing indelicately against her corset, but it had been such a long time since there had been a jug of cream on the kitchen table and it was almost her favourite thing, so she couldn't in good conscience waste any.

Next to her, her mother sat back and sighed, looking over the empty plates with a matriarch's contentment. Across from both of them, Harry and Dottie took turns glancing at each other and blushing. Jessie didn't believe either of them had touched their pudding, having only moved it around the bowl to give the impression they were eating it. If she'd anticipated that, she might have cut herself a larger slice.

'I think it's time for gifts,' Win announced. Dottie jumped to her feet to help and together they cleared the table, scraping the last of the roast vegetables into a pan to keep for supper, and the bones of the goose into a large pot on the stove for making stock the next day. Jessie cleared the remains of the Christmas crackers they'd helped each other open and straightened the tablecloth.

Harry fetched the presents from the dresser and carried them to the table. When everyone was seated, he read each tag and distributed the gifts. One by one, they were opened and thanks offered. Jessie received a pair of slippers from Win and a pincushion from Harry. Win looked exceedingly happy with her new handkerchiefs from Harry and the bath salts from Jessie, lavender scented—her favourite flower. Harry received socks and a new scarf from Jessie and Win, and Dottie fixed the scarf around his neck right there and then and they all laughed at how dashing he looked.

Win opened the present from Dottie and thanked her profusely for the jellies, which she promised to share after they'd all had a cup of tea.

There was one present remaining and Harry passed it to Dottie.

Something in his expression had Jessie holding her breath. Under the table, she reached for Win's hand and they squeezed each other's fingers so hard Jessie lost all sensation in hers.

Dottie looked at the package, looked at Harry, and then looked at the package again. She was unsure what to do next.

'Well, open it,' Harry laughed, and when she tore at the paper, she revealed a small, pale blue box inside. When she opened the lid, cotton wool fluffed up as if it had been held captive for months.

She went pale and looked to Harry.

'Go on,' he said tenderly.

Dottie lifted bolls of cotton and laid them carefully on the table as if she might collect them up to be used again. Then she burst into tears. 'Oh, Harry!' She held a plain gold band up to the lamplight.

'I would kneel if I could without falling over,' Harry said, chuckling. And blushing.

'You don't have to kneel!' Dottie cried.

'And I haven't been to your father yet because I'm not sure what he'll say when he sees that a man like me is asking for his daughter's hand.'

Dottie's tears became laughter in that moment and Jessie had never seen a happier woman in her entire life. 'We'll go together,' she said, clutching Harry's hand. 'And times are changing, Harry. I'll marry you anyway, no matter what he says.'

Win gasped. 'That's a yes, then?'

Dottie nodded, beaming. 'Yes, Harry Chester. Put that ring on my finger. My answer is yes.'

Plans for Harry and Dottie's future had been made so swiftly that night that Jessie's head was still spinning as she lay quietly in her room, trying to sleep.

Almost as soon as Dottie had said yes, Jessie had gathered every magazine she had in the house and she and Win had begun looking at designs for the dress. Harry had announced that he'd like to wear his father's suit because if he couldn't be there in person, Harry would feel like he was if he was wearing it, and Win had cried. Dottie had begun writing a list of all that needed to be done between now and the day of the nuptials.

Harry and Dottie would go to her father on Boxing Day, both to allow Harry to ask for her hand and to ignore his refusal if, in fact, he did refuse. There would be no engagement party because it would seem ostentatious when the King and prime minister and everyone else was beseeching people to be frugal in their spending and their habits during the great crisis.

The wedding would be in June because, as Dottie had giggled, 'Who doesn't want to be a summer bride?' Win had insisted that Dottie move into their home once she and Harry were married because his room was downstairs next to the kitchen and it was best he lived in a house with no stairs. Jessie felt excited too at the idea that her best friend would be there every morning over breakfast and every night at supper, that the Chester family would grow in such a way.

The plans had spun as fast as fairy floss at a confectioner's.

Jessie pulled her blankets up over her nose. It was bitter outside and rain was thumping down on the roof above, as if a hundred little drummer boys were up there summoning Father Christmas.

The next day was Boxing Day and then a week later, New Year. And then it would be 1916. She would be turning twenty-three years old in February and she wondered if another year would pass that would, in every respect, be just like 1915. When she thought ahead to Christmas 1916, she saw four people at the table, but not five. She didn't see a sweetheart for herself. Her chances of finding the kind of love Harry and Dottie clearly shared seemed further and further away than ever. What was to become of her?

1916

Chapter Twenty-Five

18 January 1916

'How cold is it out there, Sister?'

'Cold.' Cora glanced up at the ward windows. It appeared as if a cloud had fallen from the sky and enveloped the hospital. By now, she was used to England's winter gloom. Low-hung grey clouds full of coal smoke from homes and the fumes from the factories nearby, all trapped under the atmosphere like cigarette smoke under a pub ceiling.

But the cold. Would she ever get used to it? She'd been out earlier that morning to fetch some more bandages from the main supply store and had decided that, given she would only be gone ten minutes, she wouldn't need her coat for the short walk across the hospital. It had been a mistake and she'd chided herself with every step across the sodden and boggy ground. Her boots were still wet and she couldn't feel her toes.

Cora scooped up a spoonful of porridge from a bowl and held it towards Private Nixon. She lightly touched it against his lips to indicate he should open them and swallow.

'Here you go. Another spoonful. I thought you might prefer this for lunch over soup.' Nixon opened his mouth and she saw a baby bird instead of a soldier, a thought that tugged at her and made her want to weep. He pressed his lips weakly around the bowl of the spoon and Cora smoothed it over his lips to catch the porridge that had dribbled there.

'You're lucky to be tucked up in bed. It's so cold outside that the tip of my nose is frozen solid.'

Her patient chuckled. He would never be able to see for himself if she was telling the truth. 'I'll have to take your word for it, Sister.'

Nixon had arrived in the week after New Year, blinded by mustard gas, his right arm shattered by German shrapnel and with two frostbitten toes on his left foot. He'd been in a bad way and wasn't out of the woods yet. William had performed two operations and had determined he should be sent home at the earliest opportunity, but there had been an ongoing and relentless battle to bring his infection under control and to deal with the residual damage to his lungs. No one believed an ocean voyage in winter was a good option, so he would remain until spring or until he was better. In Nixon's case, Cora had a suspicion spring would come first.

'You don't believe me?' Cora rested the spoon in the bowl and pinched her nose, rendering her voice a nasal squeak. 'Peter Piper picked a peck of pickled peppers.'

Her performance elicited a weak smile and her heart was lighter for it. This boy had a long road ahead. What else could she do but nourish him and ensure he was in one of the beds closest to the fire?

'I haven't heard that one since my school days,' he said. 'My teacher, Mr Whittell, used to make us recite it every morning.'

'Where are you from, Private?'

'Baan Baa. New South Wales.'

'I can't say I've ever heard of it.'

'It's in the northern inlands. Wheat country.'

Cora lifted another spoon of milky porridge and waited while Nixon swallowed it.

'Are your parents still there?'

He nodded slowly, the padded bandages around his eyes making it awkward to move. 'They are. And my sisters—Margaret, Julia, Mary and Jane—are all still home.'

Unmarried, Cora thought.

'And where does the only precious boy fit in then?'

'Right in the middle,' he whispered and Jessie saw in the slight upturn at the corners of his mouth that a part of him was back in Baan Baa, chasing his sisters around the farm, milking the cow, searching for firewood or feeding the horses. She'd hoped his thoughts might carry him away far from his bed, the ward and the war.

'Goodness me,' she exclaimed. 'I can't imagine growing up with two older and two younger sisters. Two older to tell you what to do and two younger to also tell you what to do.'

He chuckled. 'You've got that right, Sister.'

Cora stirred the porridge, wishing there was a swirl of honey on it to make it sweeter and to give him some much-needed vitality. 'I have two sisters and I find them wholly impossible. They never listen to me, no matter what I tell them or how kindly I put it. They must all be so proud of you.'

Nixon's smile faltered. 'My mother and father wanted me to stay on the farm.'

'They wanted you to take it over one day?'

'That was their thinking.'

Nixon would never run the farm now. He would return to Baan Baa a changed man. But he would return. Wouldn't any family be grateful for that?

She raised another spoonful of porridge to his lips. He swallowed and cocked his head towards his heavily bandaged arm.

'If only I'd been born left handed,' he said. 'I'd be able to do this by myself and you could get on with more important things.'

She leant in close to whisper in his ear. 'You're actually doing me a favour, Nixon. It's rather a relief to take a moment to sit down for a minute or two and have a good old chinwag with a handsome young man.'

Nixon blushed. Cora was relieved he couldn't see the tears in her eyes and the lie on her lips.

What was this young man doing here, damaged and broken, his youth stripped from him before he'd had a life? In her mind she gathered up the faces of all the young Australian boys she'd tended and they became a hundred football teams of strapping young men with tans and smiles as wide as the horizon. How many cheeky grins had been stolen from them? How many of them had enlisted looking for adventure, waving their families and sweethearts and grandparents goodbye with a promise to come home?

And who had they left behind? Who were their mothers and fathers and sweethearts and brothers and sisters and friends? How many stars went unseen by their wide and innocent eyes? Who would look up to the Southern Cross if they weren't there?

'You work too hard, you sisters. You're all bloody marvellous.'

'It's my job. To see that patients like you eat your porridge.' She tapped the spoon against the now-empty bowl. 'And look at that! You have. You are a champion, Private Nixon.'

'It's *my* job,' he murmured. 'We're all doing our bit for Australia, aren't we? However we can. No matter the cost.'

And he had paid a mighty one. With his words, Cora held out some hope for him, that he might hold on to what made him *him*, that he would somehow survive and thrive, even with the burdens he would bear forever.

'Bloody hell!'

She turned at the sound of a deep-voiced exclamation. One of the boys was balancing precariously on his crutches by a window, looking out into the soupy fog. He reached out and rubbed a palm on the glass in big circles.

'You won't believe it!' he exclaimed, his eyes as wide as saucers. 'It's actually bloody snowing!'

Taylor, the patient in the cot next to Nixon, harrumphed. 'Seen enough of the bloody stuff in France to last me a lifetime. No offence, Sister.'

'Didn't see any in the Dardanelles, mate. I've never seen the stuff. I'm from Townsville,' the deep-voiced man announced to the ward.

The men who could get out of bed unaided scrambled to their feet and hobbled and hopped to the nearest window.

'Crikey,' someone said with awe. 'It's floating around like someone's standing on the roof dropping cotton wool balls on the ground.'

'Sister?' Nixon murmured.

'Yes, Private?'

He was exhausted from their conversation and was barely able to lift his head from the pillow. 'Will you take me outside? Help me have a look at the snow?'

She paused, scrambling for an excuse. 'It's very cold out. You're still very weak.'

He breathed deep. 'Please, Sister. I've never … I've never seen it. At least I want to feel it once in my life.'

How could she deny him this simple request? 'Only for a minute or two. And then it's back to bed. Is that understood?' Cora put the bowl on the soldier's bedside table and let him loop his left arm through her elbow. She held firm as he used all his strength to pull himself up. With her free hand, she pulled back his sheet and blankets and moved his legs to position his feet on the floor.

'You might be dizzy. Take it slow now.'

Nixon sat for a moment, moving his head in the direction of the commotion at the windows. 'Is it still coming down?'

'It is. You won't miss it. Take your time.'

'Let me help, Sister.' Taylor was next to the bed, a crutch under one arm, one pyjama leg flapping.

'Thank you, Taylor. That's very kind.' With an arm each, they helped Nixon to his feet.

'I'm Keith Taylor, 28th Battalion. Nice to meet you, Nixon.'

'Cheers, mate.' Nixon swooned a little and Cora steadied him.

Step by faltering step, they made it to the end of the bed and then down the aisle towards the door. Cora opened it.

The icy air seeped through her and she shivered but she had to admit it looked beautiful outside. Snow fell gently and silently on the lawn. It looked for all the world like icing sugar dusting a sponge cake.

'Look at that, cobber,' Taylor said.

In a few moments, the ramp was crowded with patients stretching their upturned palms out from under the veranda into the open air. Fingers fluttered as snowflakes landed silently on scars and burns and blisters.

'Those flakes are as big as plates!'

'Certainly is a sight better than mud, boys, isn't it?' Her question was met by universal acclamation.

There was a round of whoops and laughter before a silence descended, a gentle, quiet peace for just a moment. Cora could feel the heartbeats of the men slow, heard their breaths become sighs of wonder, and felt her own shoulders loosening and slackening.

'What a story I'll have to write home about, hey?' Nixon said quietly and his voice caught in his throat. 'The country boy makes a snowball.'

And as they watched, the men who could gambolled out into the falling snow, turning their faces up to it joyously, letting the flakes fall into their open mouths. Those who had the strength reached down to the ground and scooped up the snow and threw it at each other, chasing and laughing like puppies.

They turned to Cora, their faces full of wonder and laughter, and her heart clenched at the possibility that among all the sorrow, these men could find joy in such a simple thing.

Chapter Twenty-Six

2 February 1916

The streets of Harefield were filled to overflowing with people yet there wasn't a whisper, a word of gossip or a laugh to fill the frigid air. It was quieter than church. Up and down the high street there was no workaday chatter from customers filing in and out of the butcher's, moaning about sausages being rationed. The newspaper boy wasn't shouting that day's headlines about the latest losses in France and the door of Read's Cash Stores was closed.

In the overwhelming silence, Jessie's pulse was a drumbeat in her ears. She linked arms with her mother and on her right side Harry stood with Dottie, holding hands. They were in black, the same dresses and coats Win and Jessie had worn at Terence's funeral five years earlier, and Harry had gone and bought a black coat out of respect.

Jessie breathed out, puffs of breath like cigarette smoke, and tugged her cloche hat down lower over her ears.

There was a collective intake of breath as the cortege was spotted rounding the corner at the top of the street.

Necks craned. A little girl stepped out from the protective arms of her parents and whispered, 'They're coming,' before her ear was pulled by her mother, warning her not to be ill-mannered on such a day.

Jessie spotted the first people in the procession, just visible turning the corner into the high street. The village undertaker, Charles Filkins, wore a top hat and a long black coat and marched solemnly. Behind him, two columns of khaki-clad soldiers, their hats tipped up on the left side in the Australian fashion, marched in time, their arms swinging in perfect rhythm, except for those whose arms were in slings. When the clouds cleared and the sun suddenly appeared and shone down on them, one soldier broke ranks and cocked his head at the sky instead of being eyes forward. Was he looking to God to bless his fallen comrade?

Two policemen walked at the side of the procession, watching proceedings with cautious eyes, but there was no need to worry about anyone behaving out of turn or disrupting these proceedings.

The first Australian soldier had died at Harefield hospital. A collective wave of respect and grief had broken out at the idea that a young man from so far away had come to England to defend it and he had given his life for their country.

Just as Harefield had embraced the living Australians, it had respectfully turned out to take care of a dead one. The local member of parliament, Mr Francis Newdegate MP, had set aside part of the churchyard for the burial of any Australians who might die at Harefield hospital. He had also promised to pay all the expenses for any funerals and he had been true to his word. The village carpenter, Frank Carter, had made the coffin. Old Mr Marsden had dug the grave, on account of all the younger and fitter men in the village being off fighting, and that final resting place was waiting for Private Robert Sydney Wake.

It seemed that every single person in Harefield had turned out to stand quietly, pray silently and pay their sincere respects.

'I can't bear this song,' Win whispered to Jessie. In the distance, the sombre and grieving tones of the funeral march drifted towards them just as Jessie caught sight of Mr Filkins's three-wheeled truck, which ferried the coffin.

Jessie whispered, and her voice caught. 'His name was Wake; 5th Battalion, AIF. He was twenty-four years old.'

Dottie dabbed at her eyes with a handkerchief and her head fell on Harry's shoulder. Jessie knew what she was thinking but would never say: thank God that would never be her Harry. Thank God indeed.

'Bless him and his family.' Win crossed herself.

The cortege made its way slowly past, the soldiers' heavy footsteps and the low rumble of the truck the only sounds, until there was a shout.

'Wait!' Heads turned and necks craned. In front of the Junior School, a man stood unfurling a Union Jack.

'Look,' Harry said. 'It's Mr Jeffrey.'

The cortege stopped. The village school's headmaster approached the truck and draped the flag over the coffin inside it. Then, he stepped back and saluted and the truck moved on solemnly. As it passed, villagers fell in behind the procession, taking care to move in at the rear of the assembled town dignitaries, Australian and British army officers and staff from the hospital. When Jessie saw nurses' uniforms she craned her neck to see familiar faces but there were too many of them, and in the sea of scarlet capes and white veils she couldn't make out one from another.

As the cortege passed, Jessie was swept along in the crowd as if someone had linked arms with her and pulled her forward, and she urged her mother to come along with her. They found themselves marching in time with the Australian diggers up ahead. Next to her, roly-poly Mrs Biggins from next door cried. 'I pity his poor mother. Imagine. A son buried so far from home that you could never visit his grave.'

'I can't imagine the agony,' Win replied.

There was simply too much grief too imagine. Who would mourn this young man? What were his family in Australia to do to mark his death, if they had no remains and no grave? Did they have the means to one day come to Harefield to lay flowers on their son's final resting place?

The procession stopped at the bottom of the hill. Private Wake's coffin was hoisted upon the healthy shoulders of six of his comrades and then lowered into the grave in St Mary's churchyard. The hospital chaplain performed the service with full military honours. Jessie squinted her eyes closed when the firing party performed its salute and she cried when a bugler played the Last Post and Reveille.

Some of the important Australians laid a wreath on his grave and then hundreds of villagers and local schoolchildren laid wildflowers, each one of them so well-behaved their parents and all who knew them must have been so proud.

Patients who had been unable to march had been brought to St Mary's in motor vehicles and they sat in their wheelchairs or balanced on their crutches.

If there was a dry eye, Jessie couldn't see it.

When the service was over, she and Win and the other villagers walked home in sombre silence while the band played 'The Girl I Left Behind Me'.

Had Private Wake left a girl behind in Australia? What was his profession? Was he a bootmaker? A clerk in an office? A factory man? What kind of life had he lived before he'd enlisted? Jessie couldn't bear to think of him as a dead man so she made herself think of all the things he might have been.

Had Private Wake missed home as he lay dying?

Jessie had patted a kangaroo and quite recently, too. Some of the Harefield soldiers had carried it into the village in a pillowcase and set up on the village green. They'd held it in their arms as if it were a baby, feeding it little bits of carrot and cabbage, and all the village children had flocked there to smooth their palms over its fur and marvel at the long tail on this strangest of creatures. Jessie hadn't been able to resist and had waited until all the children were done before stepping forward to see it for herself. She had asked a soldier how it had come to be in the village and he'd told her it had been especially brought over on a boat to be a mascot for the soldiers and the doctors and nurses.

'To remind them of home,' he'd said, trying to be jovial but she had seen the sadness in his eyes, this Harefield hospital soldier.

Had Private Wake lived in the outback with snakes and lizards or had he lived in a place like Harefield, a quiet little village with its own history and traditions and neighbours he'd known since he'd been a lad? As he'd lain dying, had someone carried that kangaroo to his bedside so he could reach out and stroke its soft as soft fur and close his eyes and think he was home?

Chapter Twenty-Seven

The nurses barely said a word to each other on the long walk
back to Harefield. Chopin's funeral march was a drumbeat
in Cora's head, her footsteps matching its sombre rhythm
along Rickmansworth Road and all the way to the hospital.
She felt a deep need to be back at the hospital, the place
Private Wake had taken his last breath, had for the last time
breathed the English air, held a nurse's hand. Gertie fell into
step beside her, linking arms with Cora, and behind them,
Leonora and Fiona did the same.

At the canteen, a wake had been organised by the village
volunteers and the doctors and nurses and other members
of the hospital's staff half-heartedly nibbled sandwiches and
slices of fruitcake. Cora had little appetite and, judging by
the plates of untouched food, she guessed others felt the
same.

When she was pouring her second cup of tea, Cora
spotted William across the room and he gave a quick nod
to a colleague before making his way to her. Was it wrong
to think of his attention as the only bright spot in the whole
dreadful day?

'Tea, Captain?' she asked as he approached.

He was dressed in his full military uniform and the sight of him in his khaki tunic, a white cotton brassard with a red wool Geneva cross around his left arm, shook Cora. She had always thought of him as a surgeon first and army man second. But there he was, looking as if he were about to head off to the battlefield that very minute. Oh, how the thought tore her in two. She dropped her gaze to his knee-length officer's boots, lest her feelings were revealed in her wide eyes. The highly polished leather almost reflected her own visage as she studied them.

'No, thank you, Sister,' he answered politely.

Cora set the pot down and lifted her cup to her lips. It was strong but not strong enough to settle her. She hadn't stopped trembling since she'd seen the cortege, since she'd heard the villagers sobbing for someone who wasn't even one of their own.

'What a day.' William shrugged as if he too knew there were no words powerful enough to convey such a loss.

Across the mess, someone began playing the piano. It was something solemn and funereal and Cora fought the urge to cry again. When she sniffed, she felt William's hand on her arm.

'Are you all right, Cora?' He'd moved close to whisper her name.

She daren't look at him or she would burst into tears, and for that Cora felt shame and embarrassment. What was her grief compared with a family's? With any of the men who'd been patients at Harefield? Early on in her nursing career, she'd learnt to distance herself from those she had cared for and their suffering and a family's grief. She had been the bearer of bad news more than once to a family.

In those instances, she had been able to retreat discreetly, shut a door and let them sob and pray in private. But where were Private Wake's loved ones? Ten thousand miles away, too far to absorb the horror and the loss and the combined enormity of it all. At Harefield, grief hung in the atmosphere like cigarette smoke from a thousand patients' cigarettes, swirling and settling in Cora's hair and in her clothes; not in her lungs, but in her heart.

Her teacup rattled in its saucer when she set it down. 'I know I should have expected this. Do I not read of death every day? I know the cause. I know that it will happen today and again tomorrow and the day after and the weeks and the months after today, but Private Wake's death has come as such a shock. That sounds so terribly naive, doesn't it?'

'Not naive, no, Cora. Hopeful. And don't we all need hope?'

Cora had never felt this low. 'If only we could gather it up from the store like we do bandages and antiseptic ointment.'

'Cora.' William paused and removed his hand from her arm. He seemed to have forgotten it was still there.

She hadn't. 'Yes?'

'I know this isn't the time, but I've barely seen you to ask in so many weeks.' William's voice picked up speed and urgency. 'I've been in surgery every hour God sends and you, well, I've looked for you in the mess. In the canteen. I even wandered into the library in hopes that you might be there reading the newspaper.'

How could she share her relief that she hadn't been alone in seeking him out? It had been weeks. She had wondered if his particular attention had waned since Christmas, perhaps if someone else had caught his eye. She had let herself feel deflated at the thought for a few days, but they had never been anything more than colleagues and, in a hospital the size Harefield had become, it was possible they might not run into each other every day.

He cleared his throat. 'I've missed talking with you. I've missed laughing with you. I was hoping you might like to join me in the village for lunch. I haven't sorted out a day. I know we'll have to coordinate our rosters, for one thing, and if a contingent of patients arrive we might have to cancel altogether. But I thought it was worth planning ahead, at least. And asking you.'

How could he know that his simple request had lifted some of the doom from her shoulders?

'I'd be delighted.'

Judging by the twinkle in his blue eyes, William was, too.

Later that night, Cora, Gertie, Leonora and Fiona huddled together near the crackling fire in their quarters. Outside, the wind had picked up and rain was sleeting on the windows, rattling them in their frames. Fiona sat in her nightdress, her woollen dressing gown knotted tightly at her waist, thick socks baggy at her ankles. Gertie wrapped her fingers around a cup of tea, muttering that she wished it were brandy. Cora leant forward, splaying her fingers nearer the fire, hoping to drive out the cold that seemed to have settled into the joints of her bones.

Next to her, Leonora had retrieved from her suitcase every letter she'd received from her fiancé, Lieutenant

Percival Jones, and was reading them silently and clutching them to her chest, crying and laughing in turn. Although the more she read, the more tears she shed.

'How is he, your Percy?' Gertie asked.

Leonora looked up with tear-filled eyes. 'Still in France. Verdun, to be exact.' She heaved a sigh and her lips wobbled. 'He's alive. After today, that's more than any girl could ask for, don't you think? I have to keep reminding myself that so many aren't so lucky. That if he's alive at the end of today, God willing, that's one more day than some get. And if he has one more day and then another and another, until the end of the war, he'll come back to me.'

'I shall say a prayer for him tonight,' Fiona said. 'If you'd like me to.'

'I would appreciate that very much. That means more to me than I can say.'

Fiona sniffed and kept her eyes down. 'I'll say one for him every night until the war is over.'

Leonora began sobbing and Fiona went to her and held her.

Cora let her tears drizzle down her cheeks. Casualties were still arriving out of Gallipoli, two months after the official withdrawal. No one wanted to say it. Private Wake may have been the first Australian to die at Harefield hospital but he wouldn't be the last.

Chapter Twenty-Eight

5 March 1916

Cora checked William's letter twice before slipping it back into her purse. He wasn't late. She was early. She wasn't nervous, simply excited at the idea of lunch at a real pub.

And the idea of Sunday lunch with a gentleman. With her free hand, she pinched each cheek five times in the hope it might promote some rosiness. Before she'd left the nurses' quarters, she'd surveyed herself in the mirror in the bathroom and decided she looked pale. Was it any surprise? Winter had been long and wet and cold and exhausting. And now, spring had arrived, only just but definitely. There was warmth in the air and the trees at Harefield Park were in bud. Around the lakes at the rear of the hospital, white blankets of snowdrops had sprung seemingly from nowhere, their delicate teardrop flowers as white as cotton wool. And the dawn chorus warmed her soul too. Skylarks and robins and blackbirds were heralding the arrival of spring as cheerfully as the patients were.

Cora wasn't sure how William had managed to slip a letter in among the patients' notes on her desk in the ward—she suspected he'd had an accomplice in Gertie but Gertie would admit to no such connivance—and Cora had found it early afternoon the Friday before as she'd been sorting through the official paperwork belonging to a new contingent of injured soldiers.

Letters arrived every day, from mothers and fathers and grandparents and wives and sweethearts and sisters and brothers and comrades in arms, all delivered to the hospital's post office via the Harefield Post Office. Those missives from home were as important to the men as bandages and morphia.

William's letter had been caught up in a pile of mail. She'd absent-mindedly sorted the envelope marked to Barker in alphabetical order with the rest—Adams, Allen, Barker, Brown, C., Brown, W., Calthorpe, Charlesworth, Clarke, Cowell, Duffy, Gilbert, Jones, F., Jones, P., McCoy, Prentice, Saunders, Tirrell, Walker, Touchell and Wright.

It was only when she'd gone back, querying who the Barker might be, that she realised the envelope read 'Sister Barker'. Inside it was a thin slip of paper, which she unfolded and read with the tiniest of thrills fluttering at her throat. William had secured a reservation for lunch at the Cricketers. His plan was to meet her at the nurses' quarters at eleven, if it suited her, so they could take the walk into the village.

Thrilled, she'd quickly slipped the letter back into the privacy of its envelope and then the envelope into the pocket of her uniform.

She needed the distraction more than ever. The evening before, after their late supper of tea and biscuits in the mess, Leonora and Fiona had had such a row on the walk back to their nurses' quarters that Fiona had burst into tears and thrown herself on her bed as soon as she was within reach of it.

'What was that about?' Cora had whispered to Gertie.

'They've been at it like cats and dogs over the slightest thing,' Gertie had replied, looking more worried than amused. 'This time, it was something about using up the last of the hot water.'

'It's so unlike them to bicker,' Cora replied.

'It's getting to all of us. In different ways.'

Gertie was right. Cora had seen more tears than ever before, born of frustration and exhaustion and a prolonged and intensifying sense of grief that had settled in like frost. Leonora had been laid low with a cold and a fever and had slept for what seemed like three days straight. Even Gertie had been short-tempered, which surprised Cora the most. Her dear friend had lately seemed to have lost her sense of humour, which Cora missed most of all. Gertie's smart wits and her ability to prick a hole in the most pompous of utterances had always buoyed Cora's spirits. She herself had lost weight. No matter how much she ate, and how many custard creams she consumed with her cup of tea at suppertime, she'd had to move the button on the belt of her uniform so it didn't hang from her tall frame. The war was taking its toll on all of them; they were each suffering its effects in their own different ways.

William's invitation for a walk into the village and lunch was the tonic Cora needed. It had been a long time since she'd wandered out of the hospital gates. She'd had so many plans to visit London and take in its sights and experiences, to visit the Tower, the Houses of Parliament,

Big Ben and St Paul's Cathedral, but in the ten months she'd been at the hospital, she hadn't had more than one single day off. That precious day was usually spent mending stockings and anything else that needed fixing, washing her hair and writing her letters. Her mother and father, and Eve and Grace, had been regular correspondents and their letters and newspaper clippings from home were now collected in her suitcase in a three-inch thick bundle tied with brown string. She was afraid her responses barely compared in detail or heft, but she did what she could and spared them the worst of her experiences, highlighting the humour in her situation and amplifying her dedication to her work.

Sunday morning had finally arrived and Cora stood expectantly at the door of the nurses' quarters. She checked the time again on her wristwatch. One minute to eleven. When she looked up, William was striding towards her. She had to smile at his gait. He must have failed marching when he'd enlisted, as he seemed to be loping towards her, one hand in the pocket of his trousers, a broad smile on his face.

There it was again, that infinitesimal thrill that shuddered through her when he smiled at her.

'Hello! You got my letter, I see.'

'Indeed, I did.' Her tan gloves felt tight on her fingers and across the broad span of her hands and she resisted the nervous urge to press her straw hat more firmly to her head.

'You look very well,' he said.

'That's very kind,' Cora replied. 'As do you.' William wore a brown suit and a dapper trilby hat.

There was something lingering between them that rendered them both mute. Cora seemed to have forgotten how to make conversation.

'Aren't we lucky with the weather?' she said, finally.

They turned their faces to the pale blue spring sky. A warmish breeze stirred and striations of clouds in the south were strung for miles and miles like fairy floss.

'We are,' William replied. 'A perfect day for a walk, I think.'

As they strolled the gravel drive of Harefield Park towards Rickmansworth Road, Cora and William fell into a matching stride, chatting about this patient and that. How busy the operating theatre had been. The boys who'd come and gone so fast their faces and names and general health were a blur to both of them. The conversation flowed as they walked. On the south side, they passed the chapel and dispensary, the first wards that had been constructed earlier that year, and the canteen and recreation hall—new buildings as alien to the historic estate as motorised ambulances and electric light. At the huge oak tree, they turned onto the main road and headed into the village.

They found an easy path along the roadway, a track sheltered by tall birches that waved their long bare limbs as Cora and William walked by. They passed farmlands filled with elms and oaks. To the west, a small river flowed through meadows fringed with willow trees, which created little pockets of shade and havens in which children might play hide and seek. Pastures had been sown to provide hay, and in the distance horses were hard at work in the fields, the occasional whistle from a farmer punctuating the sound of the breeze through the birches. They passed the market gardens and orchards that provided the food for the hospital, and as the village came into view, Cora had to stop to take in the beauty of it.

'Is everything all right?' William reached a hand to her forearm. 'We can stop on the bench by the bridge up ahead if you're tiring.'

Cora met his concerned eyes and wanted to laugh at the idea that a splendid walk through nature this beautiful would tire her. Wards full of injured men tired her. Funerals depleted her. The war had exhausted her. But this had energised her.

'It's so beautiful, don't you think?'

The village was a romantic rural idyll. At the spot where two soaring cedars reached their limbs into the sky and almost met overhead, three little girls carrying wicker baskets stopped to smile at Cora, before setting their bounty to rest on top of a brick wall.

Past the trees, the windows of Goddards' family butcher shop were obscured by hanging joints and lamb carcasses, and open tables full of chops and sausages and steak at nine pence a pound. Cora had counted three churches on the journey, a school at the end of the main street and two pubs. A doctor's surgery with two names inscribed on the brass plaque near the bell by the front door, Bishop's bootmaker, a chemist and a grocer. The confectioner's window was filled with tins of biscuits and golden fruitcakes. When they reached the Harefield Post Office, they stopped to take a considered look.

'So this is where all the letters from Australia arrive,' Cora said.

'I suppose they do.' William sounded like he wasn't paying much attention. She felt his intense gaze on her.

She turned to him and nodded to the shop window. Lord Kitchener's face and enormous moustache stared back at them, his pointing index finger so large it seemed to be reaching right out of the poster and poking Cora in the chest.

'"Join your country's army,"' William quoted. '"God save the King."' He let out a short blast of a sigh. 'Get shot by a Jerry. See the delights of a muddy trench. Come to Harefield hospital where the doctors are bloody exhausted and the nurses are top notch.'

'And bloody exhausted too,' Cora said and William laughed cheerily.

When they stopped in front of the Cricketers, William announced rather superfluously, 'Here we are then.'

The building looked to be older than the manor house at Harefield Park. Its walls were daubed white and in the roof a dormer window had been thrown open in the warmth of the afternoon. Three upstairs window boxes were filled with bright red geraniums, and next to the pub two whickering horses were tethered in a stable. Painted advertisements for Wellers Celebrated Pale Ales and Amersham Ales decorated its walls, and large black plaster letters above the main entrance boasted that luncheons, dinners and teas were available inside.

Once they were settled at a table and William had ordered drinks and menus for them both, Cora slipped off her gloves and stretched out her fingers over and over. With two fingers, she rubbed her opposite palm in short strokes.

William reached across and went to take her hand in his but pulled himself up. 'May I?'

Cora nodded.

He pressed a thumb into her palm and massaged the muscles above her wrist. 'You've been having pain in your hand?'

She didn't feel the need to pretend it didn't hurt and she didn't feel the need to take her hand from his in a display of decorum lest anyone was watching. 'It's ached terribly the past week.'

His gaze moved to her face. His earnest expression encouraged her to continue.

'I'm not sure exactly what I've done.' She shrugged her shoulders. 'Those who've lost fingers or hands or arms need help to sit up and that means reaching under their armpits and pulling them forward. Multiple times a day. And I've drawn so much blood, cramped my fingers around so many syringes, that sometimes both my hands feel numb.' She exhaled. His touch was soft now and his thumb was warm.

'Does your back ache? Your elbows? Your shoulders?'

'I'm a nurse,' she sighed. 'There are parts of me that always ache. And I think I've aged ten years in the past ten months.'

'I beg to differ. You've not changed one bit since the first time we met.'

William lowered her hand to the table, as gently as if it belonged to a dying patient. His gesture had been simple but intimate. How openly and without conscious thought he'd held her hand. Cora lowered her gaze to the table and studied the silver salt and pepper shakers that sat on top of a lace doily like plump toddlers.

A waitress arrived with bread and William quickly chose lamb's fry with bacon, while Cora settled for vegetable soup and sandwiches. William lathered butter, as thick as jam, on a piece of bread, took an enormous bite and smiled a satisfied smile.

'If I have to live on bread and butter the rest of my life, I'll die a happy man.'

'It's only bread and butter. A workingman's meal. Surely you're used to much finer things?'

'I survived months and months on Red Cross rations, Cora. Ideal Milk. Tins of coffee au lait and nothing but Huntley and Palmer biscuits. If we had soup, it came from dirty water and a dehydrated cube of god knows what. And Maconochie's meat and vegetable stew. I'm convinced it was made entirely of gravy and lumps of congealed flour. And bully beef.' He shuddered dramatically. 'Ever had it?'

'On the boat over to England,' Cora remembered. 'It was to beef what mutton is to lamb, if I remember correctly.'

'Ah yes. And those army biscuits, which I swear were created by dentists to drum up more business. Hard as rocks. Terrible, half-cooked porridge, prunes to make you regular and rice to bind you up. I didn't see bread, butter or even margarine the whole time I was in Egypt.'

'What else did you crave when you were out there?' Cora asked.

He considered her question. 'The silence. I miss the quiet.'

Cora thought about the places at the hospital in which she found her peace. On night shift in the ward, when the boys were asleep and their moaning and sobbing had ceased, just before one or more of them began talking and shouting in their sleep about the Turks. And then, in her bed, whatever time of day or night that was, in those precious moments just before she drifted into half sleep, when thoughts of the day, as crackling and unpredictable as sparks of electricity, seemed to finally stop flashing and flaring behind her eyes. In that moment, when her limbs became heavy and her mind was slipping away, she forgot everything and everyone and succumbed.

'I know what you mean,' she finally replied.

William reached for the pack of cigarettes in the inside pocket of his jacket and Cora waited while he lit one with jittery fingers. He took a long drag, filled his lungs with the smoke and exhaled it into the air above him. She watched it rise until it hit the long dark-stained beams crossing the ceiling.

'We don't get much quiet these days, do we? But we make do. I love my spot by the lakes but it's been too damned cold to sit out there the past few months.' He frowned for a moment and then recovered, finding a smile. 'What about you? What do you miss most, Cora?'

She pressed her back to the chair, settled her hands in her lap. 'The smell of gum trees. The singing of rainbow lorikeets and magpies. I miss my family and hearing about their adventures at the end of every day.'

'Your family?'

'My parents and two sisters.'

'Older or younger?'

'I'm the eldest. Then Eve, and Grace is the youngest. And your family, William?' She'd been curious to know. 'Do they write often? Are they as disappointed in you as mine must be at my failure as a correspondent? I don't think they understand what it's like here.'

He stubbed out his cigarette in the glass ashtray on the table. 'My mother writes. Dr Kent Senior—my father—is working with veterans in Melbourne and my three younger brothers are all in practice or in training. Medicine is in the

Kent blood, you see. Being the oldest, I was the one assigned to do the family proud and serve the King.'

Their lunch arrived and they thanked the waitress as she set their plates on the table. Cora took advantage of the pause to direct the discussion. 'You promised to tell me one day about Egypt.'

'I did?'

'What was it like?'

He slowly met her eyes, his fork paused in mid-air. 'Hot.'

'That's not what I meant, exactly.'

'When I managed to scrounge a day off, I saw the pyramids and the Sphinx. I lunched at Groppi's Confiserie in Cairo, just near Tahrir Square, where I found the most delicious Swiss patisseries. Have you ever tasted Turkish Delight, Cora?'

'Can't say I have.'

'There were French and Swiss wines and Egyptian dates.' He glanced around the pub ruefully. 'What a pity that army food—or the Cricketers' fine cuisine—isn't more like it.'

'It's perfectly fine,' she chided playfully. 'On our way over to England, we stopped in Cape Town, but only for a day. How lucky you were to see Egypt. I've always thought it would be fascinating.'

'It was.'

'What was it like, treating the boys direct from the front lines?'

William suddenly became very interested in his lamb's fry. 'You don't want to hear about that, Cora. It's a lovely day. The sun is shining, at last. The lamb's fry is … edible. Let's talk about something else. How is your soup?'

She wouldn't be brushed off. 'I want to learn, you know.'

'You seem quite accomplished to me.'

Cora glanced around, careful that she not be overheard by any of the other diners, and leant in. 'I've seen the injuries, William. I have so many questions that it's not really my place to ask on the ward or in theatre. I know I'll be told it's not my place to know. And I find that infuriating.'

William continued to eat in silence. Cora waited for him to respond and when he didn't, she finished her sandwiches and washed them down with her lukewarm tea. She wasn't about to give up so she tried a different tack, hoping it might spark his interest.

'Harefield Park has a famous connection to medicine, you know.'

He raised an eyebrow. 'How so?'

'I'm supposing you've heard of *The Lancet*?'

'The medical journal? Of course.'

'The founder of that very journal, Dr Thomas Wakley, lived at Harefield Park for more than ten years from 1845. He was quite a man from what I've read.'

The tension in William's shoulders eased and his eyes brightened. 'Indeed. A peerless surgeon and a reformer. He had no truck with corruption and pushed for more doctors to use evidence when they made decisions for their patients. And he called out the incompetent, the ignorant or the idle among his colleagues. You can imagine how well that went down.'

When he saw Cora's smile, he smiled back. 'You can't grow up in a family of doctors and not know about Wakley. On top of everything else, he campaigned for the abolition of slavery. Quite the radical for his time.'

'How marvellous to think he may have walked the same groves as we have today.'

William sighed and smiled. 'You are rather clever, aren't you?'

'I like to think so.' Cora smiled back at him.

'Let's go.' He set his cutlery across his plate. 'I'll tell you everything you want to know on the walk back to the hospital.'

'Thank you.'

'Once we've had dessert, that is.'

Chapter Twenty-Nine

2 April 1916

'I'm sure you'll find the French lessons very useful, Private Mott.'

Jessie had just finished sweeping and Bert had followed her as she set the broom in the cupboard at the rear of the ward.

'Useful? You mean for when I go back to France?'

'Yes, of course,' she replied. 'Won't it be handy to have a few phrases in the local lingo so you can talk to the French? And besides, I need to mop the floor and the fewer of you there are still here, the better. Go on. Off to French,' Jessie commanded, and if she'd still had the broom in her hands she would have shooed him away as if he were a flock of chickens. 'You don't want you to be late.'

'I know all the French I need,' Bert replied cheerily. He crossed his arms and leant against the wall by the nurses' desk.

'You do?'

'I'll show you. *Alley*. That means go.'

'Doesn't sound French,' Jessie replied.

'Listen and learn, Miss Chester. *Alleyman* ... that's how the French say German.'

'Really?' Jessie had never learnt French or any other language at the village school. She took Bert at his word. 'Tell me something else.'

'*O'vwah.* That's goodbye.'

'O'vwah,' Jessie repeated. It sounded quite sophisticated.

'And *bon*? That means good. So they say *bon chance* for good luck. *Bonjour* for good day and *bonsoir* for good evening.'

'I think you might be right. You might not need French lessons, after all, Private.'

Bert smiled, warm and wide, and something felt tight in Jessie's chest. How did he manage to do that? To make her feel embarrassed and excited all at once?

'You could escort me over to the mess if you'd like,' Bert said. 'Just to make sure this leg of mine doesn't give out on me.'

Jessie scoffed. 'You don't seem to be having any trouble walking these days. You must be nearly fully recovered.'

'Almost,' he grinned.

Jessie wasn't supposed to have a favourite and she would never have admitted it, but when she arrived at the hospital she always hoped she might see Bert. His recovery had been slow and steady, and as the days and weeks passed, she had found herself growing fonder and fonder of him, this larrikin Australian with the blue eyes and the cheeky smile. Something seemed to bubble inside her from deep down when he was near and despite all the hard work, despite the lifting and the lugging and the fetching and the cleaning and the scrubbing, there was nowhere on earth she would rather have been than in a ward with him in it. She loved being there when he woke, his sleepy eyes blinking into an awareness of where he was and then who was leaning over his bed to welcome him to another day.

'Well, hello there, Miss Chester.' They were his first words when he saw her, a glint in his eye and a softness in his tone that was absent in the other patients' greetings.

'And hello to you, Private Mott. Are you quite rested?'

'All the better for seeing you.'

His attentions made the hard work bearable. He made it possible to cope with the sadness of some of the patients and the agony of the constant goodbyes to those who were returning to the front, or those who left on stretchers in their blue flannel pyjamas to make the journey to Plymouth for the long voyage home.

When he thanked her, there was something behind his words that she didn't hear in the other patients' whispered thank-yous. It was a tenderness that was unfamiliar and exhilarating and addictive.

Jessie propped her fists on her hips. 'So are you going, Private?'

'Please. My name's Bert.'

'Short for Albert?'

'I was named for my grandad. Albert Reginald Mott.'

'What a lovely name,' Jessie said. 'And I'm Jessie.'

'Jessie,' he replied. 'You a local?'

'Yes,' she nodded. 'Born and bred in the village. Went to school here. I work here. Nothing quite so fancy as that place on the river where you were born.'

'You remember that?' Bert asked and his cheeks flushed.

Jessie felt the heat rise in her own. 'Of course I do. You talked about swinging from a rope and jumping into the river. And your mother's Christmas pudding.'

'Murray Bridge. That's the name of the place. It's a little town on the river in South Australia. Struth, I miss it. I know the lay of the land there like the back of my hand. Where the banks overflow when the flood waters come down from New South Wales and Victoria. Where the river shrinks when we're hit by drought, it gets so narrow you can walk across to the other side and not get your chin wet. The Murray twists and turns, you see, snakes and loops around and I know all the places to pitch a swag so no one could ever find you. That's what I want to do when I get home. Ditch the khaki and take off with a swag. Camp by the river for as long as I want. Maybe weeks. Fish for perch and callop and cook them over an open fire. And swim in the river. I miss that. Every summer when I was a kid. My mum and dad called me a water rat.'

Jessie listened, spellbound.

'And it's so hot in the summer you could fry an egg on a piece of tin if you left it out in the sun long enough. Bloody hell, I miss the sun. No offence, but the English summer doesn't hold a candle to Australia's.'

Jessie imagined Bert swimming in the river, his skin tanned and brown, water dripping from each limb. She imagined his lovely face held to the sky, the sun drying it and tousling his hair.

'It sounds marvellous.'

'It is.' He paused. 'Listen, Jessie. I'll make you a deal. Tonight there's going to be a moving picture show right here in the ward. If I go to French lessons and get out of your hair, will you come and watch the film with me? And the other lads, you know. It's Charlie Chaplin.'

Jessie couldn't remember the last time she'd been to the cinema. Sitting in the ward with Bert might be the closest thing to a night out she would have for some time. She wasn't expected at home at any particular time. Win had supported her decision to volunteer and knew that Jessie would do what needed to be done with no eye on any clock.

'I'd love to.'

'Bonza,' Bert exclaimed.

'Lights out!'

In the aisle between the rows of beds in the ward, a film projector sat on a wooden trolley and whirred as its twin reels slowly cranked and began turning. The clicking of the machine sounded like a swarm of crickets, Jessie thought, or a plague of locusts. A bed sheet pegged to a ceiling truss was a makeshift screen and the moment the first image appeared—two little boys pushing a go-kart, a scruffy dog racing alongside them down a crowded street—rousing whoops rocked the wooden beams.

The flickering light began casting shadows and creating mirages around the ward. It looked like lightning without the thunder and Jessie was transfixed by it. How did images on that tiny film become so large in the air? She shifted her gaze to Bert, sitting propped up on his bed, extra pillows at his back. His eyes were full of wonder too, and, in the dark, the flickering images were reflected in his eyes. She could see a new world in them.

The entertainment committee had organised the screening and they'd supplied little gift baskets for the patients, filled with Cadbury's chocolate and barley sugar wrapped in cellophane. Jessie and another volunteer had made a pot of hot chocolate and both fires on the ward warmed the room.

'Jessie?' Bert whispered as he offered her a square of chocolate.

'Oh, no, I can't.' She held up a hand. 'It's a treat just for you, Bert, to help you regain your strength.'

He winked and his smile was warm. 'Go on. If it's against the rules, I won't tell anyone. Your secret will be safe with me.'

Jessie glanced around. All eyes were on the screen. She cheekily snatched the chocolate from Bert's fingers and popped it in her mouth. It melted luxuriously on her tongue and she decided nothing had ever tasted so good. She'd eaten chocolate before. She'd lost count of how many times. But not like this, in the dark with a young man. How could it possibly make chocolate taste sweeter?

'He's a funny little fellow, isn't he?' Jessie whispered.

'Charlie Chaplin, you mean?'

Jessie nodded. 'His trousers are too short. His shoes are way too big. And,' she laughed, 'he has a funny little moustache.'

'He just struck a match on his strides!' one of the patients called out in the dark.

'Stop walking on the racetrack, you idiot!'

'Watch out, Charlie, you're gonna get bowled over!'

The men's laughter competed with the clicking of the projector and every time the racing automobiles came within inches of knocking over the little tramp, the men roared.

Jessie's mind wandered as she watched the black-and-white images flickering on the hanging bedsheet. Imagine if she was in a real picture palace, sitting with Bert. Perhaps he might be wearing a suit and tie, not a khaki uniform or blue pyjamas. His hat would be in his lap and his shoulder might be pressed up against hers. Or perhaps they might be holding hands in the freedom of the darkness. There would be no need for a chaperone—the war had put an end to that formality—and she wondered if, in the anonymity of the dark, he might reach for her hand.

She had never held hands with a man who wasn't her father or her brother. She had never been kissed, either. Those adventures of young womanhood had passed her by. And yet ... there she was, sitting with Bert in the dark, a square of chocolate melting in her mouth and the sweet scent of hot chocolate on his bedside table.

On the screen, the tramp was oblivious to the danger all around him. In the ward, the men—for six minutes and twenty-one seconds—were too.

When the projector's reels stopped cranking, the men burst into applause and the projectionist bowed. Someone flicked on the lights and everyone blinked at the brightness.

Jessie got to her feet and collected the chocolate wrappers from Bert's bed, sweeping them with one hand into the other. As she did, Bert reached for her fingers and gripped his around hers.

'I've got news, Jessie.'

She stilled.

'I saw the doc today, after French. He says I'm good to go. One more week and I'll be shipped back to France.' As he told her, his quavering voice gave him away. He was trying desperately to put on a brave face but his bottom lip was betraying him, too.

Jessie gripped his hand with both of hers and held tight. 'That's wonderful news, Bert. I'm so glad for you that you've recovered. You'll be back with your comrades before you know it. Taking it to the Jerries, isn't that what you said?'

'Yep. The Jerries.'

She released his hand from hers. 'It's time for bed. If you're to build up your strength, you'll need to get as much sleep as you can. I'll be seeing you, Bert.'

He managed a thin smile and Jessie turned quickly, overwhelmed with the need to scurry away home.

'Jessie?'

She took in a deep breath and looked back over her shoulder.

'Will you come back and see me before I leave? One last time?'

'How could I not?' she said. 'I owe you some chocolate.'

Chapter Thirty

6 April 1916

The sound of raucous laughter from inside the mess made Cora laugh too. She pressed her ear to the gap between the double doors and held a finger to her lips to silence the others.

'We are not supposed to be here,' Fiona said with a scowl, but Cora noted she was listening in just as intently.

Leonora giggled and clapped a hand over her mouth when Gertie elbowed her.

'It's "the talk", isn't it?' Leonora asked Cora.

'I assume so. It's the only time the men are all called together like this.'

'Captain Kent didn't give you a special preview?' Leonora grinned, one eyebrow lifting archly towards her hairline.

Cora sighed and rolled her eyes. 'You are incorrigible, Leonora. And no, he didn't.'

'Sshh,' Gertie whispered, a finger to her lips. The sounds from inside the mess settled. Chairs scraped on the wooden floor. There was an order to hush and a pair of heavy boots struck the wooden floorboards in a determined stride. A waft of tobacco reached the nurses and Fiona silenced an imminent sneeze by pinching her nose.

'Sorry,' she whispered with watery eyes.

A booming voice from inside the mess commanded, 'Order', and the men were finally quiet. The women dared not breathe. They weren't supposed to be anywhere near the mess that afternoon. The subject of the captain's lecture was for soldiers only.

'Diggers,' he began. Cora knew the timbre of his voice and felt it seep deep inside her, warming her, exciting her.

'There are so many new men here at Harefield hospital that I find myself having to deliver this lecture—this warning—again. Many of you, I know, have leave this coming weekend and in the weekends to come. The delights of London no doubt await you. The kind people of Harefield village have been good enough to arrange motor rides for some of you and I'm sure you'll enjoy yourselves. I can vouch for the Anzac Club on Horseferry Road, where you'll get a warm welcome and an afternoon tea served by Australian women volunteers.'

A wolf-whistle pierced the air and there was more cheering. Cora knew there would be more things on the boys' minds than cups of tea.

'You'll also run into many other Australians on Victoria Street and the Strand if you're looking for mates from home. But I feel it's safe to say that you're not heading into old London town to shop at Harrods or see Shakespeare at the Old Vic.'

'What light from yonder window breaks,' someone yelled out and laughter pealed through the mess.

'Now, now. It's the other temptations I'm here to warn you about. A day and a night in London might be just what you need to lift your spirits but I'm compelled by the AIF to tell you about what and whom you might encounter on your adventures.'

'It *is* the talk,' Leonora whispered and pushed the swinging door just slightly more ajar. Was this how the men behaved when they believed there were no feminine ears nearby, Cora thought to herself. The kind boys who called her 'Sister' and 'Australia' and blessed her when she ministered to them when they were cocooned in that feminine environment had become changed men in the mess, surrounded by other men. It was as if they had emerged to spread their wings in all their ferocious masculinity. She hadn't had brothers growing up, had never been exposed to this side of male behaviour. It was a reminder that they were more than patients in pyjamas, more than their pain and their injuries. Before the war, they had been alive and vital and young, full of life's passions and with a thirst for thrilling adventures that involved women, not killing Germans and Turks.

William's voice grew louder. 'Men, I'm to remind you that despite what you might have heard, or been told—'

Leonora leant forward and pushed Cora into the door just enough so it opened and she found herself half-in, half-out without even setting a black-laced boot into the room. She froze. Hundreds of men were seated with their backs to her, their hair neatly combed, dressed in their pale blue pyjamas and a rainbow hue of dressing gowns sent from volunteers at home in a patchwork of fabrics; boys short and tall, brown hair and blond and red, all hanging on William's every word.

He stood on the stage in a civilian suit, not his army uniform or the whites he wore in theatre. He looked as if he might be heading somewhere for afternoon tea and scones.

Had her heard her breath? His eyes darted to hers and for a moment—a moment only they shared—he paused. It was only as long as it took him to swallow. His expression changed. His medical mask slipped. In that infinitesimal moment she saw not a man of medicine, but a man, and he must have felt it too, for his mouth softened and he lifted a hand, and when she thought he might be about to wave at her, he raked it over his hair instead.

Cora knew she should have stepped back and closed the door. She should have pretended she wasn't listening to his lecture that was intended for men's ears only. But she had become impatient with the rules of what she should and shouldn't do and had no desire to pander to others' expectations and rules.

William cleared his throat. His eyes were glued to hers. 'Despite what you've heard or what you might have convinced yourself, it is not harmful to one's physical well-being to refrain from indulging in sexual intercourse.'

'Speak for yourself, doc!' The interjection was met with more whistles and cheers.

William looked about the room, waited for the raucous laughter to subside. His gaze returned to Cora's and she felt held by it, unable to move and unable to shake the feeling that his words were advice to her, to them both.

'Physically, there is no necessity for it and one's good health is not injured by avoiding sexual intercourse. It is purely your imagination, your constant thoughts of sexual matters that create in you the need for sexual gratification. The answer to this? Don't be a slave to unhealthy literature, obscene pictures or postcards. Avoid them at all costs.'

'Bloody hell, doc. All this talk of obscene pictures and postcards isn't helping!'

Cora didn't need unhealthy literature or pictures or postcards. All she needed was a look, a smile, the graze of a shoulder, the brush of his fingers against hers, a note in his curlicue handwriting, like *Dear Cora* when he'd invited her to lunch. A cup of tea in the mess. A glance across the operating theatre. There had been so many moments since they'd lunched together. She had found herself living from one to the next.

What must he think of her desires, those that rose up each time she saw him in theatre, in the queue at the mess, across the body of a suffering soldier, those rare snatches of time they'd shared at their favourite place by the lake? There hadn't been time for another lunch as they hadn't had days off together in months but that didn't mean the ache and longing to be near him had subsided. Did he really believe her hunger to be near him was unnatural too?

'Enough with the backchat, diggers. If you don't listen to my advice and, importantly, take it, you will suffer great and harsh penalties with venereal disease. If you avail yourself of the offerings of one of the streetwalkers of Leicester Square, Horseferry Road in Waterloo or the streets around the Strand—'

'Wait on, cobber. Let me write that down!'

'—you'll be taking a souvenir back home that you'll rather have left right here in old Blighty. Syphilis, gonorrhoea and warts. All just as bad as each other. And it's not just the streetwalkers who are nearly all infected with disease. Other women, the so-called amateurs, are just as dangerous as the regular prostitute, no matter how clean they might look.'

William paused and looked down at his notes. 'So, what are the risks to you?'

She had asked herself that question during many a long, restless, English night. What might have seemed like unconquerable risks a lifetime ago, half a world away, when the world was as it had always been, now seemed like relics of the past that she had no material or social links with. Her sisters, Eve and Grace, might still be a part of that world, in which women weren't supposed to entertain thoughts that might strike them down, but here, in among the wounded detritus of war, she saw no God, saw no social order that made any sense any more.

She was flotsam, just as each of these boys were, cast adrift by those who made decisions without consulting them, compelled to enact orders that in real life would be unthinkable. And that's why the unthinkable might now be considered the new normal. When the past is history and the future is unknowable, who makes the rules for life right now, in this moment, the unknowable minute-by-minute present? Was it up to Cora to make the rules for herself?

'If you pick up the clap, you'll have to report to me at once. If it's syphilis, you'll be treated for eight days, give or take, with daily injections of silver, arsenic and mercury. Treating gonorrhoea can take six weeks. We'll have to wash out your old fella with a douche and apply lotions and ointments in places that will sting like a bastard. You'll have your pay docked for all those days you're being treated. Any pay allotted to your family back home, your mother, your wife, your sweetheart, will be forfeited and it'll be marked in your pay book.'

Cora had to pretend she hadn't heard the curse words uttered like an echo all around the mess.

'Think about that when you've had a skinful up in London and you feel like blowing off some steam. It will come as no surprise to you that things aren't going as well as anyone would like with this war. Many of you are on the road to recovery and will be back with your units before long. We can't afford to lose a man from a disease that is preventable. For those of you recuperating here before you head home, don't take home a souvenir that will put the health and happiness of Australian womanhood and the welfare and happiness of the Commonwealth at risk.'

At this, there were no cheers or whoops. A solemn silence descended over the men.

William read from the piece of paper in his shaking hands. 'In closing, keep your bodies and minds pure, for venereal disease is the great destroyer of national and individual happiness.' He looked up and pocketed his notes. 'But if you are unable to control these urges, for God's sake, make use of the prophylactic outfits you're supplied. Wash yourself before and after intercourse, buy some condoms, and, for pity's sake, use them. And come and see me as soon as you see any sign of infection. Look out for sores on your privates. Any discharge from your penis. If it stings when you piss. If something itches, remember: you're not on the battlefield now and it won't be lice. Get it treated. Sergeant Willcox here is going to pass out these handy cards full of useful information, including the addresses of some of the Early Treatment Centres. Go and see them if you should find yourself afflicted while you're on furlough. Yes, soldier?'

Cora couldn't make out the mumbled question.

'Yes, that's it. The Blue Light clinics. If you see a building with a blue light shining, you can go in there any time of night and get your treatment started, no questions asked. Anything else? Oh, one more thing. If you do show up with the clap, some of my more generous medical colleagues might have no ethical problem describing your symptoms as "rheumatism". Don't test me. Don't expose yourselves in the first place. Righto. Dismissed.'

At the first scrape of a chair, Cora stepped back and the door to that world of men and sexual intercourse slammed shut.

The heads of two hundred soldiers turned to look over their shoulders as the nurses scurried away from the doors of the mess like mice who'd heard the twitch of a cat's whisker.

As they returned to the ward, safely ahead of the men who were smoking and dawdling on the lawn by the main house or heading off to craft lessons or French instruction, Cora linked an arm through Gertie's as they strode purposefully along the wooden walkway.

'Tell me, Gertie,' Cora said. 'When has it ever been a successful strategy to convince people to avoid what they so desperately desire by trying to frighten the life out of them?'

Gertie shrugged. 'If simply telling men and women to stay away from each other had ever worked, the world would have ended with Adam and Eve.'

Cora laughed. 'And who are we to judge the men, anyway? They're in the prime of their lives twelve thousand miles from home. Away from loved ones. From their wives and sweethearts. They carry with them the knowledge that they could be blown to bits at any moment. They've seen it happen to their comrades. Who can blame them for wanting to obliterate the past and forget the future?'

'And as for the women who sell themselves?' Gertie asked. 'Might they be desperate too in an entirely different way? I hardly picture them as the whores of Babylon that the top brass like your captain portrays them. His lecture sounded like a whole lot of ...' she looked about to ensure no one was listening in, '... poppycock.'

Cora snorted with laughter.

'I thought it rather apt for that lecture, I'm sorry to say. I'm sure he hardly believed a word of it. There's only a market for the services they provide if men want sex,' Gertie said. 'As if these temptresses are luring these young, innocent soldiers into sin. I don't believe the boys need convincing. Have you noticed the way some of them look at us nurses? For every boy who wishes we were their mother, there are five who wish we were something else. I've lost count of the marriage proposals I've had. Or other proposals.' She rolled her eyes.

'And I've lost count of the times their hands have accidentally groped my bottom or my breasts.'

'I know. Usually when I'm leaning over their beds to tuck them in or check on a bandage.'

'I'm quite accustomed now to the sight of an erect penis,' Cora added matter-of-factly. 'Goodness, when did that happen? If my mother were to hear that, she'd die of fright. We weren't supposed to even think they existed, much less say the word out loud.'

'Such prudishness,' Gertie said. 'Imagine all the misery and suffering we might have spared people if we were simply honest enough to say, generations ago, that the parasites that cause venereal disease are spread by sexual intercourse. Millions might have been spared the consequences. All that disease. Blindness. Suffering. If only we were honest about so many things.'

Cora came to a slow stop.

Gertie stopped and asked, 'What is it?'

'Can I ask. Have you ever …?'

'You mean intercourse?'

Cora nodded. 'Yes. Have you?'

Gertie squared her shoulders. 'Once and it was entirely underwhelming. I was twenty-two years old and he was the boy next door. Literally. I found the warm water douche afterwards more pleasurable than the act itself.'

Cora laughed at Gertie's wink.

'And since then, I've seen more genitals wrapped in white sheets in a hospital bed than I ever have in the privacy of my own life. Both those in full working order and some barely recognisable after what shrapnel has done to them. Can't say they've moved me to feel anything, actually. And anyway, if I married, I'd have to give up the career I love, so it's something I've learnt to live without.' Gertie looked quizzically at Cora. 'Have you ever …?

'No.' Cora felt knocked off her feet by a sudden rush of longing for William.

'Is that something you're planning to do something about?'

Cora thought about it. 'Weren't we always reminded how wrong and dangerous and immoral it was to indulge in that kind of thing outside of marriage? I'm not so sure now. Is it so wrong to seek comfort in the arms of another? The men certainly seem to be.' She sighed. 'And, by the way, he's not my Captain Kent, if you must know.'

'Funny how your thoughts went straight to him during a discussion about sexual intercourse.'

When Cora opened her mouth to object, Gertie cut her off. 'Oh, Cora. I'm not blind. I only wonder if he will be able to practice what he preaches when it comes to you.'

Over dinner, Captain Kent's lecture was all the nurses could talk about.

'Imagine recommending the men buy … I can't even say the word.' Fiona's spoon clattered on the table as she grasped her hands together in her lap. She dipped her chin. Was she praying?

'Condoms, Fiona? Is that the word you're grasping for?' Gertie asked matter-of-factly as she tipped her soup spoon politely towards her lips, waiting for the steam to settle on the ox tongue soup.

'Pass the bread, please, Gertie?' Leonora reached an arm across the table.

'Surely we should be entreating the men to refrain. I heard the captain's warnings as clearly as you all did. The ravages of syphilis and gonorrhoea have been known to civilisations for centuries.' Fiona's pinched lips and frown revealed as much about her thoughts on the subject as her words. 'If prophylactic devices are made available to the soldiers, it will only encourage more illicit intercourse, not less. And what will they do once they've learnt such practises? They'll simply carry on that behaviour when they return home to Australia. And what will their wives have to cope with then? The men will be so used to prostitutes and we will have been part of convincing them it's permitted. It *can't* be permitted. It's a sin in God's eyes.'

'But Fiona,' Leonora said, laying a hand on Fiona's arm. 'I dare say it happened before the war and will happen when this is all over. We all know a woman who got into trouble, who was pilloried and cast out, their reputation ruined, disowned by their families. And we all know a child who was born on the wrong side of the blanket.'

'With no damage at all to the man's reputation,' Cora added. 'And everything to the woman's and child's.'

'If women like that even know who the man is,' Fiona spat.

'Fiona,' Cora said quietly. 'That's a little unkind. You're casting all women as the sinners. Can men not be sinners, too?'

'I'm not naive, Cora. But according to God, it's not acceptable and never has been. "Thou shalt not commit adultery." It's in the Holy Book.'

Leonora scoffed. 'It's only adultery if two people are married to others and—'

'I'm allowed to have my beliefs, Leonora,' Fiona insisted. 'And according to me and millions of other God-fearing people all over the world, those connections outside of marriage are a sin. Congress between a man and a woman should be for the purposes of procreation, to bring children into the world, not to satisfy carnal lust. Men must fight against their natural urges and do what's best for the good of their family and we must do all we can to help them in that fight. Who are we if all the things we believed in, all the lessons we learnt about what is good and what is right, are cast by the wayside because of the war? What are we fighting for if not to preserve the things we hold most dear?'

Cora and Gertie exchanged glances.

Leonora rested her elbows on the table and leant forward. 'I grew up going to church every Sunday, morning and night. My mother still goes to the cathedral every morning. She was quite pleased, I'm sure, when the black sheep of the family sailed off over the seas. She probably said good riddance on the dock as she prayed for my soul.'

'I know you like to exaggerate, Leonora,' Fiona said. 'But speaking so ill of your mother ...'

'This is no exaggeration. She doesn't have to be embarrassed by me and my wayward behaviour now that I'm twelve thousand miles away.'

'Why on earth would she be embarrassed by you?' Cora asked.

'I'm too outspoken. Too opinionated. Too loud. Too flirtatious.' Leonora's smile was wobbly, as if at any moment she might cry instead. 'She always told me I didn't know my place. My trouble was that I knew it. I just didn't want to be there. And now I'm engaged.'

'You still haven't told your parents?' Gertie asked kindly.

Leonora shook her head.

'Well,' Cora said, as she pushed her plate of toast crumbs to the centre of the long trestle table and stood. 'Your place is here, with us. Seeing to injured Australians. And I believe they're waiting for us right now.'

Chapter Thirty-One

10 April 1916

Jessie ran almost all the way from the village to the hospital on the day Private Bert Mott was to go back to the war.

She didn't care who thought it inappropriate that she was running and not politely sauntering. So be it if Mrs Pritchard were to see her and tut-tut about the behaviour of girls these days, chasing after soldiers. And if her skirts flew up and a man were to see her stockings? She didn't care a jot.

Her only concern was that she arrive in time to see Bert before he left. She'd had three fittings that morning with her mother, during which their client Mrs Beard had changed her mind four times on the colour of the cotton she favoured for her four little girls' new summer dresses. Jessie had been restless but had crushed every urge to be impolite to the woman and, once Mrs Beard and the girls had stepped onto the street, she had flown around the house tearing off her work apron and searching for her purse.

'I'm going to be late,' she'd cried as she'd dropped to her knees looking under the sewing table. If one of the Beard girls had hidden it as some sort of game, she might ...

'Here it is.' Jessie looked up to see her mother dangling it from a finger above her heard.

'Oh.' Jessie stood and thanked her mother.

'And you'll be needing this.' Win held up Jessie's straw hat. 'It's full sun out there today.' Jessie jammed it on her head and checked the clock on the mantel. She'd quickly kissed her mother's cheek and flown out the door.

In the months she'd been volunteering at the hospital, Jessie had watched hundreds of troop trucks arrive and load and unload their precious cargo. On their busiest day, three hundred men had left in a convoy of army trucks, in ambulances, touring cars and sometimes a motor lorry when there were no other vehicles available. As the soldiers left Harefield, they shouted hearty farewells to the nurses and the doctors; kissed the cheeks of the village ladies who'd served them in the mess, and politely thanked the women who'd hand-picked books for them among the library's vast collection and who'd taught them how to embroider and make tapestries. For the ones returning home to Australia there would be a special train fitted with bunk beds waiting for them at Denham Station to take them down to Plymouth.

The men who were returning to their battalions exhibited, without fail, a raucously cheerful demeanour—standing tall, their legs slightly apart, their arms busy with back slaps and smoking and shaking hands. Their pride in being back in their khaki uniforms, their broad-brimmed hats with one side turned up firmly placed on their heads, was evident in both their broad shoulders and their smiles. They were men again, not cot cases. They'd been patched and stitched like a pair of old trousers and were now neatly washed and pressed. Perhaps there was a relief in sloughing off their status as a patient and at being able to stand alongside their mates once more, to do the job they had been sent to do. Perhaps there wasn't much pride to be felt in having been a patient for months when so many had sacrificed so much in their places. The sheer relief of it puffed out their chests with pride.

Smoke from a hundred cigarettes rose in columns into the air above the crowd of soldiers. Above them, the sun was shining as if God and all the angels were guiding their safe passage.

Jessie stood on tiptoes searching for Bert, her gift held tightly in her hands.

'Jessie!' Bert emerged out of the crowd of soldiers and swept his khaki slouch hat from his head. 'You made it.'

She could barely speak she was so out of breath. 'Just, by the looks of things.'

Behind him, the ivy-covered house whispered to them as the wind rustled its leaves, and all around them trucks and men and kitbags and staff jostled for space.

A troop truck was parked at one end of the circular driveway, its engine still chugging, and men were hopping into the back of it, their uniforms freshly laundered for possibly the last time in months, and the kitbags on their shoulders carrying fresh clothes and toiletries and, most importantly, cigarettes.

'I've only got a minute,' Bert said, looking back over his shoulder. 'We're about to head off. I thought you might have changed your mind or something.'

'Here.' She held out a package wrapped in brown paper and tied with string.

Bert looked dumbfounded and then roused into action and took it from her.

'I'm a woman of my word, Bert.'

He looked confused.

'Chocolates. I promised you chocolates. It's Rowntree's in a special tin. I thought you might find the tin useful when you've eaten what's inside. And I thought … well, I thought you might like some more socks. Autumn will be here before you know it and then it'll be winter. It'll rain in France, there's nothing surer.'

Goodness. Jessie knew she was babbling but she couldn't seem to stop.

Bert's eyes glistened and Jessie felt her cheeks heat. The way he was looking at her right in that moment? No man had ever looked at her in such a way. As if she was precious.

Bert slipped the package under his arm and put his hat back on. 'Thank you. That's bloody marvellous.'

The truck's horn sounded and Jessie almost jumped out of her skin at the sound of it.

'Jessie? You've made my stay here at Harefield … well, something I'll never forget. I'm right as rain thanks to the doctors and nurses. And you.'

Bert handed his kitbag to the soldier behind him and it moved like a pass-the-parcel game into the truck. Someone slapped him on the back and he motioned down to his leg, bouncing on it to show how well-healed he was, as if to say, 'Those Jerries can't keep me down.'

'It was nice to meet you, Bert.' Jessie's stomach quivered and she was suddenly dizzy. His eyes grazed her face, settled on her mouth and lingered there.

She knew in that instant what he wanted to do. And that she wanted him to.

He stepped forward. She looked up at him.

'It's farewell, then,' he said.

'Au revoir,' she whispered, and he laughed.

Without thinking, Jessie reached up on tiptoes, grabbed Bert by the lapels of his uniform and smacked a huge kiss on his left cheek. When she was back on solid ground she wobbled. Bert looked stunned. All around them, soldiers began cheering and whooping. The truck impatiently blasted its horn.

He walked backwards, holding her gaze, until he reached the truck. 'What's your address?' he shouted.

'It's inside the package,' she yelled and waved and waved and waved until her arm ached, until the truck turned out of the grounds and into Rickmansworth Road and took her lovely Bert back to the war.

Chapter Thirty-Two

'Listen to this one, boys:

> *In Berlin there's a Hun called the Kaiser.*
> *Of all devilish schemes the deviser;*
> *Though he wants to get France,*
> *He has no earthly chance,*
> *And he'll soon be an apologiser.'*

Raucous laughter echoed on the ramp outside the ward and as Cora tipped a bucket of dirty water onto the ground off to the side of it, she let herself laugh at the limerick. It was certainly the cleanest one she'd heard for a while and she let the boys have their fun without her admonishment.

She didn't know how they managed to find anything to laugh about but she was so glad they were able to share it and revel in it. She knew the truth of it—that they cried at night when they thought no one else could hear and that their smiles and laughter hid a world of pain—but it was more than pride and shame that kept them so determined to laugh. They took pride in being the most incorrigible larrikin, competed as to who could make the nurses laugh the hardest, played practical jokes on each other that she sometimes had to look away for fear they would lead to more injury than the men were already suffering. They worked hard to distract themselves from their realities of their situations.

'What about this one—' But before the next limerick began, the air was split with a sound that caused hairs to prickle at the back of her neck.

Cora dropped the metal pail and it clattered on the duckboards and rolled off into the dirt below. Were Zeppelins in the skies overheard?

She spun around to face her patients. Shrieks of laughter suddenly burst forth from the doorway of the ward.

What on earth was going on? Cora leant forward, dropping her head to her knees so she didn't hyperventilate. It was the same advice she gave to the boys on the ward who found themselves struggling for breath during a bout of nerves.

'Sorry to scare you, Sister. It's our mascot.'

'Your what?' she demanded. She straightened, her heart still thudding. Four of her patients were gathered in a semi-circle and when she moved closer, they stepped back. She blinked in disbelief and looked up blankly at the laughing and guilty faces.

'What on earth ... how did that get here?' She was face to face with a sulphur-crested cockatoo, its body a mass of white with a spray of lemon yellow feathers on the top of its head like a dancer's fancy headdress. One black eye examined her as it cocked its head sideways. Its worn beak was aged and battered.

The boys found Cora's reaction even more amusing, which made her angrier still.

'How the ...?'

'He's from Gallipoli, Sister. That's where he learnt to screech like that. It sounds just like a Turkish shell, doesn't it, cobber?'

'Oh, for goodness sake ...' she spluttered. 'Just make sure it doesn't come inside or I'll have you down on your hands and knees scrubbing my floor to clean up its droppings.' She wagged a finger at the men and pushed open the door of the ward, her hands shaking, her heart thumping in her chest.

The shock of seeing the bird, cocking its head, staring at her, had more than discombobulated Cora. Just as she sometimes woke in the mornings forgetting where she was, the sight of the bird had for an infinitesimal moment shocked her into a haze of confusion. Cockatoos had swarmed in the gum trees in her street at home, feasting on the blossoms and leaving the evidence of their gluttony all over the footpath and the street in the form of empty gumnuts and shredded leaves.

As she stepped into the silent ward, she looked around at the empty beds in various states of disarray. A waft of cigarette smoke hung in the air.

Where was Jessie? The young volunteer was working in the ward today and a moment before she'd been making beds up with fresh linen.

'Jessie?' Cora called.

There were footsteps and then Jessie appeared at the far end of the ward, by the door to the storeroom.

Even from a distance, Cora knew by the wide, teary eyes and pale expression on Jessie's face that something was wrong.

'What is it?' Cora asked as she approached the young volunteer. 'Don't worry. It was only a bird. A ... a blooming cockatoo.'

Tears streaked Jessie's cheeks. She turned slowly to the open doorway of the storeroom and Cora followed her gaze. A patient was in the corner, his back pressed to the wall. Tucked up into a ball, he was quivering inside his blue pyjamas. His eyes were squeezed shut and his hands balled into fists over his ears. Cora recognised him as one of her shellies. That's what the other men called them, the boys who were suffering shell shock.

'I'll be right back,' she whispered to Jessie, and anger lit a fire inside of her, so intense she almost ran to the front door of the ward and pushed the door open so hard it banged on the frame.

The cockatoo squawked and spread its flapping wings wide. It would have flown away if it wasn't tied by a chain to a little collar around its leg.

The boys looked up at Cora, stunned.

'We've got a shellie in here,' she shouted, and she shocked herself at how ferocious she sounded, a stranger to herself. 'Get rid of that bloody bird, will you?'

Cora stood at the ward's front door and tore at a hangnail with her teeth. She watched as it bled, bright red. Snow White apple red. The blood drizzled into the corners of her nail and underneath it. She stuck it in her mouth, sucked on it, tasting metal and feeling a sting.

She needed a moment to find a path through her racing thoughts to one that made sense. The bird. The screech. The boy. She closed her eyes but she could still see him, her hunched-over patient, the man-child, cowering in the corner as if he was expecting a blow; the ridge of his spine visible through the fabric of his pyjamas; his hair stuck up in spikes and patches of bloody scalp where he'd pulled it out, strands of it between the fingers of his clenched fists.

When Jessie had looked to Cora for guidance, Cora found herself unable to provide it. Her anger had frightened her and stunned her patients. The shame of how she'd talked to them stung. Cora looked down at her nail. Her fingers felt numb, the blood still running red against the white of her calloused fingers. She looked at the blood. She'd seen so much blood. It was as if the hospital ran red with it.

She wished she had taken to cigarettes like every single soldier seemed to have. Perhaps if she smoked, the tobacco might settle the deep-down bone-shaking quivering that was rumbling inside her like a bomb had gone off.

'Sister?' William's voice. He could have been ten miles away and she would still know him. He jogged to her side, his white coat flapping behind him, a stethoscope around his neck bouncing against his chest. 'You sent for me?'

'We've got a shellie,' she said, nodding towards the storeroom. 'He's in a bad way.'

For a moment, his reassuring hand was on her arm. 'I'm here.'

A silence descended. The boys who'd been out with the cockatoo had returned to their beds, suddenly reading letters from home. Others dragged on their cigarettes and looked glumly at Cora. They knew. They'd heard the screaming and she could see by the looks of resignation in their eyes that that were thanking God or whoever they prayed to that they hadn't lost their minds, too.

William and Cora crossed the ward and when they reached the storeroom they looked on at the silent scene before them.

Jessie sat on the floor next to the patient, an arm around him, her knees pulled up tight. His head was on her shoulder and he'd uncovered his ears to listen to the gentle words of comfort she was whispering into his hair. Cora's anger evaporated, replaced with a terrible guilt. She should have sent Jessie to find William. She should have stayed with this young man.

William's calm demeanour was instantly reassuring. 'How's he going there, Miss Chester?'

Jessie looked up at them, her eyes full of tears. 'He's calm now, Captain.'

William approached the boy, knelt down at his side. 'What's your name, soldier?'

'G-Gordon.'

'You look like you need a smoke.'

The boy's doleful eyes turned upwards and Cora tried not to gasp. They were swollen and bloodshot and bloody scratches trailed down his face. She turned to William. Except for the almost imperceptible tightening in his jaw, he remained calm. His only movement was to slip his hands in the pockets of his white coat.

'Sister,' he said, looking to Cora. 'Would you mind fetching us some warm water and a washcloth, please?'

Cora nodded and when she returned a few minutes later, Gordon was on his feet, standing shakily, the wall supporting him on one side and Jessie on the other. Cora went to him, waited until he met her eyes and then gently smoothed the washcloth over his cheeks and his mouth. When his eyes fluttered closed, she washed the blood away, wishing she could wash away his terror as easily as she could remove the blood.

'There you go.'

'Thank you, Sister.'

'It's no trouble at all.'

'I'm still cold,' Gordon said into the middle distance, his gaze focussed on the open door. 'I've got three pairs of socks on, see, and a double pair of gloves and I can't get warm. Are my boots still frozen?'

Cora and William exchanged glances.

'I'll get your coat,' William said. 'Still up for that smoke?'

When Gordon nodded, William held out an arm and the boy took it. Slowly they walked through the ward, Gordon's feet shuffling in his slippers, his whole body shivering.

Cora and Jessie held back.

'You did very well, Jessie.'

Jessie hugged herself tight. 'Oh, Sister. I couldn't think what else to do. He was calling for his mum.'

'They often do,' Cora replied. 'And not just the young ones.'

'I told him it won't be long now and he'll see her again. That she must be so proud that he came all this way from Australia to help protect me and my family. My brother and his fiancée. The whole of Harefield and the whole of England.'

'They're very kind words. That must have given him so much comfort.'

Jessie began to cry. 'I didn't know what else to do.'

And in that moment, Cora didn't know what to do for Jessie either, other than to go to her, wrap her arms around the young woman and give her as much comfort as she could.

Chapter Thirty-Three

3 June 1916

'Three cheers to Matron Gray!'

Staff who were able to be relieved of their duties on the wards and the operating theatres and the stores, and those who were off duty, gathered in the mess to celebrate the awarding of a birthday honour from King George V to one of their own.

Lieutenant Colonel Hayward stood on the makeshift stage and held a letter up high so all could see it. Then, with great ceremony, he lifted the flap on the envelope, slipped out the letter and unfolded it. He straightened his shoulders, stood at attention and cleared his throat.

'To Matron Ethel Gray. A Royal Red Cross, First Class, awarded in the Birthday Honours by the King himself.'

The room erupted in applause.

Hayward held up a hand to silence the crowd. 'How proud we all are of you, Matron.'

Cora's hands hurt from clapping and she wasn't ashamed that tears were streaming down her cheeks. The recognition meant so much, not only to the matron, but to all the nurses who had made that journey to Harefield with her thirteen months before, and every other Australian in the room.

Gertie nudged Cora in the arm and leant in close to whisper, 'I think she's blushing! Our matron!' She went up on tiptoes to take a closer look. 'She is!'

'Shh,' Cora replied, laughing.

'We couldn't be prouder,' Hayward continued, his booming voice well-suited to both the battlefield and the crowd. 'Matron arrived in Harefield last year with a commanding officer, Captain Southey, to establish this hospital. I believe there were only a handful of nurses with her and with some help from the people of the village, they performed a remarkable transformation with what can only be described as ... limited resources.'

Matron Gray performed the subtlest of eye rolls and Cora had to laugh. That was about as critical of the army as the matron would ever allow herself to be and, judging by the laughter rippling through the audience, Cora wasn't the only one to notice her silent commentary.

'If I may say, Matron, you really did pull off a miracle.' Hayward swept an outstretched arm over the crowd. 'We were established at a time when the powers that be believed we might need one hundred and fifty beds in the height of summer. And look at us now. One thousand. Matron, I commend you and congratulate you. Hip hip hooray! Hip hip hooray! Hip hip hooray!'

Clapping hands were raised to punctuate the hoorays, and whistles bounced off the walls as Matron Gray stepped up onto the stage. When a uniformed soldier presented her with an enormous bunch of flowers, she seemed utterly and genuinely surprised.

It was a few moments before the applause died down and the matron had gathered her thoughts enough to reply. 'Thank you,' she began. With her free hand, she pushed her wire-rimmed spectacles back up her nose. Her apple cheeks blushed red.

'Lieutenant Colonel, it has been a great honour to serve the Empire, the King and, of course, our patients, every single one of them an Australian. Our journey began with the kind philanthropy of the Billyard-Leake family, who are still involved with the hospital today.' She shared a knowing smile with Hayward. 'We've had our battles, haven't we? The British have recently told us we've grown too big. That we're not fit for purpose and that we should be closed down.'

The mess was filled with a chorus of boos and someone yelled, 'Shame.'

'They say we're too far away from London and it's too expensive to treat our patients here. As if anyone could put a price on the care we Australians provide to our countrymen.'

A roar erupted and Matron Gray swept her arm from one side of the mess to the other, indicating the view of the lakes and the fields and, beyond, the two hundred and fifty acres of grounds surrounding the hospital. 'How on earth can the men be expected to recuperate in the middle of London?'

'Not in the big smoke!' someone yelled, which elicited uproarious laughter.

'No matter what they say about our finances, they can't fault our practice, our doctors and nurses. We were the first Australian hospital formed in England. That will never be taken away from us. I'm honoured to serve with you. Thank you to you all.'

Afterwards, Cora, Gertie, Fiona and Leonora sat together, nursing cups of cocoa and eating egg-and-lettuce sandwiches. Lieutenant Colonel Hayward's reminiscences about the earliest days of the hospital had served as a reminder to them all of those weeks, of their first patients, and how long ago and far away that all seemed.

'I remember those first nights in the nurses' quarters,' Leonora said. 'It was so cold. I thought I'd never get warm. And now? I thought nothing of stomping all over Harefield in the snow during winter. Funny, isn't it, how we become used to things?'

'Yes,' Cora said. 'Like Gertie's snoring.'

Gertie gave her an unladylike shove. 'Or your constant recital of articles in the newspaper.'

'I like to keep well-informed.'

'Despite the fact that I'm not a believer, I've become used to Fiona's prayers,' Gertie said. 'Even though you're quite loud, you know.'

'I want Him to hear me, don't I?'

'I quite like Fiona's prayers, as a matter of fact,' Leonora said. 'Especially now she's praying for Percy. When I wrote him that he was in your thoughts, he sent back a very humble thank you.' Cora saw something sisterly in the knowing smiles Fiona and Leonora shared. War had thrown together two completely different women and, remarkably, a friendship had blossomed that had clearly become a comfort to them both. The flamboyantly elegant Leonora and the cautious and pious Fiona. Who would have thought?

Cora sighed. 'How's the new job, Leonora?'

Her eyes brightened. A fortnight before, Matron Gray had requested that Leonora begin working with the artificial limb patients in a special clinic on the grounds, and so she'd said farewell to the recovery wards and working alongside her friends. 'Honestly, I can't imagine doing anything else. I've learnt so much working alongside the masseuses, about how and why they perform physical therapy on the men. The boys are learning to make the limbs themselves, which is marvellous. The idea is that it might help them find work when they go home. There'll be lots of men who'll need wooden legs.' She hesitated, resignation in the tremor of her lips. 'Most of them won't be able to return to the jobs they used to do, especially the farmers and the other labourers.'

'I expect not,' Gertie murmured.

'How do they make a new leg?' Cora asked. 'Isn't the wood heavy? Doesn't it rub against their wounds when it's attached, when they bear weight on it?'

'It really is fascinating.' Leonora leant forward, her arms crossed on the table. 'They're made from willow and they're rather light and quite pliable and hollow in the middle. Each patient is measured and the limb is carved to meet their specific measurements and then leather straps are attached to keep it in place. And then the poor things have to learn how to use it.' She laughed at a memory. 'The boys are quite determined, as you can imagine. There's been more than one tumble to the ground.'

'It sounds very rewarding,' Gertie said.

'I've been thinking that I might train as a masseuse when I get home.'

'Really?' Cora exclaimed. 'What a wonderful idea.'

'Massage and electrical therapy really helps the men. I'd like to do more of that. When the war is over, that is.'

When the war is over.

The phrase had become an oft-repeated prayer. The words signalled so many things to them. When the flow of injured might stop. When there would be no more deaths. When peace might be allowed to flourish. When they might sleep in. When they would be able to go home. When they could see loved ones again. When they might turn the clock back and resume those lives they had left behind. Cora sometimes dreamt there was another version of herself preserved in amber back home, a woman who had no idea of what she had done and what she had seen, and when she stepped off the boat on the docks in Port Adelaide she would easily and comfortably slip back into that person's skin and resume that life. Her time so far in England felt like a halt in the calendar, a shift in time, not days and months and now years in which time had moved on in that other life. She half expected her family and the other people in her street and in her life to have been suspended in time, too. That when she arrived home, her parents and her sisters would be waiting there on the dock, their arms still held high in farewells, her mother's handkerchief still pressed to her wet cheeks, her father still staring at the sky to avoid her seeing his tears. The seagulls flying above them would be frozen mid-squawk. The sea breeze ruffling hats and hair and skirts stopped, as if God had had a change of heart and had attempted to suck it back into his lungs.

But they would not be going home any time soon.

More and more patients were arriving day by day, and the latest news from France was dire. The fighting in Verdun, which had begun that February, had been disastrous for the Empire but they were slowly gaining the ascendancy and the fighting had begun to move towards the River Somme, with millions of men on both sides preparing to do battle.

Cora looked around at her friends. How would they survive what was certain to follow?

Chapter Thirty-Four

Mr and Mrs Harry Chester were married on a warm July Saturday afternoon at St Mary's Church in Harefield. Half the village had turned out to wish the newlyweds well—Dottie had become part of their lives, their triumphs and tragedies, after all—and shower them with rose petals as they left the church. Dottie had worn a wedding dress sewn by Jessie and Win, and Harry beamed in his father's suit. The frock had turned out better than Win and Jessie could have hoped, but perhaps that had something to do with the fact that their love was sewn into every stitch. Given how petite Dottie was, Win and Jessie had found just enough cream silk crepe in their fabric collection for the wedding suit. It sported a wide shawl collar, a belted design at the waist and a flared calf-length skirt. Dottie had gone to Uxbridge to buy a new hat to match and fresh flowers had decorated its wide brim. When Harry had turned to watch her walking up the aisle, he'd cried tears of happiness.

So happy with their lot and with each other did they appear that Jessie believed their picture should be in a magazine as evidence that amid all the doom of the war there was still hope. And love.

Because of the war, they had decided to keep things simple. They hadn't opted for a best man or a maid of honour or flower girls—much to the disappointment of the two little Parsons girls who lived on a farm next to Dottie's family, but they made up for it by coming along with their mother and father and giggling excitedly.

When Jessie had arrived at the church with Harry and their mother, he'd held her hand and whispered, 'This is truly the happiest day of my life, Jess,' and she knew that to be true by the twinkle of unabashed pride in his eyes and the tremble in his lips. Dottie had sniffed back tears throughout the whole ceremony and sobbed with happiness when it was all over. Win spent the entire service sucking in deep breaths and exhaling them as if she were blowing out smoke from a cigarette, hoping the exercise might prevent her from bursting into happy tears.

'One day you'll have this proud moment,' she'd whispered to Jessie behind her lace handkerchief. 'When your own child starts their own way in the world. You'll understand then, Jess.'

Jessie had watched her brother and her dear friend—and now sister-in-law—gaze at each other openly and confidently, unafraid to show the depth of their feelings for one another in front of everyone they knew. How truly blessed and lucky they were. While Jessie smiled and cried for them, she swallowed her sadness, and then her guilt about her sadness, and put on a brave face.

If Bert were still in England, would he have stood with her? Would he have met her family and become mates with Harry? His letters had been arriving with great regularity, much to Jessie's surprise and delight. In the past week alone, Dottie had delivered three, and when Jessie had marvelled to Dottie that it had only taken three days for his post to arrive in Harefield all the way from Pozieres in France, Dottie had exclaimed, 'Nineteen thousand mailbags cross the Channel each day, Jessie. It's important to the morale of our troops, don't you know. As important as the delivery of ammunition and rations. It's the duty of everyone in service.'

Harry and Dottie had decided against having a honeymoon just yet. Dottie had taken to heart the slogan she'd read on a poster in the Harefield Post Office. Field Marshall Sir Douglas Haig had implored the people of the British nation to forgo any idea of a general holiday until the goal of victory in the war was reached. Dottie and Harry had decided that the best way to support the men at the front was to stay home, so they'd put away their brochures for a train trip to Brighton and had bought war bonds instead with their little bit of savings.

After the ceremony, the Chesters and Dottie's mother, father and siblings had joined together for lunch at the Cricketers and feasted on the sanctioned wartime meal of two courses—not three even for special occasions—by dining on roast beef with all the trimmings and raisin roly-poly for dessert.

And from that day on, Dottie had lived with her husband and his family.

Having an extra person in the house hadn't inconvenienced Win or Jessie. Dottie worked long hours as it was, and if Jessie had spare time she was at the hospital.

Win and Dottie got on like a house on fire and the four of them had slipped easily into life together.

Jessie's life had taken on a new pattern and she liked the rhythm of it. She worked with her mother, volunteered at the hospital and when she had a spare moment, she was either writing letters to Bert or reading his. She was more familiar with the routines at the hospital and the tasks she'd been assigned to, and she was less nervous about making errors and of the men's injuries. She had learnt to spend a little time with each of them, to give them each a small measure of her attention. Bert had taught her how precious that was. When she shaved them, when she skimmed a razor over their throats, they stared up into her eyes as if she were the kindest girl in the world. When she helped a soldier dress or tie the laces on his boots, sew on a loose button or fix a rip or a hem, when she helped them out of bed so she could change their bedsheets after they'd vomited or sweated through the night or soiled themselves, they looked at her with such a mix of embarrassment and relief that it seemed as if they might never have had anyone in their lives treat them with such gentleness.

When Jessie lay in bed at night, her body willing her to drift off to sleep, her mind whirred with thoughts of Bert and the words of affection from his most recent letter. His blue eyes had always sparkled when he'd turned them on her; his gaze made her stomach twirl and swoop like a kite on a fierce wind.

Was this what an attraction really felt like? Before meeting Bert, she'd believed herself deficient in some way, that she hadn't engaged in flirtations like the other women in the village had. The way Arabella Pritchard had with the man from Harrow. Where had this desire come from, unspoken and seemingly innate, to spend every waking minute with someone, the ache to feel their touch, for their eyes to turn to you and see you and only you?

Chapter Thirty-Five

9 July 1916

England in the summertime was glorious.

As Cora walked around the main house and towards the lakes, she decided that she would be perfectly willing to trade a scorching Adelaide summer for this northern hemisphere version of it any day. The days were long and warm with a soft twilight that lasted until nine o'clock, and everything seemed to be alive after the dormancy of the autumn and winter. The soft leaves in the trees were so thick that they cast enough shade underneath to create leisurely and somnolent spaces for relaxing. England did not need a verandah when it had elms and cedars.

The fields around Harefield were carpets of colour. Jessie had told Cora their names one day and Cora had laughed at how pretty they all sounded. They were primroses and bluebells and kingcups and buttercups and anemones and, beyond those fields, a woodland filled with nut trees and wild fruit trees.

She and William had arranged to meet at the end of her shift and she walked purposefully to the spot under the spreading boughs of the elm tree where she'd spotted him the first time they'd really spoken as friends. When they had decided they were no longer doctor and nurse to each other, but William and Cora.

She needed this little sojourn more than ever.

In the past few days, the grim news from the battlefront had cast long shadows over the hospital. Something had gone terribly wrong at Pozieres, and wards that had previously been closed when the flow of injured from Gallipoli had ceased were now reopening with great haste.

Within days, hundreds of soldiers had arrived at Harefield from the bloody battlegrounds of France. The trucks came chugging up the hospital's driveway every hour, filled with the injured and afflicted. There was a constant stream of them in and out of the operating theatre and many of the men barely had time to rest before they were moved out on trucks to board trains to Plymouth so they could make the journey home. The hospital had marked a grim new record of caring for eight hundred and twenty-seven patients at one time.

They never seemed to have the calm before a storm. The storm continued to rage.

As Cora approached William, one hand on her straw hat to keep it firmly in place, the other holding a paper bag with two apples inside it, her heart leapt at the sight of him already there. She quickened her pace, trying not to skip like a giddy schoolgirl, and her skirts rustled against her ankles.

He sprang to his feet and waved. It had been so long and Cora felt alive for the first time in months. Was it possible for someone her age to feel like a schoolgirl?

'Cora.'

'William.'

And she couldn't rush to his side fast enough.

'I brought apples,' she said, feeling breathless.

He pointed to a brown paper package on the bench. 'I have a piece of cheddar.' William motioned for Cora to sit and she took a position on the bench on the other side of the wrapped cheese and her bag of apples. Did they need a no-man's-land between them? William produced a knife and they chatted inconsequentially about the weather, the sunshine, the swans parading on the lake as if they had been painted there by a landscape artist. 'It's a wonderful evening.'

'It is. Delightful. And to sit here and see the swans?' Cora pointed to the lake where the elegant creatures were sailing. 'I believe there are six of them.'

William held a hand over his eyes to shield them from the sun. 'I see seven.'

'Are you sure?'

'Perhaps I need glasses.'

Cora laughed at his self-deprecation. She had watched him sew ligaments and tendons with the smallest, most delicate stitches with no trouble at all.

William passed Cora a slice of red-skinned apple topped by a crumbly chunk of cheese and she studied it.

'I can't say I've ever tasted cheese in quite this way.'

'I'd prefer a loaf of bread myself, but there wasn't any to be found in the kitchen. And what there is seems to be made of potatoes these days, not flour. You can't know how much I miss real bread.'

Cora nibbled. 'And butter.'

He stilled. 'You remember that?'

'Of course.' Cora nibbled. 'This is delicious.'

They sat in silence, watching the sky. In the distance a hawk hovered, its wings quivering as it kept a steely eye on its prey in the grass below. A gentle breeze swept over the wildflowers and they waved back and forth as if greeting the bird above. Cora felt as if she could sit there with William all day. Perhaps forever.

'How do you do it, William?'

'Cheese and apple?' He grinned. 'Well, it's rather complicated. It begins with a walk to the cheesemonger in the village and then a negotiation about the price and the size of the piece. And then,' he lifted his Swiss Army knife in the air, 'I perform surgery on the unsuspecting fruit.'

How he made her laugh. 'That. How do you do that? Maintain your good humour? I've found it harder and harder just lately. But you? The boys admire you. They can't believe you stand around in the ward sharing cigarettes with them.'

'I like a cigarette and why shouldn't I? It's the least I can do. Often, the very least.'

'You're not like most doctors—or officers—they've met, I expect.'

And you're not like any doctor I've ever met.

'These are the most extraordinary circumstances. Everyone's bunked in together here. That's what I like about it. Soldiers, NCOs, officers. Rank means nothing and the injury means everything.'

'Half the nurses adore you, you know.'

He raised a solitary eyebrow. 'Only half?'

'Would you like me to do a survey to give you a more precise answer? What I'm asking is … how do you not let this get to you?'

He shrugged and turned his gaze from her. 'I'm part of a machine, just like the men are. We're all part of it. They fight. I patch them up. You care for them. And then we put them on trains like cattle to go back to the slaughter. I cope with it because I don't look for any honour in it.'

'But that's why I do it. To honour their sacrifice.' She searched his eyes and saw something familiar. She had seen that look in some of her patients. A blankness, a vacancy. Was that how he coped with the madness of the war? By trying not to look at it?

'Imagine if the war hadn't started in the first place,' he asked. 'Do you ever run through that in your mind? The what-ifs? And if you weren't here right this minute with me, and there was no war, what would be you be doing? Where might you be this July day in 1916?'

Cora had tried to hold on to her life before the war but it was growing more distant with every day and week that passed. At first, it had been her comfort when she felt homesick and overwhelmed to think of her parents and Eve and Grace. She imagined her mother in the kitchen on a Saturday morning, brewing tea and vigorously beating butter, sugar and eggs together in a bowl to make the fruitcake that was supposed to last all week but rarely did. On a Sunday afternoon, her father might be smoking his pipe in the living room while reading *The Register*. Eve would no doubt be curled up in an armchair with her nose in a book while Grace was sure to be sewing or knitting something to donate to the war effort.

And sometimes she thought of the hospital on North Terrace and how sternly her matron had treated all the new nurses. In those first few months in England, she had been able to imagine each step of her walks through the Botanic Garden. How the heavy wrought-iron gates opened at precisely nine o'clock each morning. The winding pathway to the Kiosk, which served the most delicious tea and scones. The puddle of a lake filled with ducks and fish. The sunlit shimmering on the glass of the Palm House. The towering Moreton Bay figs and their searching, thick limbs.

But all she could see in her mind's eye now was a blur of water and reflection and green. Her memories were disappearing a little bit each day, in inverse proportion to how much she needed them.

'What might I be doing?' Cora asked. 'Something inconsequential, I presume. If I wasn't working ...' She paused, tried to hold on to a memory but it slipped away. 'I'm too tired to imagine things these days. Aren't you? I wanted to be a matron one day. That I remember. I helped at home. Occasionally, I went to the theatre with some friends from the hospital to see a revue or a play. I didn't have a big life, really.'

'You've more than made up for it now, haven't you? Isn't this a big life?'

She sighed, found a smile in all the sadness. 'My life is too big now. I can barely take it all in. When the war is over, I want to sail back home, go straight to bed and not wake up for a hundred years.'

'Sleeping Beauty,' William whispered gently.

'That's such a cruel story. What if there are no handsome princes to bring her back to life? She's cursed forever. Or what if they're only moderately handsome or simply rather plain looking. Might not they be allowed to be her prince?'

'Surely there are handsome princes to be had.'

'Name one!'

'Let me see. King George V, Tsar Nicholas II and the Kaiser. Surely there must be a prince among them who can help, although, medically speaking, since they're all first cousins the gene pool might not be that strong. There are royal families in Britain, of course, Germany, Russia, the Austro-Hungarian Empire, Italy, Belgium, Serbia, Bulgaria, Romania, Greece—and even little Montenegro has a king now, I hear. Surely there must be a spare prince somewhere. Let's see. Doesn't King George V have four sons?'

'I'm older than all of them so they won't do.' Cora sighed. 'Perhaps I'll have to settle for a commoner. Sounds about right for an Australian gal, don't you think? I couldn't abide anyone full of airs and graces and they'd be shocked to find out I barely know how to use cutlery in the right order.'

William squeezed her hand. 'You are anything but common, Cora, in background or thought or deed.'

And if Cora heard a little stumble in his voice as he said her name, she didn't mention it.

'By the way,' he said, and then waited until he'd finished chewing his chunk of cheese and apple. 'I finished the book.'

Cora waited for any further details of his review but he offered none. 'Did you like it?'

'Well, Austen is no Conan Doyle—'

Cora gasped and reached across to slap his arm and he pretended to flinch. He moved fast and grabbed her hand to prevent her inflicting any further injury but held on, his fingers softening around hers. Cora looked down at his hand, so familiar to her. His fingers were long and fine, as lanky as he was, and his nails were trimmed short and neat, as always. The fine hairs on the back of his hand caught the sun and seemed even more blond.

'I liked Miss Anne Elliot very much. What an appalling father she had.'

'Despicable,' Cora agreed with a confident nod.

'What I liked best about her was that she finds her steel by the end, doesn't she? She is quite determined.'

'Yes, she does. It's what comes with being older, I think. And wiser. Being no longer willing to bow to what anyone else thinks is best for your life. About having the strength to make your own decisions.'

'Cora,' William said gently. She heard his intake of breath, watched his chest rise and fall. 'You have to know. The moments I'm able to share with you are the only things that get me through the day.'

And when he pressed his lips to the back of her hand the world seemed so bright it was as if the sun had risen at the end of the lake just for the two of them, shining its light and its heat down on them like two players on a stage.

William squeezed her hand and then slowly let go. She felt bereft all of a sudden.

'Cora, I can't … there's something I must tell you.' He got to his feet with a groan, slipping his hands into the pockets of his trousers. He began to pace. Cora had been reaching for another slice of apple but pulled her hand back. The tone of his voice had in a heartbeat flicked from intimate to serious and she felt unsettled. Was he leaving Harefield? Was he going back to work in a battlefield hospital?

William stopped, met her gaze straight on. 'Until last week, I was engaged.'

Her mind spun and every single thing she wanted to ask suddenly jammed up in her mouth.

After a long moment of silence, William said, 'You must have questions.'

She breathed deep and long. 'I do.' A hundred of them.

'I fear I have broken a good woman's heart so I can pursue what's best for my own. And I don't know what that makes me. I need to tell you so I can explain my behaviour towards you since we met in the operating theatre last June.'

How had he behaved in the thirteen months since they'd met? Cora thought back, her mind a photograph album of all their moments together over the past year. All the time he had been engaged to someone else. He had always treated her kindly. He had respected her profession and her work. He had let his guard down too, and she had managed a glimpse of the man behind his standing and his profession. And yes, he had been flirtatious with her. Too many long gazes, perhaps. The time he'd kissed her hand. Yes, he had spent too much time alone with a woman to whom he had no formal commitment. Perhaps that had been wrong, but she couldn't fault him for it. The war had changed the way everyone thought of what was proper and normal. She had held the hands of more soldiers than she could count. She had flirted with her boys in the full knowledge that she meant nothing by it, and they took nothing from it but, for those few moments, they believed themselves to be men again, which doubt and injury and cruel circumstance had robbed from them. She had let herself be flattered and hadn't wanted to hide her interest. She knew herself: she had been made more confident by his attentions, by the longing gaze of a man with such intelligence and warmth in his eyes and kindness in his heart. How could she blame herself for that?

'Please, William. You've been nothing but ...' How to explain? 'A friend to me.'

'That's very generous of you but I've carried around such guilt.' He clutched a hand to his chest. 'I had to put a stop to it. Miss Anne Elliot may have helped me see what it is I really want. Who I really want.'

She didn't need him to explain. She saw the longing in his expression, in his soft eyes, in the fullness of his lips, in the dip of his gaze to her own mouth.

He pulled a pack of cigarettes from a pocket and lit one. 'Alice Dennis and I became engaged just before I embarked in November 1914. I wish I could explain it to you so I might understand it better myself. Looking back, and I've done a lot of looking back in the past months, I can only think I had a rush of blood to the head. All those thoughts about adventure and travel and duty. Back then, I didn't think about the possibility of not coming home. Of being killed. It was all going to be over by Christmas, remember? I believed that I knew my own mind, when clearly I had no idea. How could a man of thirty-two years of age make such a mistake?' He inhaled, his jittery exhalation sending a cloud of smoke into the sky. 'It hadn't been a long courtship. I was convinced I was in love with her and I know she was in love with me. I have beaten myself up a hundred times about what I wanted to do ...'

'William, it's not necessary to—'

He held up a hand to silence her. 'I can barely remember what her voice sounds like. I should remember that, shouldn't

I? If I truly loved her? But when I lie in bed at night, I only hear you. I only see you.'

He swept aside the obstacles between them—apple cores, a chunk of cheese, a tea towel, a knife—and sat close to her. He lifted an arm behind her and it was on her shoulder. There was a gentle urging in his touch and she hadn't realised how she had longed for it. Every muscle in her body slackened and lengthened. Her shoulders dropped as she breathed out and she lay her head on William's shoulder. Where there had been two of them, separated, there was now one, almost as close as two people could be: Cora tucked up inside his embrace, her breath on his neck, their thighs pressing together. She splayed a palm on his chest and underneath her fingers, underneath the wool of his waistcoat and the cotton of his shirt, his heart beat firm and strong.

It was the closest she had ever been to any man and she waited for the guilt and shame to rise in her, legacies of a lifetime of warnings and lectures and moralising, but her mind was blank to that historic hectoring. There was only so much shame to go around in wartime and shouldn't it be reserved for those men who had started it in the first place, not forced into the thoughts of those who were mopping up the pieces of shattered men and minds?

All Cora could think of was what she wanted. The chance of love with someone sitting right by her side. Something so unexpected, something she would greedily hold on to, no matter the cost to a woman she had never met. Did one person's sadness make another's happiness less important? Did that make her a monster?

William pulled Cora's hand to his mouth and pressed his lips against the back of it. Then he turned her hand over, exposing her palm, red from soap and tough with callouses, and kissed her there, her softness becoming his softness, lips against skin, and she knew she shouldn't crave it but she did.

'I had to put an end to it. Every other letter I had written to her was a lie. She will hate me. I can't blame her. Who knows what my father will say when he finds out. But life is short and so, so precarious. I should know ... I hold it in my hands every single day and watch it while it slips away.'

'Are you certain? I've seen what loneliness does to people. I see it in my patients. Half of the men fall in love with a nurse. Mostly Leonora, I must admit.' Cora let out a little laugh but heard the falseness ring in it. 'We are not people to them, really. We are a uniform. We comfort them. We give them medication to take away their pain, something to send them into oblivion when their reality is too much to bear. People see in us things that aren't real. Perhaps you've been caught up in that, too.'

'I've never been more sure of anything in my life, Cora.'

'Then I'm happy. Very happy.'

She studied his face. She had wished for him. He was a fine, educated man; a skilled surgeon and a kind one, too. A man equally at home crowded around the fire in the ward hut sharing cigarettes with his patients as he was discussing medicine with the surgeons and specialists who visited the hospital.

There was so much she had wished for herself when she had first come to England. A journey without seasickness. Some nurses to work alongside with whom she might become friends with as well as colleagues. Interesting and meaningful work, her own glorious deeds to match the bravery and sacrifice of the boys who'd enlisted. An adventure that might be over by Christmas 1915 and a chance to see some of the world she'd only ever read about in books.

What did she wish for now? She wished her job would end. She wished for the steady stream of injured men to cease arriving. She wished never to see another prosthetic leg or another face half-missing or a mind shattered along with bones and flesh.

She thought for a moment, tore off a crumble of cheese with her fingers and threw it out on the grass. Perhaps a bird flying free in the sky above them might notice it, land and perform a little dance. She envied them their feathers and their freedom to fly away whenever they chose.

'Cora?'

She turned her face to him. 'Everything I've ever wished has just come true.'

She pressed her lips to his and they held tight to each other.

Harefield Hospital
Middlesex
England
August 14th, 1916

Dear all,

I apologise that I haven't much time to write or much to say. I've not been up to much of anything lately except work. The terrible fighting in the Somme has meant we've been very busy and we're now at capacity with more than one thousand beds and each one full. It's hard to believe the hospital has grown so quickly in just a year. The boys are in the best of spirits, as ever, as am I. I can't put into words how brave and courageous they are when they come to us, injured physically but not broken spiritually. If people back home were to see it, they would be so proud of the way our soldiers carry themselves and represent Australia.

Although they're recovering themselves, they are already making plans to do something for Christmas for the children of the village. Together with the entertainment committee, they have in mind a Christmas concert and celebration here at the hospital. The local children haven't remained untouched and innocent about events. Whenever we've buried a man at St Mary's, the village children lead the funeral procession through Harefield, sombre in their Sunday best, carrying little posies of wildflowers they've picked especially to lay on the graves of the Australians. Who can protect them from the realities of war when a cortege makes its way past their living room windows?

I must go. It's lights out shortly and I shall try to get to sleep before my dear friend Gertie drifts off. It's my only hope of getting a full seven hours if I don't want to be kept awake by her snoring.

Much love, and thinking of you all.

Cora

Chapter Thirty-Six

16 August 1916

If Jessie hadn't given the notice pinned to the noticeboard in the mess more than a cursory glance while she was waiting for a toasted cheese sandwich, she might have missed it. But there it was, situated next to offers of rides into London in motor cars, announcements about that week's concerts and an upcoming picnic in Fassnidge Park in Uxbridge, weather permitting, which seemed to involve a procession of motor cars and a trolley bus.

Jessie squinted to read it again.

New record for the No. 1 Australian Auxiliary Hospital at Harefield. One thousand and ten patients.

The number seemed unfathomable. Just a few months before, they'd been down to one hundred and fifty patients and Jessie had heard the talk everywhere: that the slowing trickle meant the war might soon be coming to an end.

But then, the battle of the Somme had become a catastrophic failure for the British, with almost twenty thousand killed and more than 38,000 wounded by the end of that first day. Jessie, Win and Dottie had sobbed when Harry had read aloud the article from the newspaper.

The trickle of injured had become a flood.

'Hello, Jessie.' It was Enid, balancing an armful of novels in one arm and a cup of tea in the other. She squinted in an attempt to keep her glasses on her nose.

'Hello, Enid. Can I lend you a hand?'

'I'm all right. I'm on my way back to the library.' She leant in close. 'But I desperately needed a cup of tea. It's been so busy this morning. I haven't stopped.'

'Neither have I. This might explain why.' Jessie pointed to the noticeboard. The two women read the number again, trying to take it in.

'Are you still writing to that Australian chap?'

Jessie nodded and pulled her bottom lip between her teeth to stop it trembling.

'God bless,' Enid said, giving Jessie a faint smile before turning away to head to the library, her cup and saucer rattling as she walked.

Jessie took her lunch to a table and barely pulled in her chair before wolfing her sandwich down. Truth be told, she wasn't in the slightest bit hungry and when she'd finished it, she felt sick. She had just needed an excuse to be out of the ward, away from the men.

She had received a letter from Bert the day before and all seemed well. He'd written of the sunshine in France and how warm it was. He'd reported that the package she had sent him—more chocolates and cigarettes—had arrived safely but he'd shared everything with his mates for fear the rats might get to the chocolate. He put an exclamation mark after that sentence but Jessie couldn't laugh at it. She'd taken comfort in his questions about her and her work at the hospital and had already been formulating her reply and, more importantly, how she would sign her name at the end.

His first few letters had been addressed to *Dear Jessie*. The first time she'd seen her name written in his hand, she'd traced a finger over it, trying to imagine where he was when he'd put nib to paper. Now she was *Dearest Jessie*.

'Stay safe, Bert,' she whispered as she swallowed her last bite.

And then she flew back to the ward.

Chapter Thirty-Seven

17 September 1916

'Jessie!'

The young volunteer looked up with a beaming smile. 'Hello, Sister Barker.'

Cora approached Private Percy Norman's bed and noticed the young patient was grinning from ear to ear. There was nothing she liked more than a smiling patient.

'I see you're making yourself useful there, Percy.'

The young private nodded enthusiastically and his cheeks blushed a deep crimson. 'Who could say no to this beautiful English sheila?' Percy's elbows were propped on his lap and he fed a roll of freshly laundered and bleached cloth, held as taut as a highwire, towards Jessie as she rolled it tightly. 'A bloke doesn't need both legs to roll bandages now, does he?'

'I'm glad you're so enthusiastic, Private Norman,' Jessie trilled happily. 'I have a whole basket here at my feet.'

'I'll sit here all day for you, nurse.'

'Oh, I'm not a nurse,' Jessie said hurriedly and shot a worried glance at Cora. 'I'm just a volunteer. From the village. You may call me Miss Chester.'

'We're all serving King and country, no matter our rank,' Cora said and winked at Jessie. 'Have you heard from Bert?'

'I have,' Jessie said with a sigh of relief. 'He's safe and well. That's all I can ask for.'

Cora saw the tug of hope and fear in Jessie's expression. Her eyes smiled but her lips trembled.

'May he stay that way.'

'From your lips to God's ear, Sister.'

Percy sighed and the taut bandage between him and Jessie became slack. 'You're not engaged are you, Miss Chester?'

'Oh, no. Not at all,' Jessie said hurriedly. 'Bert—Private Mott—was a patient here. He's back in France now. He's a … friend.'

'So there's hope for me yet?'

'You never know, Percy. You never know. Oh, Sister Barker. I forgot to mention that Captain Kent was here looking for you earlier.'

The skin on the back of Cora's neck prickled. 'How long ago?'

'I'd say half an hour perhaps? I'd just given Soames a bed bath and helped Fry with a quick postcard home. When I told him you were expected back on the ward soon, he said he'd be back shortly.'

'Thank you for passing that on, Jessie.' Cora thought back to May the year before, when she'd first met Jessie Chester. Could this possibly be the same young woman? The timid young thing had blossomed in the past year and it had been a joy to observe.

'Very good work there, Percy. Nice to see you're earning your keep.'

Percy chuckled. 'I reckon I've paid my price, don't you, Sister?'

By four o'clock, most of the patients were still outside taking in what was left of the day, or were scattered all over the hospital undertaking embroidery lessons or on picnics and excursions. French lessons had been cancelled that afternoon due to Miss Tarleton being ill, and the attractions of the pubs of Harefield, although supposedly strictly off limits, were obviously too hard to ignore.

A door slammed and William strode into the ward. 'Sister Barker,' he called, efficient and professional. She shouldn't have been expecting anything else in the middle of the ward but she found herself disconcerted by his tone. 'I need you to make up a bed at once.' He pushed back a lock of unruly hair that had fallen over his forehead. He was not himself. His tie was loose at his throat. His coat seemed to be on inside out.

'Of course, Captain.'

'I have a patient in the post-operative ward. I operated yesterday and he's still in a terrible state but I have no choice but to move him here. We're overflowing and as soon as we can move some out, the beds are filled.' He swore under his breath. 'As I'm sure you know.'

Cora thought quickly. Bed seven had been vacated that morning with the departure of a patient to the 1st Australian Dermatological Hospital in Bulford for the treatment of his venereal disease. Or rheumatism, as it was described in his discharge notes. 'I don't have a volunteer at the moment. She's out with a patient. Give me five minutes to make up the bed.'

'I'll help you.' William looked around the ward, as if the sheets might be stacked in a pile somewhere close.

Cora stared at him blankly. 'That's not necessary, Captain.'

'Many hands make light work and he's on his way over as we speak. Where is the linen?'

They worked briskly, efficiently, unfolding sheets, shaking out blankets, tucking and fluffing the stiff old pillows, and almost as soon as they were done, a porter wheeled the new patient to the freshly made cot. The soldier was drowsy and flaccid, flushed and moaning. William assisted the porter to transfer him to the bed. Cora stroked the damp hair on his forehead, using the inside of her wrist to quickly gauge a quick read of his temperature. He was burning up.

'He's pyretic,' she said.

'Yes, I can see that.'

Cora stepped back and allowed William room to take the patient's observations. She had always admired his technical efficiency and his polite manner with the patients, whether they were awake or barely conscious, able to respond or not. He lowered his voice in their vicinity, as if he was aware they might be startled by a rough one. He gently sat himself beside them, aware that their cot was the only private space they had and that he was entering it.

'He was doing well after surgery yesterday. His temperature was stable, his heart rate, too. I don't like this.'

Cora lifted the hospital gown covering the patient's torso and legs and gently peeled back a section of the cloth bandages encircling his thigh.

'The wound is clean.'

William rubbed a hand over his face in frustration. 'He had a compound fracture of his femur, thanks to the Kaiser. We set it and everything looked clean when we did. I'm thinking latent sepsis.' His face fell and he turned away from Cora, indicating with a nod that she should follow him. They stepped away from the cot, aware that the patients might hear something frightening.

'I must have missed a piece of shrapnel. Or a fragment of bone that was forced deep into tissue. I should have seen it. I ...' His voice cracked. 'I did fourteen surgeries yesterday.'

She gripped his forearm. 'Then anyone would have missed it. Yours are the safest hands I know.'

He glanced over his shoulder at the patient. When he spoke, it was gentle and quiet. 'You're very kind, Cora. Kinder than I deserve.'

A wave of longing rose up in her and she swallowed it away. She realised in that moment that it wasn't only the patients who needed reassurance. Men were men, no matter the uniform. They could all break just as easily.

'Let me help you. Talk to me.'

The ward door opened with a creak. Jessie had propped it open with her bottom and was urging Percy's cane wheelchair inside with a huffing effort. She came to a sudden stop on the linoleum strip between the rows of cots, and Cora realised what Jessie was seeing. She and William standing close to each other, as intimate as lovers.

'I beg your pardon, Sister.' The poor girl had turned white as a sheet.

Cora stepped back, gathered her hands behind her back. 'We have a new patient,' she managed to say. 'Captain Kent and I have been discussing his care.'

Jessie moved Percy's wheelchair to his bed. After a quick and quiet word to him, she joined William and Cora. All three looked down at the new patient. He was lying motionless, beads of sweat on his forehead and drizzling little trails into the creases at the sides of his eyes.

'Please tell me what I can do,' Jessie said. 'What's his name?'

'Private Neil Wiseman,' William explained.

'Hello, Private Wiseman,' Jessie said. 'You're in safe hands. Don't you worry.'

The boy's eyes flickered. Judging by his almost hairless chin and the cluster of pimples on his sunken cheeks, Cora couldn't imagine he was more than eighteen years old.

William sighed wearily. 'Thank you, Jessie. Sister, he'll need close observation. He's likely to need to go back to surgery if that temperature doesn't go down. If I may have a word?' His eyes flicked for a millisecond to the back of the ward and Cora nodded her assent. At the chair by the nurses' desk, she stopped and turned, but William strode right past her towards the storeroom. With a quick turn of the knob, it flew open and he stepped inside.

She followed him, holding her breath.

He didn't ask before kissing her. In an instant, his hands were on her cheeks, guiding the tilt of her head, keeping her pressed up against him, his mouth on hers, his lips open and devouring her. She wanted this but more, of him and of his body and his hands and mouth and fingers. Her arms encircled his neck and she held on as he pressed himself against her. He moved back only long enough to look into her eyes before kissing her cheeks, her nose, the sensitive skin at the nape of her neck and finally bringing his forehead to rest against hers. He'd pushed her back against a wall and she was glad he had because she wasn't sure she had the strength to hold herself up otherwise.

His breaths matched hers, ragged and fast. 'I'm sorry.'

'I'm worried about you, William.' She cupped his face and forced him to meet her eyes.

'Don't worry. I beg you. If I look into your eyes and see pity, I don't know what I'll do.'

'I pity everyone here. Not just you.'

He exhaled deep and long. 'I need you. Cora. More today than I ever have.'

Cora kissed him, soft and slow, and she felt him tremble in her embrace.

'You have me,' she whispered against his lips.

'I don't know why. I'm a bloody mess.'

'You're a doctor in the war. Who isn't a mess?'

He waited, and then his words came out in a rush. 'I received a letter from Alice yesterday.'

Cora had tried not to think about Miss Alice Dennis. Not whether she'd been waiting at home, knitting for William, pining for him. Not whether she'd been planning her future as a doctor's wife. Not whether she'd picked out names for her future children. Not whether she'd already had a glory box filled with linens and lace and beautiful china. Not about how heartbroken she must have been to read William's letter breaking off their engagement. Cora was surrounded by too much sadness already without taking on another woman's.

'She must have been very upset.'

'What did she call me that I didn't deserve? A liar, a cheat, a—'

Cora held a finger to his lips to silence him. 'Stop. I don't want to hear it. I know what you are and who you are. You're a good man, William.'

He kissed her finger and then lifted it from his lips. He kissed her mouth, full and soft; deeply and desperately.

'Every day when I wake I should curse the war and all the damage it's wrought on so many. But how can I curse it when it delivered you to my life? How can I pray for the war to be over when the woman I love is here?' He smoothed a hand up her back and over her ribs and cupped a breast. 'I love you, dearest Cora.'

Cora's words escaped in a sob. 'I love you, too.'

Chapter Thirty-Eight

7 October 1916

The windows along the front of Harefield House shone and glittered, as if stars had fallen from the sky and been caught up in the creeping ivy that decorated it. Cora pressed a hand to her cloche hat and looked up in awe, trying to take it all in on that cool October evening. The soft fall of her deep purple velvet dinner dress—the one formal frock she'd brought with her from home—swished about her legs in a way her crisply starched uniform never did, and she relished the sensuous feel of it.

That night, Harefield Park was as lush and fecund as a jungle. Every possible inch of space in the gardens between the house and the ward huts had been transformed into a scene so joyous one might blink and imagine it was a dream; a dream in which there wasn't a war raging across the Channel. A parquet dance floor covered the grass and around it were khaki canvas tents with their flaps wide open, revealing trestle tables covered with silver platters overflowing with sandwiches and cakes and biscuits. Union

Jacks strung from flagpoles fluttered in the evening breeze and hung from the ropes holding up every canvas tent.

In glass bowls filled with punch, sliced oranges floated flat and swollen like leaves in a lily pond. By the side of the dance floor, a dapper older gentleman in a black bow tie and tails, his pate bare except for a few lonely brilliantined strands, played an upright piano with a flourish, his shining black shoes dancing on the piano pedals. On the east side of the dance floor, tables covered with starched white tablecloths, as stiff as a nurse's veil, were decorated with little posies of wildflowers in glass jars. Crowds of people mingled at tables, the ladies' smiles warm and the men's neatly trimmed military moustaches all turning upwards in laughter.

Matron Gray had told the nurses that dignitaries from the village and the county would be attending and Cora guessed them to be the people gathered in familiar groups. The Billyard-Leake family must be somewhere among them, along with the Steddalls, the Tarletons and members of the local Red Cross, who had all become involved with providing entertainments and diversions for the patients.

Hundreds of boys were out of their beds, smiling and smoking. Some were in full uniforms, one trouser leg pinned at the knee, a sleeve sewn up at the elbow, a hat at a jaunty angle because it sat on top of layers of bandages. Others wore their blue hospital pyjamas and a rainbow assortment of chequered dressing gowns. Pairs of crutches lay flat on the grass and those in wheelchairs blended into the crowd, a haze of cigarette smoke slowly rising into the air, creating shadows in the light.

Some days, when exhaustion was as familiar to Cora as her pale and drawn face in the morning mirror, the idea of the party had been all that had kept her going. In that half-asleep, half-awake state of a morning, as she dragged herself out of bed, splashed cold water on her face and shivered in her nightdress, her toes clenched into claws on the floorboards underfoot, she had to remind herself where she was. It only took a blink or two to remember and, in that moment, she had swallowed the feeling of dread that rose in her throat, thick and viscous, at the idea of what that day might bring.

But there was no dread tonight. She'd even let Leonora make up her face.

'We have to spruce up for our poor boys,' she'd exclaimed. 'They have to put up with us without make-up every day. Please let me add just a little to your face. To highlight your very pretty features.' She'd positioned a finger under Cora's chin and tipped her face up to the lamplight. 'You could be rather pretty if you tried.'

'I don't view being pretty as one of life's major accomplishments, Leonora.'

'Why ever not?'

'Pretty doesn't make me a good nurse. And pretty is rather a random quality, don't you think? My two younger sisters were born that way. They took after my mother. Fine-boned beauties with big eyes and silky blonde hair. Look at me! I'm my father's daughter. As tall as he is. And look at these hands!' Cora held her hands up, spreading her fingers out wide.

'What's wrong with your hands?' Fiona had asked, puzzled.

Cora studied them. 'They're rather large, don't you think? I used to make a game of it. I'd hold up my hands and my sisters would hold their dainty little fingers up against mine and we'd compare. I swear mine are double the size.'

'But Cora,' Gertie had said. 'Big hands are all the better for lifting patients and long arms are perfect for leaning over a bed to tuck in the sheets.'

That was so like Gertie, Cora thought, practical down to her bootstraps.

'Yes, they may be so, but they're not pretty.' Cora had tucked her hands under her thighs. 'So you don't need to worry about making up my face, Leonora.'

'Oh, yes, I do. Tonight, you'll be dancing with your Captain Kent and there is nothing on earth wrong with wanting to look a little less Florence Nightingale and a little more Lillian Gish.'

Cora had given up pretending he wasn't her Captain Kent.

Gertie had snorted. 'Do you really think he'll give a jot about whether or not Cora has rouged her cheeks?'

'And we're not allowed, anyway,' Fiona had added. 'With very good reason. It's not sterile.'

'And we're not here to be beauty queens, Leonora,' Cora had reminded her.

Cora had quickly learnt her protest was pointless and she had relented. Leonora had snapped open a gold compact and applied a dusting of face powder with a puff as soft as a dandelion flower, which had made Cora sneeze. She'd rouged Cora's cheeks and then patted a little brush into a tin of cake mascara and combed her eyelashes. When Leonora had shown Cora her reflection in a little handheld mirror, Cora had looked at a version of herself she hadn't seen in months, perhaps years. Her face glowed. Her eyes sparkled. And the little slick of red lip gloss gave her mouth a pout she'd never seen. She felt giddy, as if the brushes and powders not only had the magical powers of giving her a glow she didn't feel on the inside but also in turning back time to a point in her life when it might have been natural.

She felt that night as glitteringly lovely as Harefield Park looked. Even the ward huts, lit from inside by flickering fires and lamps, seemed welcoming.

Cora shivered a little and held her bag tight in her fingers, looking around to find her friends. In the light from a lamp, Leonora was flirting with one of her patients, which didn't surprise Cora in the slightest. Leonora possessed a skill that few people had, Cora had determined. She managed to attract attention and deflect it at the same time. People were drawn to her smile, her beauty, her poise and her charm, but she quickly diverted it back to its admirer and before long, people were telling Leonora things they might never have told another living soul. It was more than a nervous response to the attention Leonora showered on them. It was as if Leonora wanted to share the spotlight whenever it shone on her, fearing it was too much for one person to have all to themselves. Her presence gave the patients comfort, more than perhaps any other nurse Cora had ever worked with and, in the circumstances they found themselves in, comfort was often all they had to give.

Across the lawn, Gertie and Fiona were at a punch bowl, having an animated discussion about which of the sandwiches on the silver tray before them to try first, judging by the pointing.

She heard her name and pricked up her ears. From across the dance floor, some of her boys were beckoning her, cigarettes hanging from their pursed lips, their hands waving. It was Prentice, Saunders, Wright and the two Jones boys, no relation. She waved back but before she'd had the chance to take a step in their direction, she felt a gentle hand on her elbow.

And then there was a low voice in her ear. 'May I have this dance, Sister?'

'Captain,' she replied with a polite nod. 'How are you this evening?'

William clasped his hands together behind his back. 'All the better for seeing you, my darling.'

'You look … better.'

'It's all down to you. Seeing you across the dance floor looking so beautiful? It's boosted my spirits more than I can say.' He held out a hand. 'Shall we dance?'

The dance floor was empty. 'Perhaps we should wait a moment or two. For another song.'

'Wait? Whatever for?'

'It might not be—'

'Appropriate? That a doctor and a nurse take a twirl? Half the medical corp would have already been sent home if that were the rule.' He leant in close. 'I want to hold you in my arms and I don't care who sees it.'

The dance floor was fast filling with couples. Cora spied Leonora leading a soldier by the elbow, the bandages around his eyes an indication that he wasn't in a state to lead her.

William's eyes were soft and so, so blue and Cora found herself a little light-headed. Why, she might have even forgotten to breathe.

She put her hand in his. 'I would like that very much.'

William led her to the centre of the dance floor.

Chapter Thirty-Nine

Until the war, Jessie had always known where she belonged, which puzzle piece she was in the jigsaw of her life in the village.

She would never feature as the centre of any scene, not like the churches with soaring steeples or bridges spanning pretty rivers or men gripping reins in their hands to encourage draught horses to continue on their way. She was in that scene, but she was always to be the shadow in the window of a cottage on the edge of the frame, the young woman toiling by lamplight, blurred, anonymous. An easily forgotten smudge of grey.

But all that had changed. Her world had spun on its axis and she'd found her feet in a place where there was absolutely nothing out of the ordinary about a girl like her standing in the middle of a party at Harefield Park in a silk organdie gown and a cloche hat adorned with feathers.

Her gown was gathered with a bright green satin cummerbund that fit snugly around the slimmest part of her waist. She'd shortened the sleeves from the pattern in her collection and they now sat at her elbow, elegantly full. A hip-length overskirt trimmed with cream lace matched the neckline and the hems on each sleeve, and she'd found a pair of long black gloves among her mother's things. She'd sewn two diamante buckles to the tops of a pair of black satin shoes and even though they could barely be seen under the full length of her skirt she knew she was wearing them and they had changed how she carried herself. She felt as if she was floating on air and, in the warm evening breeze, she might actually have been floating, because the walk to Harefield Park from home seemed to take no time at all and before she knew it she was showing her invitation at the front gates. She'd been directed to the towering oak tree and it was there she now stood, observing, summoning up the courage to step out from its shadows.

Oh, she would have so much to write about in her next letter to Bert. The decorations. The food. And the people!

She was as familiar with the hospital now as she was with every street and laneway in the village, but would it always seem like another world?

Jessie leant against the oak tree and took in the scene. Soldiers in khaki uniforms stood in clumps smoking casually and laughing. Others, speaking more seriously in little huddles, wore dark worsted suits. Men sitting at the tables and on wooden chairs wore their dressing gowns draped over their shoulders like smoking jackets.

She walked slowly, letting herself take it all in. The dance floor was filling with couples, turning in time to the music from the piano.

'Why, Miss Chester.'

Jessie startled. 'Hello, Sister Grady.'

'Come now. Leonora will do just fine. I must admit that I saw your dress before I noticed it was you wearing it. It's simply beautiful.'

'Thank you.'

Leonora reached for a fold in the fabric of Jessie's sleeve and ran her fingers along it. 'Is that silk?'

'Yes.'

'I simply must come and see you and your mother. I've been meaning to but I just haven't found the time.' Leonora clapped her hands together. 'But I'm making a promise to myself right now. I shall come and see you on my next free day.'

'We'd be delighted to create something for you, Leonora.' Jessie couldn't help but think that any frock on the beautiful woman would look well-sewn and glamorous.

'Now, I expect you're looking for a young man to dance with? There are plenty here who would be delighted to take your hand. But first, come with me.' Leonora guided Jessie around the edges of the dance floor to a long table on which dainty china plates of sandwiches, cakes and petit fours were set out in a tantalising display.

'Gertie! Fiona!' Leonora called and the women greeted Jessie with waves and raised glasses.

'How lovely to see you,' Gertie exclaimed. 'And isn't that a lovely frock.'

Leonora held out a hand with a flourish. 'Isn't it ravishing?'

Jessie felt her cheeks flush but didn't mind them seeing it. Fiona and Leonora examined it closely, their fingers smoothing the full sleeves and over the silk organdie.

'Such fine stitching,' Fiona said.

'I've never seen fabric like this,' Gertie declared.

And when pride swelled in Jessie's chest, she found herself smiling and the words poured out. 'I had a little left on a bolt. No one's wanted it since ... since the war broke out.' And she decided she could tell these women because they, more than anyone else, would understand. 'I was going to make a dress, you see, for a young lady in the village, the daughter of one of the managers at the Asbestos Works. She wanted a very special frock for her engagement party. She was very happy with my design and I was about to cut out the pattern when her fiancée was killed on the Western Front. There was no celebration, of course, after that.'

'How dreadful,' Fiona said quietly, her voice breaking just a little.

'Yes, it truly was,' Jessie said.

And they all shared a moment of reflection at the loss of so many young men, English and Australian both, until Leonora clapped her hands together in a movement that made them all look towards her. Leonora always seemed to be the centre of attention, no matter where she was and who she was with.

'So what do you think, Jessie?' Leonora looked around the party and her chin lifted, as proud as if she owned the property herself. 'Ignore the music. The piano player can't seem to play and turn the pages of his sheet music at the same time.'

'Please don't be so hard on old Mr Thomas,' Jessie implored. 'He can barely see at the best of times and in this evening light, he's struggling to see a note, I expect.'

'Of course,' Leonora said, chastened for a moment. 'But isn't it all marvellous?' Her eyes gleamed. How could Jessie not envy her beauty, her charm and her kindness?

Old Mr Thomas finished his song with a jittery flourish and the crowd broke into applause. Jessie looked around at all the men. How could she dance with anyone but Bert? A hand drifted to her lips and she remembered how clean and smooth his cheek had felt when she'd kissed him on the day he went back to the war. All the words of affection from his many letters were imprinted on her memory.

When the war is over, I'll be making a beeline for Harefield, Jessie, to see you again. Nothing would give me greater joy.

'Sister Grady?'

The nurses around Jessie turned almost as one. A man in a crisp Australian uniform stood, ramrod straight, a letter in his hand.

'Yes?' Leonora said gaily as she stepped forward.

'Sister Leonora Grady?'

Fiona gasped. Gertie clapped a hand to her mouth and both of the nurses crowded Leonora. There was an arm around her waist and another at her shoulders.

'I have an urgent telegram for you.'

Chapter Forty

A shrieking scream split the air.

The piano player stopped mid-song and a heavy silence descended in waves across the dance floor.

'What on earth was that?' William asked, pulling Cora in close. 'I hope to God it's not a Zeppelin. Thirteen of them bombed London last month. Carnage. Absolute carnage.'

Something shuddered in Cora's chest. Her head began to pound. She knew what it was. She shook free of William's arm and pushed her way through the crowd of revellers, of smokers, of drinkers, dancers, patients and porters and villagers.

Leonora had fallen to her knees on the grass and was hunched over, sobbing so hard the sound of it pierced Cora's heart like a sniper's bullet. Jessie stood at her side, holding a pink piece of paper in her hand. Tears streamed down the young woman's face. Wordlessly, Jessie handed the telegram to Cora.

'Oh no,' Cora murmured. Gertie crouched near Leonora, a gentle hand on her friend's back. She looked up at Cora, stricken. Fiona was at her other side, stroking her hair, whispering in Leonora's ear. Was she praying?

Cora didn't need to read the pink telegram to know what it said. Pink meant only one thing. With shaking hands, she held it up to a hanging garden light and read it anyway.

We regret to inform you that Lt Percival John Jones was killed in action 14.10.16. His Majesties the King and Queen and the Commonwealth Government send deepest condolences.

Cora wanted to crush the pink telegram in her hands, rip it up into a hundred pieces and scatter it into the wind.

'Let's get her home,' Cora said. Gertie and Fiona helped Leonora to her feet. The guests silently formed an impromptu guard of honour for Leonora as her friends escorted her to their sleeping quarters.

'That should help her sleep.' William and Cora stood side by side at Leonora's bedside, watching over her. Fiona and Gertie had pulled up chairs across from them and Cora knew they would take turns watching over Leonora until she woke. And beyond that, for as long as she needed.

Cora led William away with a hand on his arm. 'Thank you.'

He nodded solemnly. 'When she wakes, and when she's ready to hear it, please pass on my most sincere sympathies.'

Cora sniffed. William pulled a handkerchief from a pocket inside his suit jacket and passed it to her. His initials had been embroidered in a corner. W.W.K.

'Walter,' he told her. 'William Walter Kent.' And then, 'A gift from my mother when I left Australia.'

Cora clutched the handkerchief in her fist. 'I feel numb, William. I want to cry for her and what she's lost, but I don't seem to have any tears left.'

'You'll cry later. When she doesn't need you so much.'

They stood together, in shock, in silence. He reached for her hands and she held on tight.

'Call me immediately if there's any change in her condition, won't you?'

'Yes, of course.'

'Goodnight, darling.' With a gentle kiss on the cheek, he was gone.

Cora pulled up a chair at Leonora's bedside. Gertie looked blankly ahead, her fingers twisting together in an angry knot.

Fiona suddenly burst into tears. 'They didn't work, did they? All those prayers for Percy. I've let her down.'

Just over a week later, on 16 and 17 October 1916, staff at the hospital formed orderly queues in the mess and had their say in the Commonwealth of Australia's referendum on the subject of conscription.

The question was:

Are you in favour of the government having, in this grave emergency, the same compulsory powers over citizens in regard to requiring their military service, for the term of this War, outside the Commonwealth, as it now has in regard to military service within the Commonwealth?

Eve had gone into great detail in her letters to Cora about the emotional and partisan debate that had erupted back in

Australia on the issue. Cora had been so busy in the past few months she'd paid only scant attention to it. All her concentration had been focussed solely on the events in Europe, not in the Parliament of Australia. As far as she could make out, forcing young men to enlist or not wouldn't change a thing about her work. Injured soldiers had been pouring in from France for months.

Before she cast her vote, Cora dug up Eve's letters and read them again to clarify her own thinking on the issue.

Our dad is firmly on the no side—he's with Archbishop Mannix from Melbourne in believing that if we put the Empire first, we're not taking into account what's best for Australia. Dad also says the Archbishop despises Billy Hughes and I can't decide if it's personality rather than philosophy that has divided them on this issue. I did read that Hughes is only taking the vote to the people because he wouldn't have any luck seeing it passed through the Federal Parliament, because the Labor Party has more representatives and they don't support it. So why not simply drop the idea?

It's all rather confusing. The Methodists, Baptists and Congregationalists are all for conscription, as is the Church of England. All the fine ladies of the League of Loyal Women, who spend Sunday mornings at St Peter's Cathedral, with its spires and stained glass looking down over the city from its perch in North Adelaide, are avidly in the yes camp. They're arguing that all men, no matter their calling or capacity, should share the burden of national service. Why should only some women suffer the loss of their sweethearts and husbands and fathers?

I'm torn, Cora. What should I think? On one hand, won't a yes vote help Australia fight off the threat of a German invasion? Then I hear Dad saying that forcing young men to enlist denies them their basic human right to freedom. All we hear in the newspapers is how dreadfully the fighting is going in the Somme and it's so hard to think about sending more men off to the trenches when so many are being killed in so horrendous a manner.

Please tell me what you think. I should appreciate your advice.

As she waited in line, Cora tried to remember the names of all the young men she'd nursed since she'd arrived in England. There were thousands. Eight young men were now buried at St Mary's churchyard. Cora had been to each funeral and wasn't sure she could attend another. If she was to survive the war with her sanity intact, she had to find a way of coping. Endless funerals were not helping.

She wasn't asked her opinion about going to war in the first place, but by casting her ballot, she could make her feelings known about what it was really like to serve in one.

She voted no.

Chapter Forty-One

18 November 1916

'Shouldn't the nerve cases have been sent home by now, William? How can it be good for their recovery to be kept here in hospital in England now that winter's coming? I'm barely coping with it and I'm in my right mind. At least, most of the time.'

William turned to Cora, stroked a finger down her cheek. 'Firstly, I can confirm you are of sound mind.' His gaze was hungry, desirous. 'And body.'

She laughed and quivered at his gentle touch.

'And secondly, is that a hint that I should put another log on the fire?'

'Would you? It's icy in here. What were we thinking going for a walk in this weather? I'm still chilled to the bone. The lakes are beautiful but what I wouldn't do for some sun. I miss it, dreadfully, don't you?'

'Sun? I've found other things to occupy me. And keep me warm, my darling.' William pulled her close, pressed his lips to hers for a long slow kiss and then threw back the blankets and walked naked to the wicker basket by the fire.

While he chose wood and then poked the flames with one of the metal implements from the stand on the hearth, Cora watched him.

It was almost a dream to be together this way, with no prying eyes, no second glances and no guilt. She propped herself up on an elbow and watched the muscles in his back move and bunch as he worked. She had seen male bodies before. Hundreds of them. But not like this. Not after it had been pressed against her in the most intimate way, not after she'd wrapped herself around the length and shape of him, had him inside her.

There was nothing fancy about their cold little room in the small Cotswolds hotel. But they didn't need fancy. They'd needed privacy and this room afforded it. A double bed with an ancient sunken mattress pushed against one wall. Near it, a low chest of drawers decorated with a kettle and a teapot, two cups, saucers and teaspoons, decoratively arranged on a lace-trimmed doily. Above the mantelpiece on the opposite wall, a gold-framed mirror reflected the thin light from the window. Earlier, they'd pulled back the heavy velvet curtains to make best use of the daylight but would soon have to pull them closed to preserve the heat from the meagre fire.

For the moment, they were enjoying the dusk, the flicker of the flames, the freedom to be truly free in each other's company. They had driven up from Harefield just before lunch that day.

They had each organised to take a week's furlough owing to them and it had been approved with no question. Cora had served more than twelve months without a break and had mentioned to Matron Gray that she would love to see Oxford, even though it may well be too cold to take a punt on the River Cherwell. The matron had thanked her for her hard work and dedication to her patients and asked no further questions before wishing her a relaxing and recuperative journey. Cora had a suspicion that Matron Gray knew Cora's motive but she hadn't said a word.

As for William, he had suggested to Lieutenant Colonel Hayward that while his plans were fluid, he was considering driving down to Bath to see a second cousin who lived there.

There were rules and both Cora and William knew they were breaking them.

Being seen together at Harefield Park was one thing. They had been able to keep up the ruse that they were professional colleagues and it wasn't unusual for friendships to develop among the staff. In times of crisis and hard work, when they were swamped with patients and overloaded with cases, there were only a few other people who could understand the frustrations and small rewards, and those intimacies were shared. Matron Gray and Hayward had made it clear, in not so many words, that the Australians were there to serve, not fraternise. Anything else would only be a distraction. But Cora had thought more than once how cruel that was, to effectively deny men and women the comfort of another's arms and affections, when they were so far from all that was familiar, so out of step with daily routines and occupations.

But there were rules of propriety that had to be obeyed, rules that governed both the professional and private lives of nurses. Married nurses were not able to serve. Single nurses were to follow the example of Florence Nightingale twenty-five years earlier, who had worked so hard—and against much resistance—to professionalise nursing as a career.

Nightingale had set down edicts about how nurses should behave and they had permeated every area of nurse training. It wasn't enough to be skilled in patient care. A nurse was also expected to be without womanly weaknesses. She should not be petty or selfish or envious or jealous. Gossip and foolish talking should be beneath her. She was to be, at all times, a good woman.

And what, in Nightingale's eyes, determined a good woman? One who exhibited quietness and gentleness, patience and endurance and forbearance. She should, at all times, obey. Obey, not question. That rankled with Cora. Florence wanted nurses to be saints and Cora knew she herself had already failed that test. She was no saint, nor had she ever had any aspirations to be one. It was impossible to be saintly during a war. She had decided that a thousand patients ago. She had become impatient and angry, selfish that she had little time to herself, jealous of those women back in Australia who were getting their boys back. She had engaged in unkind thoughts about people who crossed her. She was more than exhausted with it all.

And she had entertained lustful thoughts about William for longer than she cared to admit. When he'd told her of his planned getaway, she had agreed readily, hungrily, *yes yes yes*.

That morning, she'd waved goodbye to her friends—only Gertie knew the truth—and had taken the vehicular bus to Uxbridge. William had picked her up outside the florist, as planned, with a smile and a peck on the cheek and she had instantly felt free. He'd borrowed a motor vehicle from one of the other Australian doctors, who'd bought it with some family money and who had intended to become an Antipodean tourist and drive it all over the countryside on weekends. In the end, there had been no weekends to speak of and he'd made it available to whomever wanted to use it.

William had booked the Cotswolds hotel under the names Captain and Mrs William Kent and if the elderly receptionist had had any suspicions about the true state of their relationship, she had given nothing away. A paying customer was a paying customer after all, and if she'd made a habit of turning away couples who weren't married during the war, she would have more empty rooms than full ones.

The fire flared and crackled and William stood back, hands on his lean hips, admiring his work. The flames licked around the wood he'd just added to the fire. 'Look at that. I've mastered the element of fire.'

'Congratulations, Prometheus.'

William turned back to her and grinned. The two of them were in a little bubble. The bitter cold outside couldn't touch them, seep into their bones or make them shiver. Cora knew what was waiting for her back at Harefield. A ward full of strangers. Two of them blind who needed to be transferred out to a mental home. Another with his jaw blown away who was waiting to be transported to Queen Mary's Hospital at Sidcup for restorative surgery. Two men who were well enough to go back to their units but who had begged and pleaded with her to stay. That would all be waiting for her when she returned. The grief was still deep inside her, embedded now, but for a week at least she was going to try to tuck it away. To let her needs take priority, as selfish as that sounded. For it was the only way she was going to survive with her sanity intact, of that she was sure.

William returned to the bed, and when he lifted an arm Cora tucked herself against him. She pulled the blankets up to their chins.

'Prometheus,' he mused. 'I believe he gave man the gift of fire.'

'That he did.' The gift of warmth and comfort and home. How many more gifts had William given her? There was no numerical way to measure them; what he meant to her couldn't be counted off on one's fingers.

How could love be measured? What was the scale of it? Was it a creek that became a raging torrent? Did it start out as a breeze and end up as a cyclone, engulfing everything in its path? Or did it form slowly, like a healing scar?

And where would her affections lie on such a scale?

She loved him. There was nothing surer. She couldn't have entertained the idea of giving herself to him if she didn't. They were in an alternate universe, in which the rules of civility, or propriety, didn't apply. And there, in the world they inhabited in England in November 1916, the past meant nothing, the future was unknowable, and all they could do was embrace the moment. Cora was ready for it. She was filled with the desires of a woman, not the flirtatious affectations of a young girl. She knew what she wanted and knew that she would lie with William that night and for five more, as lovers.

He lit a cigarette and took a leisurely puff, turning his head slightly to considerately blow the smoke away from Cora. He knew she didn't like the smell of tobacco.

'Everything will be fine without you for a week, Cora. You know that.'

'I know they'll be fine with Gertie in charge. She won an everlasting place in their affections when she helped two of them sneak into the ward after curfew.'

William laughed. 'She did?'

'They'd had a few too many at the Cricketers and arrived back at the hospital after ten at night. She ushered them in and kept their secret.'

'A true war hero. How's Leonora?'

It had been a long eight weeks since Leonora had received the news about Percy. He'd been buried almost where he'd fallen, so there had been no funeral. His personal effects had been sent back to his parents in Australia so all she had were his letters, which she read each night, still. She'd returned to work after two weeks furlough, which seemed to have given her purpose, but she was a shell of the woman she'd once been.

'She gets out of bed every morning. That's something, isn't it?'

'It's a start. How's her mood?'

'Low. I would expect nothing less from someone who loved as much as she did. She hadn't told her family about the engagement, you see, knowing her parents wouldn't approve of him. Too low class, or some such rubbish. That's made the whole situation sadder for her. Unbearably so.'

'They sound like Austen's Mr Elliot.'

'They do, don't they? Shouldn't anyone celebrate finding love in among all this?'

William kissed the top of her head and she moved so she could look at his face. 'Yes, we should.'

She could stare at those soft blue eyes forever. However long forever was.

He stroked the soft curls at her forehead, tucked them behind an ear in such a gentle way. She wrapped an arm tighter around his warm body.

'I'm prattling on, I suppose. I'll stop now.'

'Please don't. I could listen to you talk all day and all night.'

'You have me for five more days. I can say a lot in five days.'

'Not if I have anything to do with it,' and then he silenced her with a kiss more intimate than anything she'd shared. She shifted her legs and he moved into the space between them. His body was a delicious and sensuous weight on hers.

She threw her arms around him and forgot everything.

Harefield Hospital
Middlesex
England
December 23rd, 1916

Dear Mum, Dad, Eve and Grace,
Sending you love and the warmest of Christmas wishes from Harefield hospital, a place decorated with so much holly that one can't help but feel in the festive spirit. Who would have thought I would be spending my second Christmas in Blighty?

The holly trees in the grounds are beautiful and so abundant—some are fifty feet tall—that there is plenty to go around. All the boys have been busy roaming the grounds here and the village to cut branches of holly to send home. Every ward—and indeed every bed—is decorated with sprays of it and it gives us all a lift to see the place looking so wonderful. In my ward, the boys sketched a large map of Australia with blue ribbon for the coastline and one of them, with more artistic skills that the others, drew a kangaroo and an emu in the middle right where Alice Springs is, with two flags crossed over them and a Rising Sun badge. Every time I look up and see the words 'home sweet home' printed above our beloved continent, I must admit to a little pang of homesickness, but it doesn't last for long as I'm surrounded by Australians here in Harefield and when we're feeling blue, we tell each other stories of home.

The weeks leading up to Christmas have been very festive. There was snow in November and some lovely frosty mornings that remind me where I am and what I am here to do. It's such an odd thing to have pipes freeze and burst, instead of turning them on only to find scalding hot water! Autumn here was so lovely. Everyone says that England is most beautiful at that time of year and I can't help but agree. The reds and oranges and tawny browns descend on the countryside and then, one by one, the trees lose their leaves in waves with every breath of wind, falling like colourful snowflakes.

I've developed a taste for chestnuts, you might be surprised to know. The boys pick them from the trees around the village and we roast them in the stoves in the ward. There is nothing like them.

My letters have been very tardy this year and I hope you will all forgive me. Did you raise a glass to me on Christmas Day? I missed your lunch, Mum—most especially your roast chicken and plum pudding.

With much love,
Cora

Chapter Forty-Two

25 December 1916

'Do you think we've captured it convincingly, Captain?'

Cora and William stood as close to the coal fire in Ward 22 as they could without burning themselves and studied the Christmas decorations. Every available surface—windowsills and side tables and trestles—was scattered with shredded paper and cotton bolls ripped into whisps like clouds pulled from the sky. In the corner, a young fir tree was decorated with daisy chains made from newspaper and a large banner reading *Merrie Christmas* hung from the rafters.

'It's a masterpiece. Well done, boys.' A round of whoops went up from the patients.

The men had embraced the Christmas spirit. They were clean-shaven and freshly bathed. Those who were able sat on beds in groups of twos and threes, smoking and chatting with their pals. Those who weren't able to leave their beds weren't alone. There was either a nurse or a volunteer at their side, playing cards or chatting to them, or another patient, showing by their actions they believed that no man should be alone at Christmas.

'Merry Christmas, Sister Barker.'

'And to you, Captain.'

They watched over their patients and Cora felt a lightness and hope she hadn't felt since she'd landed in England.

'I have something for you.' William held a hand out between them, his palm upturned. There was a small gift, about the size of a bar of soap, wrapped in brown paper and tied with a piece of string.

The heart that had been fluttering now beat fast. 'Is that for me?'

'Yes. Unless you'd like me to give it to one of the men.'

A hand flew to her chest, as if by pressing it there against her breast she might calm herself. 'I hope you don't mind if I open it later when I'm off duty.'

'I'd prefer it,' he replied.

Cora took the gift, surreptitiously slipped it in her pocket and trembled at the idea of his secret wrapped up and hidden away in her uniform.

'Sister!' Wright called from halfway down the ward. 'If you weren't stuck here in Blighty in the middle of winter, what would you be doing for Christmas back home?'

Cora motioned for William to follow her, and they went to Wright's bed. Smith, Touchell and Hurst were in the group. Four men and only five legs between them. She sat next to the Queenslander and tucked her hands under her knees, taking a moment to remember.

'C'mon, doc. Take a load off,' Hurst said, patting the blanket and moving along as best he could to make space.

'Kind of you, Corporal.' William sat too.

'The name's Alexander,' Hurst said, holding out a hand.

'William.' They shook hands and the men repeated the gesture with respectful nods.

'Smoke?' Smith held out a packet. William nodded his thanks and took one, leaning close to Touchell to light his cigarette from his patient's.

'Sister? Tell us about your Christmas back home, won't you?'

Cora gazed into the middle distance. 'Let me think. It would probably be hot as Hades in Adelaide this time of year. I might be working the early shift at the Adelaide Hospital. Because the rest of my family would always wait until I'd finished work, there would be a lovely Christmas dinner of roast chicken and vegetables and freshly baked bread. My mother and two younger sisters would have spent all day preparing it, which means I wouldn't have to lift a finger. And last Christmas I was here, working.'

There was a wolf-whistle. 'You've got two younger sisters, Sister?'

Cora laughed. 'I promise to introduce you when you get home.' And she didn't hide the hope in her words, that they would get home, that they would be well enough and strong enough in their own minds to want to romance a young lady, one kind enough to overlook their missing limbs and their battle scars.

William repositioned himself on the small bed and as he did, his thigh pressed against hers. He didn't move. Neither did she.

'And here we are, a year later, and you're working on Christmas Day again.'

'True.' Cora nodded, and transformed her smile into an exaggerated frown. 'But, then again ... in Adelaide I was looking after *very* old men with gout and piles.' It wasn't the exact truth but she forgave herself the lie. 'Here, I'm surrounded by brave and handsome boys, sitting in a ward decorated with artificial snow. I'd pick here any day.'

A round of cheers broke out and Cora nodded graciously, letting their affections warm her. Their acclamation was better than the stove.

'And what about you, doc? Where were you last Christmas?'

William took a long drag on his cigarette, lifted his eyes to the ceiling for a moment. 'Last Christmas, I was here at Harefield. But the Christmas before that?'

He paused, glanced from soldier to soldier, and took a puff of his cigarette. 'I was at sea, sailing on *Kyarra* with the 1st Australian General Hospital. We were bound for Egypt. If I remember rightly, there may have been whisky involved and some heavy breathing over the side of the ship.'

'Some of the boys from Gallipoli ended up there,' Hurst said. 'At Heliopolis.'

'That's right. They did.'

He was there. In the midst of the disaster. He saw it all.

A bell rang out and all eyes turned to the door. Gertie and Fiona arrived pushing a dinner wagon into the ward, so heavily laden with boxes they could barely be seen behind them.

'Gifts from the Red Cross,' Gertie announced and there was another rousing cheer as the nurses began distributing one to each patient.

'A new comb!' Bassett announced. 'Just what I need. I threw my old one away in the trenches. What use was it against the lice?'

Touchell laughed as he waved a new shaving brush and shaving soap above his head.

'Hope you use it to shave off that sodding moustache,' his mate called out.

Gertie and Fiona continued down the rows of beds, stopping to chat and have a laugh with the boys as they went. Even if the respite was brief, it was a welcome one. These emotions would disappear by night-time, Cora knew, when memories of Christmases past and families and sweethearts would rise up and overwhelm them, bringing tears and nightmares and grief. But for now, for today, this was enough.

Cora called out to Gertie. 'I hope you're staying for the ward judging. I think we're in with a shot for best decorated ward.'

'Absolutely.' Gertie winked. 'That artificial snow will clinch it for us, I'm certain.'

'But Gertie, we can't,' Fiona huffed. 'We have thirty-six more wards to visit and loads more parcels to distribute.' She blew a strand of hair from her eyes. 'I was hoping we'd be finished before lunch but it's not looking likely.'

Cora sighed dreamily. 'I hear there are fruit jellies and custards for dessert. Do you know how long it's been since I've had a fruit jelly?'

'Lunch had better be as good as everyone's expecting. What a dreadful let-down if it turns out to be meatloaf and turnips.' Gertie pulled a face. 'But we'll see Leonora. She's with her amputees this morning.' Since Percy's death, Leonora had thrown herself even further into her work. There were so many amputees that needed care and treatment.

'Sisters.' William saluted the nurses. 'A merry Christmas to you all.'

The nurses returned his greeting. Cora pressed a palm against the pocket of her uniform, William's present a little secret treasure inside it, like a seashell discovered on a seaside holiday.

Fiona gave the trolley a shove to get it moving. 'Come on, Gert. We'll see you all in the mess for lunch. And if not, at the concert this afternoon.'

'Concert?' William asked.

'Word is going around that a comedian has come up from London to perform for the troops.' Gertie sighed. 'He'd better be funny or I'll ask for a refund.'

William suddenly snapped to attention and saluted. The nurses knew to quickly form a line. Matron Gray and Lieutenant Colonel Hayward had arrived in the ward to judge the competition.

'Merry Christmas, Captain. Sisters,' Hayward boomed. He looked down at his feet and chuckled. 'What's this then? Do I have to pay my respects to the Kaiser?'

Matron Gray smiled. 'Some of the men laid it there.'

'It shows such patriotic spirit to the King.' Hayward and Matron Gray each made a great show of wiping their muddy shoes on the German flag that had been laid out to form a doormat.

Hooting and hollering echoed throughout the ward.

The official judging party began their inspection, greeting each patient and chatting to them for a moment, sharing warm wishes and smiles, praising their service and their stubborn determination for their own recovery. William and Cora followed a few respectful steps behind.

'I think your lot will win,' he murmured.

She shrugged. 'Honestly, while the men might like the one pound prize money to buy extra cigarettes or to shout themselves a beer at the White Horse Inn, it's the getting here that has been so important. We've spent weeks making all this.' She swept a hand around the room. 'It's given us all something positive to look forward to.'

William regarded her curiously. 'I would never have thought about it that way.'

'And the men have grown to know each other better, too. Imagine what it's like for them. Waiting to recover. Waiting for more surgery. Waiting for the medical board to wave its magic wand to determine their future.' The board's members assessed a soldier's fitness for duty. A determination of Class A meant a soldier was fit to return to general service. Class B meant more time was needed for recovery before returning to the front, while Class C meant a ticket home. So many of the men they treated were deemed to be Class C from the moment they arrived: they'd lost limbs or were blinded or deafened from exploding bombs or their injuries would need more than six months of treatment in England.

Cora held her hands together behind her back, her fingers tightly wound. 'I don't know how they bear it. I honestly don't.'

'Cora?' William spoke her name so quietly she almost hadn't heard him.

'Yes?'

'Will you be at the concert this afternoon?'

'I expect I will.'

A smile flickered and then disappeared into a stoic expression. 'Might we go for a walk while the men are being otherwise entertained?'

She nodded. *Yes yes yes.*

When Cora returned to the nurses' quarters, her heart full and warm and her fingers feeling almost frostbitten, she found the place in darkness. As she'd walked past the

canteen, too distracted to join the others singing carols at
the top of their lungs, she'd spied Gertie, Leonora and Fiona
inside leading the chorus, and had been thankful they were
experiencing such Christmas cheer. As for herself, she'd had
other more pressing plans.

She fumbled for the light switch and a dim light shone
down on their beds, each one made with regulation hospital
corners, none tauter than Fiona's. Despite the neatness of
the beds, there was a ramshackle quality to the place. The
curtains at the windows clearly required a clean. The floor
needed sweeping and she knew that if she were to look
closely there would be cobwebs along the ceiling trusses but
she chose not to. They had only expected to be in Harefield
for six months. What point had there been in making their
accommodation more homely? And anyway, if they had any
energy for cleaning, it was directed to the wards, not the
nurses' quarters.

When she shivered, Cora walked across the hut to the
stove and loaded coal onto its glowing embers before pulling
up a chair to warm herself. She held out her gloved hands to
the meagre warmth and let her attention drift.

She and William had shared a wonderful afternoon
together. They'd found some privacy in the hospital's
store and, while everyone else was distracted by Christmas
celebrations, they'd been distracted by each other. Should
she have felt guilty? Before the war, Cora would have found
herself torn between the thrill of being with William and
the propriety of her role. Now, she barely gave the rules
another thought.

Life was short. And brutal. Cora needed a reminder that
amid the carnage of war there was life, and she had found

that in her love for William. Each day, as the newspapers were filled with dreadful headlines and the hospital was flooded with more injured men, the future seemed further away than ever. Her life was a day-to-day proposition.

Whatever she and William shared here in Harefield was of the moment. Who could guarantee them more than that?

Cora shivered. As she pulled her coat lapels tighter around her, she felt the square form of William's present in her pocket.

She tore at the fingers of her gloves and they tumbled to the floor in her haste to get to the present. When she tore off the brown paper, she gasped at the sight of a deep green velvet box. Inside, on ivory satin, sat a brooch pin. She lifted it from its box and held it to the weak overhead light.

The cameo in the centre was small, perhaps half an inch in diameter, flanked on either side by gold swallows, their wings and forked tail feathers formed in such a way to suggest they were in full flight.

Her eyes filled with tears.

Yes, life was short and brutal. But there was joy to be found, no matter how fleeting, if you knew where to look.

Chapter Forty-Three

'You all right, Dottie?'

Across the Christmas table, Dottie looked white as a ghost. She'd just pushed away her full dinner plate—goose, vegetables and all the trimmings. Jessie thought it most uncharacteristic.

'Dot?' Harry's chair scraped back and he rounded the corner of the table to be at her side.

Dottie pressed a hand to her stomach. 'I feel a little gippy in the tummy, that's all. I'm so sorry, Mum. It all looks really delicious. I think I need to go and lie down.'

'You've been working too hard,' Harry exclaimed, his voice tight with worry. 'Four deliveries a day and that mailbag. It must weigh a ton.'

Dottie got to her feet. Harry slipped his arm through hers and together they shuffled off to their bedroom.

Win brought an elbow to rest on the table and put her chin in her cupped hand. 'The poor love.'

Jessie surveyed the table. Her stomach rumbled. She was famished.

'Do you mind if I …'

'Go ahead, love. I hate to see all this good food go to waste. Those hens will get spoilt if we give them roast vegetables.' Win got up from the table, picked up Harry's plate and set it on the stove to keep warm.

There was a knock on the front door.

Jessie's fork was perched mid-air, filled with meat and gravy. How she loved her mother's gravy. Win looked curiously at her daughter. 'Whoever can that be? The carollers came yesterday.'

Jessie quickly filled her mouth. 'I'll go, Mum. You might want to put Dot's in the oven as well.' Jessie wiped her hands on a napkin and walked through the workroom.

She opened the door a peep, careful of both who it might be and of the bitter cold. When she spied khaki, Jessie threw open the door.

'Bert!' Had she screamed his name? She wasn't sure but when Win and Harry came running to the front door she supposed she might have.

'Jessie. It's so good to see you.' Bert slipped off his slouch hat and out of the shadow of its brim, she saw a grin so wide she thought he might hurt his face if he kept it up. 'I hope you don't mind. I've come right from the train station.'

'What ... what are you doing here?' She struggled with the urge to throw her arms around him and crossed them against her chest instead. It wouldn't do to be seen hugging soldiers on the doorstep, even if it was Christmas and even if he had turned up so entirely unexpectedly Jessie thought she might be imagining the whole thing.

He looked past her and nodded. 'Hello there.'

Jessie looked over her shoulder. Win stood open-mouthed and Harry looked suspiciously at the Australian soldier on the doorstep. Dottie, drawn by the commotion, joined them, asking, 'What's going on?'

'This is Private Bert Mott,' Jessie announced. 'The Australian I've been writing to.'

Dottie breathed deep and pressed a hand to her stomach. 'I believe I've delivered all your letters, Private Mott. Dozens and dozens of them. Regular as clockwork, you are.'

Jessie nodded her head in Dottie's direction. 'This is my sister-in-law, Dottie.'

'You must work for the post office then,' Bert said.

'I do,' Dottie replied and her cheeks flushed with pride. 'And this is my mother.'

'Hello, Private,' Win said. 'Isn't it nice to meet you.'

'Now, now. Please call me Bert. You must be Harry,' Bert said, nodding respectfully at her brother. Harry reached out his left hand to shake Bert's outstretched one, and Bert didn't bat an eyelid at the unusual gesture. Jessie almost burst into tears.

'It's always an honour to meet a soldier.'

'Nice to meet the man of the house, Harry.'

Win suddenly fluttered her hands in frustration. 'What's with all this standing in the cold? Come in, won't you?' Win bustled Harry, Dottie and Jessie back inside the house. 'You're just in time for Christmas dinner. I hope you haven't eaten.'

'I hope I'm not interrupting. I can come back later if that's more convenient.'

Jessie was stricken at the thought and she stepped forward to take his hand. 'No,' she said quickly, smiling up at him. 'Please come in. We have plenty to go round.'

Bert stepped inside, set his black canvas kitbag on the floor and took off his greatcoat.

Jessie stepped forward to take it from him and hung it on a hook on the wall. She didn't care if anyone saw her press her face into the soft wool. She inhaled the scent of Bert's shaving soap. She had never hung up a man's coat in her home. Had never had one sit with her family for a meal. Had never had a man to parade before her family as a way of saying *he's mine and I'm his and I want you all to like him as much as I do.*

'Sit down, Bert. Please,' Win implored. 'I'll fetch you a plate.'

As they all settled at the appropriate positions at the kitchen table—Harry at the head, Win nearest the stove, Dottie, who seemed to have miraculously overcome her gippy tummy, on the other side nearest the sink and Jessie next to her mother. Bert sat opposite her. She was directly in his line of sight and Jessie relished the opportunity to stare unashamedly at his lovely face.

'There you go,' Win said, setting Harry's plate in front of him.

'This looks absolutely blood— excuse me. Absolutely delicious.' As Bert devoured the hot dinner, he seemed blissfully unaware that he was being observed as if he were an exhibit in a glass case.

Dottie and Harry tucked into their dinners. Win picked at hers, too focussed on Bert, and Jessie ate because eating stopped her staring at Bert quite so much. Which was all she wanted to do.

The village had been full of Australians for more than a year but this was the first time the Chesters had ever had one in their home. Jessie couldn't blame her family for staring at him so inquisitively. Win was eyeing him up and down, sizing up the cut of his jib, as she so often said about a stranger. She was no doubt assessing his gaunt face and congratulating herself for feeding the poor boy. She was probably already thinking about what she might serve up for supper—would there be enough leftovers?—and what to present him with when he was next invited.

And then there was Harry. Beyond a shadow of a doubt, he was assessing Bert for his suitability as his sister's sweetheart, because surely she wouldn't just write to any Australian soldier, would she, and so frequently? With their father gone, and Harry now a husband himself, it was only natural that he assume his role as protector. Jessie thought how the tables had turned: she had grown up thinking she was his. She had never seen him so confident or so happy since his marriage to Dottie. His physical restrictions seemed somehow less of a burden, even though nothing about his body or his abilities had altered. Jessie knew this change was all down to Dottie and the love they shared.

And as for her? She simply couldn't believe Bert was sitting in her house. Alive. Whole. Looking as bright and cheery as a new penny, with a smile on his face that not even the Jerries and the mud and the trenches had been able to erase. Surely Bert Mott was the handsomest man she had ever met. And the kindest. And the funniest. His letters always made her laugh, filled with tales of his adventures in France with his cobbers, as he called them, his attempts to communicate with the locals—'They don't seem to understand me when I parlais Francais'—and the long and boring hours he'd spent waiting for something to happen. Every night she had wished for more long boring hours for him.

How his letters had thrilled her. Every word he'd written had convinced her that she might be just a little bit in love with Private Mott. How was it possible to fall in love with someone she'd barely spent any time with, really. Had they ever truly been alone? Had he ever kissed her on the lips? Did she need those displays of affection to know if he felt the same? Was turning up at her home direct from the train station evidence of his affection? It was a thrilling thought but one she'd shared with no one, not even Dottie.

'So, Private. Bert.' Harry cleared his throat. 'You must be on some kind of furlough or something.'

Bert set his cutlery across his plate and wiped his mouth with a napkin. 'That's right. I have a week's leave and I was given permission to come back to England for it.' His gaze fixed on Jessie. 'I promised you I'd come back when I could.'

'You did.' Jessie felt hot all of a sudden. 'Where will you be staying?'

'I thought I'd take a room at the Cricketers. It'll be nice to be in the village.'

She smiled.

'I hear you're starting a new position soon, Harry.'

All eyes turned to Harry. 'I am.' Harry puffed up with pride and Dottie looked at him as if he were her prince. 'I'm going to work in the post office in Harefield. Sorting the mail. They need all the help they can get, even if I'm a little slow.'

'Being smart makes up for that, Harry.' Dottie popped a kiss on his cheek.

'You can't know how important letters and packages are to us boys.' Bert shook his head. 'To know that our families

… and friends … are thinking of us?' He glanced at Jessie. 'Well, it's what keeps us going.'

'We appreciate what you boys are doing for us.' Harry said. 'For all of England.'

'It's an honour to do my bit with my comrades. We've still got some work to do. The Huns are still on the march. So are the Turks.'

'To the King,' Win declared, holding her cup of tea aloft.

'To the King,' the others entreated.

Two hours later, with conversation exhausted, pudding devoured, and cups of tea drunk, Bert prepared to leave. Dottie and Harry had said their goodbyes before retreating to their bedroom.

'That's the best Christmas dinner I've ever had.' Bert grinned at Win and then winked. 'But don't go telling my mum that, will you?'

Win looked fully pleased with herself. 'You're too kind. We hope to see you again while you're in England.'

Jessie held her breath. Bert smiled down at her. 'I hope so, too.'

They exchanged goodnights with Win before stepping out to the street. As the front door closed behind them, they gazed into each other's eyes, oblivious to the biting cold and the wind that howled down the high street.

'I still can't believe you're here,' Jessie whispered. 'Why didn't you tell me you were coming?'

Bert shrugged. 'When I got word, I hopped on a train as quick as I could. There was no time for writing and I reckoned I'd get here before any letter did.' He winked. 'Don't tell Dottie I said that.'

Jessie felt bold. 'Seeing you is better than any letter.'

'You're even prettier than I remember, you know that?'

Bert moved closer. Jessie held her breath. Just as she was sure he was going to kiss her, whistles and shouts erupted from across the street. Bert stilled.

'The Andrews boys,' Jessie huffed. 'The little blighters.' The three tearaways were still in short pants and their cheekiness had gone unchecked since their father had enlisted and their mother had taken up work at the Asbestos Works. Their grandmother was all that stood between them and the rest of the world and she was as soft as they came.

'You got yourself a sweetheart, Miss Chester?'

'Kiss him, Miss Chester. Mwah mwah mwah.' The brothers laughed themselves silly and Jessie felt the blush creep up her cheeks.

'Mind your manners, boys,' Bert called out in a tone that suggested if they didn't hush up he might walk over to them and give them a shilling each to spend at the village sweet shop after Christmas.

Jessie laughed nervously. Bert was still close. His eyes were fixed on her mouth. How she wished they could be alone together, away from her family's attention and the prying eyes of the street. She wanted to be somewhere so private that when he held her in his arms no one would see or hear or care.

'Are you free tomorrow?' he asked.

'Yes.'

'And for the next week?'

'Yes,' she laughed. Was there anything lovelier than staring into Bert's blue eyes? 'They like you,' she said. 'Mum and Harry and Dottie.'

'And I like them. They were very bloody generous to a stranger who turned up on their doorstep on Christmas Day.'

'No Australian is a stranger in Harefield.'

A truck ambled past with a red cross on its flapping canvas sides. Jessie and Bert watched it pass. They both knew without saying there was human cargo inside it, heading to the hospital. And that's when reality almost bowled her over. Bert had been one of those men. In one week he would be getting back on a truck just like it to head back to the front.

'Don't worry, Jess.' He reached for her hand and squeezed it between both of his. They were warm and strong. Her fingers felt suddenly icy cold. She sucked in a breath and held it so she wouldn't cry.

'I'm not worrying. Truly.' She hoped he heard reassurance in her voice.

'Harry's a decent bloke.'

'He's the best brother a girl could ever ask for.'

'He reminds me of some of the fellas I met when I was in hospital. The blokes worse off than me, I mean. Before the war, I would have thought losing your leg or your arm would have been the worst thing that could happen. I thought you'd be better off dead, you know? But they're still blokes. They'll never be the same as they were before the war but they've kept their spirits up and they keep laughing and playing pranks on each other. The blokes with one leg? They strap on their wooden legs and hobble around like they've just struck it rich. They've made me see things in a different way. I expect having Harry for a brother has made you see the world in a way that other people don't see it.'

Bert was right but she had never been able to articulate it so succinctly. 'People in the village have never been able to see in Harry what we do.'

'That's their loss, then, isn't it?'

He had passed the test. He had passed it with leaps and bounds. Jessie was certain that Win and Harry and Dottie were as taken with him as she was. Bert had simply been himself and that had been enough.

'What are we doing tomorrow?' she asked.

'It's a surprise,' he grinned.

Jessie closed the door behind her and pressed herself against it and held her hands to her heart. When she closed her eyes, she saw Bert smiling at her, so close he might have been about to kiss her.

'He's gone then?'

Jessie blinked open her eyes. She nodded.

Win came into the front room from the kitchen doorway, wringing her hands together.

'He's a lovely boy. No doubt about that.'

'Mum ...' Jessie demurred. 'You don't mind about him being a soldier?'

'Love, have you thought about what it means to fall in love with such a man? One who'll be going back to fight? Or if not to fight, back to Australia when it's over?'

Jessie hadn't let herself think that far ahead. It was a window in her mind that, unlike the windows in her house, was kept tightly latched. She couldn't think of tomorrow when tomorrow was so uncertain. With every bomb that rained down on the streets of London, uncertainty grew about the war. So many young men had been killed in battlefields across the Channel that dreaming of tomorrow seemed like a fool's errand for anyone.

'I can't help it. I think I love him, Mum.'

Win teared up and sniffed. 'Oh, Jessie.'

'He's asked me to spend the day with him tomorrow. Is that all right?'

'Of course it is. This sweetheart of yours is determined to have you and to win the war.'

'He is, Mum. That's exactly who he is.'

Chapter Forty-Four

27 December 1916

The journey to London had only taken twenty minutes in the motor vehicle ably piloted by one of the volunteer ladies at the hospital, a service rendered to all Australian soldiers with a connection to Harefield.

Mrs Hall-Smith was the same age as Jessie's own mother but had the vitality of a woman half her age, judging by the speed and agility at which she careened around every corner and roadway and the strength of her foot on the brakes as she deposited Jessie and Bert at the corner of Shaftesbury Avenue and Charing Cross Road.

'Are you sure you don't want me to drive you to Victoria Street and the Strand? I'm told by all the other boys that the Anzac Club on Horseferry Road is the place to be. And it's rather cold out.'

'That's very kind of you,' Bert called out above the traffic. A motor vehicle behind Mrs Hall-Smith sounded its horn angrily. 'But this'll do just fine. We're happy to walk, aren't we Jessie?'

Jessie smiled at Bert.

'I'll be back here, right at this spot, at seven o'clock tonight to pick you up.' Mrs Hall-Smith winked at Jessie, beeped her horn twice and raced off.

'Good Lord,' Jessie said, clutching her purse to her chest.

'I don't know who's more frightening. Mrs Hall-Smith with a motor vehicle or a Hun with a gun.' Bert clutched his stomach in uproarious laughter. 'I've faced both and it's a close call!'

Jessie shivered in mock fright. 'I swear I will never be able to tell my mother about that. She'll forbid me to ever ride in one again. She's just come round to the idea that I can go out unchaperoned. The escort from Mrs Hall-Smith certainly helped settle her nerves at the idea that I would be in London with you all alone.'

Bert held an elbow out and Jessie slipped her arm through it. 'You'll always be safe with me, Jess. I swear it.'

They took Greek Street to Soho Square, craning their necks high to take in the Georgian architecture of the houses on the street. The square itself was busy with meandering couples and well-dressed children laughing and playing.

Bert whistled. 'Imagine having the coin to live here, hey, Jessie?'

Jessie thought the folk who lived in these houses would be as rich—perhaps even richer—than the best families who lived near Harefield. Living in the country was one thing, but London? Surely those homes with their flat Georgian roofs needed the top floors to house all their servants; their butlers and housemaids and cooks. 'These aren't my people, Bert. How would I know what to do with all those rooms?'

'And aren't I glad of that, Jess? You wouldn't be stepping out with an Australian digger if you were one of those toffs.'

Jessie laughed gaily. She felt giddy at the thought that she was walking in London with a fellow. And one in uniform, no less. Was it the Australian sun that he'd carried with him to England and saved up just for her? He seemed to glow with it and she basked in it.

'Now, to somewhere for a bite to eat, Miss Jessie Chester. And then there's the surprise I promised you.'

Jessie and Bert walked out of His Majesty's Theatre into Haymarket. Jessie was abuzz with excitement. Absolutely everything had been beyond her imaginings. She looked up at the theatre and couldn't believe she had just been inside so grand a building for almost two hours. Outside, there were four colonnades on the first floor creating a set-back area where the fancy people might sip their champagne and their sherries and look out over the street. Domes pointed skyward and a glass canopy reached out over the ground-floor entrances to protect theatregoers from the rain. She and Bert had seats in the stalls and when she'd looked up she'd developed a crick in her neck, it was so high.

Had everyone in London come to the theatre that afternoon? There were more people on Haymarket alone than Jessie believed she had ever seen in her life, jostling each other in their thick coats and scarves and warm hats. Who were they, these rushing hordes? Whoever they were— ladies walking together, husbands and wives, mothers with a clutch of children, hawkers, men on bicycles and post women—they seemed to be in perpetual motion, barely stopping to look for motor vehicles as they crossed the road, ignoring the news boys holding aloft that afternoon's copy of the *Daily Telegraph*, ducking and weaving around street sellers with paper bags of roast chestnuts and walnuts. It was life in a way that Jessie had never seen it before and she was overwhelmed and ecstatic at the same time.

They found a tearoom and when they were seated inside, their orders placed, Bert reached his hands across the table. 'What did you think of the show, Jess?'

She reached for his hands and squeezed tight. She was bursting with all she had to tell him. 'I've never seen anything like it in my life and I don't think I will again. The costumes, Bert!' The female characters had worn the most extravagant stage attire. Little tops that looked like the new brassieres the modern girls were wearing. Daring bare arms and bare stomachs had been in full view, wrapped with ribbons and decorated with exotic glittering stones hanging from long necklaces. Headdresses created from ostrich feathers that must have been four feet long at least, and enormous bows fastened to headwraps, and crowns of glittering gold with flowing satin.

'The boys made me swear to take you to see *Chu Chin Chow*. And they were right. What a show. Who wouldn't love a song and dance about Ali Baba and the Forty Thieves. The live camel!'

Jessie covered her eyes. 'And the snakes! I thought I was going to jump right out of my seat when I saw them.'

'Never you mind about snakes.' Bert reached for her hands across the table. 'I know what do with one of those creepy crawlies. All you need is a shovel and you slice it right in half if it comes close.'

Jessie peeped through her fingers. 'I expect you had snakes as pets back in Australia?'

'Bloody oath,' Bert grinned. 'And goannas and kangaroos. We ride the roos in races around Murray Bridge and then we hang on for dear life as they swim across the Murray. And we have pet koalas in our apple trees too.'

'Really?' He shot her a warm smile and she forgot to breathe for a moment.

'I'm pulling your leg. If you get a bite from a brownie, it'll kill you before you realise you've been bitten. Best not to go anywhere near 'em.'

Jessie laughed. 'Despite the snakes, it was wonderful, Bert. This has been the best day of my life, I swear.'

'Really and truly?'

'Really and truly.' And Jessie squeezed her eyes shut, wanting to hold the memory of that moment—the show, the crowds, the feeling of at last being fully alive—in her heart forever. She had never been so happy.

She opened her eyes, her silent wish tucked away in her heart.

And judging by the tears that welled in Bert's eyes as he held her hands across the table, he felt the same.

Chapter Forty-Five

31 December 1916

At the front of the main house at Harefield hospital, Jessie and Bert stood staring into each other's eyes. Troop trucks were waiting, their engines throbbing, but all Jessie could hear was her heart beating furiously.

She'd had Bert to herself for one whole week. They'd seen each other every day. The theatre. The cinema. Lunch at the Cricketers. A visit to the hospital so he could say cheers to some of the fellows he'd met when he'd been a patient. He'd brought them cigarettes and sweets and had reeled off jokes about his comrades back in France. They'd shared their first kiss and then so many more.

Each day had been a precious gift to Jessie. And each day had been one day closer to this one.

'I can't believe you're going,' she said, as much to convince herself as anything. The last time they'd stood there together, when he'd left to go back to the war in April, she was saying goodbye to a friend. Now, she was waving goodbye to the man she loved.

'How did one week fly by so fast?' Bert entwined his fingers with Jessie's and tugged her close.

There was so much she wanted to say but she couldn't speak a word of it. They'd professed their love for each other and had shared their plans for a life together when the war was over. Those words and declarations seemed unnecessary in that moment. And they would share words again in their letters to each other but it was this she had to memorise: his face, his smile, the touch of his hand, his kiss. She wanted, needed, to imprint on her memory every bump, every line, every crease in his forehead. The curve of his long lashes. The shape of his jaw and his bottom lip, so full, as plump as a cushion.

My Bert. My darling Bert.

'I promise I'll write.'

'So will I,' Jessie replied tremulously. 'Every day. Even if it's only a few lines, I'll write. I promise.'

His lips began to quiver and he waited to speak until he'd regained some semblance of composure. 'Look at our photo every night, will you? Imagine us together in real life, hey?'

When they'd visited Harefield hospital to see the patients, Gertie had offered to take their photograph with her camera. Jessie and Bert had readily agreed. Gertie had found a sunny position in the library by one of the large windows that overlooked the front garden—'The morning light here is perfect'—and snapped away. The village's volunteer amateur photographer happened to be at the hospital that day taking a class for the patients and had offered to develop the photographs in the well-equipped darkroom in the main house.

'It's on my bedside table in a frame. You'll be the last thing I see before I go to sleep.'

That made him smile. 'And I have my copy.' He patted the left side of his uniform's jacket. 'Right here in my wallet.'

Jessie lifted a hand and pressed it to the pocket. She could feel his heart beating fast under her fingertips.

'That's the wrong pocket.'

Jessie met his eyes, confused.

'Try the other one.'

She moved her hand across his chest, across metal buttons, and felt a square shape under the heavy woollen khaki fabric on the other side.

'What do you reckon that is?'

'Chocolate?' Jessie offered with a laugh. 'Jellies?' He already knew how much she loved jellies.

Bert reached across and undid the button on the pocket.

He pulled out a small black box.

He got down on one knee.

'Bert!' Jessie squealed and clutched at her throat. Soldiers gathered around, forming a crowd as tight as ladies in a queue at the butcher's on the high street when word had got around that there were chops.

'Miss Jessie Chester.' Bert opened the ring box and looked at her, his eyes welling with tears. 'Will you do a digger the honour of marrying him?'

A simple gold band sat in the velvet lining. It was the most beautiful thing Jessie had ever seen. She tried to speak but it felt as if a gust of wind had whooshed past and sucked all the air from her lungs. And then she felt dizzy and when she gasped for air she was finally, joyfully, able to exclaim, 'Yes, I will.'

Bert jumped to his feet so swiftly it was as if he'd never been shot by the Jerries and Jessie fell into his embrace, clutching his arms, looking up into his eyes and thinking this was surely the best day of her whole life.

'She said yes!' he shouted to the sky and then he swept her up into his arms and swung her feet off the ground. She felt as if she were flying as high as her heart was soaring. When Bert finally set her down, he pressed his cheek to hers and whispered in her ear, 'You've just made me the happiest man on earth, Jessie, I swear it.'

'And me the happiest girl in the whole of England,' she cried.

Around them, the troop's cheers became a roar and the men starting singing 'For He's a Jolly Good Fellow' at the top of their voices.

Bert slipped the ring on Jessie's finger and it fit perfectly. He pressed his lips to it and pulled her in close, kissing her lovingly and long. And she kissed him back. She didn't give a hoot about decorum or what people like Mrs Pritchard would say if they were to walk by. She was engaged to be married—married!—and if a young lady couldn't publicly kiss her fiancé who was going back to the front, then what was the war for in the first place?

Emotions flooded Jessie's heart and head. She was suddenly filled with hope for her life and for the future. In that instant, she saw it all unfurling before her like a flag: a husband who loved her, children, a home, sunny days and happiness. Simple, unfettered joy coursed through every vein.

Her arms were around Bert's neck and his were at her waist. She laughed and then sobbed or perhaps it was the other way round. She couldn't tell. 'Come back to me, Bert Mott. I'm counting on you.'

Bert's eyes glistened. 'You can count on me, sweetheart. I've already had my brush. I'm the luckiest bloke in the world, I swear.'

'And I'm the luckiest girl, I reckon.'

'I'll be back before you know it.'

'I know you will.' She had to believe it. There was simply no other alternative. 'Stay safe. Be careful.'

'I will. For you, my darling.'

A horn sounded and the first truck set out, its engine croaky and choking as its wheels spun on the gravel driveway. There were only precious moments left. Jessie pulled him closer and kissed him again, pressing her lips so hard against his that her teeth hurt. She pulled back, tasted the metallic bite of blood in her mouth.

'I'll be back when the war's over and we'll have a slap-up engagement shindig with champagne and all the cake you can eat and anything else you want. I promise.'

Jessie nodded. She could already taste the rich fruitcake heavy in her mouth and French champagne bubbles exploding on her tongue. Under her fingertips, the fine silk of her wedding gown and the stiff lace of her bridal veil pressed against her shoulders.

'And,' he said hurriedly as the men massed around him moved towards the next truck, kitbags on their shoulders. 'We'll have a honeymoon here in England before we go back to Australia. The boys say Brighton's beaut.'

'Brighton sounds lovely.'

His voice quavered and his eyes shone as he spoke. 'And after that, when you come home to Australia with me, I'll show you Murray Bridge and the river. We'll make a life there, Jessie. My family's going to love you. My brothers will be so jealous I've managed to nab myself a proper English rose.'

She laughed joyously at the idea of a life with Bert, of Australian sunshine and swimming and kangaroos. 'You'll have to teach me how to swim!'

He was trembling. 'I'll do anything for you, Jessie. Anything.'

'Oh, Bert.'

A whistle blew. Bert glanced around quickly. Duty was calling and they both knew anything else would have to wait.

'It's my job, Jess,' he told her, his voice jittery with emotion. 'It's what I signed up to do. We'll keep fighting until the war is won. Until we avenge every bloke on our side who we've lost.'

'I'm so proud of you.'

He gave her one last kiss. 'I love you with all my heart, Jessie.'

She gripped the sleeves of his coat so hard he had to pry her fingers loose. 'And I love you, Bert Mott. To the moon and back. Stay safe.'

He nodded his final goodbye and turned away, walking to the troop truck with heavy, shuffling feet.

Bert looked back once. His smile was as bright as the sun and Jessie waved frantically until he stepped up on the back of the truck and the tarp came down.

'Come back,' Jessie called but it was swallowed by the grumbling noise of the truck's engine.

She stood, fixed to the spot, unable to move, as the truck turned its half circle and made its rumbling way down the driveway onto Rickmansworth Road and back to the war.

Win burst into loud sobs. Dottie joined her and Harry fetched what was left of the bottle of whisky stowed in the dresser for special occasions such as this.

'Both my children married. I can't believe it.' Win pulled a lace handkerchief from the pocket of her apron and dabbed at her eyes.

'Sit down, won't you, Mum?' Jessie implored. Win was taking in air in quick little exhalations and beads of sweat had broken out on her forehead.

'I'm feeling a little … oh, goodness me. Light-headed.'

Dottie poured a glass of water from the jug on the dresser and set it on the table in front of Win. 'There you go, Mum.'

'You all right?' Harry went to her side, peering down into his mother's pale face.

Win's arms suddenly flew up like a frightened chicken's wings.

'Make room, everyone. No wonder I can't breathe.'

They did as they were asked. Win began fanning herself and slowly the colour returned to her cheeks.

'Are you having heart palpitations?' Dottie gasped.

'Mum. I swear. It all happened so fast. Bert was about to hop on the truck and he got down on one knee and …'

'I'm not having heart palpitations,' Win huffed. 'Aren't I allowed to be upset when my daughter tells me she's moving to Australia?'

Jessie opened her mouth to speak but paused. How had she been so carried away that she'd not realised what this would mean to her mother? Guilt overtook her in a cold shiver.

She laid a hand on Win's heaving shoulders. 'You'll never lose me, Mum. I'm getting married, that's all.'

And as she said the words, Jessie knew they were a lie. Marrying Bert meant saying goodbye to the three people she loved more than anything, packing up her life and stepping onto a ship for a six-week-long voyage to Australia and never coming home.

Dottie burst into tears. 'You'll never meet your niece or nephew, Jessie.'

'I beg your pardon?' Now Jessie needed to sit down.

'I've seen the doctor. It's true. You're going to be an aunty.'

'Come now, Dottie,' Harry whispered as he slipped an arm around his wife's shoulders, urging her to sit too, but when he looked at his sister, Jessie saw the joy in his face. Harry was going to be a father. She looked at her mother.

Win started crying again. 'Perhaps I'm having heart palpitations after all. A grandchild and an engagement on the one day? I wish your father was here. He'd be so proud he'd burst. And then no doubt he'd head directly to the White Horse. Harry? Give me that whisky, will you?'

Win poured a slug down her throat and blotted fresh tears. 'I'm so happy for you, Jess, I really am,' Win sobbed. 'Bert's a lovely Australian boy and I can see he loves you. Who would have thought, with so many of our own lost, that you'd find such a fine man. It's a miracle, it really is.'

'We didn't have much time to talk about it but we're going to get married right here in Harefield. You won't miss out on that, Mum. I swear. And Harry? You'll be Bert's best man, won't you, on account of his brothers being back home?'

Harry nodded, unable to form a sentence. She could see in his eyes how much the question meant to him.

'And Dottie. You'll be matron of honour, of course.'

'Of course,' Dottie managed between her sobs.

Harry reached for the whisky and poured a mouthful into each glass on the table. Win, Harry, Dottie and Jessie lifted them high and clinked them together.

'To Jessie and Bert,' Harry said before downing the shot.

'To Jessie and Bert,' Win and Dottie replied.

'To my grandchild,' Win added.

'To life,' Jessie said. 'And to 1917. May it bring us peace.' The whisky burnt hot down her throat. She slid her glass to Harry for another shot.

1917

Chapter Forty-Six

25 April 1917

By Anzac Day 1917, twenty young Australian men had been buried in Harefield.

Three had died in just the previous two weeks. Thirty-seven-year-old New South Welshman Private John Hayden of the 55th Battalion had been admitted to hospital in December 1916 half deaf with a chronic ear infection and had died four months later from pneumococcal meningitis.

Twenty-one-year-old Lance Corporal Charles Dines of the 36th, who hailed from New South Wales, had spent three months in hospital before succumbing to testicular cancer. And thirty-seven-year-old Private William Tuck of the 41st Battalion was felled by an amoebic abscess of the liver, a complication of amoebic dysentery.

Each of them had suffered long and painful deaths; such cruel deaths in the scheme of things, Cora believed. A gunshot could fell a soldier in an instant. An exploding shell shredded a body into so many pieces that nothing would ever be found in the mud and detritus of a battlefield. These soldiers' suffering had been painful, prolonged and public. Yet, Cora thought, was any death not cruel? Did it not rob loved ones of a last moment, of a final goodbye, of promises and apologies for past wrongs, a redemptive moment before they slipped away?

She had been in England a month shy of two years and she had seen too much death.

There had been a simple memorial service at the Australian cemetery at St Mary's Church in Harefield on 25 April. As many staff as were able attended and seventy of the men who were well enough walked from the hospital to the church for the service. As ever, it seemed the entire village had turned out too, waiting at St Mary's for the Australians to arrive, to express their gratitude to the fallen, their respect to the dead and their commiserations to families so far away.

Hospital staff were met with respectful silence by the adults and waves from the children of the village. Cora and William had walked together to the church with the other doctors and nurses. Huddled in their overcoats, their gloved fingers tucked into their pockets, they remarked on the dull day and the threat of rain. At the church, the hospital band played and Lieutenant Colonel Hayward spoke of the sacrifice of all those buried there, and all those who'd lost their lives in other places in Europe.

Cora had heard the same speech too many times to want to listen to it. She had found it sadder and sadder each time, and when she heard about sacrifice and courage and duty and honour all she could see in her mind were the anguished faces of loved ones in Australia receiving a telegram from the AIF. A mother, a father, a sister, a brother, a grandmother, a grandfather, a lover. All would mourn a loved one gone forever in foreign soil.

After the service, people filed out of the church and set flowers on the final resting places of all the diggers buried there: Wake. Keeley. Regan. Taylor. Rowlands. Hitchins. Kennedy. Moffatt. Farthing. Knox. Giddins. Anderson. Johnston. Cookesley. Graham. Mickels. Hingst. And the three new arrivals. Cora saved her bouquet of wildflowers for Private Robert Wake, the first. In the middle of the graveyard, a six-foot-tall white cross loomed eerily and the Australian flag that had been draped over it was decorated with a laurel wreath, a crown of thorns.

As the Last Post played, William came to stand by Cora's side. At the final note, there were salutes and murmured prayers and the crowd broke into small groups, sharing solemn conversations and quiet reminiscences.

'What a bloody waste,' he muttered as he dragged on a cigarette. His hands trembled with fury.

'It's hard to think anything else.'

'Do you know what we tell them, these men, to convince them to enlist?'

Cora had never heard him speak with such bitterness.

'"Come on chaps. Vindicate your manhood. Prove yourselves to your country and the King. Stand by your comrades. Be men."'

He stopped, turned away from Cora. She fought the urge to reach for his hand. He didn't seem in the mood to welcome such a gesture.

'What is a man? Is it braver to lie in bed dying of cancer and wish with everything you possess to be back on the battlefield with your mates? Or is it braver to be shot and die instantly?'

'Doesn't the act of bravery lie in enlisting in the first place? Or in knowing the risks and still putting on a uniform?'

'What about me, then? How brave am I here in England, hiding behind a scalpel instead of wielding a gun like these boys did?'

She knew how hard he and the other doctors toiled for their patients, struggling through fourteen-hour stretches in surgery without a break, trying to create some semblance of normality and a future for men who'd been hastily and often haphazardly patched up on the battlefield under a hail of gunfire and cannon shells. He'd been in Egypt treating casualties freshly evacuated from Gallipoli. He had always treated patients with gentle care, tending to them with kindness and good humour when it was called for; taking pulses to reassure them, checking wounds, palpating stomachs while telling a joke to distract them from their agonies. She had never once doubted his commitment as a doctor. Why, suddenly, did he? She could only reassure him with words and she thought a moment to find the right ones.

'This isn't hiding, William. This is serving. We are all doing what is required of us, where it is required. Isn't that all we can do?'

William studied her face and for a moment she saw a flicker in his eyes, a harshness, an anger that was unfamiliar. When he spoke, his eyes were fixed on hers but he didn't seem to be seeing her.

'"Do the honourable thing. Don't want to be the kind of man who failed to do his duty. Imagine what will happen if you come upon a man who did? He'll cut you in the street.

His wife won't speak to yours. She might even hand you a white feather in a place where everyone might see. They'll call you a traitor to the cause, and the other children will avoid yours like the plague. The offspring of cowards. That's what they'll call them. Do you want to be branded and to pass on that brand to your own boys to wear?"'

A sudden and urgent anger radiated from William, like heat, from the twisted contortion of his lips, from his clenched fists. His eyes were narrowed and blazing, his mouth pulled tight, his teeth gritted. His words had been forced from his mouth like sputum.

'And now a million Americans are on their way. You know what that'll mean? More lambs to the slaughter, not less.'

She barely recognised this version of him and it scared her. She had seen men lose their senses. She recognised the vacant stare, the limbs that refused to work, words trapped in a tight throat that might never be spoken. This was different. It was rage.

Cora leant in. 'Shall we go back to the hospital? I think you need a rest, William.' And this time, she didn't check who might see before she put her hand on the inside of his elbow, gently urging him to follow her. 'There's a cricket match on this afternoon in one of the fields and there will be tea and cakes. It might be nice to sit and watch the nurses play the patients, don't you think?'

William stiffened under her grip and shook her off. He gazed at her as if he'd momentarily forgotten who she was.

'Cora … I need to go.' He strode purposefully and urgently away from her, away from the graves and the church, passing under the outstretched branches of the oaks and elms, their new leaves shimmering, north to the hospital.

Cora took her time on the journey home. When she walked through the wrought-iron gate onto Church Hill, she'd stood before each grave in the cemetery, making sure to read the name of each fallen soldier, saying it out loud to honour them, to somehow help their families understand, if they could hear from so far away, that these boys weren't forgotten, that their names lived on her whispered breath. That their names lived forever more.

The sun had appeared from behind the morning clouds and it shone down meekly on her upturned face. Years before, she would have thrown herself down in the nearest meadow and turned her face up to it, just as she had in the Botanic Garden in Adelaide, drinking it in, warming her through her clothes to her very bones.

But she was too restless and agitated to try to relax in such a way that day. William had articulated what she had been feeling all morning, as she dressed, ate breakfast and drank her weak tea. What a sodding waste.

She felt the burden of grief tighten her shoulders. Pieces of every man's life and memory and tragedy had stayed with her, each one a stone in an invisible sack on her back. She had grieved when families couldn't. She had grieved for those with no next of kin. She had grieved for sweethearts and fiancées and wives.

Now, she was feeling swamped by it.

Cora walked the dirt path that ran along Church Hill, sticking close to the hedgerows. Along the path, pink and purple and white blooms unfurled fresh and crisp from their beds of greenery. Bees flitted from stamen to stamen and birds sang their welcoming chorus above her. She breathed in the spring air. When she'd arrived in England, she'd meant to learn the names of the birds that flew overhead and chirped and nested in the trees in the meadows surrounding the hospital but, like so many of her plans, it had fallen by the wayside.

The path veered left and as she continued along it, a group of slow-moving waddling birds came into view. A surge of delight swept over her and she stopped walking and watched, pressing herself against the hedgerow so as not to startle them. The gaggle of geese, led by a graceful mother goose with an elegant black neck and a brilliant white patch under her black beak, led seven little goslings, her head bobbing up and down like an exotic dancer. The goslings waddled along, their webbed feet looking for all the world like clown shoes, and Cora found herself smiling at the thought. The birds were silent as they shuffled past, not even pausing to look in her direction.

It was a reminder, if she needed one, that life carried on. The sun would rise again tomorrow, no matter how many patients died. Birds would continue creating new life, bees would collect pollen and make honey.

She would continue to be the best nurse she could be and William would treat patients to the best of his ability, no matter the state of his nerves or his exhaustion. What else was there to do?

When she reached the hospital, Cora walked up the drive and past the Long Ramp on her way to her quarters to hang up her coat. On the open field to the north of the main house, there were shouts of howzat and she detoured over to see if William was watching the game. She searched among the crowd but saw only patients.

'Cora!'

Gertie was striding into the centre waving a cricket bat aloft. 'I'm going to hit him for six!'

Cora applauded her friend and waved. The bowler ran in and Gertie swung so fiercely she might have been batting away a German bomb. Her skirts danced and her veil flew behind her but, despite her valiant effort, she managed to merely nick the ball, which edged into the hands of the one-legged man hopping at second slip.

There was a roar from the soldier players and from the crowd and hearty applause as Gertie left the crease. She jogged over to Cora.

'Out for a duck,' Gertie laughed. 'I wasn't even at the crease long enough to lose my breath. Oh well, it could have been worse. I could have copped a ball in the head from Walker. He could have played for Australia one day, the boys reckon, if only he hadn't lost an eye in France. It doesn't stop him, though. His delivery comes at you so fast you can barely see it, I swear.' Gertie's excitement was palpable. When Cora didn't reciprocate, Gertie looked her up and down. 'You took a while to get back. I lost sight of you in the procession. Have you been out on a sojourn with you know who?'

Cora pinched her lips together to stop herself from crying.

Gertie's cheeky smile faded. 'Is something the matter, Cora?'

'William's a bit out of sorts today.'

'I'm sorry to hear it. I can't say I've seen him here, though. Perhaps he's in the canteen? In his quarters?'

Cora bit the cuticle on a thumb. She hated that she did it, but she did it nonetheless.

'I don't know. I'm sorry. I'm totally distracted.'

Gertie sighed. 'I hear there are fresh scones in the canteen today.'

'I don't have time. I have to get back to the ward. I'll see you for dinner?'

Gerties saluted. 'Cora?'

'Hmm?'

'Whenever you need me.'

Cora nodded her understanding and walked back to the ward.

Chapter Forty-Seven

9 May 1917

'What on earth is that?' Cora lifted her eyes from the pile of patients' notes on her desk.

Leonora almost dropped the prosthetic leg she was fitting to an amputee and had to steady herself by grabbing his good knee. He in turn steadied himself by reaching for the top of her head. It was all very precarious.

From the fourth bed on the left came a tune so professionally sung it might have been one of the regular entertainers who came to Harefield. Cora checked her notes. It was Private John Collinson. He'd arrived the day before and had had surgery on both arms for shrapnel and bullet wounds. He'd been injured at Gallipoli and recovered. He'd re-joined his unit and then he'd been sent to the Somme. He was a miracle.

The last time Cora had checked his vitals, he'd still been drowsy from the chloroform. A glance across the ward revealed he was still lying flat on his back in bed, his arms heavily bandaged at his sides. In each bed around him, men were rousing. Heads lifted from pillows, those who were able to clapped their hands and surprised laughter pealed around the ward.

'Why, it's …'

'It's Waltzing bloody Matilda!' One by one, the other soldiers joined in, voices weak and strong, struggling and booming, all in chorus. Cora walked to Collinson's side in a daze.

'How wonderfully strange,' Leonora said as she came to join her. 'I'm not even certain he's awake.'

'And he's singing like an angel,' Cora added. The two women grasped each other's hands and listened as Collinson's fine tenor voice rang out. Patients and staff alike belted out the words as if the King himself was there to hear a special performance.

And singing of billabongs and swagmen and coolabah trees and billies boiling meant there wasn't a dry eye in the ward.

The next morning, the troops roused at Reveille to a bright, clear morning. Cora threw open the windows and she and Gertie helped the men wash, shave and dress before breakfast. As the men who were able to leave their beds walked over to the mess, Cora stood by Collinson's side and studied his peaceful face. His dark hair was swept up off his forehead, his deep-set eyes were still closed. His face, that might have tanned easily back in Australia, was pale. How had he survived both Gallipoli and the Somme?

He exhaled and his eyes fluttered open, then they widened when he realised Cora was watching him.

'Good morning, John,' she said quietly

He blinked, attempted to press his arms into the mattress to sit up, and moaned.

'Oh, no. Don't try to sit up. Not yet.'

'Thanks, Sister.' His voice was a rasp. Cora reached for the jug of water on his bedside table and poured a glass. She slipped one hand under his head, lifting it forward and held the glass to his lips. He slurped as if he hadn't seen water for weeks.

'How are you feeling this morning?'

When he spoke, his voice was weak. 'Just dandy, Sister.'

'You're due more pain relief. I'll fetch it for you. It'll help you settle. You've had some major surgery on your arms and it'll hurt for a while.'

Collinson glanced down at his bandaged arms and a shimmer of something crossed his face, as if he'd just remembered what had happened. 'I'm in good hands now though, aren't I?'

'You are indeed.' She paused but had to ask, 'Do you remember singing yesterday? When you came back to the ward after your surgery?'

He furrowed his brow in confusion. 'Singing?'

'We had a real singalong with you. It was wonderful. It lifted everyone's spirits for the rest of the day.'

'I ... I don't remember anything. I can only apologise If I offended you or any of the other nurses.'

'No, no,' she replied quickly to settle his doubts. 'It wasn't that at all. You sang "Waltzing Matilda". It was wonderful. You made us all cry.'

'I did?' John gasped.

'You certainly did. Ask any of the other men. They'll vouch for me.'

'Well, I'll be.' He chuckled. 'Funny thing is, I'm not even Australian. I went out to Australia just before the war and signed up for a free trip home. I was born in Northumberland, worked on the shipyards. I'm the proud son of a coalminer.'

'How astonishing,' Cora replied. 'You've never had a singing lesson?'

'Not a one.'

'You should definitely sing at one of the afternoon concerts. We have them every week. You'd be so welcome.'

He shook his head wearily. 'Oh, no. I couldn't get up on stage and sing in front of everyone.'

'You most certainly could. I'll mention it to the village ladies who run the entertainment committee. They organise all sorts of things for you boys, you know. Concerts. Recitals. The best of the vaudeville entertainers come direct from the West End. I can't believe you weren't a singer before the war ...'

He managed a grin. 'Only while shaving, Sister.'

'A talent like yours deserves to be shared. You should be on the stage, Private.'

And Cora knew, even as the encouraging words fell from her lips, that John Collinson was in no state to stand, much less climb up on a stage and perform. But if encouraging him were to aid in his recovery, she would mention the possibility of his performance every single day. Sometimes medicines alone weren't the best medicine, she had found.

The weeks that followed the spontaneous and mysterious performance of 'Waltzing Matilda' were the darkest days at the hospital since the losses at the Somme twelve months before.

When rumours spread that the German army was close to collapse, the Allies decided that a new offensive at Ypres, followed by a push into Belgium, was necessary to capture the ports from which German U-boats set out into the Channel and across to England.

Among the injured men, those who'd been evacuated from Passchendaele and Pilckem Ridge told the story in whispered conversations with the other cot inmates, who'd been injured in other places and in other battles. They never seemed to think that Cora was able to hear them. Perhaps the anonymity of a nurse's uniform rendered her so invisible that she was able to hover and hear what had really happened on the battlefields of Europe and the Middle East. She'd only ever trusted firsthand accounts since Gallipoli, when the numbers she'd read in the newspapers sent from home were in inverse proportion to the numbers of injured she had seen. She had learnt that the army didn't tell the war reporters the entire truth of what was going on.

A group of patients had gathered their cane chairs into a semi-circle around one of the cot cases, in deference to the fact that he'd had his legs blown off by the Germans during the Nivelle Offensive.

'It was a bloody disaster.' The speaker was a grey-haired man of middle age, with a salt-and-pepper moustache and jagged healing scars down one side of his face. His right arm was a stump just below the elbow. 'Thirty-two thousand blokes died and the Brits advanced three thousands yards. That's ten yards a bloke, give or take.' He took a noisy drag on his cigarette and his smoke was a bitter cloud above his head.

Exclamations and curses followed.

'We went down the Menin Road, south east of Wipers. Ypres, as the Frenchies call it. The whole place was a quagmire. The locals reckon they hadn't seen summer rain like that in years. Just our luck, hey?'

Cora sat quietly, pressing her fingers into the carotid artery at Private Cecil Roy's neck to check his pulse. She listened as intently as a fox in a field.

A whisper. 'Some of the boys are saying it's worse than Gallipoli.'

Hisses and seething exclamations. 'You're joking.'

'It was a right bloody mess, let me tell you. Bits and pieces of your mates as far as the eye could see. You didn't want to look down in case you were stepping on someone you'd just sat next to at breakfast. It's as near to damn hell than any place else I can imagine.'

Perhaps it was possible to know too much. Cora shook off the thought of arms and legs and hands and feet and jaws and eyeballs scattered in a French field somewhere, mixing with mud and manure to become part of a macabre mix of new soil. How long would it be before those green fields would once again become something productive rather than places of destruction? Battlefields as instant cemeteries. It was all so cruel.

When she sensed a presence at her side, she looked up and was relieved to see William.

'How is he, Sister?' He pressed a hand on her shoulder. She didn't move for fear he would stop touching her. It had been weeks since she'd been able to be with him, to touch him openly and let him touch her. She needed him and the connection with him, no matter how slight, to help chase away her thoughts of despair and gloom.

'Stable. He sleeps heavily and often.'

'We'll have to keep a close eye on him for these first twelve hours. With head cases, it's the most important thing,' William said. 'They do what they can in the field hospitals, your colleagues and mine, scraping out what they can, packing the wounds with cyanide gauze or packing them with salt when there's no gauze to be had. And then we take on the impossible task of mending them.'

He swore under his breath. 'I don't know if I can do it any more, Cora.' His voice faltered and Cora recognised what was behind the exhaustion. War-weariness was settling over everyone at the hospital like a London fog. Cora saw it in the eyes of the nurses, frequently teary and vacant. The worst of it was that she had always believed she was stronger, that it was her task to keep everyone else from going under, but she could feel the cold clouds of that fog seeping into every pore, every muscle and tendon, into her heart.

'We all do the best we can. That's all anyone can expect.'

'So they say.'

Cora realised the patients' conversation had quietened. Someone was reciting a limerick. There was weak laughter at the punchline. Another talked of cricket.

William cleared his throat. 'I didn't see you at Private Power's funeral the other day.'

Cora couldn't meet his eyes. 'No. I wasn't there.'

'I looked for you. I thought we might have had the chance to talk on the walk back to the hospital. I wanted to apologise.'

'There's no need. Honestly.'

'I've been a bear with a sore head. The past few months …'

'You don't need to explain … '

They turned their attention to Private Roy. The patient's breathing had slowed and his face seemed to have grown more pale. His slight body tucked under the sheets looked like a little boy's waiting for a bedtime story.

William pressed a hand to Roy's forehead and kept it there. 'He's clammy.'

Cora checked his blood pressure again. 'It's higher.'

William widened the private's eyelids and searched them for signs of life. 'I have a nasty feeling about this one. When they close up the wound on the front they don't have time for a drainage line. They wash away the brain pulp and any clots, poke around in the hole to find any remaining fragments and then close. I think they've missed something.'

'If there's an infection, it has nowhere to go.'

William tensed. 'Call theatre, will you? And hurry. I've seen evidence to suggest that if we get in there fast, search for and remove any foreign material or bony fragments, we might be able to avoid permanent disability. It's highly unlikely this bloke's still got a bullet in his brain, but there's something else, I'm sure of it.' He leant over Private Roy, and said, 'You'll be right, mate. We're going to do all we can to help you.'

Cora ran to the telephone on the nurses' desk.

France
June 2nd, 1917

My dearest, darling Jessie,
Please forgive me for not answering your letter sooner. It took a while for yours to arrive here (I can't describe exactly where I am) and in the days since, well, there hasn't been much time for writing. I'm sitting in a trench now, a stubby pencil in my hand, my boots encased in mud, and I haven't shaved in weeks. It's pretty bloody messy shaving with a blunt razor and cold water, I can tell you, so you might have a hairy sweetheart for a little while longer.

It's a sunny day here and we're hoping it might dry things up a bit. Pity is, there's not much of anything to hold all the dirt in one place. All that is left of the trees are thin slivers of trunk. The place where I'm sitting right now, before it was dug into trenches and blown to bits, might have been a field once, green as England is and a home to cows and sheep, but I don't reckon an animal has grazed here in years.

We've had a lull the past twenty-four hours and after a spot of marching, drilling and a few overs of cricket, a few of my cobbers are catching up on sleep. I'll have a few winks when I finish this letter and hopefully will dream of you.

We've also had some exciting news. We're all to get a complete change of underclothing. Which means we'll get the chance to have a bath. At bloody last!

Please know that I love you with all my heart. I am confident I will make it through and be reunited with you once more. The Jerries have already had a shot at me and missed, so luck must be on my side.

I have to sign off now. Please write back to me as soon as you can. You can't imagine how much it gladdens my heart to hear from you.

I remain, ever yours,

Bert

Harefield
June 14th, 1917

My dearest Bert,
Your letter was waiting for me when I returned home
tonight and I can't explain the excitement I felt in having
received it. Mum had set it on my pillow and it was the
first thing I saw when I lumbered upstairs with tired feet
at the end of a long day at the hospital. Everyone in the
house is excited when a letter from you arrives, my darling.
Mum, Dottie and Harry remind me to send you their best
regards. Dottie is doing well, although perhaps a little more
tired than usual. Harry fusses over her like a mother hen,
which pleases Mum and me no end, for in his actions we see
ourselves fussing over him when he was younger. It warms
my heart to see them so happy.

The house is quiet as I write. Everyone is asleep and it
feels like you and I are alone together. How is that possible
when there is so much distance between us?

Dottie has promised that if I leave this letter on the
kitchen table tonight, she'll post it tomorrow as soon as she
can so I hope it reaches you quickly, wherever you are.

We have a fresh crop of boys in the ward and I assure
you that none of them are as handsome or quick-witted as
you. Two of them have already proposed but I took great
delight in telling them that I'm already spoken for. You
should have seen the expression on their faces when I told
them I'm marrying a 'cobber'.

The warmer days are here and the evenings are growing
long once more. I think I love summer more than any other

*season and I can't wait to experience one in Australia. I've
longed for the sunshine all those long winter months.*

*Life continues on as it ever did, except now I have the
memory of you to fill my waking hours. Come back to me,
dearest Bert, and we shall make a happy life together. I am
counting the minutes, hours and days.*

*Well, darling, I must close. I'm tired and it will be a
blink before I'm up again tomorrow. Goodnight and sweet
dreams.*

*With fondest love, I remain your ever-loving sweetheart,
Jessie xxxx*

Chapter Forty-Eight

1 July 1917

Jessie ran into the storeroom in the ward, pressed herself against a wall, and sobbed, great racking quivering cries that rattled her bones. She slammed her palms against her face to muffle the sound of her tears and squeezed her eyes closed against the stinging. When her legs felt so weak she feared they might buckle, she sank slowly to the floor until her knees were pressed up against her chest.

It was all too much. The ward was full of newly arrived boys, all in pieces, as if the powers that be had decided to put them all together to see if a few whole men could be made out of the physical wrecks they were now, like pieces of a puzzle. In each pair of eyes wincing in agony, she saw Bert. The sight of any patient with short red hair and a stocky build sent her quivering with fear and she had wanted to unwrap the bandages from each of their faces to see for herself that it wasn't her beloved Bert.

In the past fortnight, nearly nine hundred patients had been admitted and three more had been buried. and if Jessie had been able to volunteer twenty four hours a day, she would have been welcomed with open arms. But she'd been feeling terribly neglectful of her duties at home and knew without her even saying that Win was tiring of carrying the load. Bless her mum: she'd never uttered a word to Jessie about it, but her daughter could tell. Win was asleep in her armchair soon after supper. She seemed to creak in the mornings now when she rose and it took two cups of tea to get her going, not her usual one.

Jessie was being torn in two. Something was pulling her towards to the hospital. Everything reminded her of Bert. It had been comforting to walk the same paths that they'd walked. To see the bed in which he'd recovered now occupied by another young soldier in need of care. She felt close to him there. And her labours helped the days pass more quickly than they might have had she been at home, working, knitting badly, listening to Dottie and Harry's excitement about the baby. At the hospital, she felt her purpose. She had carried the weight of her responsibilities with courage and conviction.

Until a moment half an hour earlier.

She'd been helping a porter transfer a new patient from a wheeled trolley to the cane chair by the side of a freshly made cot. Almost his entire head was wrapped in bandages. All that was exposed was a two-inch strip of his hair and one eye. The bandages had been wound in layers, clearly in a hurry. Had it been days or a week since they'd been changed? They were fraying and ragged at the edges, a rusty discolouration seeping through from about the position of his mouth. How on earth was he breathing?

She'd found her cheeriest voice. 'Welcome to Harefield. Are you a private? A lance corporal? A sergeant or a sapper? I must admit I'm still trying to learn the differences, and I've been volunteering here almost eighteen months.' Jessie was fully aware that the soldier wasn't able to answer but she had to chat anyway. It was simply a way to fill the awkward silences in the men who didn't speak or couldn't, who either had nothing to say or who could hear nothing above the Kaiser's shells still exploding in their ears. She knew they didn't want pity. No 'you poor thing' or 'that must be painful'.

She had grown to know the Australians by now: the cheeky sense of humour they used liberally with whomever they pleased—from the Lieutenant Colonel in charge to the many hospital volunteers; the lack of respect they had for rank and privilege and formality; the peculiar knack they had for teasing her and including her at the same time.

But there was none of that from this man. Above the wrapped bandages, his weeping eye remained focussed at a fixed point in the distance. Was he blind on top of everything else hidden underneath those bandages? How much cruelty was a man supposed to bear?

'There you go, Private,' she'd said as she'd settled him in his chair, trying to decide which muddied piece of his uniform she should remove first so she could wash him. She looked him over. His hair was matted with dirt. He'd lost his shoes somewhere on his journey from the battlefield. Every piece of clothing he was wearing seemed to be covered in mud or dried blood or dust, as if he'd collected souvenirs of France and pressed them into the seams of his jacket and trousers.

'I'll clean you up in no time and once you're in a pair of clean pyjamas, you'll sleep the sleep of the angels. You can count on that.'

When Jessie was certain he wouldn't move from his chair, she went quickly to the bathroom at the back of the ward and returned with a bucket of water she'd stirred into suds with soap flakes, two flannels and a clean towel. She rolled up her sleeves and sat down on the bed.

'Now, we might start with your head. I'm sure you're in dire need of a shave.' She moved forward, tracing her fingers along an edge of the bandage to discover where it began and once she found it, she slowly peeled it away, as if she were peeling an apple, the skin all in one long thin piece. As she unrolled it, the bloodstains were thick and crusted and she slowed.

'You all right there? You let me know if this is pulling, won't you?'

She studied his eye. Tears began to well and suddenly, his hand was on her forearm, gripping so tight she jumped.

'It hurts? I'll go more slowly.' It was hard going. The congealed blood had worked as efficiently as cement between the layers of bandage but finally, the apple peel of cloth lay in his lap, almost unwrapped. That's when Jessie noticed the dip where his nose should have been. She paused, steeled herself and removed the bandage altogether.

A chill stiffened her spine and stole her breath.

When tears spilled from the boy's right eye, they disappeared into a cavity where his nose, upper palate and half his jaw would once have been. There were hasty battlefield stitches in a line from his ear to a flap of skin that had been the corner of his mouth, pulled tight to cover the stumps of his teeth and his nostrils. Nausea roiled inside her and the guilt that swept over her was worse than feeling sick. This poor young man. This poor, poor young man. He'd been shot right through his lower face.

Jessie had looked down at the bucket filled with water and dizziness overcame her. She lowered the flannel, squeezed it and took a deep breath in as she sat upright.

With every bit of strength she had, she'd given him a little smile. 'Let's get you cleaned up.' She pressed the warm and clean flannel to his eyes, washing his tears away, wishing she could wash away his pain just as easily.

When he was as clean as could be, dressed and breathing noisily through what was left of his septum, Jessie emptied the bucket of blood and dust and tears into the sink at the rear of the ward. That's when she allowed herself to collapse with the burden of the soldier's grief. She'd absorbed it into her bones just as the bandages had absorbed his blood and flesh.

In that moment, it all overwhelmed her. There was too much death and too much damage. Patients were back and forth to the operating theatre in the main house every hour of every day, it seemed, to treat joint injuries, the amputation of festering stumps, chronic bone sepsis, burns and shattered limbs and faces and minds. Her job was to clean their bloodied and soiled sheets soaked through from raging fevers. To mop up vomit. To start all over again with clean sheets and new patients who repeated the same patterns over and over.

She wanted to help these men, these volunteers who'd crossed the sea to save her and her family and every English man and woman. But the burden suddenly felt too heavy for her slim shoulders. There was nowhere to hide at Harefield from the reminders of what might be happening to Bert that very moment.

The door slowly opened.

'Jessie? Are you all right?' Cora stepped into the storeroom and closed the door behind her, shutting out the bustling noises of the ward. Fresh mortification stiffened Jessie's shoulders and she dropped her head into her crossed arms.

The compassionate concern in Cora's voice only made Jessie feel worse. She lifted her head. 'I'm sorry, Cora. I don't know what's come over me. I …'

Cora came to her side and sat on the floor beside her, her stockinged legs outstretched, her black boots shining as always.

'I do. The things we see sometimes … beyond anyone's worst nightmares.'

'I … I've never seen an injury like that. What bullets can do to faces. It's so cruel.'

Cora paused, as if she was expecting Jessie to say something profound, something that might be worth listening to, but what fresh words could Jessie find to explain the depths of her revulsion about the damage done to that man in the name of defending England?

'I expect you can't help but think about Bert.'

Jessie nodded, fighting back fresh tears.

'He's well?'

'Oh, yes,' Jessie replied quickly, wiping her tears. 'And as jolly as I remember him. But when I see the men … I'm just so glad it's not him and then I feel absolutely terrible. I don't want to be glad that it's someone else lying there, I truly don't. I wouldn't wish those injuries on anyone. Not even a German.'

'I understand,' Cora replied heavily.

The wars Jessie had read about in story books were battles between swashbuckling swordsmen in spanking uniforms riding snow-white horses, wearing hats with enormous plumes that shimmered as they rode, and, if they were shot at by enemies, the bullets always missed. Heroes lived another day and returned home to marry their sweethearts and revel in the glory of their victorious battles. Where was the glory in returning home with half a face?

'The French have a name for men like our new patient. They call them *les gueules cassées*,' Cora said quietly. '"Men with broken faces".'

Fresh tears welled in Jessie's eyes. 'I never learnt French at school. Can you tell me how to say it?'

'Le girl cassay.'

Bert had taught her how to say *allez* and *bonsoir*. She added *les gueules cassées* to her repertoire.

Jessie repeated the phrase in a whisper, hoping the unfamiliar sounds would imprint in her memory so the next time, for there would inevitably be a next time, she might remember that even if they were unrecognisable, they were still men. They had beating hearts and minds probably gone half mad, a home somewhere far away and a family who would get their boy back.

Cora heaved a sigh. 'The steel helmets they wear? They don't protect the face, you see.'

'I suppose not.'

'You're wonderful at your work, Jessie. The patients love you. It's only natural to be shocked and upset at the things you see. Many of us feel overwhelmed at times. Even the doctors.'

'Really? I thought it was just because I'm not a nurse.'

'It's hard for all of us.'

'But surely the doctors get used to it?'

'No. Quite the opposite, in fact.' Cora's gaze was fixed on a point in the distance, something only she could see. 'It's simply dreadful. The war and every single thing about it.'

Jessie sniffed and wiped her tears away with the hem of her uniform.

'And what I wonder is …' Cora paused as if she were about to reveal a secret. 'How a man injured in such a way can ever recover? How do they become *unbroken*?'

The two women sat in the quiet and contemplative silence for a full five minutes before duty returned them to their feet and back to the ward.

Chapter Forty-Nine

23 August 1917

'Remember when we all thought the war would be over by Christmas? And I mean Christmas 1915?'

Sitting beside her, Fiona harrumphed. 'Pity we weren't specific about exactly which Christmas.'

Cora moved her cane chair closer to the stove in the nurses' quarters, tipped her head forward and ruffled her fingers through its damp strands. It was so long now, the wet ringlets almost touched the floorboards. She hadn't been intentionally growing it for vanity. It was purely practical. Long tresses were easily tucked up in a bun that could be hidden under her nurse's veil. It was all so practical and neat, except for when it came time to washing and drying it. It always seemed to take days, especially now summer was at its end. She unfolded the towel on her lap, wrapped it around her head and tucked one end under the fold at the back of her neck like she was wrapping a turban.

'It's more than two years since we enlisted. I can't believe it. Can you, Gertie?'

'I feel as if I've aged ten. Is that biologically possible, I wonder? Do I have any more grey hair?' Gertie pushed the hair away from an ear so Cora could more closely inspect her roots.

'Can't say I've noticed,' Cora replied. 'Although it is a little dim in here.'

They allowed themselves a laugh at each other.

Sometimes it seemed two years had passed in the blink of an eye. Other days, when the wounded had arrived in a never-ending convoy of vehicles, body after body after body, it seemed whole days and months would pass before Cora even remembered to look at the date on the calendar. Two winters had passed, long and slow and cold. There was no novelty left in the snow any longer. Clothes froze into stiff sheets and the nurses discovered that chipping the ice from them hardly compared to hanging them on a clothesline strung from one fence to the apricot tree in an Australian backyard. She had forgotten that scent of summer and sunshine on her clothes. Here, her uniform always smelt vaguely of smoke from having been draped over chairs to dry by the fire.

Why had the war gone on so long?

'And you know what else that means?' Cora asked.

'Other than that the war hasn't ended, you mean?'

'That we've been wearing those blinking uniforms for two whole years, give or take a week away on furlough.'

'Furlough?' Gertie looked to the ceiling. 'What's that?' She reached to the floor for her cup of tea and took a loud sip. 'Let's play the game.'

'Oh, not again,' Cora groaned.

'I quite like the game,' Fiona said quietly. 'It helps remind me of ... you know, my other life.'

Cora had trouble remembering that other life these days. Everything that made her happy—her friends, William, her work—was here in Harefield. And everything that filled her with grief and that overwhelming exhaustion that only those in war could understand was here, too.

'Yes, again.' Cora laughed. 'All right. What will you do when the war is over?'

Gertie nodded her approval. 'Fiona?'

Fiona set her knitting on her lap. 'I think … I'd like to go home and work with veterans.'

'Really?' Cora asked.

'Patients just like the boys who've been through here.'

'Won't that kind of work just remind you of,' Cora swept an arm around, 'all this?'

Fiona held her chin high and Cora saw a new pride in her eyes. She'd always thought of Fiona as a cautious crow, perpetually on the lookout for danger and perhaps, out of all of them, the least prepared for it. Cora clearly hadn't been looking closely enough at her colleague lately.

'That's why I want to do it. They need nurses like us who aren't frightened by their injuries, who understand what they've been through. There are repatriation hospitals back in Australia now who'll need nurses like me. More than one hundred thousand of our troops have been injured in the fighting. They'll need care.'

'And they'll be lucky to have you,' Cora said.

'What about you, Cora?' Fiona asked in return.

'Nothing as noble as you, I'm afraid.' Cora leant back in the cane chair, crossed one leg over the other and narrowed the gap in her woollen dressing gown. 'I want to lie around in my nightdress for a month. No, perhaps a good six months.

I want to burn my corset. Who on earth ever believed a nurse could do her job trussed up like a turkey? I want to let my hair loose all day, floating down my back.'

'Like Rapunzel,' Gertie noted.

'Exactly like Rapunzel. Except perhaps for the tower and I can't say I'm all that keen on being held captive.' She let herself imagine for a moment. 'I want to eat butterscotch from a tin as big as a wash trough and drink endless cups of real tea. You know, the kind we had before the war.'

'Tea?' Gertie smirked. 'I shall down an entire bottle of gin without a care in the world about who might judge me for it.'

Fiona picked up her knitting and kept her eyes focussed on her knits and purls as she asked, 'Will your future involve your captain?'

The fire crackled and shadows flickered on the walls around them. Cora hadn't discussed William with anyone but Gertie. She hadn't even mentioned him in her letters home, fearing the same questions from her sisters and, in a roundabout way, from her parents. A single woman's future prospects—or lack of them—seemed to be everyone's business. How could she describe to anyone else what she and William shared? Nothing was permanent. How could two people thrown together by war think anything else?

As for Fiona, Cora had always slightly feared her friend's judgement and had never wanted to argue with her about their differing beliefs. But it seemed like Fiona was opening a door.

'I don't know, Fiona. Who's to know what the future holds?'

She and William had never spoken of it, either. His affection for her was evident, in word and deed, but they'd never discussed what might happen after the war. She was conscious of his broken engagement and the effect that would have on him when he returned to Australia. His humiliation of a young woman would not have gone unnoticed. In that sense, he was fortunate to be ten thousand miles away.

And as for her wishes? They seemed to have disappeared with any dreams she'd had about the future.

'Indeed,' Gertie said. 'For any of us.'

'I wouldn't mind digging my toes into the sand at Henley Beach again. I'll swim so far out into the ocean that I might reach the Yorke Peninsula.' Cora twisted the towel from her head and combed her fingers through her hair, imagining it was salt water and not soap that had tangled it in clumps.

'How far across is that from Adelaide?' Fiona asked.

'So far that it disappears over the horizon. Miles and miles and miles of nothing but blue skies and the ocean.'

At the end of the quarters, the bathroom door opened and closed and Leonora shuffled out, pulling the ties of her dressing gown into a knot at her slim waist. It had been a long ten months for their friend since she'd lost her fiancé. Grief had shrunk her inside herself. The war had been too long for her, too tragic, filled with not enough glamour and far too much grief. The old Leonora was there sometimes, in a laugh or a joke, but those glimmers of light were few and far between. Who could expect anything more from one who had suffered such a loss?

'Was there any hot water left?' Fiona asked, looking up from the sock she was knitting. She lifted the ball of wool and unspooled some more thread.

'Just enough.' Leonora smiled. She came to sit by Fiona, who patted her leg as a gesture of comfort. Leonora leant into her friend's shoulder.

'We've been playing the game,' Gertie said. 'What we're going to do when the war is over.'

Leonora pulled her lips tight. 'My war is over. I'm going home.'

Cora strangely wasn't surprised and judging by the looks on Gertie's and Fiona's faces they weren't either.

'I spoke to the matron today.' When tears welled in her eyes, she didn't attempt to stop them. 'I need to go home. I'm on the boat from Plymouth next Wednesday. I'll be nursing patients on the voyage. That's fitting somehow, isn't it?'

Fiona's knitting tumbled to the floor. She held her arms open wide and Leonora leant into her shoulder, sobbing.

'You've given so much,' Fiona murmured. 'No one deserves this more than you do.'

'We'll miss you,' Cora said, her words catching in her throat.

Gertie sniffed. 'It won't be the same around here without you.'

Leonora lifted her head and looked at them all in turn. 'I don't know what I would have done without you three. Honestly. I would have fallen to pieces if I hadn't had your friendship. Please come and visit me in Sydney. You'd all be most welcome.'

As her three friends starting making plans for walks to Mrs Macquarie's Chair and boat rides on the harbour, Cora thought how lucky they were to have been together for so long. The four of them, for more than two years, had somehow turned their nurses' quarters into a home, a respite, a haven.

How fortunate they had been to have had each other.

She caught Gertie's attention and passed her a brush. 'Can you plait it for me?'

'Of course.' Cora turned and Gertie repositioned her chair behind her. She felt the tug on her hair as Gertie manipulated it into three sections and then bound it into one.

Gertie's voice was a whisper in her ear. 'It doesn't seem fair, does it? What's happened to her.'

'Nothing seems fair any more, Gertie. None of it.'

Chapter Fifty

12 September 1917

Cora quickly closed the ward door behind her before the wind caught it and slammed it shut. Removing her coat, she draped it over an arm before striding through Ward 22 towards the nurses' desk at the other end. The ward was quiet. At that time of the day, the men were involved in activities all over the hospital. Only the newest and most unwell patients were still in their beds and that was where Cora found Millie, staring.

'Is everything all right, Sister?'

The new nurse's eyes were wide and her hands were shaking with nerves. She opened her mouth to speak, stopped, and then began again. Millie Stuart had just arrived from Australia to fill the vacancy created by Leonora's departure.

'Private Wainwright ...'

'Yes?'

'He's ... he's an Aborigine,' Millie whispered as she stepped back from the bed.

'Yes. I believe he is.'

Cora and Millie looked down at the sleeping patient. His left arm was in a sling strapped awkwardly across his body. A bandage was wrapped around an eye and the top of his head.

Millie whispered, 'I've never seen an Aborigine in my life. To think I've come all this way to England and there he is.'

'Which means he's a soldier first, Millie. Fighting for King and country just like any other man here.' Cora walked to the nurses' desk a few feet away, draped her coat over the chair and looked through the new patient's file. 'He was injured in France.' She read on. 'He's from Adelaide. Like me. It says here, "Sir, as Legal Guardian of all Half Caste Aboriginal Children ... I hereby give consent to Gerard Arthur Wainwright to enlist in the Australian Military Forces, he being under the age of 21 years."'

Cora squinted at the fine print. 'It's signed by the Chief Protector of Aboriginals. I wonder what Private Wainwright needs protecting from? Millie, he needs fresh water, can you fill his jug, please?'

'Yes, Sister.'

Cora gently pressed his forehead and confirmed for herself he was feverish. She untucked the blanket from his chin and lowered it to his chest.

Millie returned with a fresh jug of water and set it on the bedside cupboard. 'I've just heard we're to expect more patients shortly.'

Cora surveyed the ward and counted five cots on either side of Private Wainwright and six on the other side all ready to take new patients. They sat expectantly, freshly made, sheets tucked in tight.

'Millie,' she asked. 'Will you find fresh flowers and some magazines for Private Wainwright?'

'What for?'

'Won't it be nice when he wakes up to see how welcome he is?'

The young nurse paused. 'From what I know of the Aborigines, he probably can't read anyway. It would be a waste.'

'A waste?' Cora made no attempt to hide the impatient and brittle tone in her voice.

'Do you really think he can read, Sister Barker?'

And before she could answer, they both heard, 'I can read.'

Millie yelped. Cora turned to look at the digger. He was awake. Cora was mortified at the thought he'd heard their conversation and shame seeped into every pore.

'In church,' Private Wainwright rasped. 'I bloody well learnt to read in church, sisters.'

The moon lit Cora's path to the oak tree by the lakes at the rear of the house, growing bare in the autumn evening. With each step, she saw another soldier's face. After more than two years at Harefield hospital, the images of the boys' features flickered through her mind as if they were printed on a deck of cards that someone was shuffling. There were blonds and brown-haired boys and redheads. Boys with hair so dark that when it was shaved they still had shadows on their scalps. Blue eyes. Brown eyes. Green and grey. Tall and short and stocky and thin. Quiet ones and boisterous ones. Some with souls shattered and others seemingly untouched by what fate had delivered to them.

What fate would await Private Wainwright when he returned home to a country as hostile to him as the battlefields of France?

She took in a lungful of air as she strode, hoping that when she exhaled, all thoughts of unfairness and cruelty would disappear. That's when she saw it—a dancing light, the tip of William's cigarette—moving like a firefly as he lifted it to his lips.

Happier thoughts flooded over her. Why should a woman of her age feel as furtive as a schoolgirl about meeting a man she was in love with? They weren't the first man and woman in history who wanted time alone, but they would be judged for it if they were found out, that much she knew. More accurately, she would be the one judged. She'd tried not to let the thought bother her but Cora knew that she alone carried the weight of expectations about her career, her sex and the time in which she lived. It was simply the way the world was: women's behaviour was judged and regulated and controlled in a way that men's wasn't. There was a raging part of her that wanted to revolt against the idea that others should determine the type of person she should be and how she should behave. As a nurse, she didn't need people to confess to know what they had been up to. Bodies and symptoms revealed secrets that patients never wanted to divulge. Puritanical Adelaide businessmen, with doting wives and children, suffering with venereal disease. Society ladies with liver damage from the alcohol they swore they never touched. Brides presenting in labour with their first child who were not primigravidae. And here in England, soldiers told not to stoop to consorting with low women while being provided with prophylactics.

It seemed to Cora that the world she lived in was full of lies.

She didn't want to be one of the liars.

Her sin would be omission.

The light flickered to the ground and then disappeared. William stepped out of the shadows, greeting her with a smile, and even in the dim night she could see such warmth in his expression that she felt heat course right through her.

'My darling Cora,' he called and she went to him, stopped when their bodies were almost touching, and held her hands behind her back. She wanted, needed to make this moment last. She tilted her chin upwards and met his gaze. He moved in half a step and she felt the warm exhale of his breath on her lips. Then his arm was around her and his hand found hers. Their fingers entwined and Cora leant against him, her ear pressed to the spot where his heart beat strong and fast.

'I wish we could go back,' she said hurriedly. 'To that little cottage in the Cotswolds. Once every few months isn't enough for me. I need that little bubble of perfect solitude. Just you and me and none of this mess.'

When they were away, they'd talked of their childhoods, their favourite books, their lives before the war. They ignored the newspapers in an attempt to remain in their cocoon and let themselves pretend it was all over, if only for a week. They made love and he was always respectful of her future by ensuring he had a supply of condoms from the hospital.

She'd been so, so happy. And Cora had believed him to be happy too. She had to believe it. And that meant overlooking the restlessness that could only be calmed by a brandy. Or two. When they'd managed to get away for weekends back in that little hotel in the Cotswolds, she'd had to overlook what he'd said in his sleep, words she couldn't make out no matter how hard she listened. And she'd had to pretend that the midnight flailing of his arms—striking her in the face more than once—were the hallmarks of some kind of sleep disorder rather than anything else.

She would put up with all that and more if it meant they could be together.

'Isn't it a perfect place?' he said wistfully. 'Perhaps we can arrange a weekend soon. Two whole days off. I know how I'd like to fill every minute. Just the two of us and a fire. I'm told I'm quite the expert.'

Cora laughed. 'I'm sure you need some more practice.'

'That can be arranged.'

Cora leant into William again, let him take her weight. 'But until then, this is all we have. These few precious moments.'

William guided her backwards until she was pressed against the tree and they kissed to the sound of a hooting owl in the woods not so far away.

Chapter Fifty-One

24 September 1917

'Did you really write this poem?'

'Ridgy-didge, nurse. I sat right here in bed and scribbled it on a piece of paper with a pencil. That new editor of *The Boomerang*, Mrs Roscoe, said it was marvellous. Let me see, will you?'

The Boomerang was the hospital's newsletter. Jessie turned it around so Ernest could see it for himself. 'Bloody hell,' he exclaimed. 'There's my words in the bloody newspaper.'

Jessie had to take him at his word. 'You didn't want your full name at the bottom? All it has here are the initials EN.'

Ernest looked sheepishly at Jessie. 'Truth is, I thought the other blokes might give me a ribbing about it. Seeing as it's about … you know … love.'

Jessie's heart seemed to break into a hundred pieces at the mention of the word. Bert had been gone for eight months and she had quite the collection of letters from him, so many she'd had to put them in a trunk. Each night before going to sleep, she would choose one at random and read once again his expressions of love.

Sweetheart I miss you.

My darling Jessie.

She had kept her promise to write to him every day and Dottie had teased Jessie that she alone was keeping the King's Mail in business. It was always the same. Jessie would write late at night in bed, the oil lamp on her bedside table burning low, Bert looking up at her from the photo in the silver frame. Just the two of them and their secrets.

'A love poem?' Jessie asked the soldier.

Ernest was blushing from ear to ear.

'Well, I …'

'Let me read it to you.' Jessie stared at the first line but when she read the words to herself she immediately regretted her decision. She drew in a deep breath. '"There's a chap they call the Anzac",' she began and stopped. Her throat seemed to have closed over.

'It's all right, love,' Ernest said quietly. 'You heard from your Bert lately?'

Since her engagement to Bert, Jessie had risen in the estimation of all the patients and, in fact, in the eyes of all the Australians at Harefield. The simple act of accepting his proposal seemed to have already made her an honorary Australian, much to her delight. Every patient in the ward knew about her connection to Bert and, if they were new to the hospital, they were soon informed of it by the others.

'This one's engaged to a digger. Private Bert Mott from the 10th. Hails from South Australia. Anyone know him?'

Sometimes a South Australian would call out and introduce himself to Jessie and they would try to find a connection to Bert and Murray Bridge. Most often they didn't, but she would share what she knew about Bert, about his brothers and about swimming in the river and that he'd worked at a grocer's. The boys always asked after Bert: when she'd received his most recent letter, if she'd had the opportunity to write back, to remind her to tell Bert that he was in their prayers too, to reassure her that the bloody Jerries wouldn't get him, that he was no doubt brave and would dodge anything the enemy threw at him. She took great comfort in these conversations. When she wrote to him, she passed on regards from all the boys in the ward, as they had insisted, along with their threats that if he didn't come back, one of them would snap her up because she was a bonzer girl.

Bert had written back, *I know you well enough to ask you to keep your affections for me alone. That's a lot to ask in these times, but I ask it unreservedly, dearest Jessie.*

She had never been one for prayers but if praying would bring her Bert home, she had pledged to get down on her knees each morning and night and every Sunday.

'Would you like me to read the rest?'

Ernest's question pulled her back from her thoughts. 'Beg your pardon?'

He rustled *The Boomerang*. 'The poem I wrote.'

Jessie sniffed, told a lie and willed herself to be strong. She needed to smile and laugh with these boys, not just for herself but for them. She needed to exemplify moral courage, an unwavering belief in the idea that Bert would return to her. They did not need to see doubt or fear in her eyes, for any doubt would be construed as doubt for every serving soldier, not just Bert. She of all people had to portray her belief in the rightness of the cause and her total belief in victory.

'Read it, please, Ernest. That would be lovely.'

Her patient cleared his throat. The boy in the next cot along stuck two fingers in his mouth and whistled so loudly Jessie swore the panes of glass in the windows shook.

'Ern's about to read us a poem,' he announced. A hush settled over the ward.

There's a chap they call the Anzac
You can see him up in town
With his smartly fitting tunic
And his face a sunny brown
And although he's but a stranger
He's as proud as any Earl.

If you leave him to his hobby
Trotting round some pretty girl.
And he'll love her, how he'll love her
While she's staying up in town
And perhaps a few days later
Till his heart has settled down
And some maiden in the country
Sets his heart all in a whirl
Then once more you'll see him walking
With the everlasting girl.

Then in hospital you'll meet him
And the symptoms here are seen
When his boots he dabs with polish
And his hair with brilliantine
Some mysterious correspondence
He'll at intervals unfurl

They you know that he has found her
That the Anzac's got a girl.

But his Dinkum girl, why, bless you
Is at home; and then perchance
The maiden has her only Boy
Fighting somewhere out in France
So they're feeling rather lonely
Don't reproaches at them hurl
For they have to keep their hands in
The Anzac and his girl.

Ernest laid the newspaper on his lap. The ward was silent save for Jessie's sobs.

'I didn't mean to make you cry, sweetheart.' He looked as if he was about to cry himself.

'It was lovely,' Jessie sobbed. 'Just lovely.'

Jessie and Cora looked over the decisions from that day's medical board meeting.

'Private Jack Hamer's being invalided home. "Permanently unfit for service".' Hamer was sitting in a cane chair by his bed, engrossed in a book, one lanky leg crossed over the other. He'd taken great comfort in books since he'd been admitted two weeks before. His stay at Harefield had been one in a long list of hospital admissions during the past six months. He'd been suffering chronic ear infections, which had been aggravated by the terrible conditions he'd endured on the Western Front. He'd survived the fighting at Pozieres but the damp and the mud and the unsanitary conditions had led to a chronic discharge that had completely destroyed his right ear and left him with no hearing in it at all. He was a quiet man, modest and polite, always saying, 'Thank you, Sister,' or 'I'll be right, Sister,' when the slightest thing was done for him. Jessie wondered if he felt a strange sort of misplaced guilt that, compared with those in the cots around him, he appeared at first glance unhurt. He'd starred in the previous weekend's cricket match against the nurses, hitting more sixes than any other patient ever had. But he'd not wanted to bask in his success. He'd walked quietly back to the ward on his own, eschewing the convivial post-match analysis with his team members. And here, back on the ward, he continued to be alone in his near-silence.

'You can tell him the news,' Cora said, and while she continued down the list of names Jessie walked to Hamer's bed and sat on the end of it.

He looked up from his book, politely closing it but keeping a finger in the pages to mark his place.

The words had formed in her head and she'd been about to speak before pulling herself up. Was anything to be judged good news these days for these men?

'I have news,' she said. Hamer's gaze was on her mouth and she became suddenly conscious of enunciating so he might, through the combination of her voice and the movement of her lips, be understood.

'Yes, Miss Chester?'

'You've been assessed as Class C. You're going home.'

Hamer stared at her.

'Home,' she repeated, more loudly this time. 'You're going back to Australia.'

He dropped the book in his lap. 'I heard you.'

'You'll be leaving tomorrow for Portsmouth. Your next of kin will get a telegram saying so.'

'My wife and my little boy,' he murmured.

'They'll be so pleased to have you home.' She stood, smoothed down her skirt and then hesitated but did it anyway: she leant down and pressed her lips to his cheek. 'Thank you,' she whispered, and she wasn't certain if he'd heard her or not

Chapter Fifty-Two

9 October 1917

'Jessie?'

At the sound of her name, she looked up from the sudsy circles her scrubbing brush had created on the wooden floorboards in the ward. When she recognised her mother, Dottie and Harry at the doorway, fifty feet away, Jessie smiled. Dottie's belly looked more enormous than ever and that familiar surge of joy and envy rose up in her. How on earth had she got to the hospital? A woman in her condition walking all the way from the high street was unthinkable.

'Hello!' Jessie sat back on her haunches and blew a strand of hair from her face. 'Well, this is a nice surprise. It's not my birthday, is it?'

Three of the dearest people in her life came towards her in a slow procession. Dottie held an envelope in tremulous fingers. Win was wiping tears from her eyes and Harry's lips trembled.

In that moment, Jessie knew. The blood in her veins turned to ice.

'This came. We had to give it to you right away,' Dottie said in a breathless rush.

'Jessie, love,' Win stammered and Jessie knew that look. Her mother was trying to be stoic but grief had already clearly overwhelmed her.

'Jess?' Harry shared a look with her that revealed more than any words could say. In it were all the times she had said to him 'I'm here. I'll help.'

He was now here for her. To help her cope with the possibility of the worst imaginable news.

Her head felt heavy and there was a thumping in her ears. She dropped her scrubbing brush into the tin pail and suds flew up and created an arc on the floor. Little bubbles sat on the surface, creating tiny rainbows as they caught the light from the windows. She tried to stand but her legs wouldn't obey. She stayed on the floor, the water slowly seeping through her skirt and her petticoat and her drawers.

'Read it, Jessie,' Dottie urged as she handed Jessie the envelope. 'I beg you. I'm sure Bert's just injured. People get telegrams for that too, I promise. I've delivered hundreds of them.'

How did the envelope find its way into Jessie's hands? She watched as trembling fingers pried it open. The telegram, the colour of clotted cream, unfolded and there were typed words on it. She took a moment to focus.

Deeply regret to inform you that Private Bert Mott is reported missing in action October 8, 1917.
Letter to follow.

The typed words swirled and spun on the paper, blurring into a black smudge.

'Missing in action.' She must have said the words out loud because suddenly there were arms around her and the sound of sobbing in her ears. Other words echoed in the ward.

'He'll be right, nurse.'

'Don't you worry.'

'God bless him and bring him home safe to you.'

'Chin up, cobber.'

And when Jessie opened her eyes, the cot cases had sat up as best they could, smiling sadly at her, and those who couldn't find the right thing to say gave her a thumbs up.

Her darling Bert. Something pulled at her lips and they contorted and then she heard a cry.

It wasn't hers.

Dottie was hunched over, her face white, clutching at her stomach.

April Jessie Chester was born right there in the ward eight hours later, weighing seven pounds three ounces and measuring twenty-one inches, just as darkness fell over Harefield hospital. The sheer novelty of having a new life come into the world on a ward—instead of having one depart it—brought joy to everyone.

When little baby April screamed for the first time, there wasn't a dry eye in the place and those patients who'd been kept outside for the sake of Dottie's privacy cheered and whooped when the news of the arrival was announced. They'd lit cigarettes and passed them around to each other, as if they themselves were the fathers and the cigarettes were cigars.

Jessie didn't remember much of it. Dottie had been bundled into the nearest bed. Sheets had been erected around her. Win had insisted on boiled water and washcloths and the nurses hovered efficiently around her like bees around a flower about to bloom.

Cora had made her cups of tea. She remembered that much. Harry had taken the telegram from her hands and slipped it into his coat pocket for safekeeping. And at the end of the day, when they had all been given a ride home in a motorised ambulance, Jessie had slowly climbed the steps up to her bedroom, closed the door behind her and wept.

In the weeks that followed, Jessie tried to hold on to the memories of that day, to the moment before her world had turned on its axis, to those last few moments when she was happy and certain in thinking that Bert was still alive and that he would still come back to her. They were fading with each minute. A fog rolled through, and it clung clammy and thick to every thought and every waking moment. Her limbs felt as thick as tree trunks, her fingers fat as sausages, every movement heavy and her head a dark cloud.

At home, Jessie seemed to hear April every time the little one cried during the night, little kittenish mews that quickly became screams of hunger, but that might have been because she wasn't sleeping herself, her dreams and her nightmares filled with thoughts of what had happened to Bert and where he was. She knew that soldiers were sometimes captured and held as prisoner of war. Was he in a cell somewhere being guarded by merciless Huns wielding bayonet rifles? Was he cold? Was he hungry? Did he hear them, the prayers she was sending to him across the Channel, wishing him safe?

On a Sunday two weeks after she'd received the telegram, the Chesters had visitors. Jessie had been absented from any duties at the hospital—matron's orders—and she sat at the kitchen table in her dressing gown and slippers, even though it was two o'clock in the afternoon. Her hair hung down her back, fastened in a loose plait, and her face remained unwashed. She held April in her arms, the baby having been foisted on her with a misunderstanding that she would prove a much-needed distraction to her aunt. The opposite was true. In every delicately clenched fist, in each snuffle, burp and sigh, Jessie saw something that now might forever be denied her. Her alternative and impossible future stared up at her beautifully and cruelly.

The front door opened and closed and there was chatter but Jessie couldn't make out the voices through the fog in her head until Cora and Gertie appeared in the kitchen.

'It's the nurses, come to pay a visit,' Win announced.

The nurses looked so different in their day clothes that it took a moment for Jessie to place them.

'Hello,' she replied meekly.

Gertie came to her side and peered at the baby. 'She's looking hale and hearty, isn't she, Cora?'

'She certainly is. How's she feeding, Dottie?'

Was Dottie in the room? Dottie stepped into the kitchen from the backyard, a wicker basket full of dry nappies propped on her hip.

'She's a hungry miss, that's for sure. I don't believe I ever did get around to thanking you both for everything you did for me and little April that day she was born.'

Win cleared her throat. 'It was a day of mixed blessings, that's for certain.'

Cora and Gertie exchanged glances. 'No more word, Jessie?' Gertie asked.

'No, not yet.'

Win fussed at the presence of the nurses. 'Can I get you both a cup of tea? I'll put the kettle on, shall I?'

'Actually, Mrs Chester,' Cora said. 'Gertie and I were wondering if Jessie might like to take a walk with us to the tearoom. It's not raining. We thought she might like some fresh air.'

'Thank you, but I don't think I'm up for it. Not today.'

'You need a walk, love.' Jessie knew that tone of voice. Win wasn't suggesting.

Gertie held her arms wide for the baby and Jessie passed April over. 'You go and freshen up. We'll have a look over little April, if that's all right with mum?'

'Perfectly all right,' Dottie answered with a sigh of relief.

Gertie sipped her white tea and sat back with a sigh. 'I miss sugar.'

Cora smiled and Jessie watched her, trying to move the corners of her mouth to mirror Cora's expression but they didn't seem to want to move at all.

'Blame the Germans,' Cora said, her expression one of sad resignation. 'The merchant ships carrying the sugar and meat can't get through the naval blockade. Imagine how much of the stuff is on the bottom of the Channel by now.'

'More than enough for my tea,' Gertie sniped.

'I don't mind about the sugar so much, but I miss butter,' Cora sighed. 'I'd rather not have any than the measly amount we're allowed.'

'What's the point of butter if we're being encouraged to eat less bread? I shall waste away before this war is over,'

Gertie said, which made Cora laugh and point out Gertie's double chin.

'You're not going to drink yours?' Cora asked and it was only when Cora and Gertie fixed their gazes on Jessie that she realised they were talking to her. She was being watched. She'd been working alongside the Australian nurses long enough to know the ways they looked after people when people didn't want to be looked after.

Jessie pushed the cup and saucer into the middle of the table. 'I'm not in the mood for it, really.' Should she tell the truth to the nurses? If not them, who? 'I'm not in the mood for much of anything, if I'm honest.'

'Well, of course you aren't. That's entirely understandable, but you must,' Gertie implored. 'You must find your strength. Not just for Bert when he returns, but for yourself.'

'Gertie's right, Jessie. We must all keep going.'

'It's so difficult when—'

'Jessie Chester?'

The voice caused the hairs on the back of Jessie's neck to stand on end. It was Arabella Pritchard. Without thinking, Jessie glanced down at her corseted stomach and then up to her perfect nose and powdered face.

Arabella noticed it and pulled herself up to her full height. 'I hear you're engaged to be married.'

'Yes.'

Arabella leant over the table, grabbed Jessie's hand and inspected the plain gold band on her ring finger. 'Oh, how sweet. Austerity has been so disappointing for regular people, don't you think?'

She dropped Jessie's hand like it was an old fish at the fishmonger's and restored herself to her full height. The delicate ostrich feathers in her hat danced like a marionette when she moved and her navy silk gown whispered its secrets.

Jessie stood out of habit. 'May I introduce you to Sisters Cora Barker and Gertie North from the Australian hospital at Harefield. This is Miss Arabella Pritchard.'

Arabella tsk-tsked. 'I'm Kirkham now. Mrs Henry Kirkham. Haven't you heard? I thought everyone in the village knew. How do you do, sisters?'

The nurses shook hands politely and then turned their attention back to their cups of tea.

'You're married?' Jessie asked and then surprised herself at the words that fell from her lips. 'The man who went to Harrow, with the black motor car?'

Arabella sucked in a fierce breath in reply and she fluttered her hand in the air to present her sparkling engagement ring and wedding band in their best light. 'I don't know who you could possibly be referring to. My husband works in insurance. In the City.' And then she turned her head curiously as if she'd forgotten something mildly important. 'And who is your lucky man, if I may ask?'

'Private Bert Mott. An Australian. He's—'

'Oh,' Arabella sighed. 'An Australian.'

From the corner of her eye, Jessie saw Cora lean forward, primed. Gertie laid a hand on her friend's forearm with the clear intent of holding her back.

'He's ... he's in France.'

'Is he? I expect you and your mother have already sewn a sweet little dress for the wedding?'

'Not yet. We're waiting until the war is over until we marry.'

'I'm sure you'll make a perfect village bride.' Something across the tearoom seemed to have caught Arabella's attention or perhaps she was simply bored with being so horrible. 'I must fly. Nice to meet you, ladies. Goodbye, Jessie.'

Arabella Kirkham nee Pritchard swished away, manoeuvring around tables and chairs and bestowing little niceties on the village people she recognised. Jessie felt bile rise in her throat and swallowed it away.

Gertie huffed. 'What a dreadful snob.'

Cora's forehead furrowed in confusion. 'Who on earth is she and what's her excuse?'

Where to begin? Could Jessie even summon up the energy to be spiteful? 'We went to school together in the village. Dottie knows her, too. She's always believed herself to be better than us all and has always taken great pride in showing it.'

'You showed great patience with her just now,' Cora said. 'And that's what makes you the better person. Being kind and being loved is far more important than riches.'

'Or sparkling baubles.'

Jessie began to cry, openly, unashamedly. Great heaving sobs.

'And you are loved, Jessie. By your wonderful family. By that little April who will adore you. By your dear Bert. And by all of us at the hospital. We will be at your side no matter what comes to pass. Do you understand?'

All she could do was nod.

Chapter Fifty-Three

30 October 1917

'I can't be certain but he says he's a South Australian, from the 10th, just like your Bert.'

Jessie stared at Cora.

Some of the patients suffered an ear condition called tinnitus, a symptom of which was a constant ringing in their ears. They'd been too close to too many shells and bombs and grenades and guns. Some had come to the hospital with split eardrums, which would render them deaf, or shrapnel in and around the ear, which meant their hearing might never be recovered.

Jessie wondering if the thudding in her ears was tinnitus or shock.

'I beg your pardon?'

Cora shook her shoulder. 'Come quick. He's in Ward 18. Captain Kent told me about him. He's just arrived.'

The two women ran along the duckboards in single file, their skirts flying, their breath ragged. They burst through the door of the ward and when Jessie saw the captain at a patient's bedside, she raced to him as fast as decorum would allow.

'This is Private Terrence Skipper. Says he fought alongside your Private Mott, Jessie. Skipper, this is one of our wonderful volunteers, Miss Chester.'

'Hello, miss.' His voice was brittle and scared.

Captain Kent stepped back and stood beside Cora. Jessie stared at the young man. He stared back at her. He was blond with sad blue eyes, and both his bandaged hands lay on top of his blanket like badly wrapped Christmas presents.

'My fiancé is Private Bert Mott. He's serving with A Company, 10th Battalion. Almost full of South Australians, he told me. My Bert was from a town called Murray Bridge and he mentioned it frequently. Perhaps you knew him?'

Skipper's mouth contorted in a grimace of thought. 'Mott?'

'Yes.' Jessie's heart raced. 'He was of medium height, stocky build with light red hair, almost strawberry blond, and blue eyes. His patch—the one on the arm of his uniform— is a dark blue bar on the top and lighter one underneath.'

'I know it,' Skipper rasped. 'We all have one.'

'He's missing in action, you see.' It was the first time those three words had fallen from Jessie's lips. Missing in action. Saying them aloud was more frightening than reading them, or hearing them over and over in her head.

'Bloody hell.'

'Can you tell me where you were and what was going on? I need to know if he was injured and taken prisoner. It's been very hard waiting for more news from the army.'

'Whatever I can do, miss.'

Jessie heard the scrape of chair legs and saw that Cora had pushed a cane chair over to Skipper's bedside, urging

Jessie to sit in it. She lowered herself, perching on its edge.

'We'd marched from Steenvoorde to Chateau Segard in the last few days of September. That's west Belgium, near the French border. We were on our way to Passchendaele. We knew things were about to get serious when we all got ammunition, bombs and rations. On the next Monday, October first I reckon it was, we had the bejesus bombed out of us. It lasted most of the night. Five blokes were killed and twenty-four wounded. And it went on like that for more than a week. The bombs and the rain. I've never seen rain like it.'

Jessie leant forward. 'I've been told Bert went missing on October eighth.'

Skipper gulped and his face paled. 'That sounds about right. We were near Ypres by that stage, in the trenches. And on that Monday, when you said your bloke went missing, we raided the German trenches. Up ours and into theirs.'

'And was Bert there with you?'

'I can't say I knew every bloke, but if he's in the 10th, he was there that day. Some of the wounded crawled back into our shell holes on our side of Celtic Wood. But those bastard Germans. We put up white flags and all, so our stretcher-bearers could get out into no-man's-land and bring back the injured but they shot them too. No mercy, Sister. No mercy.'

That night, Jessie sat at the kitchen table and squinted in the low lamplight as she wrote her letter, heart thumping with hope, her hand jittery with dread.

October 30, 1917

Dear Sir,
Could you please give me any information concerning
      3649 Prv A.R. Mott
      A Company, 10th Battalion AIF
      I have had the news from a chum in France, saying
that he went over with the boys to attack and has been
missing since October 8. Would you indeed be kind enough
to let me know as soon as possible, hoping that I have given
you all the needful details.
      Yours very sincerely,
      Jessie Chester

Chapter Fifty-Four

15 December 1917

Jessie stared at the date on the envelope. The telegram inside would bear the same date stamp: December the fifteenth.

For the past ten weeks, she had done nothing but sleep, eat and work like a machine, making the same monotonous movements over and over like she was a hulking metal contraption in a factory. She drank tea. She ate breakfast, because her mother watched her until she ate every last spoonful of porridge. She sewed pretty stitches until her fingers bled. She walked to the hospital and swept and cleaned and fed boys and changed bandages and mopped brows and changed sheets and said goodbyes and hellos to soldiers whose names and ranks and faces she would never remember. Every time the ward door creaked open she looked up instantly, hoping it was her mother and Dottie and Harry holding the telegram that would announce that Bert had been found and was safe and that he would be home to her soon.

A fresh tree had been cut for the Chesters' Christmas that year—even though little April was only two months old, the entire family believed they were doing it for her benefit. She seemed to appreciate the tinsel when it caught the light and sparkled. Win and Dottie had made paper chains, which were strung along the kitchen window, and over the doorway from the front room, branches of holly to make the house look merry.

Time had passed but it was as thick as sludge. Jessie had waded through it endlessly during those past weeks, hovering in the place in which death was expected but not confirmed, in which her heart was broken and was not, in which she was either to take a step into her life or shut the door on it.

15 December 1917.

Next to her at the table, Win sobbed with either joy or grief, none of them could be sure which, until Jessie opened the envelope. Win was preparing herself either way. Next to Win, Dottie sat stoically, cradling April in her arms, a shawl over her breast where April suckled. Across the table, Harry smoked a sad cigarette.

No one wanted to rush the moment. Whatever news the telegram contained had already been determined by fate or a bullet or a chance discovery in a German prisoner-of-war camp and nothing Jessie did—waiting, tearing it open in a rush, leaving it on the sideboard to open another day— would change the truth of what it contained.

Had the news also made it to the other side of the world? Was Bert's family—his mother and father and two brothers—staring at an envelope that very moment too?

Jessie opened it. The room was completely still. Win gasped and it seemed as if she had sucked in all the air from the kitchen because the silence was louder than anything Jessie had ever heard.

She pulled out the pink telegram and read it through trembling lips.

"Fifteenth December, 1917. Re: 3649 Priv Albert Reginald Mott 10th Batt. AIF. Dear Madam. We regret to inform you …'"

Dottie startled and April let out a shriek, her little fists flailing in the air. Harry's chair scraped and he limped to Jessie's side. She felt the comforting pressure of his hand on her shoulder.

"'… that the above named soldier who has previously been reported missing is now reported as killed in action on 8.10.17. We are making further enquiries with the hope of learning details of his death and will send you any information that we receive. Regretting the distressing character of this news, yours faithfully, et cetera'."

Jessie set the pink telegram on the kitchen table. The draught from the open window created flickering lamplight that shadowed the creases folded into the paper. It sat there, pink and ugly.

She had gone over this moment in her mind every day since she'd heard Bert was missing. She had imagined she might wail and fall to the ground, that she might crush the telegram in her fist or cry so much that its thin tissue would disintegrate in a flood of her tears.

The truth was nothing like she'd imagined it.

She felt nothing but a cold realisation, one thought that settled in behind her eyes and lodged there like a bullet in a soldier's brain.

I have lost Bert, my dear brave-hearted fellow.

*

Five days later, a wooden box was delivered from the AIF, addressed to Jessie.

She politely thanked the Australian who had delivered it and carried it to the kitchen table.

She had been at home since the news of Bert's death. The matron had insisted she take a week off to help her recover from the shock and she had taken to her bed, giving in to the exhaustion that had set in, rendering each limb leaden, her head scrambled like eggs. Win and Harry had made sure the fire in her bedroom was always stoked and, in a rare concession, Win had closed all the windows to ensure her daughter's broken heart was kept as warm as it could possibly be.

Dottie brought April up the stairs when the little one had had a bellyful and was settled so her aunt could cuddle her. There had been deliveries every day: bunches of flowers from neighbours, cards from the patients at Harefield and a special letter signed by the matron and all the nursing sisters, expressing their deepest sympathy.

If Jessie were able to feel anything, she would have been overwhelmed by all the kindness.

She pulled out a chair and sat. Harry was at work at the post office, Dottie and the baby were spending the day with her family on the farm and Win had left early that morning for Uxbridge to queue for meat, on account of the butchers there being bigger and the likelihood there might be more beef mince to go around.

It had been a long while since Jessie had heard the place so quiet. There was no fussing over her or the baby, no Dottie chatting about the goings-on in the village or Harry talking about the machinations of the post office that he had learnt about since he'd been working there. Win wasn't in the front room sewing or getting ready to go out delivering garments. The only sounds were the rumble of trucks from the street and the howl of the wind outside.

She opened the box. Inside it, there was a letter listing all Bert's possessions and a note saying that Private Mott had requested that for the purpose of the delivery of his final possessions, Miss Jessie Chester should be considered his next of kin.

There were two leather wallets. A bundle of her letters tied with brown string. Postcards and letters from Australia. A metal watch (damaged) and a leather strap. His testament. A coin—a kangaroo on one side and the King on the other— and a pencil. There was his copy of the photograph of the two of them, the one Gertie had snapped in the days before he'd left for France. Jessie turned it over. An inscription on the back read, 'If anything should happen to me, the finder please return to Miss Jessie Chester, High Street, Harefield, England.'

She turned it back over and stared at the two people in the photograph. A brave soldier and his smiling girl. Oh, how happy they'd been that day. Gertie had implored them to stand still for the photograph 'or it will come out all blurry' and it had taken them a full two minutes to stop laughing and giggling at each other before they could settle and be still.

How had she let herself be so naive as to think she wouldn't be touched by the horror of it all? What made her so special that she should be singled out for exemption?

She held the photo close to her eyes in the dim room. Bert was smiling, his blinking eyes blurry in the shot. She wanted to remember the touch of his hand on the small of her back. His kiss, gentle and loving. His dreams of a life together in Australia in a home by a river.

There was one extra letter without an envelope. Jessie unfolded it and blinked the tears away to focus. It was dated 7 October. The day before Bert had been reported missing. He'd not even had a chance to post it.

Somewhere in France
October 7th, 1917

My dearest Jessie,

I hope you're well and not working too hard. Everything here is tickety-boo. It's getting a little cold and as I write I'm wearing some of your mother's socks. Tell her from me that all my mates are dead jealous. I reckon I've got the warmest tootsies in all of France.

Please keep your letters coming. You can't know how welcome they are. To think that your precious hands have unfolded the paper, pressed a pencil onto it, written such words of love, and then sealed the envelope with a kiss. Well. It all fills me with such a joy and hope for our future.

I think back to the day you said 'yes' and I still count myself the luckiest man on earth. I can't say I have much to offer you except my heart and my promise that as long as I live, all I want to do is make you happy. You'll be pleased to know that the photo of the both of us that I sent home to Mum and Dad now sits proudly on the mantelpiece. Mum says she cried when she saw it, that's how happy she is about having a daughter-in-law, and Dad says I'm a lucky so-and-so on account of you being so pretty.

I think of you every day when I need reminding about what I'm doing here.

And I see you in my dreams each night.

I can't wait to teach you how to swim in the Murray, to swing you from the rope than hangs from the outstretched branch of the old gum tree and see the look on your face when you fly through the air, the sun on your face, freedom in your heart. And a wedding band on your finger.

I'm counting the days until we can be together again.

I remain ever your loving sweetheart,

Bert

xxxxxx

Jessie folded the letter and set it on the table. She lowered her head to the kitchen table, the energy leaching from her like blood seeping from a wound, and closed her eyes.

December 20th, 1917

To Whom It May Concern,
I received the letter you so kindly sent to me concerning the
death of
    3649 Prv A.R. Mott
    A Company, 10th Batt AIF
    If you can find out for me how he was killed, I shall be
very glad, and thanking you for your kind attention.
    I am yours very sincerely,
    Jessie Chester

Chapter Fifty-Five

22 December 1917

The fire in the library was roaring and it had become Cora's favourite place to sit to write her letters home. In her hand she held an unopened letter from her sister Eve, which was well overdue a reply.

The room felt a little like what she had imagined England to be before she'd arrived in 1915. Country manors with libraries bursting with books. Comfortable settees and billiard tables on which highly polished balls sat in their triangular rack, just waiting for men in fine black ties and wing-tip collars to enter after dinner with their cigars to pick up a cue and chat about world affairs while they puffed. Walls hung with full-length portraits of important men wearing wigs and breeches and white stockings

The truth was altogether different. There was only one billiard table and it had been covered over with board to transform it for the playing of table tennis. The bookshelves were no longer neatly stacked. Books travelled between wards and staff and patients, some had likely been packed in kitbags to be read on the long voyage home and there were empty spaces on the shelves now.

The settees were worn at the corners from years of constant use and if there had been curtains over the windows, there were none now to keep out the bitter cold. The weather had turned a month before and it mirrored the mood of everyone at Harefield. Skies had been grey for weeks and it had rained and rained and rained. The duckboards leading from ward to ward and to the Long Ramp looked like bridges hovering over muddy pools. There had been some snow and some of the new nurses had caroused with the able patients and taken part in snowballing. Cora hadn't wanted to warn them that the novelty of it would wear off before they knew it, because surely to God this would be the last winter of the war.

The Germans had had a morale boost: the collapse of Russia and its twin revolutions meant the Germans were no longer waging war on their eastern and western fronts, but there was still fighting in the Caucasus. The Allies' naval blockade was biting deep and the arrival of the Americans earlier that year had been welcome news but had they yet made a difference to the war? There were mixed opinions among the armchair experts in the patients' canteen.

When Jerusalem had been captured in October during the battle of Beersheba, there had been much rejoicing among the Allies. Every battle won was a step closer to ultimate victory and they leapt on the news as if it might instead be the end of the war.

'Onwards to bloody Mesopotamia!'

'Let's get those Fokkers!'

The fire in the library's hearth crackled. Cora put another log on the flickering flames. She stood for a moment, rubbing her hands together to warm them through. She really should read Eve's letter and craft a quick letter in return. What lies could she invent this time for her family? Would it shock them to know she'd lost the ability to pretend?

Should she write to them about the anguish of a young man she'd nursed that week who felt he was all alone in the world. One of his best mates had been gassed and was in hospital in England although he didn't know where. Almost all his battalion had been killed or wounded in France.

Or another, who'd cried like a baby when he'd described what had happened to him and his cobber. She would not forget the anguish and her utter inability to make anything better for the young man.

'I stepped on him, Sister,' he'd said.

'Oh, you couldn't have,' Cora said as she tucked him in bed. The lights had just been turned off for the night despite him begging her to leave them on.

'He was right next to me. Bullets ripped right through him and he fell and sank into the mud and it's like quicksand, you know? If I'd stopped to pull him out, well, that just would have killed me too. So,' he sobbed unashamedly, 'I left him there in the mud and the puddles.' Tears had streamed down his face and his jittery hands had been clasped together so hard his knuckles had been white with the strain of it.

'And you know what we call that, Sister?'

She didn't have an answer.

'Anzac soup. And I'll be in that soup when I'm all fixed up and they send me back.'

Was it Cora's place to tell him he would never go back? Not judging by the growing size of the wound on his foot. He'd already endured two operations to stop the gangrene from trench foot spreading from his toes, but they hadn't arrested its bloom into the arch of his foot.

She had no words of comfort for a man who'd endured such a loss, and a primal fear that he had pushed his dying mate, his best mate, further into the French mud, suffocating him.

She had sat with him, clutching his hand, while he'd sobbed until he'd fallen into exhausted and fitful sleep.

Perhaps that was not a story to tell in a Christmas letter home.

She fidgeted and began to pace, a fingernail between her front teeth, nibbling at it, tugging the cuticle from her nail bed until it bled and she could taste the metal in her mouth.

Forty-two Australians were now buried at St Mary's churchyard and it would soon be forty-three if Private William Duddle succumbed, as he was now expected to do. The popular twenty-five-year-old from Goulburn had survived his first knock at Louverval in northern France but had then been wounded again at Ypres, knocked unconscious by an exploding shell. He'd had an eye removed while at Harefield and had seemed to be recovering well but had taken a turn for the worse in the past forty-eight hours.

Cora hadn't been to a funeral in months. Word around the hospital was that the people of the village still turned out loyally and faithfully to every single one, lining the streets of Harefield, draping the coffin with a Union Jack and following the cortege to St Mary's churchyard. She wished she could thank each of them personally for the kindness they had bestowed on every Australian buried there.

The war's routines and rhythms had become so familiar to her that she no longer jumped when the sound of bombs dropping on London floated on the wind to where she sat at a patient's bedside. When someone spotted a Zeppelin hovering ominously in the sky, she no longer felt paralysed by fear, but experienced a stoic sense of acceptance about its presence. Unless it was shot by anti-aircraft guns in the capital, it would unleash its load somewhere. What else could they do from a distance, other than wait for it to drop its weapons?

The sound of trucks arriving with new patients didn't send a fizz of adrenaline up Cora's spine, and when the men whistled at the land girls who came every morning to deliver milk she no longer felt the need to chide them for being cheeky. Those English land girls could handle themselves well enough without Cora's interference.

She had found other ways to endure her work in England, to distract her from the brutal truth, and one of them was William. She longed to be with him in a way that shook the foundations of everything she knew about herself.

They had slipped away for another weekend earlier that month, back to their favourite place in the Cotswolds. They'd spent it in each other's arms, making love and talking and sleeping the sleep of the dead. The future beyond the war seemed so distant and unreal that grasping the truth and reality of what it might be was like trying to hold steam in your cupped hands.

Cora walked across the ancient woven rug to the large bay windows, steamed up from the heat in the room. She sat on the cushions propped there, pulled a sleeve between her fingers and her palm and rubbed a circle so she could see out to the lakes. She saw nothing through the drizzle but smudges of brown and grey.

She opened the letter.

Adelaide
November 1st, 1917

Dearest Cora,
I'm writing this letter with my Christmas wishes very early,
I know, but I want to make sure you don't miss out on all
the greetings from home.

    Our plan here is to have a roast chicken dinner with
all the trimmings and we've held back a plum pudding
from our batch of donations to the Trench Fund to save for
ourselves. We'll exchange presents, Mother, Father, Grace
and I, as usual. We will add to the collection of gifts we
have been keeping for you since you've been away. This will
be the third Christmas and the wicker basket on the hearth
is now full to bursting. When you come home, it will seem
as if you were never away at all.

    We have so much to catch up on, dear Cora.

    My volunteering with the League of Loyal Women
is over. It was made clear to me that I was no longer
welcome because I cast my vote for the negative in both
the first and second conscription referenda. After reading
over and over what you had written to me, I could not,
in good conscience, send more boys to endure what your
patients have endured. I was told that I had voted against a
resolution of the executive committee, an order which, it was
made extremely clear, I had been expected to obey. There
were two of us who admitted to voting against conscription.
Molly Dunnart voted yes the first time but no in the second,
her opinion changed so dramatically by the loss of her dear
sweetheart in November. There has been so much loss and

the thought of sending more men into the trenches was not something I could condone. I've let Dad think I simply followed his lead and voted the way he and Archbishop Mannix had instructed, rather than making up my mind for myself. But I thought long and hard, considered both positions, and when I walked into the ballot box, I made the decision on my own views and beliefs. What a privilege it is to have the right to make one's opinion known. I pity the poor women of England who don't have it. I hope when the war is over they will take up the cudgels once again and demand that equality for themselves.

Maybe I'll volunteer for the Red Cross's Cheer Up hut. I find myself needing to do something. There are too many boys on the streets, legless, injured, limping. The obituary pages in The Register *are filled with notices from families who've lost someone. Imagine never having a grave to visit, nor a headstone to decorate with pretty flowers on anniversaries and birthdays? It's heartbreaking.*

Sorry to end on such a morbid note, but there's not much else to think about these days. I don't know how you've done it, being in the thick of things.

With my fondest regards and in great admiration of you, as always,

Eve

There was another page with the letter, a hastily scrawled note.

Cora—on my way to the post office to mail your letter I ran into Myrtle Hickinbotham who shared the terrible news that Eddie Bagot from number 73 has been killed. Mrs Bagot is inconsolable. Imagine. Two sons now lost.

The pages of the letter slipped from Cora's hand and fluttered to the Oriental rug like snowflakes. Her sister's cursive was so neat and ordered compared to Cora's, which had become rushed scribbles from too much hurried notetaking. Eve's handwriting, like her life, had been preserved in amber like a prehistoric insect and Cora had never felt more distant from her sister, her family or home.

And now Eddie Bagot was dead.

They had grown up together on the same street, the Barkers and the Hickinbothams and the Bagots. Cora had been the eldest by a few years, and in their games had always somehow managed to convince the other children that she would play-act as their teacher and they would be her students. Little Eddie Bagot was the youngest on the street, a scrap of a thing who perpetually seemed to have skinned knees and blood running down his legs in rivulets into his dirty old socks, until he grew tall as a young man and filled out after he took on a job as a bootmaker in Rundle Street, working with his older brother Horace. The boots Eddie had made for Cora, tucked up in a trunk at home, were the most comfortable shoes she had. How many times had she wished for them at Harefield? Eddie had been sweet and artistic and gentle. She blinked her eyes closed at the idea that his flesh and bone had been torn to shreds.

She had seen death before, and injury and malady, but she had never known any of those men as boys. Eddie had been a lad who liked cricket and collecting tadpoles and who had made a kite that had soared into the sky on windy days. She had known him in short pants and knitted jumpers, with jam smeared over his mouth from freshly baked bread.

'Oh, Eddie,' she said quietly and the sobs came too easily to hide.

Chapter Fifty-Six

24 December 1917

'I hardly know where to begin, Sister North.'

Jessie wiped her forehead with the back of her hand and blew at a strand of hair that seemed to be growing more disobedient as the day wore on. It was three in the afternoon, the day before Christmas, and they'd just been notified by the matron that truckloads of new patients were on their way to Harefield, once again. They'd started flowing like a river when the Battle of the Somme had begun that July, and for one hundred and forty-one days the battlefields had run with blood and soldiers had flooded to England injured, gassed, blinded, limbless, dying, half mad or a combination of all of those things.

There wasn't time to change one bed much less all twenty-two, sweep and scrub the floors, wash all the dishes from lunch and find fresh supplies from somewhere for all the new patients. As soon as the beds were vacated, new patients arrived to fill them.

She didn't want to cry, she really didn't. When she'd first started at the hospital, she had successfully managed to save all her tears for the evenings when she was in bed at home, alone with her doubts and insecurities and the images of injured men that played in her mind.

All that strength had gone. Traitorous tears threatened to drizzle from her eyes as she tried to fix her mind on the task before her. Every organised thought seemed slippery as an eel. Humiliation rose up in her and she felt sick.

She'd come back too early.

'Now, now, dear girl. It's all right.' Gertie laid a hand on her shoulder and patted her there sympathetically.

'I'm sorry, Sister. I can't seem to think. Please tell me what I should do first?' she pleaded, her palms on her cheeks. When she realised they were wet, she turned her face away.

'We'll get it sorted, Jessie. Don't you worry. Two minds are better than one, as they say.'

They stood at the nurses' desk and surveyed the ward. Beds were dishevelled and sheets had been thrown back so hurriedly they draped on the floor. The muddy footprints of porters created trails back and forth to each bed, as they'd picked up kitbags and belongings for the men who couldn't manage the task on their own. Two thin lines on the floorboards were tracks from a wheelchair, still muddy from having moved another patient. A vase of flowers had been knocked over, leaving scattered stems and a puddle of water on the floor. The windows were streaked with rain. The fires in both stoves had gone out. It looked as if someone had sounded an evacuation signal and everyone had left in a panic.

Jessie stared at the mess. 'We ... we need to strip the beds first, I think.'

'Yes, I agree.'

'And then, well, as you can see for yourself, the floor is filthy. Best we do that before we make up the beds?'

'Yes,' Gertie said, with an authoritative nod. 'Why don't I clean out the ash from the stoves and get the fires going. If it's warmer in here, the floors will dry more quickly. And we won't freeze while we're working.'

Jessie's breathing settled. 'And while the floors are drying I'll go to the stores for pyjamas and clothes and toiletries for the new patients.'

'See?' Gertie smiled. 'You know what to do after all. You just needed to take a breath.'

Jessie took one in, deep and long, filling her lungs. She blinked away the light-headed feeling that had made her slightly woozy. 'Thank you, Sister.'

'Don't let this little stumble worry you. We all have days when we'd rather have stayed in bed. None of us have had barely a moment to breathe since July. And it's not getting any quieter, that's for certain.' Gertie sighed, barely hiding her frustration. 'And you've had a terrible shock to cope with as well. How are you going, really?'

'One day at a time. That's what my mother says.'

'She's right. Will a cup of tea help?'

'I'd love one, thank you, Sister.'

Gertie headed to the small kitchen at the rear of the ward and Jessie got to work. At the bed nearest her, she tugged the sheets from the mattress so violently the bedframe squeaked and the mattress lifted into the air. It was very satisfying.

By eight o'clock that night, the ward was ready for the twenty-two new patients who'd been waiting in the mess. Some of the men were stretchered in, others pushed in wheelchairs, and the blind were led by their comrades who managed on crutches and walking sticks. They were a sorry lot, their faces drawn, sad, stoic. They didn't betray any emotion but exhaustion and once they'd scrubbed themselves clean or been bed bathed, they collapsed between clean sheets in the warm ward. Before long, the sound of gentle snoring filled the air. The fire crackled and the scent of fresh flowers competed with wood smoke.

Jessie pulled a chair from the bedside of a sleeping patient and set it behind the nurses' desk. Gertie looked up from her notes and sighed.

'Very good work today, Jessie.'

'Thank you, Sister.'

When her tears fell this time, they weren't from frustration or humiliation but from a deep-seated sense of pride. She had never experienced such a feeling of accomplishment. Certainly, she'd felt a little puffed up when a customer had admired her needlework or the fine seams of a gown she had crafted, and she'd felt pride as a sister when Harry and Dottie had married.

But this was different in a way she was still trying to define. When the weary Australians had entered the ward, they'd looked around in disbelief at the calm cleanliness of it. The fresh flowers and the fire. The piles of neatly folded clothes on the end of each bed, accompanied by a new toothbrush and Euthymol toothpaste in its blue box, a rosy-cheeked officer on the front. None of the patients looked like him and likely never would again. They had shuffled up the middle aisle and chosen cots. Two boys wanted to be next to each other and the other patients accommodated them. They inspected their fresh clothes, and tired smiles had broken out among them; smiles that had lasted until they'd drifted off to sleep: calm, warm and safe.

'The men seem settled,' Gertie said. 'Why don't you go home?'

The mere mention of the word had her yawning. 'Is there nothing else to do?'

'Not here.' Gertie picked up her pencil and closed a file before opening another. She was making notes on all twenty-two of the patients. 'Go and get some sleep.'

'Thank you, Sister North. You've been very kind to me.'

'It's nothing you don't deserve. I'll see you tomorrow?'

'You will. Oh, and Sister?'

When Gertie looked up from her notes, Jessie realised she'd never seen the nurse looking so tired.

'Merry Christmas.'

1918

Chapter Fifty-Seven

6 February 1918

'Well, will you look at this.' Cora rustled the *Middlesex and Buckinghamshire Advertiser* and held a page close to her eyes so she could read the small print. She firmly believed she needed glasses.

'Watch out. You'll spill my tea,' Gertie exclaimed as she moved her cup and saucer on the mess table to the side.

'Mark this day down in history. The Representation of the People Act has received Royal Assent.'

Gertie frowned. 'What's that when it's at home?'

'Women in the United Kingdom have won the right to vote.'

'Have they now? They've been very patient, that's all I can say.'

'Oh.' Cora continued reading. 'Hold on. Only if they've reached the age of thirty.'

'Thirty?' Gertie exclaimed. 'So you and I would be able to vote if we were English, being the old spinsters that we are, but young Jessie can't. Nor her sister-in-law, Dottie. Who is married and already a mother.'

'So it seems.' Cora affected a stuffy old man's voice. '"Mature women can now engage with politics but younger women are too flighty. A new hat or a man with a car is more important to them than the fate of a nation."'

Gertie scowled.

'Men can vote at the age of twenty-one. But a woman has to be an occupier of a property or be married to an occupier, which means *two-thirds* of British women will now be able to vote.' Cora didn't feel as exhilarated for her English sisters as she thought she might.

'Hurrah,' Gertie harrumphed. 'We've had the vote in South Australia since 1894. And the right to stand for Parliament.'

'Maybe the colonies aren't so far behind after all.' Cora glanced at her watch and sprung to her feet. 'We'd better get moving.' She took one final slurp of her tea. 'Some of the boys are heading off to the London Hippodrome and the Paddington Bowling Club today. We'd best make sure they're up and dressed.'

That evening, Cora and William snatched some time together, sharing a hot chocolate and a plate of scones—no cream—at the canteen. No one blinked an eye any longer at the sight of the two of them spending time in each other's company. While not a word was said—to Cora's face at least—they were accepted as a couple around the hospital. And while they were careful never to engage in public or unprofessional displays of affection such as holding hands or kissing each other where patients or other staff might see, every spare moment Cora had that happened to coincide with any spare moment of William's was spent together.

The length of the war had made them both suspicious of being optimistic but by late February, Cora had let herself develop a cautious sense of optimism about the way the war was heading. Germany's allies were failing and the involvement of the Americans had provided a welcome boost of strength to the Allied forces, with thousands of troops landing in Europe every month. After Russia had collapsed, the Germans had withdrawn all their troops from the eastern front and diverted them to the battle in the west.

William had placed great store in the deployment of the Sopwith Camel, a newly developed English fighter plane fitted with two synchronised machine guns. 'It'll change things forever. Mark my words.'

If the end was close, the price had already been too heavy. On one horrific day in July 1915, 5,533 Australians had died in one twenty-four-hour period at Fromelles. During 1916, more than forty thousand Australians had been killed or wounded on the Western Front.

In 1917, the casualties had been nearly double that— nearly seventy-seven thousand Australians had been killed or wounded in places with names Cora was now so familiar with: Bullecourt, Messines and Ypres. The battle of Passchendaele. The battle that had killed Private Bert Mott, Jessie's fiancé.

The fighting on the Western Front had largely reached a stalemate, with heavy losses on both sides for so little territory gained. They had seen thousands and thousands of patients at the hospital, so many that Cora found herself numb to the sheer volume of broken men.

'What news from home?' William sat back in his chair, smoking, turning his head to blow the smoke away from Cora.

'My mother and father are well. They worry constantly about me, of course.'

'Totally understandable.' He smiled.

'My sister Eve writes that the streets of Adelaide are filled with the walking wounded.'

William's expression fell. 'They must be. I must say I hadn't thought about that, that people at home would be as exposed to the war as we are.' He stubbed out his cigarette on a metal ashtray. It was already full of ash.

'And you?' Cora asked. 'What's the latest from Melbourne and your family?'

He lit another cigarette and didn't reply until he'd taken a first puff.

'My mother wrote to tell me that Alice is married.'

'Oh. Congratulations to her.' Cora tried not to feel guilty at the mention of William's former fiancée, but it came anyway, a burdensome weight on her heart. Was it alleviated somewhat now she had found someone else? Cora tried not to think about that. 'One wouldn't wish anything else for her. Is your father a little less angry at you now?'

'I have no idea. He hasn't responded to one of my letters since I broke off the engagement.'

'That's unkind of him.'

'But exactly like him, I'm sorry to say. There's no one who bears a grudge like my father.' He shrugged. 'But I can't change him. I made him proud when I enlisted and

I've clearly disappointed him by being a cad. I'm not the son he imagined I'd be. But … you know what I've realised? I find myself caring less and less about his approval the more time I'm away from Melbourne. There, I was the doctor son of my doctor father who was the doctor son of his own doctor father.' He laughed at himself. 'Do you know how good it's been to work in a place where no one knows—or could care less—about the family name?'

'You're a wonderful doctor. And that's all down to you, not your family or your good name.'

'Could you still love a man who wasn't a doctor, Cora?'

She blinked and studied him for a moment. 'I'd love you if you were a streetsweeper. Where is this coming from?'

'I've been thinking about what I'll do when the war is over. I'd always been so determined that I was going to go back to Melbourne and resume my work as a surgeon, take everything I've learnt here and in Egypt and put it into practice to change the way we operate. Now … I don't know. It feels like another world, doesn't it, that life? I don't know how I'll fit in to it any more.'

Cora heard his doubts and recognised each one of them. 'I understand,' she replied. 'I don't know if I can go back to what I was before the war. I'm not the same person I was in 1915 when I enlisted. My work can't be everything to me any more. There's more to being alive, isn't there?'

'I believe there is.'

'I thought myself to be happy with my lot in life. I had my work. I was very good at it and I was glad, because I had nothing else. I didn't have expectations, ever, that I would meet someone who would love me. My age and my profession were always going to be strikes against me.' William's face was blurred through tears she hadn't expected. 'And then I met you.'

'Cora,' he murmured and reached for her hand.

'I don't know what the future holds for either of us. But I'm not sure I want this to end when the war does.'

William hesitated. 'I can't make promises, Cora, if that's what you're asking. Not while I'm questioning everything. How can I be trusted to make a decision in the state I'm in? War weary. Battle scarred. Exhausted in both mind and body.'

Was her heart breaking just a little?

He reached across the table for her hand and his grip was firm and so familiar. 'All I know is that the joy I feel when I'm with you? The ease of what we share? It sustains me. You keep me sane, Cora. You are mine. You are mine here, in Harefield, for the war. Can that not be enough?'

'I see,' she said quietly. She understood what he was saying, perhaps even felt the same, but it still hurt to hear the words fall from his lips so assuredly.

'I don't think it helps to have dreams here, now. They're too easily shattered, don't you think?'

Chapter Fifty-Eight

10 March 1918

Dear Madam,

I am writing to ask if you have had any more news concerning the death of Private A.R. Mott.

I last heard from you sometime in December and you said you were trying to find out more details of his death, as I cannot get to know how he died, but if anything has come to light, or if you could get to know for me I should be very grateful, as I feel very unsettled in my mind, owing to different reports.

Hoping I am not worrying you too much, and that you will do your best for me.

I am enclosing an envelope for your reply.

Yours very respectfully,

Jessie Chester

Harry passed the letter back to Jessie and frowned. 'Are you sure about this?'

'What do you mean am I sure?'

'Can't you just ... I mean, what good will it do you, Jessie, to hold on like this?'

A tremor rose from her gut and made her stutter in anger. 'He was my fiancé, Harry. I owe it to him to find out everything I can.'

Harry lit a cigarette and took his first puff angrily. 'How is it going to help you to know exactly how he died? That's my point. You've read it for yourself. He was killed, Jessie. As bloody awful as that is, he's dead. He died in October. Five months ago.'

Had it really been five months?

She had been measuring the days and weeks against April's young life. The little girl could roll over now when they set her on the rug on the floor, and they clapped when she turned and showered her with kisses when she giggled. Win had sewn her the prettiest dresses in preparation for the time—and it wouldn't be long, Win assured Dottie with a grandmother's knowing—when she was walking and wouldn't get the skirts caught up on her knees when she crawled.

April was proof that life went on. Her grief hadn't stopped the clock. Bert's death hadn't stopped the war. It all lingered like a stench in the air. All of it.

'I have to know, Harry.'

'Can't you see you're torturing yourself with these letters, Jessie?'

'It's not just for me, Harry. It's for his mother and father and his brothers. Don't you think they want to know where Bert is? Put yourself in their shoes, won't you? Their son and brother dies on the other side of the world and all they have is a telegram. They don't know if he was struck by a bullet or blown up by a bomb or …' She stumbled over the words and the thoughts that had never left her mind each day and night of the past five months.

'You'll give yourself nightmares, you will,' Harry huffed, and although she knew he was only thinking of her, only saying what he was because he hated to see her suffering, her anger flared unbidden.

'I've had them all. In my dreams he's been gassed and shot and blown to bits and crushed and strangled and mutilated in a hundred kinds of ways. Nothing ... nothing can be worse than what I've imagined, Harry. The trouble is, I've seen it all. At the hospital. I've seen what war really does to men.'

She closed her eyes against the images but they flickered as vividly as the Charlie Chaplin moving picture she'd watched with Bert in the ward a million years ago.

If she could find out how Bert had died, she could write to his family and give them the details she instinctively knew they would be yearning for. Where had he drawn his last breath? Where did his mortal remains rest? Was there a cross to mark the spot in a Flanders field so far away, somewhere she might one day take a photograph so his family would know? Would it settle their minds and bring them some peace to know? Would it bring her peace to know?

In her heart of hearts, she knew that nothing—not a letter from the AIF, not an investigation, not an eyewitness account from a chum in Bert's battalion—could give her the answer to the question she desired the most.

Had Bert been thinking of her as he'd scrambled up out of that French trench, clutching his .303 rifle in his hands, in the moments before he'd died?

14th March, 1918

Dear Miss Chester,

With reference to your further enquiry of 10th, for Pvt A.R. Mott, who is now officially reported Killed in Action 8.10.17, having previously been reported Missing on that date, we regret to inform you that up to the present we have been unable to obtain any particulars of his death and burial in spite of our efforts to do so. As you will readily understand, it often takes a long time before such information is received.

Assuring you that we are doing our utmost to obtain the desired information and that we will advise you as soon as we succeed.

M. Ryan
Secretary

25th May, 1918

Dear Miss Chester,
We write to advise you of an unofficial report we have received concerning 3649 Pvt A.R. Mott, 10th Battalion AIF.

One informant, a man in the same unit, 3734 Cpl A.J. Duncan, when interviewed in an Australia Military Camp in France certified as follows:–

Mott was going up to be attached to C Company. I knew him in England during our training: he was sharp featured, about 5 feet 6, clean-shaven, thin. I was going up at night with a party of details to join the Battalion in the Celtic Wood, Ypres Sector. When we got there I found Mott was missing. I was told by Cpl Anderson, 10th Battalion A Company (who went to England wounded in November and has not joined the Battalion since) that on the way up he was behind the details with Pvt Mott. A shell dropped near them, and he saw Mott on the ground; he did not know if he was wounded or killed; he had to carry on.

We regret this information is so slight, but we have now written to Cpl Anderson and will at once advise you as to his reply.
With a further assurance of our sympathy,
Yours faithfully,
Miss McConnell,
Secretary

1st June, 1918

Dear Miss Chester,
We have now received an unofficial report from 3452
Cpl Anderson, AIF, to whom we wrote for information
concerning your friend Pvt Mott.
He certifies as follows:

Mott had been away in England after being wounded.
I knew him well, but did not know his Christian
name or number. I think he came from Adelaide.
He was of a good sturdy build and about 5'6" in
height. We were close to Menin and Ypres Road
about 1 mile E of Ypres and were at the time going
up to the firing line about 2 miles off. He was hit
by a shell burst and wounded by the explosion.
I was 10 yards away from him at the time and I think
he was killed instantaneously. I do not know where he
was buried but probably near the spot where he fell, 1
mile E of Ypres.

Trusting this report may be of some value and with a
further assurance of our sympathy.
Yours faithfully,
Miss McConnell
Secretary

Chapter Fifty-Nine

1 June 1918

Jessie, Harry, Dottie and Win stared down at a map in the atlas Win had brought home from the village library. Belgium was so close to England, really. A hop across the Channel from Dover. The only association Jessie had in her mind with the small country had been chocolate. That had changed forever. For four years Ypres had stood in the path of Germany's planned sweep into France from the north and had experienced the deadliest fighting of the war. Bert had been one of half a million casualties on all sides during the Battle of Passchendaele: Brits and Canadians and French and her dear beloved Australians had lost so much and Jessie couldn't help but feel for the mothers and fathers on the other side who'd lost their sons, too.

'One mile east of Ypres,' she said. Had Bert died in a field? On a cobbled street? Had his bones been sucked into the earth by the quicksand of a muddy bog?

'You have to wonder what's left of the place after four years of fighting,' Harry said, staring at names he didn't know how to pronounce in a country he would likely never visit.

Win crossed herself. 'God bless them all.'

'Oh, Jessie,' Dottie said, swaying back and forth to settle April, who was dozing in her arms. 'Now you know.'

That night, Jessie lay in bed, a warm early summer breeze playing with the curtains in her bedroom, and read all Bert's letters.

He had loved her.

And he was dead.

Chapter Sixty

23 June 1918

'There's nothing more to do for her, is there?' Standing next to Cora, Gertie's voice caught on a sob that was muffled by her improvised face mask, and she reached out a hand to her friend.

Cora gripped Gertie's fingers tight. 'She's tolerated some aspirin for her pain and she's as comfortable as she can be in the circumstances … but.'

The patient's eyes were closed, her breaths shallow. Cora pressed a damp cloth to her clammy forehead and smoothed it down her cheeks and her neck. 'Ruby,' Cora whispered. There was no reply.

Gertie adjusted the damp sheet. Ruby's flaccid arms rested on top of it and her fingers lay prone, as if they knew they would never grip anything ever again.

Nothing was going to save Staff Nurse Ruby Dickinson from New South Wales. She'd reported herself ill that morning and had become poorly so quickly she'd taken to bed and hadn't left.

Cora and Gertie both knew she would be dead by dinnertime.

'Influenza,' the doctors had announced after they'd assessed her, a prognosis which surprised no one but scared them all. There had already been two deaths from it that month and three other nurses were sick too, their conditions grave. Boys had come back from France with what everyone believed at first to be the common cold. They even called it by its French name, *la grippe*, and it came with the usual symptoms of sore throat, headache and a loss of appetite.

'I lost my desire for bully beef,' one soldier had joked and the patients all around him in the ward laughed and commented that they must have had *la grippe* since they'd enlisted.

By early spring 1918, word had come from the battlefield hospitals that a three-day fever was spreading like wildfire among the troops in the trenches. The men would become very sick for the first two days, with intermittent temperatures of 102, severe frontal headaches, constipation and a general malaise. Fortunately, by day three the temperature spikes would subside and they would begin to eat, even though they continued to cough up a lot of muck from their lungs. By day five, the boys were up and about, even if they were a little shaky on their legs. The entire unhealthy episode would last about seven to ten days and they all seemed to recover after a little rest. Influenza had been added to the long list of conditions to strike down men living in such cramped, filthy and degraded conditions. And there were confident predictions that once the warmer weather came, *la grippe* would disappear.

But reports had begun to circulate of an entirely different nature. In early June, influenza had hit London but there was no seven- to ten-day recovery in sight. Thousands were dying from it. Policemen were keeling over in the street in Hull. The virus was spreading like wildfire among factory girls and post office workers and schoolchildren, and there was talk that churches and cinemas and mills would have to be closed to contain the spread. Tramways and buses were no longer running because too many drivers and guards had been stricken. The ill were being treated with ammoniated quinine, eucalyptus oil, sweet nitre and Turkey rhubarb. Some believed taking cocoa three times a day would ward it off and the canteen had been doing a roaring trade.

No one seemed to know where it had come from. Had the virus been rampant at Gallipoli and the Somme and every other battlefield, buried so deep in paratyphoid, rheumatic fever and influenza diagnoses that it had been able to remain hidden in plain sight? How many men had arrived that summer with a diagnosis of 'pyrexia of unknown origin'? The French had taken to calling it *La Fièvre des tranchées*. The Germans, *Flandern-Fieber*. The Spanish described it as the French flu while the Italians referred to it as the German disease. In England, at Harefield hospital, it was the Spanish flu.

Ruby's sudden turn had cast a pall over the entire hospital.

'She's one of ours,' Gertie whispered, cutting right to the reality of it, the heart-shattering truth of it. The staff had grown worried about the reports of the severity and speed of the illness but they had no other option but to carry on. Who would look after the sick? How on earth could they isolate the ill from the healthy in a hospital with more than one thousand patients and no extra beds?

'It's here, isn't it?' Cora didn't need an answer to her question. Harefield was about to lose one of its own, one of its medical staff, to a virus that was already ravaging England and the Continent.

Cora hadn't known Ruby at all, really, until that morning when she'd dragged herself into the ward and collapsed onto one of the beds. Cora, Gertie and Jessie had hastily thrown bed sheets over the wooden ceiling trusses to afford her some privacy from the male patients in the other beds, but they were too ill to even notice. And there had been a pall of despair among the rest of the men in the ward, as they'd woken to the news that two of their bedfellows, Privates Grubnow and Jones, had died in the early hours. The new patient could have been the Kaiser for all they cared at that point.

Cora had tucked her in and mopped her brow, and scrounged a few extra pillows to prop her up so she could try to press a feeding cup to her lips in a vain attempt to convince her to swallow some beef soup.

'For your strength, Ruby,' Cora had urged.

Ruby had turned her watery-eyed gaze to Cora. 'Frederick?'

Cora smoothed her hand over Ruby's brow. Her dark hair, pushed back from her face, was wet from perspiration. Her brown eyes looked like stagnant pools in her pale and fading face.

'Just a couple of sips now.'

'It's hot in Egypt, you know.' Ruby's voice was a struggling rasp. Cora surmised her lungs must already be filling with fluid.

'I hear it is. As hot as Australia?'

'Australia?'

'Where are you from in Australia, Ruby?'

Ruby sucked in a huge breath as she tried to speak. Think of home, Cora thought. Home and family and whoever Frederick is. Remember gum trees and kookaburras and the Australian sun on your face. Remember your mother's arms about you and the first patient who ever smiled at you and pineapple and mangoes and white sand and skies that go on forever.

'Forbes,' Ruby managed. 'I've never seen a bluer sea than in Greece. As blue as Frederick's eyes.' And saying his name again seemed to cause her such pain that Cora wished she hadn't asked her anything.

'Sister Barker. Sister North.' Matron Ross moved the sheet curtains aside and stepped into the makeshift private room. She was a tall, imposing woman but her usually perfect posture had deserted her. Cora wondered if this was what she'd expected when she'd taken over from Matron Gray, who was across the Channel in France now, in charge of nursing staff at the 2nd Australian General Hospital at Wimereux.

Matron Ross's chin hung low, her complexion so pale it was as if she hadn't slept in a week. She looked as Cora felt. Utterly defeated.

She exchanged glances with Gertie, who bowed her head mournfully and then slipped away into the ward.

'How is Nurse Dickinson?'

Cora found some strength. 'I was here when she came in this morning. I can't believe how quickly it's advanced. She's febrile. She's been coughing and her sputum is blood-streaked. As you can see by the blue-purple shadows around her ears and encroaching here on her jaw, she's cyanotic. If she's anything like our other cases, it won't be long now before her whole face is the same pallor.'

'Some of my colleagues describe it as heliotrope cyanosis.'

'Heliotrope?' Cora asked.

'After the flower. It's purple. It's such a pretty flower, too.'

Such a pretty name for such a deadly symptom. Soon, every breath would come sharply and with an effort that would drain every last ounce of strength from her and, eventually, her lungs would fill with fluid and she would drown. This was how Ruby's war would end.

'She's a truly wonderful nurse,' Matron Ross said reverentially. 'This is a tragedy is so many ways.'

'Ruby signed up a few months after me, I believe,' Cora said. 'I was March 1915.'

'She sailed directly to Greece and the 3rd AGH on the island of Lemnos. All those wounded men straight from the beaches at Gallipoli.' The matron's voice trailed off into the silence.

Cora knew. Thousands and thousands of them. Too many to imagine being sacrificed for naught in those early days of the war.

'After that, she served in Egypt and actually went back home as nurse in charge of the hospital ship *Seang Choon*. But she came back and went to France when the 3rd AGH was re-established there.'

'How many men must she have treated.'

'That hospital ship? The *Seang Choon*? It went down in July last year on the way back to Sydney. It was torpedoed. Nineteen lives were lost.'

How had Ruby dodged death so many times only to be felled by a particle no one could see, but one that could strike with deadly aim? Which death was worse, Cora wondered. If she'd had the chance to choose the manner of her own passing, would Ruby have chosen to be killed by a shell hitting her canvas tent on a battlefield in France? A sinking ship in the Aegean? Or this?

Ruby roused and gasped for air. Cora laid a hand on her arm and quieted her gently. 'You'll be all right, Ruby.' She was running such a fever Cora could feel it radiating through the sheets.

'You've both done your duty with great steadfastness, Cora.' Cora felt a hand on her shoulder and that gentle gesture from the matron nearly tipped Cora over the edge. She bit back the tears she couldn't let flow. Not now. Not here. Not when Ruby was slipping away before her eyes. There would be time for tears later. Tonight and tomorrow night and next week and next month and for the rest of her life, no doubt. How would she recover from so much death? She would see ghosts forever.

'My service is nothing compared with hers. I've been so … safe. I don't deserve to be thought of in the same breath as this woman.'

'We have all sacrificed. No matter where we've served. And no one here is safe from death.'

Ruby had nursed patients so near the battlefield that she would have heard the shells whistling overhead. 'I wish I'd got to know her, Matron Ross.'

'You're with her now when she needs a friend the most. It will be of great comfort to her that a fellow Australian is taking care of her. I know that for certain.'

There were more than seventy nurses on staff at Harefield and while Cora knew many of them by sight, becoming familiar with their faces across the mess or in the gardens or in one of the therapy rooms, there was so much movement in and out nowadays that she couldn't remember names. She had given up long ago with the men as well. Tens of thousands of soldiers had passed through Harefield's beds and if the war continued as it had begun, there would likely be thousands more. The Harefield hospital conveyor belt had become a well-oiled machine: soldiers in, soldiers out. Fifty-four Australian men would never again be enveloped in the loving embraces of families and loved ones, the churchyard at St Mary's their final resting place.

Before long—and for the first time—a woman would be joining those hallowed ranks. A nurse. An Australian nurse. Someone just like Cora, who had joined the profession to care for the sick, then enlisted to serve King and country and to honour and care for wounded soldiers. Cora tried to take herself back to the day she'd signed her enlistment papers. Had she imagined it would be like this?

It seemed like a hundred years since that first funeral in February 1916, when Private Robert Wake had been buried. The war had made days pass in a blur but years stretch out like wisps of cirrus clouds, like strands of silk and just as fragile.

'Would you like a cup of tea? A glass of lemonade?' Matron Ross asked gently. 'The volunteers in the canteen have just made some fresh. Why don't you walk over and have a glass. Take a break. Have you eaten?'

Cora found the matron's concern touching rather than officious. 'No, thank you, Matron. I'm perfectly fine. I'll stay with her.'

The matron nodded her understanding and left Cora with her patient.

Cora tried to shut out the noise from the ward. There was a commotion of some sort that ended with someone admonishing another. Footsteps signalled the hob-nailed boot comings and goings of soldiers. Someone whistled 'Waltzing Matilda' and Cora fought the urge to leap from Ruby's bedside and tell whoever it was to hush this instant. A window was opened—Cora recognised the squeak of the frame—and a moment later she felt a flutter of fresh air. Could Ruby feel it on her pale blue cheeks? Ruby roused and coughed and the gauze Cora held to her mouth came away bloodied. Each breath was growing more shallow, each gulp of air a wet rasp.

It was Sunday. Shouldn't there have been church bells pealing somewhere in the village? Something to herald this loss, this hole in the hearts of the nursing staff?

The curtain was swept aside and it was Gertie, her eyes glazed with unshed tears, her lips trembling. 'So many want to come and pay their respects. What shall we do? Shall I let them?'

'Let them come,' Cora said, nodding. 'It might comfort Ruby. If she can hear them. Just have them stand back by the end of the bed, won't you, Gertie? And make sure they all wear face coverings.'

Chapter Sixty-One

24 June 1918

Cora had held Ruby's hand.

She'd mopped her brow and spooned water into her mouth until her last ragged and laboured breath.

And now she was dead.

Once a doctor had pronounced her, and the requisite matters of the removal of her body to the morgue had been taken care of, Cora had ripped her face mask off and stormed out of the ward in a seething rage. She needed to walk and breathe freely. Wasn't that the advice? To take in fresh air as often as one could to flush the influenza out of the lungs?

Her strides grew faster and longer, despite her exhaustion, as she rounded the main house and headed out to the lakes. She approached the bench where she'd sat with William so many times and almost stumbled onto it, her breath ragged, her rage coiled, her mind a hurricane.

She pressed her hands to the bench on either side of her hips, feeling the cool smoothness of the wood under her fingertips. She closed her eyes and took in the earthy scent of pastures and wildflowers and fresh leaves and tried to find any birdsong but the buzzing in her head was too loud.

Her breath came quick and shallow. She felt woozy and furious and useless and it all came together in a primal scream she at first heard in her head but then was echoing all around her.

She screamed until her head throbbed and her throat was raw.

And when she had no voice left the tears flowed down her face like spring rain.

She had a wish buried so deep inside her, one that was so private she hadn't allowed herself to think about it until that moment. She had been so scared of what it would let loose. But it wouldn't be contained any longer.

She had made a mistake back in 1915. She should never have enlisted, should never have naively followed the exhortations to serve, to protect, to nurture and to care. She had thrown her other life away and sacrificed it for this one of despair, this agonising life of injury and war and death. Regret sat like a huge stone in her gut but something heavier had lodged in her mind the past month, scattering her thoughts, sending her heart racing, her chest tight and her breath shallow and scarce. Sleep had become a stranger to her. Was it going to be possible to see the war out with a skerrick of her sanity intact? Was she losing her mind?

She'd seen so many men lose theirs, whittled away on the battlefield by shells and tortured flesh and unimaginable sights and sounds. A warm bed and a comforting hand on theirs hadn't restored their sanity. A nurse's care and medical attention couldn't bring back limbs hacked off by the enemy's bullets. All the aspirin in the world hadn't been able to cure them of influenza or cancer or return their shredded eyeballs or lungs.

She dropped her head in her hands and let the sobs rack her body. How cruel for Ruby to have made it through all these years of the war only to be felled by influenza. Who needed guns and bombs when death lurked in every cough and sneeze?

When the sun had finally set behind the fields in the western sky and the stars were flickering above, Cora walked wearily to the nurses' quarters. As she pushed open the door, she thought back to her first days at the hospital with Leonora and Fiona and Gertie. The four of them, so young in some cases and naive in others, had believed themselves to be setting out on some kind of heroic adventure in which they would save the world and all the soldiers in it.

As she entered the quarters, dragging her feet and her heart, desperate to slip between the sheets, she heard her name.

From behind, running footsteps echoed across the floorboards.

'Sister Barker.'

Cora turned. A nurse rushed at her, one of the young women who'd recently arrived, fresh-faced and eager. Cora was too exhausted to try to remember her name.

'What is it, Sister?'

The nurse's red and calloused hands covered her mouth, her eyes were wide and frightened.

'You must come quickly. It's Gertie.'

'She's gravely ill, Cora.'

Cora couldn't know what it felt like when a bullet tore through flesh but if it was anything like the power of

William's words tearing at her, it hurt beyond anything she had ever known.

Standing at Gertie's bedside, wearing gloves, a face mask and a surgical gown, William looked like a stranger. But he didn't sound like one. There was as much concern for her in his tone as for Gertie. He knew how much they meant to each other.

'I can see it,' she whispered. Gertie was moaning, her face white and sweating. Her beautiful thick hair was damp round her forehead and little ringlets framed her gaunt face. They were so tired after so many years of war. How could they be expected to summon the energy to fight anything?

William shifted on his feet, moved slightly closer to Cora. He lowered his voice. 'Her temperature remains stubbornly at 102 degrees. I've tried three different thermometers in case one is faulty. When she's lucid, she's complaining of severe headache.' William's blue eyes, the only part of his face not covered, were faded and weary and there were dark smudges of grey in the puffy bags underneath. He reached a hand out to Cora then drew it back to his side. No one was allowed to touch any more or stand close. Cora knew she shouldn't touch Gertie and that pained her more than anything.

'Please hold on, dearest Gertie.' Cora sat on the very end of the bed, her voice muffled as she whispered through her white linen face mask, 'Just make it to day three, will you?'

Seventy-two hours. The fever would need to break in seventy-two hours if she were to have any chance.

'I need you to get well. I can't get through this without you. You promised me a fancy hotel in London and French champagne.'

Gertie's eyes flickered and she rasped, 'The Ritz.'

Cora gasped and cried. 'Yes! The Ritz or Claridge's or the Savoy. We're going to blow our savings before we get on the boat for home.' What else? What else? 'I'll find you the best bottle of gin I can find and every single book in the world. We'll pray for you, Gert. Fiona, especially. You know we will.'

There was a rush of footsteps and someone skidded to a halt by Gertie's bed.

'Oh, dear God,' Jessie gasped. 'Gertie?'

William quickly raised his hands in warning. 'Stay away. You need to leave the ward. And for God's sake put on a mask.'

Cora saw the confusion in Jessie's expression. 'I do apologise, sir. I didn't mean—'

'It's influenza,' he blurted.

The young woman's eyes widened and then hardened. 'Please. Tell me what I can do to help.'

Cora barely slept for three days. Nor did Fiona or William.

Jessie had insisted she be of service, even though it would mean she wouldn't be able to go home, and when Cora had protested, Jessie had sloughed off the concern as she might have batted away a bee on a hot summer's day.

'This is Gertie,' she'd insisted. 'I would do the same for any of the nurses here. But you and Gertie? You've always been so …' Jessie couldn't finish her sentence and Cora didn't need her to. For someone so young, she had gone through so much already.

Jessie made herself busy fetching sandwiches for Cora and William and making them fresh pots of tea when she thought they needed it.

The ward was filled with other broncho cases, all in various stages of the disease. Some were a cyanotic blue, others already heliotrope, all suffering laboured breathing and high temperatures. It was all absolutely pitiful. The patients moaned from the splitting headaches and vomited from the nausea. Cora rarely took her eyes from Gertie, checking her temperature and breath sounds every hour, and William continued to hover nearby.

At some point in the night, when Jessie was asleep on her crossed arms at the nurses' desk and the patients were quiet, drowsy from drugs, Cora stood to stretch her back.

'How are you holding up?' William asked.

Cora shrugged. 'I don't honestly know.'

'We're in the thick of it, you know.'

Cora looked up at him. 'There's worse to come?'

William looked grave. 'Tens of thousands of people across the country have died. Pneumonia and septicaemia follow the initial illness and there aren't enough hospital beds in all of England to cope with what's to come.'

Tears drizzled cold down her cheeks. 'How much more are we expected to bear?'

'This gargantuan parasitic debauch has only just begun. Cora …'

She felt as cold as her tears.

When Cora blinked open her eyes, it took a moment to realise where she was. It was night. She was cold, shivering under a thin blanket. She was on the floor, wearing her uniform. Someone was shaking her shoulder.

As her eyes adjusted to the dark, she saw Fiona. A shadow at first. Then her features became clearer. Tears, her mouth a grim line.

'Cora.'

A wave of fear skittered through Cora and she sat bolt upright as if she'd been shocked.

'She's gone.'

She thought of every whispered conversation they'd had lying in their cots at night. Every cup of weak tea they'd sipped together and her complaints about sugar rationing. Gertie's shock at the realisation that she snored.

Cora would give anything to hear it again.

Chapter Sixty-Two

23 July 1918

Cora's veil was soaked through.

The sleeves of her dress clung to her arms, sopping, and she should have felt cold but felt nothing.

A dozen trucks emblazoned with red crosses had just turned in to the hospital from Rickmansworth Road, a sad convoy sure to be full of injured troops. Land girls from a nearby dairy had just departed, having delivered that day's milk in silver cans, but Cora was overcome by the thought that it would never be enough. There would never be enough milk. There would never be enough beds. Every day, every hour it seemed, more broken and ill soldiers were arriving. How were there enough boats and trains to transport them all from France? How were there so many young men in the world that these boys could be sacrificed like lambs to the slaughter?

Somewhere, a horn sounded and throbbed in her ears. Cora looked down at her sopping boots and thought she should really try to move her feet but they seemed to be fixed to the gravel driveway.

Something was wrong but she couldn't decipher it. Suddenly, she needed to sleep and she surrendered to the pull of it, the relief of giving in, and her eyes flickered closed, the weariness sweeping over her like a wave.

She was back home in Adelaide, on the warm sands of Henley Beach, wet from the ocean's waves that broke gently at her knees. She lifted her face to the sun and tried to feel the heat of it on her cheeks. She needed to be warmed through, was desperate for her cold heart to feel alive again.

'Cora!'

She knew that voice, didn't she?

Large hands gripped her shoulders. 'Bloody hell, Cora.' And then those same hands pushed her backwards and she stumbled and then an arm was about her waist and a horn blared like a thousand air raid sirens in her head.

Cora roused. She became aware of her breathing first, steady, slow, and when she blinked her eyes open, the long shadows in the nurses' quarters were a hint that almost the whole day had passed.

She was in her bed. She recognised the hint of lavender from the oil she dripped on her pillow. Gertie had told her once that it would help her sleep and she'd become religious about it.

Cold tears coursed down her cheeks.

Oh, Gertie.

And now, forever, she would think of Gertie whenever she saw the pale purple buds of the flower, or smelled it or saw a sachet of its dried heads hanging in a wardrobe. She lifted her head but two strong, familiar hands urged her down again.

'That's enough of that.' William sat on a wooden chair by her side. He must have been reading a book, because a novel lay open on the bed by her knee. 'You need to rest.' She felt his cool fingers on her carotid artery as he checked her pulse, all his concentration on his ticking fob watch.

She felt a stab of fear in her abdomen. 'What's my temperature?' She laid a wrist on her forehead trying to judge by touch if she was pyretic.

He shook his head. 'No. Thank God.'

'Why am I in bed? Why are you taking my vitals?'

He sighed as he wrote something on a piece of paper attached to a clipboard. 'Your blood pressure is low. You're likely anaemic.' He leant close, laid a finger on the bone under her eye and guided her lower lid down. He peered at her eyes. 'Obviously exhausted. Do you remember what happened this morning?'

How to describe the wave of it as it had crashed over her, knocked her off her feet, rendered her mute and unable to think enough to will her feet to move to save herself. That she hadn't cared about saving herself. 'This morning?' And then she remembered. 'I was daydreaming. Wishing I was somewhere else.'

'Where?'

She didn't dream any more. It was a figure of speech, a cruel one, because each day was a nightmare, not a dream. And if each day was a nightmare, her nights were nothingness. Her exhaustion was so complete at the end of every day that when she laid her head on her pillow, the picture show behind her eyes was filled with every soldier she'd ever nursed: their scars, their missing jaws and eye sockets and noses, their gaping wounds, their empty eyes and their haunted screams. And now Gertie was there too, her lips and ears and cheeks purple, her breathing rasping and gurgling as she drowned.

She would give anything not to dream those dreams of death. Sometimes as she lay there in the dark she wondered if she was indeed dying too and whether the thoughts haunting her would be her last on earth. Sometimes it was a shock to wake in the morning with the realisation that another day had dawned and she would have to do it all again.

'I don't dream any more,' she said groggily. 'I sleep the sleep of the dead.'

The dead. There were so many dead. She studied his sad face. 'Do you dream, William?'

'I'm like you,' he said grimly. 'Dreams are impossible these days.'

His hand was gentle on hers and she didn't dare move lest he think it wasn't wanted there, or needed or so desperately desired. If she'd had the strength, she would have curled her fingers around his, pulled his hand to her lips and kissed it.

'This morning.'

'Yes?' He watched her.

'Someone pulled me out of the way of the truck.'

He said nothing.

'It was you, wasn't it?'

'I was concerned you were going to throw yourself under it.' His lower lip trembled.

'Maybe I was. I … I don't remember.'

'You scared the hell out of me. You haven't been yourself since Gertie died.'

It had been one month since that dreadful day. The hospital was treating more patients with influenza than war wounds and donning a face mask had become as automatic as pinning a veil. In the past few weeks alone, another five patients had died of it.

Even speaking was exhausting. 'I can't seem to find the energy to do much of anything. Sometimes I don't know how I'm going to get up in the morning and carry on.'

'I understand. More than you know.'

'I'm tired.'

'I've spoken to the matron. You're on bed rest. Doctor's orders.' The corners of his lips almost quirked up in a little smile.

It took her breath away. 'Thank you, Doctor.'

'Rest now.'

She closed her eyes so she didn't have to see him go. There was pressure on the mattress. She felt him next to her. Then, his lips pressed ever so gently against hers and he whispered her name as he kissed her.

'My mother and I made it. Well, it was mostly Mum on account of me being here, but I added the finishing touches around the collar. I hope you like it.'

Jessie stood nervously by Cora's bedside. On the bed, rumpled butcher's paper lay open, the gift of a new dressing gown unfolded on Cora's lap.

'It's just beautiful, Jessie.' Cora ran her fingers along the blush-pink satin edging that decorated the collar and each seam. The buttons and belt were covered with the same fabric, so soft under Cora's fingers that she stroked it for a while for the comfort of it. Once, before the war, she had worn dresses that soft and the memory came back to her like a long-forgotten dream.

'It's not much really. But we thought it might help you be more comfortable.'

Cora held the woollen fabric up to her face, pressed it softly to her cheeks. Autumn was on its way and she would make great use of this gift. 'Thank you. And please thank Win, too. This is ever so kind of you both. Please. Pull up a chair, won't you?'

Cora needed conversation. Since Gertie had died and other nurses and patients had been struck down by influenza, quarantine measures had been instituted across the hospital. There was a distance between people now. There were no embraces or handshakes or comforting arms about her shoulders. Face masks rendered people strangers. Familiar voices were muffled into unrecognisability.

Jessie carried a cane chair to Cora's bedside and positioned herself at the foot of the bed. She sat, straightened her skirt and rested her entwined fingers together in her lap. Cora thought back to their first meeting. Jessie had struck her as a quiet young village girl who could barely say boo to a goose.

The young woman had such a self-assuredness about her these days. Her shyness had transformed into a quiet confidence; her grief meant she had metamorphosed from naive girl into knowing woman.

'You have some colour back in your cheeks,' Jessie said, peering at Cora's face.

'It must be all the liver,' Cora said and then laughed as Jessie twisted her face into a contortion of disgust.

'I know it's supposed to be good for you, and sometimes it's all Mum can get from the butcher, but I absolutely hate it.'

'Even cooked with a little bacon?'

'There isn't enough bacon in all the world—rationing or not—to make it taste any good. But I'm very glad it's working for you, Cora.'

'So tell me. How are you getting on?'

Jessie reached for the butcher's paper, folded it into a small square and tucked it in her pocket while she thought over her answer. When she looked up, her eyes were wet with unshed tears. 'Every day is still hard, even though it's almost ten months now since Bert died.'

'You'll never forget him. You'll never want to.'

'No, I never will. Seeing so much here at the hospital has made me think that I'm nothing special.'

'What do you mean? Of course you are.'

Jessie shook her head. 'That came out the wrong way. What I meant was that I'm not the only one to have lost someone. I'm not the only one who grieves. I see it in every face here and in the village. Everyone in England knows someone who's been killed. Every family has been touched in one way or another. Every one of us.'

Cora began to cry.

'I wanted to say, Cora, that I'm so dreadfully sorry about Gertie. I know what it's like to lose someone so dear.'

Cora's voice caught in her throat. 'That's very kind.'

'She was always so lovely to me. She taught me so much. And she was funny, too, always making everyone laugh.'

They sat in silence for a long moment while their tears flowed as freely as their memories.

'She was a remarkable person,' Cora managed to say. 'I don't know how we'll get on without her.'

'It gets easier, Cora. A little each day.'

'When I wake up in the mornings, I still turn around in my bed expecting to see her in the next cot, snoring like a train like she used to do.' Cora roughly wiped her eyes. 'I wrote to her family to tell them about her last hours.'

'Best coming from you. A true friend who knew her. A telegram can be so blunt and those few sentences don't really tell you anything or answer the questions you really want to know. That was true in my case, at least. But I found out what I needed to know.'

'How did you find out?'

'Since I got the telegram about Bert, I've been writing to the AIF, asking questions about what happened. About how he died, I mean. I didn't think I could rest until I knew. Really knew. It took eight months. Letter after letter. I would have thought the Australians would get right sick of me but they never did. I think finally I know everything there is to know.'

'Did finding out make it any easier?'

'I think so. I found some consolation in knowing that he didn't linger, that it was quick.' Jessie drew in a deep breath to steel herself. 'He was walking up a track in single file, one mile east of Ypres in Belgium. Wipers, the soldiers call it. A German shell burst right next to him and he was killed instantly.' She hesitated. 'Blown to pieces.'

'Oh, Jessie.' Cora saw in Jessie's expression that she needed physical comfort, a tender arm about her, the warm understanding of someone who truly understood. It burnt that she couldn't give it.

'I needed to know. At first I thought that one day I might go to Belgium and visit his grave, see the white wooden cross they put where men are buried. But there is no grave. There was nothing left to bury. His body is in a field somewhere near Ypres but his heart is here with me.'

Jessie laid a hand over her heart. 'And will be forever.'

Chapter Sixty-Three

8 October 1918

Exactly one year to the day since Jessie had received the news that Bert was missing in action and April Chester was born, the chubby blonde-haired girl took her first steps.

The moment was met with joyous laughter and tears from Win, who seemed to cry at the drop of a hat these days. Harry looked down at his daughter with a look that was more like relief than joy, as if he had been carrying a burden of guilt and doubt since his daughter had been born that she might have inherited his affliction. Dottie dropped to the floor, her full skirt fluffing up like a dandelion flower, swept April into her arms and smothered her with kisses.

Jessie stood in the doorway and cried.

Their little delight, born in war, might grow up in peace, it seemed. Harry had taken to bringing home the two newspapers every night and the family's after-dinner conversation, once April had been put to bed, was dominated by Harry reading accounts of the war. In every theatre, the Allies had been gaining superiority in the latter half of 1918. Germany had suffered losses on the Western Front.

Turkey's campaign in Palestine had collapsed and seventy thousand Turks had been taken prisoner of war. Australian and American troops had broken through German lines at Bellicourt in northern France—breaking the Hindenburg line. And just the week before, Germany and Austria had requested an armistice from United States President Woodrow Wilson.

'It'll be over soon,' Harry said authoritatively every night as he folded the newspaper closed and lit his final cigarette for the evening.

'From your lips to God's ear,' Win said, every night, without looking up from her sewing.

'It's so wonderful to think that April will grow up never knowing war. She's so young that she won't even remember it. Won't that be a blessing.'

For months Jessie had believed the pronouncements to be nothing but war-weary wishful thinking but there was evidence at the hospital that the end was in sight. The cases of battlefield injuries had slowed, only to be replaced with cases of bronchitis and pneumonia related to influenza—but the deaths continued. Sixty-nine Australians were buried at St Mary's and some of the boys were so poorly that it wouldn't be long for them, either.

In 1914, Jessie had been asleep to the world, both its pleasures and its pains. Her world had been this house and the people in it and she'd thought that might be all she would ever know.

But now, she was awake to its possibilities and its agonies. She had matured ten years in just four, she was certain, and the life she had led, sheltered and quiet, didn't exist any more.

Because that version of herself didn't exist any more. She had loved and she had grieved and she would be forever changed because of it. Three hundred and sixty-five days ago, she had lost her love and grief had moved in alongside it in her heart.

She knew her grief would be everlasting, that it would remain with her as long as her heart was still beating.

It was stitched into her now, this new Jessie Chester.

Chapter Sixty-Four

11 November 1918

At 8 am, a note was pinned to the cinema noticeboard in the mess at Harefield hospital.

There hadn't been a change to that night's moving pictures or to excursions planned into Harrow and London.

The note announced that the armistice had been signed at seven-thirty that morning and that hostilities would cease at exactly 11 am, the eleventh hour of the eleventh day of the eleventh month.

Word had circulated as fast as *la grippe* had spread through the trenches, and as Cora and Jessie watched each minute tick over on the clock above the nurses' desk in the ward, the minutes seemed to pass as slowly as days.

Twenty-three men had been buried at St Mary's since the beginning of autumn, and the signing of a piece of paper in a railroad car outside Compiègne, France, would not put an end to the deaths at Harefield hospital as quickly as it would bring an end to the hostilities.

All twenty-two beds in Ward 22 were full of men. Cora knew that her war would not end that day. As sure as the leaves in the ancient trees in the village had crisped and burnt and then fallen that autumn, there would be more deaths in the weeks ahead, Cora was certain.

In Harefield, the bells of St Mary's Parish Church rang at 11 am, echoing throughout the village. The hospital fell silent for a few moments of mournful remembrance.

Cora and Jessie had wrapped themselves in coats and stepped onto the duckboards to mark the turning of the hour. Those patients who were well enough joined them and silently smoked their cigarettes. There wasn't rejoicing or celebrating; there was no whooping or dancing or kissing. Not yet. There was only an empty silence filled with ghosts.

All Cora could think about were the faces of the eighty-six people buried in Harefield, Australians who would always call this little corner of England home. She saw her dearest friend Gertie's laughing face, not her heliotrope one. She saw little Eddie Bagot from home with his skinned knees. She thought of Jessie's Bert, blown to pieces in a Flanders field. She thought of all the families who would never have their sunny boys back home with them.

She was so tired. So dreadfully tired and broken-hearted. She folded her elbows on the nurses' desk and lay her head on top of them. She could barely summon the strength to hold her head up.

That night, there was a celebration in the canteen and everyone was mad with excitement about the end of the war, throwing their arms around each other singing 'For the Red, White and Blue' and 'Rule Britannia' and 'Waltzing Matilda' in rounds until they collapsed into confused laughter. One of the more musically inclined patients hauled himself up on stage with his one leg and pounded the piano keys as if his life depended on it, and a crowd of enthusiastic singers, their voices muffled by masks, joined him in belting out the chorus of every tune they knew.

The Cricketers had delivered beer and sherry and both were being consumed with great enthusiasm by patients and staff alike.

When the commanding officer, Lieutenant Colonel Yeatman, strode up on stage and raised his hands to silence the crowd, it took a few moments for people to settle.

'The King has sent a greeting to Australia, expressing his heartfelt gratitude to his overseas peoples for their wonderful efforts and sacrifices that have contributed so greatly to secure victory. He says, and I quote,' the lieutenant colonel cleared his throat, '"Together we have borne this tremendous burden in the fight for justice and liberty and together we will now rejoice at the realisation of those great aims for which we entered the struggle. The whole Empire pledged its word not to sheathe the sword until our end was achieved. That pledge is now redeemed."'

And there were hoots and shouts of 'God save the King' and more music, and Cora watched all of it feeling hollow.

Jessie crossed the room to her with two glasses of sherry and sat down. 'I've been told to give you this.' She cocked her head over her shoulder and Cora saw William at the makeshift bar, a cigarette hanging from his lips as he poured beverages—beer for the men and sherry for the women.

'Thank you.'

Jessie pulled down her mask, held her glass to her lips and downed the brownish-reddish liquid in a single swallow. When she grimaced, Cora couldn't help but laugh.

'I've never done that before,' she announced. 'I think today of all days we should, don't you?'

'Here's cheers.' Cora didn't think about it for more than a second and a moment later she too grimaced from the warm hit down her gullet. 'I've never done that before either.'

Jessie leant in close to be heard over the tuneless singing. 'Half of me wants to cry. The other half wants to drink more sherry.'

Cora raised her empty glass and clinked it against Jessie's. 'I should be happy. Like they are.' A conga line had begun snaking its way through the mess, legs kicking out to the sides like a drunken caterpillar.

'When will you go home to Australia, do you think?' Jessie asked.

Cora shrugged her shoulders. 'When there are no more patients.'

'I'll miss you terribly,' Jessie blurted. 'You and the other nurses. Well, you've inspired me more than any suffragette has.'

Cora stared back at the young woman across the table from her. 'I'm honoured.'

'I was thinking about something and I hope you'll give me your advice.'

'Of course.'

'I'd like to be a nurse. I'm going to apply to the Nightingale Home and Training School for Nurses at St Thomas's Hospital.'

It was the best news Cora had heard in so long she slapped her hands to her cheeks. 'You are?'

Jessie nodded and the pride and excitement flaming her cheeks were evident in her smiling eyes and her wide smile. 'It's in London, right on the Thames.'

'That is absolutely wonderful news. You'll be an excellent nurse. If you'd like a written recommendation—if you think it would help—I'd be happy to do it. More than happy, in fact. And I'm certain Dr Kent would do the same for you. What you've overcome … you're a wonderful young woman, Jessie.'

Jessie wiped happy tears from her eyes. 'I believe I've found my calling.'

'I can see. I'm so proud of you.'

Suddenly, Jessie's hand flew to her mouth. 'Oh my goodness, I forgot to tell you. When Captain Kent handed me the sherry to give to you, he asked me to pass on a message.'

Cora held her breath.

'He said something strange. "The tree".'

Cora saw the flickering and dancing light of a cigarette in the darkness under the bare branches. She pulled her coat tighter around her, shivering with the cold.

The light dropped and was extinguished.

Above the night sky was cloudless, and in the pale moonlight she made out his form. He was leaner now than he had been when she'd first met him over the body of an unconscious patient in the operating theatre. Older too, with streaks of grey through the hair at his temples.

He stepped out of the shadows and her heart leapt.

'I had hoped my message wasn't too cryptic.'

'No, it wasn't,' she replied. 'I'll miss our little place here by the lake.'

He stepped closer, reached for her hands and she held them out to him. 'I will, too. Not everything about it, obviously. But this tree and being here with you.' He waited, pulled her closer and kissed her slowly and gently. 'My orders came through this afternoon. The army wants me back in Melbourne.'

'Of course.' Why did she feel so blindsided by his news? 'When?'

'Tomorrow. The repatriation begins immediately and I'm to leave on one of the medical ships.'

Cora released herself from his arms and lowered herself to the bench. The wind was bitter and she wrapped her coat around herself. It didn't help warm her.

'The headlines might be trumpeting it, but our war isn't over, Cora.'

Would it ever be, she wondered? The past four years were imprinted on her, in every cell in her body, in every fibre of her being. She would never look at the world in the same way, would never see a young man without thinking of the slaughter. She would never see a young woman without thinking of Jessie Chester and all she, and so many other young women, had lost. The idea of a future. Hope. And would she ever stop seeing Gertie in every nurse's uniform she saw across a hospital ward?

'I'm to stay, for a few months at least. There are men here who aren't well enough to travel, more still who will die of influenza in the coming months.'

William stood before her, his hands pushed deep into the pockets of his trousers.

There was nothing more to say. He had said it himself. What point was there in having dreams? They were too easily shattered these days.

'You're a very special woman, Cora Barker. You have made the war …' He rubbed a hand over his face. 'I don't know if I would have survived it without you. Without your love.'

Once, in thrall of him and in thrall of being in love, she would have done anything to have him as her own.

But the war had changed her, too. Precious things were so easily crushed that it might be better not to find them so precious in the first place.

Would things be the same between them if they were to meet again in Melbourne or in Adelaide, without the war? Would she want them to?

Cora lifted her chin to the night air, listening for the hoot of the tawny owls that lived in the woodlands around Harefield.

It was over.

1921

Chapter Sixty-Five

25 April 1921

Nurse Jessie Chester took the train from Paddington Station to Uxbridge and then caught a motorised bus to Harefield for the Anzac Day ceremony in the village.

Win greeted her with smiles and sobs, as ever. Harry and Dottie stood at Jessie's side during the service while they kept watchful eyes on April and Mavis, and rocked little Pearl in her perambulator when she cried. Dottie missed the post office but Harry kept her in touch with all the news as surely as if he were a newspaper correspondent himself.

The Chesters continued to live on the high street with Win, who had since retired as a seamstress. The front room had largely been cleared of all its fabrics and notions—although the Singer still took pride of place—and she was these days fully occupied helping raise her granddaughters.

As they had since the end of the war, the villagers turned out each Anzac Day to pay their respects to the one hundred and twelve Australians who were buried at St Mary's and to the tens of thousands of Australians who'd passed through the village.

After the church service, the village schoolchildren laid wreaths of wildflowers on all the graves in the churchyard, bearing the names of the honoured dead.

Jessie found Private Robert Wake's grave and stood silently in front of it for a moment, remembering the day five years before when she'd followed his cortege through the streets.

Attached to the wreath was a little white card and she knelt down to read it.

In grateful remembrance of the brave sons of Australia who fought, suffered, died and conquered many on the battlefields. We will remember them.

She laid a hand against her chest and felt Bert beating there. He was stitched into her, and as long as her heart was still beating, she would remember him.

Chapter Sixty-Six

Adelaide
18 July 1921

Cora walked down Grote Street, rubbing her gloved hands together to warm them against Adelaide's brisk and wintery July morning. It had been a clear night, cloudless, the sky star-speckled, and she knew that because she hadn't been able to sleep the night before. She hadn't been able to sleep properly for years, if truth be told. She'd pulled the blankets off her bed and wrapped them around her like a cloak before tiptoeing out the door and into the front yard to light a cigarette.

Her parents hadn't approved of the habit she'd acquired since she'd left nursing. The first time her father had seen her with a cigarette in her hand, clouds of smoke drifting about her short bob, he'd stood in shock for a moment or two and then chided her. She'd thought it faintly ridiculous for a father to be chiding his thirty-five-year-old daughter but she let him anyway.

It had been night-time then too, the week she'd returned from London in September 1919, when her father had caught her smoking. He must have seen the bright tip of her cigarette in the twilight as he'd walked back up the street from the pub, his limping footsteps echoing in the quiet street.

'That you, Cora?' He'd stopped at the front gate and clutched it to get his balance.

'Hello, Dad.' She'd dropped her cigarette in the garden and stepped on the guilty, glowing butt.

'You smoking?'

'You been drinking, Dad?'

Arthur unlatched the gate, stumbled up the path and joined her on the wooden bench, which sat under the bedroom window of her parents' cottage in Mile End.

'Just the one,' he'd replied.

'Same.'

They'd sat on the bench in silence for a long while. Oh, how she'd missed it: the simple, uncomplicated silence of her father.

Finally, he said, after hiccupping. 'I blame the army, you know.'

Cora chuckled. 'For my smoking?'

'All those smokes they gave to the soldiers. And your sister and that League of Loyal bloody Women. You don't want to know how many thousands of ciggies they posted off to the boys and to you lot. How was it a good idea to give a bloke in a trench a smoke?' He shook his head ruefully. 'It's like giving them a bloody flare. "Here I am, Jerries. Come and get me." Madness.'

'The boys always appreciated the cigarettes, Dad.'

'I'm sure they did.'

'I suppose you cadged some off them, did you?' He held out his hand and Cora put the pack in his palm.

'I'm my father's daughter, all right.'

And that conversation the first week she'd been home had led them to a nightly ritual, which Cora cherished more than anything else in her life. Until she had moved out, they'd had a quiet cigarette on the front verandah every night.

She wished she had a cigarette now but propriety would prevent her from smoking it in public. She may have become a modern woman in so many ways but there was still a part of her that believed smoking in the street was common.

In the distance, across the city and towards the east, the Adelaide Hills were purple and grey, clouds hovering over them like umbrellas. She had become soft after so many years at home, she realised. She'd endured four bitter English winters and was now feeling cold in fifty-nine degrees.

She crossed the street and, as she entered the gates of Adelaide High School, she opened the clasp on her purse and pulled out the invitation she'd received three weeks before.

Please accept this cordial invitation
to the presentation of the historic Union Jack
presented to Adelaide High School by Harefield School
Monday July 18th, 1921

Cora followed the signposts and made her way into the Price Memorial Hall just in time for the official proceedings to begin. The Governor began by reading a letter from the headmaster of the Harefield School:

To the scholars of the school receiving our flag.
Dear Children, I'm asking you to exchange flags with
us. I feel sure that our flag, although not a new one, will be

of very special interest to you, and when you hear its story, will prize it very highly.

Our school is situated in the county of Middlesex, about 15 miles from London, and in common with most schools of the Empire, we have a flag, which is hoisted on the flagstaff in the school playground on important occasions.

On Empire Day we have a special celebration, the chief feature of which is the saluting of the flag. At the commencement of the war with Germany, the Australian Government took over a large park and residence in our village and established the First Australian Hospital there. This was chiefly used in the first place for convalescent patients recovering from sickness and wounds, but as the fighting grew more severe it was used as a general hospital for the treatment of Australian soldiers brought direct from the fighting line.

Unfortunately, many of these brave fellows died and now about one hundred are buried in the churchyard of our village church. Sometimes there were two or even three buried at a time and on these sad occasions this flag we are now sending to you was used to cover the coffins of those who had died for King and Empire.

Thus we feel that no one could prize this flag more than the children of Australia who have every right to be proud of the part Australia and the Australians took in the long struggle for defeat of our enemies.

The audience stood solemnly while the Governor unveiled the flag. A verse of 'Recessional' was sung and a bugler sounded the Last Post.

Cora felt a stab of grief as the familiar notes of the mournful tune drifted across the crowd. How many nights had she heard it played at Harefield? How many times had it echoed through the village after the one hundred and twelve funerals held at St Mary's churchyard?

She'd been home for more than two years but sometimes, when she closed her eyes, every thought was about her time at Harefield. The men. The rain. Each Christmas. Those who'd gone mad. Those who'd died.

Sister Gertrude North.

She looked over at the Union Jack that had travelled so far to commemorate Australians' service and sacrifice.

The flag that had been draped over Gertie's coffin during the processions to St Mary's. Cora looked up as it was hoisted into the sky and it unfurled and fluttered grumpily.

It was so Gertie.

Cora had worked at Harefield hospital until the end of May 1919. The week she resigned, three young men had died within the span of just six days. They were the 104th, 105th and 106th Australians who would forever lie buried at St Mary's churchyard, so far from home. In Gertie's honour, she left the village and the war for good and booked herself in to the Ritz on Picadilly, indulging in French champagne and more than one very hot and luxurious bath. And then, she'd criss-crossed England by train for months, seeing as much of the countryside as she could, allowing her restlessness to guide her, taking it all in to help create new memories of the country that, for her, had seemed to be full of death.

'Cora?'

There was a gentle hand on her arm.

'I'm sorry I'm late. Too many patients in the surgery this morning, all believing themselves to have urgent conditions that needed my immediate attention. Which made me late for this.'

On the day she had disembarked at Port Adelaide, her family was there to meet her with tears and sobs. They had gone straight home to Mile End for a roast chook with all the trimmings, a bottle of sherry and more hugs and kisses than she'd ever had from her mother, her sisters, and especially her father.

When she could eat no more, Eve and Grace had dragged Cora to her room and insisted she open the years' worth of Christmas presents they had faithfully kept in a wicker basket in her bedroom. There were embroidered handkerchiefs, a novel or two, bath salts and a folded piece of fabric for a new dress. When she'd thanked them all, Grace had huffed impatiently.

'For goodness sake, Cora. There's something else.'

Nestled at the bottom of the basket was a bundle of letters tied with string.

There must have been thirty. They were all from William.

She'd shooed her sisters from her room and read each one.

As the crowd milled about then, Cora turned to William and held out her hand. He took it in his, stepped in closer to her and kissed her cheek.

'Not in front of the Governor,' she admonished with a smile.

'If a man can't kiss his wife in public, what did we fight the war for?'

She kissed him back.

When she closed her eyes, she still saw destruction and waste and agonies. She saw her boys: the shattered ones. The limbless ones. The faceless ones. She saw Leonora. She saw Fiona. She saw Gertie. She saw wooden huts and duckboards and mud and rain and the beautiful English summer sunshine.

All of it was still with her, and would forever be.

Author's note

As authors are wont to do, I have written a mix of real and imagined characters in this novel to bring the story of Harefield hospital to life.

Sister Ruby Dickinson was a real nurse and the only woman who is buried in St Mary's churchyard. Matron Ethel Gray really existed and was held in such high esteem that she was awarded the Royal Red Cross, First Class, in the Birthday Honours of June 1916. After leaving Harefield, she was posted to Wimeraux in France and served there until March 1919. She was appointed CBE at Buckingham Palace in 1919 and returned to Australia in January 1920. After being demobbed she converted another old house, this time in Melbourne, into a hospital and was its first matron. She died in July 1962 at 86 years of age.

Cora, Gertie and her other colleagues are fictional.

However, there is more than a note of truth to the story of Jessie Chester. She is based on the real-life fiancée of Private Bert Mobbs. He served in World War I, was injured and sent to England, and then returned to his battalion, only to die in action on the battlefields of Ypres. He was my husband's great uncle, his mother's uncle. While in England recuperating, he became engaged to an Englishwoman named Jessie Higginson. I can find no trace of her, except her letters to the Australian Army searching for information about her dead fiancé, all of which are included in Bert Mobbs's records at the National War Memorial. I used—word for word—the real Jessie Higginson's letters for my Jessie and the letters she received from the army are also used verbatim.

The quote at the front of the book is from a letter from an Australian soldier, 7 September 1916 (Australian War Memorial 2DRL526 Dora Wilcox).

The poem reproduced in Chapter 51 was credited to E.N. in the *Harefield Park Boomerang*, and reprinted in the *Yea Chronicle* (14 June 1917, page 6).

Two books were particularly helpful while writing this book: *Heart of Harefield: The story of the hospital*, Mary P. Shepherd (Quiller Press, London, 1990); and *The Accidental Heiress: Journey of a Glencoe Squatter's Daughter*, John Berger and Carol Grbich (National Trust of Australia Glencoe Branch, 2020).

World War I remains Australia's deadliest conflict. From a population of fewer than five million, 416,809 men enlisted, of whom more than 60,000 were killed and 156,000 wounded, gassed, or taken prisoner. It's estimated that more than 3,000 Australian nurses served in theatres of war and in England during that time.

The Harefield flag has been restored in recent years and still sits in Adelaide High School, the school my three sons attended.

Acknowledgements

I would like to thank my husband Stephen and our three sons, once again, for understanding what it means to be a writer—for not asking me 'Aren't you meant to be writing?' when I clearly wasn't—and for indulging me when I determinedly went ahead and found us a Golden Retriever puppy to bring into our family, even though we were still heartbroken at the loss of our dear spoodle, Charlie. Maisie, they will now readily agree, has changed our lives and helped us get through the pandemic. Dog people will completely understand that it's hard to be cross at the state of the world when you have a dog in your life.

To my mum, Emma Purman, as always, for your love and support. And food.

To my dear and beautiful friend Sally Eckert, who has shown me that it is possible to move on after devastating loss, something that is woven into the pages of this book. We think of Andrew every day. He never got to meet Maisie but we know he would have loved her—and she him.

To my friend Dr Amy T. Matthews who came up with the book's title in about a minute flat—after we'd been pondering it for twelve months—and absolutely nailed it. So grateful.

To the entire team at HQ/HarperCollins: it's a miracle that you've been able to keep putting books into readers' hands during the past two years. To booksellers, the same!

To my brilliant and talented daughter-from-another-mother Natika Palka who spruiks my books to the world: thank you.

To Annabel Blay, who has edited this book—and many of my others—so skilfully and kindly. Not only is she a fact-checker extraordinaire, but she pours her heart and soul into making sure my stories work for readers. (I don't know how you do it.)

To Jo Mackay: my own personal Ted Lasso. Thank you for encouraging me to think big—and then bigger—and your cheer-squading when I've needed it so desperately.

To my readers. Without you, I wouldn't get to do what I love so much. I'm so thankful.

And finally, to my dear and much-loved mother-in-law Vilma Halliday (24.7.1928–16.11.2021). From the day we met, you welcomed me into your family with open arms and a loving heart. We bonded over our love of books and it's something we shared until the end.

A chapter completed

A page is turned

A life well-lived

A rest well-earned.

Turn over for a sneak peek.

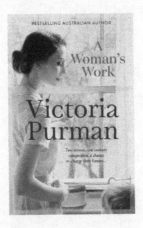

A Woman's Work

by

Victoria Purman

Available April 2023

Chapter One

Kathleen

'Mummy!'

Kathleen O'Grady could usually tell which of her five children was trying to get her attention by the particular tone of the screaming coming from one room or other of the square-edged weatherboard house in St Kilda, not so far from the streets she'd walked as a child and the frightening, gigantic leering face of Luna Park's clown.

But not today.

She hadn't had enough cups of tea to decipher which child was bellowing. Their house wasn't big—three bedrooms, a kitchen, a living room, one bathroom and an outside laundry—but it was going to be fully theirs one day and that made her a very happy wife. Mr and Mrs Peter O'Grady had secured a loan from the Commonwealth Bank, back in March 1951, on the strength of Peter's wage as a car mechanic. Each year since he'd been busier than ever, now that the hardest days of austerity after the war were over and everyone was buying new cars, and the more cars on the roads, the more cars needed fixing. Back then, when they'd bought their house, there had only been two children and one on the way. Kathleen sometimes looked back on those days with a sense of wistfulness. The whole family had been able to fit in one car back then, the baby in a Moses basket on the back seat and the other two squeezing into the space on either side.

Now there were five little O'Gradys, almost exactly two years apart: Barbara, James—although he'd always been called Jimmy—Robert, Mary and Little Michael, who was two years old and still in nappies.

It was Monday evening and Kathleen was bone-tired. Washing day took it out of her like no other day of the week. When she'd heard the radio forecast for a dry and windy day, she'd washed and hung out the sheets from the children's beds, the crisp white cotton tugging on the spinning Hills hoist so boisterously that if Robert hadn't been at school with his two older siblings, he would have announced it was a pirate ship and then climbed on top, hoisting aloft an imaginary sword in a battle for mysterious buried treasure. Once, Kathleen had tried to imagine what the view from the sky might be like on washing days. If she could transform herself into a magpie and soar above all the houses in the street on a stiff breeze, would they resemble a flotilla of ships with so many sails energetically flapping? She imagined green lawns, lemon trees, and white sheets whirling like dervishes in every backyard, snapping to a mysterious symphony from the sky.

Peter was always gone by seven so mornings were hers to organise. After breakfast for the five children— Barbara, Jimmy and Robert liked porridge in winter, Mary liked toast with jam and Little Michael ate whatever was left—she waved Barbara, Jimmy and Robert off to school, with a stern warning to Barbara to mind her brothers, and commenced the weekly washing.

By the end of the day, she'd soaked and washed and hung and dried and folded Little Michael's nappies and had balled thirty-five pairs of the children's socks and seven of her husband's. She'd read stories to Mary to keep her quiet while Little Michael was down for his afternoon nap. She'd peeled and diced potatoes, covered them with water in a saucepan and left them to sit, ready to be boiled and mashed for that night's dinner. A bunch of carrots and a brown paper bag filled with peas sat ready to be sliced and shelled. Sausages were wrapped in butcher's paper in the fridge. She'd made all the beds and tidied the children's rooms. She'd picked up her husband's singlet and underpants from the bathroom floor and left them to soak in the concrete trough in the laundry, in the vain hope the odour of car grease and petrol might dissipate with a good dose of Rinso because those suds really got to work on washdays and left whites and coloureds simply dazzling. Or so the advertisement told her.

'Mummy!'

She'd mopped the kitchen floor and dropped to her knees to scrub away the black scuff marks from the children's school shoes and then mopped the bathroom too while the mop was wet. While she worked, she had the radio tuned to 3AW. At nine o'clock it was *Hour of Stars*, followed by one of her favourites, *Housewives' Quiz*. Kathleen loved the company of the voices from the radio. While she washed and mopped and cleaned and scrubbed and cooked, it was easy to imagine she was privy to real adults in the house engaging in stimulating conversations, even if she couldn't answer back. There was a certain familiarity and comfort in having friends from inside the radiogram fill her days.

At precisely five minutes to one Kathleen had stopped, washed her hands, made herself a cheese and pickle sandwich and settled down at the kitchen table for fifteen minutes to listen to *Portia Faces Life*, 'a story taken from the heart of every woman who has ever dared to love', as the slick-voiced announcer purred at the beginning of every episode. How Portia Manning managed to combine her high-flying career as a lawyer with her motherly duties was a mystery to Kathleen. Poor Portia. Every time she'd dared to love, she'd been terribly let down by men.

Kathleen had sliced a loaf of bread and prepared a plate of Vegemite sandwiches cut into neat triangles for the children to share when Barbara, Jimmy and Robert tumbled through the front door after school, satchels and legs akimbo and tummies rumbling. She had laid a blanket on the back lawn between the lemon and orange trees to tempt them outside, because even though it was July in Melbourne, it hadn't rained so they could do with the fresh air after being stuck in their classrooms all day.

And then, with the children playing after school, or arguing or jousting with pretend cutlasses or wheeling dolls in little prams in the backyard, Kathleen tried to remember to slick on a touch of lipstick so she might look slightly more presentable when Peter arrived home at the end of the day.

'Mummy!' Which child was it? Kathleen rested an elbow on the kitchen table and cupped her chin in her hand. Her back ached. Her feet ached. Perhaps she was getting her monthlies.

Across the kitchen table, his eyes firmly fixed on the form guide in *The Argus*, Peter muttered, 'You gonna see to that, love?'

She stood and followed the sound of the shouting. Ah, yes. Robert.

'What is it, Robert?' Kathleen retied the bow on her apron. In her experience, when boys called there was sure to be some protection required.

'Mummy! Come quick!'

Two steps into the hallway and she could smell the trouble before she set foot into the boys' bedroom. Robert had backed himself into a corner, his chubby little fingers firmly pinching his nostrils together. Little Michael stood in the centre of the room, grinning proudly. His nappy was open on the rug. His hands were smeared with poo.

'It's a horrible stink, Mummy,' Robert squeaked, squinting in disgust.

She let out a deep breath. After five children, nothing was a surprise to her any more. 'It is, isn't it?' Kathleen scooped up Little Michael and he clamped his hands firmly around her neck. The warm smear of excrement soaked through her cotton frock. She tightened her lungs, forcing herself not to breathe.

Barbara, Jimmy and Mary appeared in the doorway and guffawed at the messy spectacle.

'Yuck!' Barbara held her nose.

'Little Michael. You're disgusting!' Jimmy taunted.

'Poo poo. Poo poo!' Mary laughed and waggled her finger at her little brother.

Robert rushed past her now the threat of being chased by his youngest brother was over and the other children ran in a gaggle through the house to be as far away from the disaster as possible. Kathleen heard the back door slam.

'Barse, Mummy?' Little Michael murmured into her shoulder.

'Yes, time for a bath. Let's clean you up.'

Kathleen stopped at the doorway to the kitchen, jiggling Little Michael in her arms. 'Peter, can you run the bath?'

Peter scoffed at the odour. 'Bloody hell, love. Not in the kitchen, I'm still eating me dinner.'

He took an exaggerated puff of his cigarette and butted it out next to the peas and carrots on his dinner plate. Every night she served him up peas and carrots next to the mashed potatoes and every night he left them.

'The bath?' Kathleen repeated. 'Michael's made a mess of himself and of me and I don't want to put him down.'

'Just one more smoke. It's been a hard day at the garage, love. Cars coming and going. Customers complaining about who knows what ...' His voice trailed off as Little Michael began to whine. The two warm smudges of his poo on her shoulders were going cold and beginning to smell worse.

Kathleen gritted her teeth as she walked through the kitchen and out into the backyard. The other children scattered to all corners of the backyard, pressing themselves against the corrugated iron fencing in the twilight, hidden in the shadows from the setting sun.

'You're stinky!' Mary shouted and her siblings joined in. In her arms, Michael began to howl at the humiliation of being taunted so. The smell of his poo, something to which she was normally quite immune, settled in Kathleen's nostrils like a good dose of Vicks VapoRub but with less camphor and eucalyptus oil. She set him down on the ground, which only made him howl even louder. The poor little thing was tired, that was all. She went to the outside tap by the laundry window, grabbed the end of the garden hose and cranked the tap. She held the frigid spluttering flow to her hands to dislodge the excrement. It stubbornly stuck like glue to her fingers so she leant over and scraped her palms on the grass.

Then she had an idea.

She held the hose skywards and the spraying water shot up in an arc like a city fountain. Drops rained down on the grass and the taunts from her children became squeals of delight at the unexpected playtime.

'It's freezing, Mummy!' Robert shrieked as he ran into the spray and, in a flash, Jimmy, Mary and Barbara had joined him, and the squeals of delight echoed from every fence of the quarter-acre block as they all became soaked through their clothes right down to their underpants and socks. Kathleen looked on in wonder as her children played and splashed like puppies in the water. Even though she knew Tuesday would bring more work to wash and dry the clothes that were now soaking wet, she suddenly didn't care. Portia took chances in her life, or she wouldn't have become a high-flying lawyer with a complicated love life. Kathleen could surely ignore what Mrs Hodge next door might say and play with her children in the backyard at the end of a long, busy Monday.

Little Michael looked up at his mother, excited and confused. Kathleen kinked the hose so the spray became a trickle. 'Wash your hands, Michael,' she said gently and her baby held his hands to the water and laughed and laughed so hard at the chill of it, ducking his fingers under the water and hastily pulling them out when he couldn't bear it any longer.

The children hovered and then bolted away as she turned the hose on them, before daring to come back, sneaking up behind her, calling out, 'Mummy!' to entice her to turn before they dashed off in another direction, as if she were a kitten and they were teasing her with a ball of unfurling string.

She gasped as she held the hose over each of her shoulders to wash away Michael's dirty handprints and then twirled the hose so the arc of water formed a figure eight in the air and Jimmy and Barbara aimed their fingers inside the parabola of the spray as they giggled and laughed.

And then the force of the water petered out and stopped.

The children's giggling came to an abrupt end.

'That's enough of that.'

Kathleen turned to the back door. Peter was scowling at the lot of them. She felt like a scolded child. She hoped Mrs Hodge next door hadn't overheard Peter's admonishment. The woman was such a terrible gossip and was the first to notice if Kathleen hadn't washed on Mondays, which led to a knock on the front door and an interrogation as to why.

'I don't know what you're thinking, Kath. The kids'll catch pneumonia,' he huffed. 'And besides, we can't afford to waste all that water. Someone around here has to pay the bills and it's not you.'

The back door slammed in its frame. A minute later, the water heater jittered as it cranked up. Peter was finally running the bath.

His bath.

Harsh words sat on the tip of Kathleen's tongue like a lozenge but they dissolved before she would ever say them out loud. Wives didn't criticise their husbands in front of their children, let alone in the backyard where Mrs Hodge might hear. In fact, wives didn't criticise their husbands at all lest they wanted to be known as an old harridan or a fishwife or a shrew or a harpy.

'Come on, children.' Kathleen dropped the hose into the grass and it lay there like a dead snake. 'Take off your wet clothes and I'll hang them on the hoist.' They obediently did as she asked, except Little Michael, of course, who had been naked to begin with. She slipped off her dress and pegged it on the line and, in her wet petticoat, she fetched fresh towels from the linen press for her shivering children. She wrapped them up in their towelling cocoons—except Jimmy, who tugged the towel out of her hands because he wasn't a baby and could do it himself. The six of them sat on the edge of the cement path that circled the house and stared up at the newly twinkling stars. Mary and Little Michael didn't like the backyard at night and snuggled in close on either side of their mother. The citrus trees were ominous in the dark, swaying and rustling, their branches like witches' fingers. The shed filled with mechanic's tools loomed large and sometimes the galvanised iron sheets creaked in the wind, while the Hills hoist looked like an enormous dinosaur skeleton.

If Peter was just hopping in the bath, it would be at least half an hour before he would be finished reading the sports pages while he soaked and until the rest of the family could take their turns. There was an order to bath time in the O'Grady household: Peter first, Jimmy and Robert and Little Michael next, then Mary and Barbara together and, finally, Kathleen.

'I'm hungry,' Jimmy muttered. His teeth chattered like rattling bones.

'You've just had your dinner,' Kathleen said.

'I know. But I'm still hungry.'

'You're always hungry,' Robert muttered.

'I can't sit here all wet like this,' Barbara said, annoyance dripping from every word. 'My hair will go frizzy and when I go to school with frizzy hair the boys say I've got steel wool for hair and they try to touch it.'

'Are there any biscuits, Mummy?' Mary pleaded.

'Oh, Mary,' Barbara huffed, turning to her little sister. 'Don't you remember? Monday is Mummy's washing day. Tuesday is baking day and that's when we get biscuits, not Monday.'

'Don't worry, Mummy,' Robert said, resting against her arm. 'I'm not hungry. I liked your dinner. Sausages are my favourite.'

'Thank you, Robert. They're my favourite too.' They weren't really Kathleen's favourite, but they were affordable and even though Peter was doing quite well at the garage, thank you, there were still seven mouths to feed in the O'Grady home.

A breeze whipped up and Kathleen shivered. The hoist slowly turned as if by a ghostly hand. Next to her, Mary shivered too and leant in against her hip. She moved an arm around her dear daughter and cuddled her close.

An hour later, after the girls were warm and scrubbed clean and in their flannelette pyjamas playing a game of snakes and ladders on the living room rug by the fire, Kathleen closed the bathroom door behind her, hung up her dressing gown on the nail hammered into the back of the door and slipped into the tepid water. It had been years—literally years—since she'd had a steaming hot bath and she missed the sting of it and the tingling in her icy toes. She missed how the soap sudsed when it was lathered against her skin; what the water felt like without a film of oil and dirt and grit on it.

That night, just like every other night, as the boys had run through the house wrapped only in their towels—except for Little Michael who was naked again—Jimmy had called out, 'I did a wee in the bath!' Every night, without fail, he would put on this show.

'You did not,' Mary sniffed, in fear every time that he actually had.

'Did so!' he teased.

'Mummy!' Mary had shouted. 'Jimmy did a wee in the bath again.'

Kathleen closed her eyes and let her thoughts drift to Hawaii and its miles and miles of tropical beaches edged with swaying palm trees, just like she'd seen in the picture *From Here to Eternity* with Burt Lancaster and the beautiful Deborah Kerr. It helped her to not think of the urine and oil and dead soap suds that she was marinating in.

After her bath, she put her dressing-gown back on and made sandwiches for Barbara and Jimmy and Robert to take to school in the morning and then it was time to put all the children to bed, with goodnights for the older ones and bedtime stories and nursery rhymes for the little ones.

At half past nine she trudged into the bedroom, slipped into bed between the icy sheets and turned on her side towards the window, away from Peter. Finally, she was able to take her first deep and calming breath of the day. On the other side of the bed, Peter stubbed out his cigarette and flicked the switch on the lamp. A faint light from the street split through the venetian blinds and cut soft lines on the pale pink chenille bedspread.

She knew what was coming.

Peter turned towards her, pressing his body against her back, his erect penis jabbing the top of her thighs.

'What kept you?' he murmured into the back of her neck as he cupped a breast.

'I was making lunches.'

'Couldn't that have waited until the morning, love?'

'Peter, I'm tired.'

'C'mon, sweetheart.'

It was late. She'd been on her feet all day. Her back ached and her wrists hurt from working the mangle on the washing machine. She would be up in the night at least once to tend to Little Michael, who still cried out for her or needed changing.

She was so, so tired. But she reacted instinctively to her husband's touch and turned to press her lips to his.